Hidden
Neath

Other novels by Kassandra Mullan

Rose Among The Thorns

Broken Pieces Shine

Hidden Neath

KASSANDRA MULLAN

To all those who love but are condemned for it

Remember:

Love always wins

CHAPTER 1

Pride. That's what he felt as he surveyed his new home. His castle outshined any other in all of the Kingdoms.

And it was his.

King Gurav walked the cobbled halls, running gentle fingers along the graceful arches that separated hallways from rooms. His smile widened as he arrived at the one doorway no one would know about. So secret, he would never tell even his family. So secret, the workers were buried somewhere on the property.

Whispering an incantation, a click echoed and the sliding of the brick slab supported by wheels sounded like music to the King. He headed down the hidden staircase, as the secret door slid close, watching the glow below become brighter and brighter.

At the bottom of the stairs, the reason he built his towering palace on this very spot. King Gurav inhaled happily as the lights in the cavern's walls greeted him. Tempted as he was to touch the glowing veins, the heat emanating from them warned him off from that thought. Ghost lights escaped the walls, dancing around him like faeries. He loved the magical power confined in that room. And it was his. His and his queen's. His ignorant family would never know about it.

After a few moments basking alone in the energy, he decided it was time to return to reality. He strolled to his bedchambers first, changing from his morning robe to his royal cloak. With a quick look in the looking glass, he puffed up his chest. Then his image faded away as a glittery swirl overtook the reflection.

"Soon," he promised. "Soon, my cimmerian Queen."

A chaotic whisper answered and he bowed to the luminosity.

Down the stairs to the main floor, he strode back to the throne room, to find his son Elixin waiting for him. Sniggering under his breath, the King knew his useless son had become quite jaded when he was ordered to move his family to the new castle. But he didn't know the next step Gurav would be taking – ensuring that his youngest son, Crenast, ruled after him. The older son never agreed with his father's vision for their family and kingdom, arguing with him even in front of others. Knowing Elixin's hopes to find allies in the courtiers, the King made him move his family to keep a better eye on him. Gurav made a mental note that he needed to finalize the announcement of his true heir, before telling the insufferable Elixin.

"What news, Elixin?" Gurav inquired as he glided up the dais.

Elixin bowed his head, as was customary, and smiled slightly at his father. "We have settled in our rooms, Father. Any other rules we must follow other than, and I believe the direct quote was, 'Stay out of my way'?"

"No, I think that was it."

"Then we will respect your wishes. But first, I wish to thank you for thinking of me and my family. We are grateful for your hospitality."

Gurav scoffed, knowing that was a lie. However, when Elixin offered his arm in thanks, Gurav begrudgingly stepped forward. As he got within reach, Gurav felt a sudden pain in his abdomen. Startled, he looked down to find a dagger hilt deep inside him. Gasping, he returned his eyes to Elixin's face. His son's smile shifted from pleasant to sinister.

"Mehdehra is mine," Elixin said, with a hiss, before twisting the blade harder and deeper.

Then the King crumpled to the ground.

Upstairs, in the fallen King's bedchambers, a distressed shriek shattered the glass of the vanity.

CHAPTER 2

The sun had already set and the moons, in different phases and rising from their chosen horizons. Splashing the landscape with various levels, the light tried to break through the leaves of the forest below. And the massive, ancient trees shifted the shadows and light by swaying gently in the wind, which had brought its song and coolness to the evening. Critters fussed because of the movement, scurrying here and there, trying to settle down for the night.

As the rest of the forest readied for bedtime, a man walked casually down the ungraded road. The stranger easily navigated the deep grooves made by the many carts and carriages that traveled over it. His white cloak lined with light violet flapped around him while the dark violet hood, lined inside with white, hid the lurking dangers from his sight.

Three man-shaped shadows moved carefully along the tree line, their attention focused intently on their prey. One moved to the road, behind the cloaked traveler, while the other two stayed in step, out of sight, on either side. When their target reached the high point in the road, they moved in.

The one from behind knocked the traveler down, laughing and watching him sprawl along the declining road. Their victim laid on the ground for a moment in surprise, then rolled into a sitting position to face his attackers. His hood fell down onto his shoulders, revealing a young man with dark blonde hair, pale skin, and hickory eyes. His attackers surrounded him, three hulking inhuman robbers who had eyes for his possessions. He looked around for options, but realized he had very little recourse other than to give up his goods or lose the most precious thing left to him – his life.

Until a voice broke the tension.

"Hello, boys."

The owner of the voice sauntered out of the tree line, smirking. She wore a dark caramel colored leather breastplate with straps that secured it over her shoulders and was cinched and tied in the front. The bodice stopped just above her hips, while petals of leather encircled the bottom of it. Underneath was a thick topaz colored tunic, saving her from the chafing of the straps, while the sleeves were held in place with archer gauntlets. Her matching suede pants were well-fitted, adjusting to her movements like they were molded to her birch-colored skin. Her pecan brown leather boots ran from toes to just below her knees, fur lining the tops to insulate.

At first glance, it looked like she had shaved off half of her black hair. But as the moonslight rained through the moving leaves of the forest's wind caressed canopy, flickers of dark emerald ran along the length of the braids. And twisted in were pale peridot bursts, as if new hair had grown in but hadn't yet been jaded by the elements. Her elliptical eyes were dilated, the round black pupils almost overtaking the cat-like hazel irises.

In her right hand, she held a haladie sword. Each blade protruded from the center handle, which looked like it had been carved from petrified wood, and they curved in opposite directions. The well-honed edges glinted in the moonlight like the eyes of vengeful monsters. At her right hip and strapped along her leg appeared to be its scabbard, while still holstered on the left side was a single bladed short sword.

If she wasn't standing in the middle of the road, the colors of her body and clothing would have kept her camouflaged from an unsuspecting eye as it surveyed the forest.

"I see you still haven't learned your lesson," she chided.

She didn't seem to be intimidated by the three massive, healthy muggers who looked like her as they all unsheathed their broadswords in one loud chorus.

"I guess I must teach it again. Let's see if it sticks this time?"

She spun her haladie sword, cocked her head and flashed a wry smile, then gestured with her free hand for them to come at her. Foolishly, they took her challenge.

The three thugs lined up in front of the woman, weapons at the ready. One brandished a broadsword, another a mace, and the last one had two short swords. Their antagonist appeared unimpressed, twirling her own blade.

The broadsword wielder stepped forward first, snarling an insult their victim couldn't hear. However, the raised eyebrow from the woman confirmed her annoyance at such slander. Then he swung. She ducked quickly, avoiding the blade easily, before charging like a bull. She rammed him in the abdomen, causing him to screech as he lost his breath. They tumbled to the ground, but before she could jump back to her feet, the mace swished over her head. She snatched the broadsword and raised it as another swing came her way. The chains wrapped around the blade, allowing her leverage. Once the spiked ball rattled to a stop at the tang, she yanked before he did. The mace wielder flew towards her and she landed a devastating punch to his face, knocking him out.

The one already on the ground grabbed her ankle, trying to pull her down. A quick look of anger flashed across her face at his audacity. With the mace still entangled with the broadsword, she slammed it down into his crotch, the spikes hitting home. The agonized scream echoed throughout the forest.

The thug with the short swords shook his head, disgusted by his comrades' lack of tactics. He cut his blades through the air, looking intimidating, but his enemy again appeared unimpressed. She dropped all of the other weapons, rising back to her feet with only her haladie. He rushed her, and she stood her ground until he raised his blades to smash into hers. She shifted her back foot before impact, letting one side lock into his tang then used his momentum to deflect and send him flying into the tree behind her.

What was a swirl of movement and deafening cacophony, she had taken them down within a few moments. All three ended up on their backs, bloody noses, lips, and swelling eyes the rewards for their arrogance.

She stood proudly, hardly out of breath. "Lesson learned?" she inquired, kicking the bottom of one thief's foot.

He groaned in pain but nodded.

"Good," she replied, spinning her haladie almost thoughtlessly. "I'll leave you all here to think over your life choices. But this will be the last time I want to see you around. If I do see you again, lessons will no longer be the goal."

She approached their intended victim, who hadn't moved from the spot where he fell. Instead of being dazed, he appeared mesmerized. She offered her hand, which he grasped readily, and she helped him to his feet. She released his hand quickly then gestured for him to follow her down the road. He caught sight of another weapon, a khukuri blade sheathed against the small of her back, with the handle angled for her right hand to grab easily.

After putting enough distance between them and his attackers, the woman - or forest elf, he realized as he surveyed the back of her neck and hair - turned around to face him.

"You should be fine from here," she reassured, looking him over. "I guess it's a good thing you were traveling through my sector or this would have ended differently for you."

"Why?" he asked.

"We don't help men."

"Then why did you help me?"

"I didn't," she retorted. "I wanted to teach those boys the lesson they failed to learn the first time. You shouldn't have any more trouble out of them. Goodbye."

She started to head back into the trees when he held out his hand.

"Wait, you have to let me thank you."

She paused, then flashed her feline eyes over her shoulder. "You just did."

"Hm, I have a better idea."

Then he held up a heavy, overly filled leather hip flask.

She raised her left eyebrow.

~   ~   ~

Deep in the forest, among a tangle of fallen limbs and exposed roots of an ancient tree, bodies writhed under a cloak while pleasured moans and drunken laughter spilled out. Once one climaxed, the other followed. The individual on top rolled off and they laid shoulder to shoulder, panting, on the thin sheet that protected them from the leaf covered ground.

"You know, Gwendin, saying 'thank you' was enough," she chided.

He laughed, breathless. "Oh but Zawn, this way is much more fun. Admit it."

"Well, again," she replied, with a giggle, "you're welcome."

"Give me a few moments and I will happily thank you again."

"Again? What, twice isn't enough?"

"Hm, never enough." He rolled onto his side, then kissed her. After their lips separated, he laid his head on his folded arm. "And I thank you for being receptive. I'll admit this is selfish on my part, seeing that this will be my last fling before living my life as the required sexless monk."

"Sad life indeed." She rolled on her side as well, using her own arm as a pillow, then her smile faded. "You know, creatures like us are not supposed to breed."

His eyebrows furrowed, as he reached over and covered her with his cloak. "Creatures?"

"Neither of us are human, are we? They say we're magic."

"You have a point," he admitted, after making a face, then he sighed. "First, don't worry, this will never be spoken of to anyone that is not me and you, even though I will dream of it nightly. Second, they finally figured out a way to magically sterilize us theurgists so we don't have uncontrollable amounts of offspring, and therefore, no worries here."

She sat up, grabbing the half-empty belt flask, and took a swig before offering it to him. "You never did say where you were headed."

He propped himself on his arm and accepted it. "To the residence of the King of Mehdehra."

"Ooh, I am sorry to hear that."

"I heard it was an unpleasant assignment. But when you are a theurgist, you go where you are sent."

"Fair warning, the King is a murderous fiend who thinks creatures like us are beneath him. The Queen will not stand up to him or for the people they reign over. And the children, well, stories say they take after their father even at their young age."

He sat up, bringing them shoulder to shoulder. "Good to know. I will choose my steps carefully around them."

"If you wish, Gwendin, I can take you up to the tree line at the moat bridge. I am forbidden to go any further."

"Why?"

She looked at him, somewhat surprised. "Elves are dirty and carry diseases," she answered, her tone dark. "To keep the women and children safe inside the castle, we are barred from crossing the gates' threshold."

"I am sorry, Zawn," he responded, gently caressing her cheek. "Humans are absurd in their ignorance."

"And yet when they need rescuing, it is always us dirty creatures they turn to."

"They forget that piece of history, don't they? If it wasn't for elves, among others, the humans would have been annihilated during the Purge."

She glanced away, grabbing the flask and taking another swig. "From what I hear, they teach their children of the men who fought but not about us or the others. Victors tell the history as they wish."

"It's not the stories we learn at the College, if that is any reassurance."

"A small one."

A long sigh escaped him. "But if they are not careful, the men here will find themselves without allies."

"They are already without allies."

"Can we be allies?"

Zawn stared at him for a moment. "What do you mean by that?"

"Well, you know," and a sly grin materialized on his face, "I am not required to stay at the castle every hour of every day."

Startled by the implications of his suggestion, she turned her back to him and started gathering her clothes. "You should really get going," she replied, avoiding his train of thought. "And I should get home."

"I could find reasons to travel into this forest," he continued, leaning over and inhaling her scent, his breath tickling the base of her neck. "From time to time."

She closed her eyes briefly, relishing the sensation. She cleared her throat, retorting, "Hm, sounds like a lonely walk for you, from time to time."

"Ah so that's how it is?" he asked, after a gentle kiss on her shoulder. "Get it out of my system now or forever hold my peace?"

"I highly doubt I will be your last conquest."

"Am I not your conquest as well?" he demanded, before whispering against her skin, "What if I don't want to pursue another?"

"We're not supposed to be together, remember?" she inquired, looking over her shoulder, then her eyebrow rose up. "Ah, so is this the reason why you were handed the worst assignment in all the kingdoms? You are a troublemaker, aren't you? Hate the rules, do what you want?"

"Every. Damn. Day."

"I would save the life of a kindred spirit."

He nuzzled her cheek, his hand sliding up her thigh toward a very sensitive region. "Is that a yes, then?"

Unable to answer him, she decided to distract him from their line of conversation. In one swift move, she straddled his lap, wrapping her arms around his neck. "What did you put in that brew?"

"Not allowed to use theurgy for selfish purposes," he replied, in a mocking authoritative tone.

"Oh, another rule to be broken?"

He ran his hands up her back and pressed her against him. "What do you say? Allies?"

"Keep thanking me and ask me again in the morning."

"Hm, it would be my pleasure."

CHAPTER 3

Their schedule was regimented and never wavered. Their leader preferred it that way and no one dared question it. Not even Zawn.

Each morning, they all met in the kith square. Their leader, Medruano, patriarch of the Emana family, their fighter, would dole out assignments then send the members of each caste to complete their morning routines. Half of the members of the farming caste moved to tend to the cattle, goats, chickens while the other half tended the fields. The worker caste headed out to their jobs, earning income outside the kith. Those in the warrior caste, archers and fighters, strode out to the east of the kith where a large meadow opened up. The archers headed out to the range where targets paralleled the tree line, while the fighters traveled to the flat spot behind them.

Zawn joined her fellow fighters there, ready to complete their daily exercises. In rows of seven, they stood shoulder to shoulder, before placing hands on those next to them. Then they pushed out and away from each other, ensuring they had enough space between them. Next, they bowed to whomever led the group that day and started moving through their forms.

The kith leader kept an eye on his warriors, making sure they were perfect in every sweep, every step, and every turn. Hands were expected to be in the proper position, feet landing elegantly, while swift turns expert and deadly. If Medruano saw something he didn't like, he would make a throaty grunt and the day's lead would hurry over for the notes. Then the lead would walk among them and tap whoever made the offending move to correct them.

Zawn hid in the back, as far from Medruano as she could get. Not that he would bother making suggestions to her because she was, after all, a lost cause, but it helped her concentrate better. She didn't have to see him or be reminded how much he loathed her. Especially since the feeling was mutual.

However, she was always meticulous, determined, and precise in her moves. No complaints could ever be waged against her forms. Her mentor trained her well and she never forgot each lesson passed on to her. Once the exercises were completed, she retreated to her small hut to finally get some sleep.

~   ~   ~

Her home sat far from all of the other huts and buildings, almost as if banished, nestled in the tree line. It was made with the same type of wood as the oldest huts, mostly poplar with cedar accents, with a thatched roof made out of dried branches and local longstraw. It was the smallest and the least desirable, but it was hers.

When she stepped in, the fireplace with its plain hearth and mantel greeted her on the left, while her bed was directly to the right. A small table was nestled on the other side of the bed with a plain wooden chair. The kitchen ran across the back wall, until it encountered another doorway, which led to a small bathing room. The only real luxury she allowed herself was a double-sized mattress that could fit two. Everything else was salvaged or built with minimal cost.

After waking from her nap and completing her chores, Zawn, heir of the Haley family, daydreamer of the Whispering Hornbeam Kith, spent the rest of the day cleaning up. She bathed a little longer than normal, while braiding her hair in several plaits before twisting them together. She grabbed a fresh pair of pants and a clean tunic, as well as her recently cleaned leather breastplate, trying to hide from her kith her interest in showing more cleavage and curves than usual. The others didn't need to know why. It had taken a brutal lesson to teach her to keep her secrets to herself.

However, before dressing in her layers, she worked on making herself soft and pliable.

Elves were nature based as much as they were magic. Depending on the natural influences, their physical manifestations always mimicked their heritage. Zawn was a forest elf, born of trees and earth. She rubbed a moisturizing cream along her rougher parts, which included her joints and lower half, since her nature made her more bark-like in those areas. She let her fingers run along her legs, feet and toes, working the thick lotion into the root-like texture of her flesh. She smeared more along her ears, especially the pointed ends that looked like twisted twigs, and her neck, where her rougher dermis mixed with her hair. She did her best working it into her spine, where the bark tracked from her hairline down to her buttocks.

As she rubbed the cream into her skin, her thoughts lingered on that first kiss, a small smile creeping across her face.

She hadn't planned on fraternizing with a human that night; that was against the rules. She thought no harm would come of it though. After all, he had only said he wanted to thank her for saving his life with a drink.

They had shared his flask, drinking his homemade spirits without hesitation, after those initial flinches at least. It had been a strong brew, one he was quite proud of as he explained his process. She had kept a safe distance from him at first but once the flask had been swapped between them a few times, and as they talked and laughed about different things, they seemed to get closer to each other without realizing it. His smile was relaxed and contagious. And well, she had found him charming.

His sense of humor became wicked the more they drank and she enjoyed laughing along with him. It had been a long time since she had reveled in any honest amusement. Then he complimented her on her fighting skills, admitting he had never paid attention to the warriors in his everyday life. But to watch her fight?

"It was like watching a dance," Gwendin had admitted. "I didn't know the steps or even hear the music, but I was enthralled all the same."

She never expected to blush at his observations. She blamed the brew at first. Until he looked at her in a way that perplexed her. His expression communicated his confusion and something else, almost as if he was debating life and death. Then he leaned in, slowly but determined, caressing her lips with his. She didn't expect his to be so soft and his intention so genuine. He tasted sweet, underneath the burn of the alcohol, and she found herself reaching out for more. And she had heard how lonely a theurgist's life could be. Giving Gwendin something naughty to remember sounded like a good plan at the time.

It hadn't even registered that she had found him attractive in that way. When she first saw him, she had determined that he was quite handsome, for a human, but she had pushed the acknowledgement to the back of her mind while she handled the thugs in front of her.

Until he kissed her.

Her smile turned sly as she thought of all the other moments after that first kiss. She shivered and blushed at the memory, still surprised that she could find such pleasure with someone human. And his enthusiasm definitely made up for his lack of confidence in the beginning.

She remembered their second meeting just as fondly. He had asked her to meet him again after a fortnight, to give him time to get settled in. Then they would discuss what they wanted, as "allies" as he had called it. She honestly hadn't expected him to show up.

However, when she ventured into the clearing and found him leaning against an old grandfather tree, talking was the last thing on their minds. They at least got a verbal greeting out before descending into a madness that stripped them of their logic and clothing. She giggled when she remembered, at that time with some trepidation, spending the majority of that following morning finding leaves in her hair. She had no idea how to explain it had someone noticed.

They never planned their visits. She always knew when he entered the forest, making her way to him each time. Their irregular meetings became exercises in pleasure and each of their meetings never failed her expectations. Their last entanglement, though, he asked her to meet him tonight. She shivered again, this time with anticipation of what laid before her.

Her smile faded. There were times where she thought about ending it. It would be easier that way. She knew eventually it would end when he fell for a human at the castle or in a nearby town. He complained that it was lonely, but there was always the chance someone new would begin employment there and catch his eye. Or he could run into a lovely maiden when visiting one of the towns or settlements. He was a young man and she knew his tastes could change in a heartbeat.

And knowing that his job as a theurgist tied him to a King who had committed several aggressions against her kind in previous years… it all made things complicated. Gwen could be removed or killed for displeasing the King at any moment. Or he could start thinking just like all the other humans who resided at the castle.

All the scenarios she came up with made continuing their rendezvous more stressful.

She shook her head. She refused to plan for the worst. It would end when it ended.

The time came for her to start her shift and she hurried to relieve her kithlin. If Teno noticed that she had started her shift just a little earlier than usual, he didn't mention it. He watched her approach, updated her about any transgressors, then headed home to his mate. Then she preoccupied herself with her duties until it was time for Taylor to take over watch.

Taylor, one of her closest friends, knew of her dalliance – to a certain extent – and only said he was happy that she found someone she could burn off her energy with. That made her roll her eyes, but she appreciated his silence on the matter to their kithlin. Even if she knew he had already told his mate Chaelene.

When the time came, she got Taylor caught up, then Zawn darted off into the forest.

~   ~   ~

Zawn jogged quickly through the trees, choosing her steps carefully. The last thing she wanted to do was twist her ankle or land face first into a thorn bush. That would end her evening of fun instantly. She made it to the clearing thankfully unharmed to find her lover already waiting. When their eyes locked, smiles were shared. She jumped down from the ledge of the impression, crossed the distance, then leapt into his arms. He spun them around until he had her held fast against a tree. They kissed and groped each other excitedly, before he kissed his way down her neck and kneeled in front of her.

He cursed quietly, fighting with her laces. "I hate that you wear boots."

"I can't fight in sandals," she replied, laughing.

"You couldn't untie them a bit?"

She loosened her breastplate's cinches and slipped it off. "Can't run in loose boots."

"Oh? You run to me, do you?" he inquired, yanking on the bootlaces.

She released and removed her archer's gauntlets. "You don't have to take my pants completely off, you know."

He finally got her boots off, unbuckled her belt, and pulled her pants off as quickly as he could. Then he sprang up and pressed her against the tree, kissing her fervently. She tried to unlatch and push down his slacks between kisses, but he didn't give her much room. Once she succeeded, she secured her grip on the available limbs above her head and he lifted her up. She wrapped her legs around him as he positioned them.

"I love the feel of your legs around me," he admitted, before starting their rhythm.

After their raucous encounter, they finally collapsed against the tree. He moved to sit down and lean back against the tree, then without hesitation, he pulled her down and made her straddle him. His dreamy eyes glanced over her face, until his eyelids grew heavy.

She tried to count his freckles again but like always lost track. She caught herself smiling, before leaning forward and resting her forehead against his. Closing her eyes, she privately enjoyed this time with him as his breath crashed against her cheek.

She chastised herself for letting down her guard again. But it was hard not to lose herself when she was with him, especially in the throes of their physical entanglements. Even though he would huff for a while afterwards, she calmed herself and listened over his noises to make sure no one got the upper hand on them. She never knew what kithless fools or hungry predators were close by. However, the trees around them agreed they would try to warn her in enough time.

Once his breathing slowed and became steady, she took that as her sign. But he tightened his hold on her when she started to move away. Surprised by his need for additional closeness, she kissed his forehead, feeling his breath tickling her neck.

"Do you have to go?" he asked, his voice faint but hoarse.

She gently tucked a lock of hair behind his ear. "Do you want me to stay?"

"Can you? Just for a while?"

The look on his face startled her. "I can."

He grabbed his cloak that laid nearby, then spread it out next to them. He rolled them onto their sides, the soft dirt cradling their entangled bodies. She wrapped her arms around his neck and shoulders, holding him close. He inhaled deeply and she felt his eyelashes brush her chin as he slowly closed his eyes. Stroking his hair gently, she listened to his breathing slow even more. He nuzzled her chin, then stopped, and she knew he had dozed off.

She laid there holding him for quite a while, somewhat confused. She reflected on the expression on his face, leaving her to wonder what was bothering him. He had never fallen asleep before or had asked her to stay afterwards. Usually, they satisfied each other, gained back their senses, and then separated, only to see each other again during another meeting. They hadn't spent any additional time together since the night she saved his life.

Then he stirred, sighing against her neck. "I'm sorry."

"For what?"

"Asking you to stay. Falling asleep. I am taking advantage of your patience."

"You are indeed," she replied, drolly. When he didn't respond, she nudged him. "Something wrong?"

"No, nothing's wrong."

He glanced up at her, seeing that look on her face telling him she didn't believe him.

"I didn't sleep well last night."

She raised an eyebrow, still unconvinced that was the only thing bothering him. "You can talk to me, you know."

"Can I?"

She loosened her hold, propping her head up on one arm. "We agreed to be allies, Gwendin," she reminded him. "That means we can use each other for things other than sex. I'm actually a good listener despite my infamously short attention span." Then her eyebrows furrowed together, unsure. "Unless that's not what you mean."

"No, I would... I'd like that."

"Then what's on your mind?"

He pulled his arm free, then tucked it under his head. "Things at the castle have been... been rough."

"What happened?"

"The prince died last week."

Zawn looked at him, confused. "The baby?"

"He hadn't been a baby for a while. He was already walking and talking, getting into mischief, and then one day he couldn't muster the energy to even cry."

"I didn't know he had been sick."

"His health had declined before I got here. The King's healers had him stable by the time I was dispatched. I thought he was recovering. We still don't know what ailed him. But I know we did everything we could. Everyone sent their best healers, even the College, but there was nothing we could do. We could only watch while that awful illness consumed him..."

She could see the sadness in his eyes, making her heart hurt for him, and she pulled him back into a warm embrace. He sighed, hard, against her collarbone, while tightening his hold on her.

"To watch a child suffer," she whispered, running her hand through his hair before kissing the top of his head. "I wouldn't wish that on even an enemy. Definitely not on you."

He scoffed. "I thought you hated the Royal Family."

"I do but I'm not completely heartless."

He nestled his cheek lower onto her chest, pressing his ear to her heart. "No, you're not, are you? Your heart is bigger than you'd ever admit."

"That, my dear theurgist, is a very big secret."

14

He looked up at her, his sad eyes memorizing her wry smile.

"Don't let that get out," she whispered.

He stretched to kiss her, those sweet lips of his gentle and appreciative. "Can you stay a little longer?"

"As long as you need."

~   ~   ~

After that night, their interest in each other slowly moved past just the physical. They spent more time together. Cuddling occurred after orgasms. Small talk turned into conversations. Tender kisses replaced flirty farewells. And random escapades became consistent rendezvous.

Each visit brought them closer to each other than they could have ever expected…

CHAPTER 4

They had enjoyed their usual romp under the twisted roots and afterwards, sat together, half-naked, on his cloak. He rested against the exposed roots, while she sat between his legs and leaned back against him. With his arms wrapped warmly around her, she felt oddly content.

"You never told me the excuse you use to leave the castle," she mentioned, when she realized his breathing was rocking her to sleep. She knew talking would keep her awake.

"Oh, I uh tell the King that I am looking for herbs and things for medicines. I don't tell him where I go, just that I'm looking for options."

"Have you seen anything interesting?"

A chuckle from him vibrated against her back. "Besides you? Of course, this forest is full of remedies and helpful herbs. Not in great quantities, at least in this area, but enough to help some. Here, let me show you. That one over there, it helps with aches and pains from arthritis. And this one next to us?"

Gwendin continued with his lesson, pointing out different plants and fungus that grew around and on the grandfather tree. Zawn listened intently as she felt awe about his knowledge. However, her stomach twisted when she realized what his enthusiasm meant.

"Don't take," she interrupted.

"I haven't, I've only observed." He looked over her shoulder and saw her expression. "I promise. I don't know who owns this land and I wouldn't wish to upset anyone. And seeing I'm here with you, why give anyone a reason to investigate me?" He wrapped his arms tightly around her again before he kissed her temple to reassure her. "Who owns this land? I know it's not part of Mehdehra."

"My kith. Our territory stretches up to the road where we met the first time. All of this, even the river, is ours."

"And if I wanted to harvest?"

"You'd have to ask the kith's leader for permission. But he hates your kind

16

more than any other elf."

He didn't respond immediately and she could sense him thinking. "What would your people do if they found us?"

"They would kill you on sight."

"No chance of talking myself out of execution?"

"It's not our way."

"I will keep that in mind. And what would happen to you?"

"Most likely, death. Maybe, if they pitied me, banishment."

He shook his head, in wonder. "Here I thought we only had to worry about the law of man. Never thought your laws would parallel ours."

"Only when it comes to mating outside our species." She scoffed. "It's bad enough we're a finnicky lot as it is."

"How do… how do elves choose who to be with?"

"Usually, the male will let the female know he's interested, either with words or with touches. They will go somewhere private. He will undress in front of her and she will decide based on what she sees if she is confident that he would be a strong enough lover for her. If she does, she makes him undress her. If not, she will walk away."

"Now you're telling me that I've been doing this wrong the whole time?" he lamented.

She couldn't help giggling. "You were the one who showed interest first. You kissed me. And I saw what I needed to see the moment you dropped your pants that first night. If I wasn't interested, we would have never mated."

"Is that what this is? Mating? I guess there are worse words to describe it."

"Mating. Breeding. Shagging. Sex. Copulating. Fornicating…"

His laughter filled the air around them. "Well, when you put it that way…" and he slipped his hands under her tunic. His fingers danced up her stomach and along her ribs. "We should find another word to describe our…" and as he thought about it, his hands cupped her breasts.

After moaning from his caresses, she suggested, "Debauchery?"

"Now I like that one," he replied, as one hand found its way between her legs. He smiled as she gasped in delight and, eventually, she returned the favor.

CHAPTER 5

One morning, after her meeting with Gwendin, her friend Chaelene stopped her in the kith square. They were both sweaty from their sparring exercises, the archers like Chaelene having been ordered to workout with the other warriors. They had avoided crossing swords that morning, but whoever worked with Chaelene had not gone easy on her.

Chaelene, or Chae as she was called by those close to her, was Taylor's mate. She looked like Zawn, at least in color as well as skin and bark patterns but her bark ran darker. She had her hair pulled back into a messy bun. The locks had more bright peridot streaks and ended about mid-shoulder when she wore it down. Her eyes were a light gray, which seemed to get brighter when she was up to no good, not to mention a glint that could frighten the uninitiated. Her body type also differed, her hips were wider and she was more voluminous in her bosom. Having given birth to three children helped in that department, but the other elf had always been curvier than Zawn. Then again, compared to all the females in their kith, Zawn wasn't very voluptuous.

"Are you coming to breakfast?" Chae asked. "Tay should be home soon."

"Yes. Just want to freshen up."

"See you in a bit, then."

Zawn cleaned up quickly, changing into an old tunic and a pair of patched lounging slacks. Then she strode across the kith to a hut that was much larger than hers. Considering it housed a family of five, the size was necessary. There were several huts on the south side of the kith that were large enough for families of various sizes. Changes and swaps had been known to happen if a family outgrew their home or if a family downsized due to children striking out on their own.

Zawn knocked before entering, but once she slipped in and closed the door behind her, she was besieged. Two short bodies landed into her.

"Auntie!" the two boys cheered.

She wrapped an arm around each child, hugging them tightly. "Good morning, Chaen and Talor," she responded, with a giggle. "What's for breakfast?"

"Momma is making omelets," Talor answered. "Mine has mushrooms."

"And mine has shallots," Chaen replied.

Chae turned and smiled at her sons' excitement. "We didn't have much from our garden. What do you want in yours?"

Zawn held up a small cloth bag. "Some peppers I picked from my sad little patch."

"Can I have some too?" Chaen begged.

"Is there enough to share?" Talor asked.

"I think so. Here, take this over to your Momma."

Both boys grabbed a part of the bag and carried it over to Chae, who thanked them. They were so close in age, that if one didn't know the family, they would assume the boys were twins. They looked more like their mother, in color and pattern, but their sister, who laid in her bassinet by the couch, took after her father. Speaking of the baby, she started to fuss because of all the noise.

"Oh, can you grab Minee?" Chae requested.

"Of course."

Privately, Zawn loved holding the baby. She lifted Minee up, laying the infant comfortably in her arms. Glad that she cleaned up and changed out of her armor, she could hold the child properly. She sat down on the small couch, near the fireplace, smiling down at the baby. Minee stopped fussing, sighing to herself. Then the boys sat on either side, talking about this and that, trying to entertain Zawn and Minee while their mother cooked. She laughed at their jokes, then asked for additional information when they talked about the new moves they learned in combat training. They even begged her to help them hone their strikes and she promised she would.

Taylor arrived then, the boys jumping up and hugging their father. He embraced them, one arm for each son, and sent them back to Zawn's side. He greeted his friend with finger taps then kissed his wife and entered the bathing room to clean up.

Taylor was at least a head and half taller than Zawn, forcing her to crane her neck if she had to look up at him. His markings were similar to hers, but instead of greens, his bark, hair and eyes ran silver and graphite. He braided his hair similarly to Zawn, but instead of twisting them together, he would wrap most of it up in a bun at the back of his head. His shoulders and chest were broad, making him almost twice the size of his friend and he could pick up both boys and Zawn at the same time without breaking a sweat. The only blemish he had marred his left arm, a scar from the days of the Purge, and it appeared granite in color and texture.

When breakfast was ready, so was he, and they all ate around the fireplace, either at the table or on the couch.

"How was watch?" Zawn asked, as she maneuvered the dozing baby to her side, still cradling her with one arm, while using that hand to hold her plate on her lap. She ate with her free hand, musing that her training was good for something besides fighting.

"Quiet," Taylor answered, chewing some toasted bread. "Not even a critter."

"I guess that's a good thing. No trespassers, no issues."

Chae grinned over at her. "I'm glad to see you more comfortable with Minee."

"I always felt like I might break her," Zawn responded. "She came out so small. But she has gained weight and grown quite a bit."

"She'll be fighting with the boys before we know it," Taylor replied, with a chuckle.

"And winning."

The two boys glared at her, making Zawn laugh.

"Finish eating, boys," their mother ordered. "Your training is going to start soon."

"Yes, Momma," both boys answered, unenthusiastically.

Chae rolled her eyes and tried to hide her smile with another fork full of food. Once the boys finished, they gathered their weapons and headed out to meet with their teacher Darend. Medruano had the children in the same three castes as the adults – fighters, farmers and workers. After the school teacher died a decade prior, no one had been appointed to that job because the kith leader decided it was unnecessary. So, the children didn't learn reading, writing, or math like Zawn and their parents did.

However, Chae refused to leave her children illiterate, teaching them behind their kith leader's back. She even created workbooks for her sons and when the other parents found out, she handed out copies to them, but each were sworn to secrecy and ensured that the books never left their huts. Mainly because no one knew what their leader would do if he found out.

Taylor and Chaelene started to clean up, waving Zawn off as she kept their baby content. She adjusted Minee again, who woke up at being jostled, and looked up with wide eyes. The baby's granite eyes always captivated her. Left to her own thoughts, she wondered what a child would look like if she and Gwendin... Would the baby look elven or human? Or would the child take on only certain characteristics? She snapped herself out of that fantasy. That was dangerous territory and she knew better. They were using each other, nothing else.

Taking a deep breath to shake her free of her foolishness, she cradled Minee a little closer. Then she started to tell her tales of their ancestors. The baby stared at her in wonder, not understanding the words, but enthralled in the sound of her auntie's voice.

CHAPTER 6

Gwendin had been used to the cacophony of the college. Voices, laughter, clattering and clanking of canisters, things one heard daily. However, the castle refused to be such a welcoming place.

It was the antithesis.

The contrast between the castle and the college was stark. The castle was built out of dark rock, while the college had been carved into the white cliffs. There were few windows, and those that did exist were small, mainly for the castle's defenses. The college had large windows, but still had enough defenses to protect the students. The halls of the castle were dank and tight, while the college's allowed several to walk shoulder to shoulder with room to spare.

The only thing that kept him above the darkness of the castle was her. Her smile, her energy, her beauty. Knowing thoughts of her gave him away, Gwendin tried to only think of her in the privacy of his chambers. However, when walking alone through the hallways, he let himself linger on her face before his surroundings suffocated him. The way she looked at him at the top of the outcropping, how her lips landed on his and thrilled him deep in his bones.

Gwendin walked down the hallway, for a quick stop in the kitchen. He knew they had tea in stock, something he could use to dilute the bitterness of the Queen's medicine. When he arrived at the doorway, a sound of unkind laughter rattled by. Stopping just out of view, he leaned against the wall and listened.

"You know he isn't right in the head," one of the cooks said.

"He's a theurgist, they worship nature," another one replied.

Another scoffed. "At night? Only evil things happen at night."

"Or naughty," the first cook responded.

"Do you really think someone would lay with him?" demanded the second voice. "You have seen him? Or do you need magnifiers?"

"Maybe the girl needs magnifiers," the first voice answered. "Blind as an old fool."

"Even a blind shepherdess would avoid him," the third cook retorted.

He heard one of the women shudder, before adding, "It's a shame the College couldn't send us someone not so repulsive."

"Come, the King should be heading into the dining room. We must hurry the food up."

"And be thankful he doesn't take his meals with the King and Queen."

Gwendin bolted around the corner and hid out of sight until the three women's footsteps receded. He peeked around the corner and saw it was clear, so he darted into the kitchen to retrieve what he needed before those awful women returned. Knowing he had time, he also grabbed vegetables and potatoes, along with some chicken cutlets, so he could cook his own food and avoid returning to the kitchen during the day. He would ensure never to enter the kitchen when those crones were around.

~   ~   ~

As Gwendin set down his cache from the kitchen, the cooks' words swam in his head. Trying to ignore their viciousness, he started the tea and gathered his pot to make a hearty stew for later. But even keeping himself busy couldn't keep their cruelty at bay. Then he started to wonder... if they saw him as unattractive, why in the world did Zawn bother with him? Their time together was the highlight of his day, his week really, but what did it really mean to her? They called themselves allies, using each other for more than just sex, but why did she choose him?

Shaking his head, he started peeling the potatoes. He focused on his food, trying to conjure her beautiful face while he chopped and boiled, but his doubts had snatched that away. He forced himself to finish off his daily responsibilities, then left the bitter walls of the castle before the sun started to set. He thought about not meeting her that night and walking in a different direction. Yet his feet took him straight to their meeting place, where he waited for her and drowned in his doubts.

Until she arrived and pressed those lovely lips against his, chasing those uncertainties away. At least temporarily.

~   ~   ~

They laid beside each other, using his cloak as a blanket beneath them. Resting on his side, he used his tunic for a pillow, giving him an angle high enough to view her properly. She laid on her stomach, with her arms tucked under her head. His one arm was still trapped under her waist, but his free hand ventured. His fingers lightly ran up and down her spine, tracing where the bark dissolved into the skin of her back.

"My skin isn't as..." and he paused, searching for the right word, "dynamic as yours."

"Yes, it is," she replied. "You have freckles, moles, scars. And hair." She smirked. "A lot of hair."

He squeezed her buttock in response to her teasing, making her laugh.

"Your derma is just as dynamic as mine," she reassured, "in its own way."

"Your eyes are different, too. They change when they see light compared to the darkness, like a feline's would."

She furrowed her eyebrows. "Am I too different?"

"No, you're beautiful. Incredible."

Her eyes widened and heat colored her cheeks, her reaction surprising him. "Was that inappropriate?" he asked.

"No, just never been told that."

"How can that be?"

"I have no curves," she recited, drolly, "I have very small breasts and my hips do not advertise a wealth of children. Best to fight and not expect much else."

"I am sorry then."

"For what?"

"For all the fools who see you every day and are oblivious to how beautiful you are."

She raised up onto her arms and kissed him ardently. He looked into her eyes, memorizing every fleck of color. She shifted to her side and propped herself up onto her arm. He mirrored her with his suddenly freed arm. But something new, something different, was bothering him and she waited for him to speak.

When he didn't, her patience waned. "What happened?" she asked.

"I uh… I didn't think castle life would be so lonely. There are people everywhere but… No one talks to each other. They stay to themselves, do their duties, and leave once their shifts are over."

"Is that why no one questions you coming back dirty and disheveled?" she inquired, pulling a twig out of his hair.

He chuckled, mirthlessly. "I get back pretty late, everyone's already in bed, and it's dark enough for the guards not to notice anything." He glanced down before adding, "If anyone in the castle does talk to another, it's never in a nice way or even kind when speaking about others. It's quite a bleak place…"

"And have they been talking a little too loud?"

Gwendin frowned. "I heard the kitchen staff gossiping."

"And were you the topic?"

"One of them."

"What did they say?"

"It doesn't matter."

"If it upsets you, then it matters. Especially to me."

He hesitated before sighing. "I guess there's been discussions about why I leave once a week. I could care less but… I heard them talking about either me not being right in the head," and he smirked at that, then it faded, "Or I had found a girl in one of the towns to lay with. But they wondered who would bother with someone like me. Even a blind shepherdess would find me," and he paused, as if trying not to choke on the word, "repulsive."

It took everything in her at that moment not to march herself straight to the castle and thrash the kitchen staff. Unfortunately, she knew it wouldn't change anything especially after all of the stories he had already told her. A deep breath stifled her lust for violence. For now.

"I find myself quite baffled as to why me," he admitted. "Why you would be with me?"

"What do you mean?" she inquired. "Do you think yourself that ugly?"

"Compared to you? Yes."

She stared at him, bewildered, then a realization. "Do you think I fantasize about someone else when we're together?"

"Don't you?"

"Why would I?" Concerned by his silence, she ran a hand from his chest to his stomach, her fingers dancing in the whirl of hair. "I assure you," she added, bringing out her lustful tone, "No fantasies required. And I'd like to think that I have better taste than a blind shepherdess." When he didn't react, she caressed his cheek. "Now I'm sorry, Gwendin."

"For what?"

"For not ensuring that you are aware of how handsome you are. Why else would I be here, naked, doing things with you that would injure most people's backs?"

"Can I ask why me?"

She shrugged. "Before the Purge, we elves lived without conflict side-by-side with mankind. During the Purge, we worked together to fight a common cause. We were brothers in arms with a common goal. But afterwards, the men we fought with started treating us like something that disgusted them. That we were lower beings even though we had fought as equals. Most men I've run into during patrol are afraid or repulsed. Granted, I am warning them off our lands, not saving their lives, but... You... When we met, you didn't treat me like that. You didn't even react differently when you saw me on the road. You offered me a drink, you shared your flask without worry, you made jokes just to make me laugh. And you talked to me like a person, not a villain you'd see in your nightmares. You have always looked at me like a person. You have always treated me like a friend."

He stayed silent, almost like he didn't believe her.

"That means so much more to me than..." and she ran fingers down his cheek, "that dangerously charming smile of yours. Or the lovely freckles that are splashed along your nose. Or those little amber flecks in your eyes that seem to shine when you are considering something..." then she chuckled, slyly, "imaginative."

He still seemed unconvinced.

She grinned impishly, pushing him over onto his back and straddling him.

"I find you quite attractive. Even with all that hair." She bent down and gave him another kiss, her lips persuading him to return the embrace with the passion she expected from him. "And if you are not to those gossipers' taste then I'm glad. I don't like to share."

Finally, he chuckled, with honest amusement, running his hands along her back and buttocks. As she kissed him again, he rolled them until he was on top. She spent the rest of their time together happily reassuring him with every touch that he had nothing to worry about.

~   ~   ~

A few days later, her kith leader called together all of the sentries who were not on duty. They met in the kith square, loosely gathering around him at the area next to the firepit.

Medruano glowered at his sentries, as if they had failed him. "Have any of you interacted with a theurgist within our borders?"

Shock ran through the ranks, stealing voices for a moment, before each sentry responded negatively. Medruano's eyes met each elf's, including Zawn's, but he apparently found no sign of guilt.

"Has there been a trespasser, Leader?" Teno inquired, the muscles in his neck tensing.

Teno wasn't the only one. Each sentry suffered in silence, thinking they had failed to catch an absconder within their borders. All of them but Zawn. She tried to keep her face unreactive and her eyes emotionless. She knew if she showed concern her leader would notice. Especially since he was used to her blankly staring at him. So that's exactly what she did.

"Not as of yet. The College of Theurgy sent a letter, requesting to let him research and harvest on our lands." Then the leader scoffed, in incredulity. "They even offered to compensate our kith in return."

Surprised murmuring rippled through the group.

"I have decided to permit him… but only so far. He will be told to stop before the river. If any of you see him past that, report it immediately. Do not interact, do not bother this… theurgist. Only keep an eye out for him in the places he shouldn't be."

"Yes, Leader!" the group responded.

Medruano waved a hand. "Dismissed."

Zawn spun on her heel and headed to her hut, to ready herself for her evening shift. Once she closed the door, she leaned against it and sighed hard. He sought permission. Not only did he ask for it, he got it. The fact that he arranged a tithe through the College of Theurgy to pay her kith, which in turn gave him permission to not only gather on their lands but be within their borders… her heart warmed at his attentiveness to her people's honor.

Then the dread set in. What would have happened if Medruano said no? And would they be caught now? The only one who had any business in that area during the time they met was Taylor, because it was their shared area of watch, but what if the others became curious, investigating what this theurgist was doing?

She made herself take a deep breath. She couldn't spend time worrying when she had to meet the expectations of her kith's leader.

~ ~ ~

Their next meetup came around quickly, and as Zawn jogged to their spot, she still struggled with her confusion. She knew she couldn't let herself drown in fears and doubts, but they had been rattling around in her head for days. He was waiting for her as usual, leaning against the tree, that smile appearing at the sight of her. As she hopped down, he grabbed her into his arms and kissed her. However, he realized she didn't match his passion and he pulled away.

She stammered for a moment. "You asked permission?"

"Why do you sound so surprised?" He furrowed his eyebrows in confusion. "Was I not supposed to ask? Zawn, did I do something wrong?"

"No. No, you did everything... right."

"Then why does it feel like I didn't?"

"They know you're here now."

"Is that bad?" he asked, frowning. Then he noticed that she had a hard time finding her voice. "I have a legitimate reason to be here now. This way I don't have to sneak around and hide and I can forage without offense. The College did ask that I not be disturbed and told your leader that I didn't want to interact with any of the kith because it was unnecessary. But if I get caught on my way to meet up with you, neither of us will get in trouble because I can say that I'm here just to harvest. As long as I stay on this side of the river."

"But you asked."

"You told me to."

"Thank you," she whispered, before kissing him.

His smile broke their embrace, making her lean back this time. "I can think of a better way for you to thank me," he replied, his lips turning up into a sly grin.

"Oh, is that so?" she inquired, her relief finally breaking through the worries that had wracked her nerves for days. "Hm, let me see if I can figure that out."

~ ~ ~

Nestled in the roots, they cuddled. Suddenly, Zawn stiffened, causing Gwendin to look over her shoulder. Her hand reached for her khukuri, which was still sheathed as it laid next to his leg. He watched as her pupils dilated into full spheres. He knew she was listening, so he tried to hold his breath and not ask her anything until she figured out what she had set off her senses. Whatever it was either moved or vanished, because she slowly started to relax.

"What was it?" he asked, keeping his voice low.

"Predator, maybe," she whispered back. "Not sure. It didn't get close enough for me to see or smell. But it's no longer nearby."

CHAPTER 7

One day as she walked toward her hut, she caught herself glaring at the matched mates in her kith. Seeing the affection those couples had for each other, as they held hands and kissed in public, she felt jealousy. It also made her bitter. She had to keep her companion secret. She knew her kithlin looked down on her, but the fact that she was still unmatched made most pity her. However, even if she had found someone, even if he were an elf, nothing would change their view of her. She would always be the pariah of the kith.

Late at night, when alone in her hut, she would fantasize those small things. Holding hands, his pale fingers entwined in her gray-green bark. She dreamed about setting up a small campsite, where they could stay the night and spend real time together. She started to think about what else their future could hold, but kept her flights of fancy to herself. Even though they had grown closer with every conversation, she feared pushing him away with talks of more, knowing that he had no real reason to want anything other than what he was already getting out of her.

She had to remind herself that it was all moot. He was a human and she was an elf. Their affair, serious or not, was a crime. Humans and elves at least agreed on that one thing. And they both had the same punishment.

It would all end eventually.

~ ~ ~

They sat together, his arm around her shoulders while she rested her head on his. Even when they suffered doubts alone, together they were reassured, even confident in their companionship. They enjoyed their time together, finding themselves trying to find ways to extend it every visit. They listened to the sounds around them, while the summer heat still ebbed up from the ground. A flask moved between them, a sweeter concoction of his own creation, with a lower alcohol content than usual.

The nocturnal creatures that broke up the silence fascinated him. He asked which creature made what noise and she happily answered. It was nice to know something he didn't, especially after he shared his herbalist knowledge. She described what they looked like, since they hid in the shadows and bushes, while explaining what they hunted or ate. She had learned so much over the years during the Purge that she knew more than even most kithlin.

He took a deep breath before saying, "I've always wanted to ask something."

"Ask me."

"Are you sure?"

She nodded.

"Why is someone in the warrior caste," then he hesitated, as if choosing his words carefully, "a sentry? Is that normal? I mean, I learned about caste structure at the College. Should you be…?"

"Stuck on border duty?" She chuckled, mirthlessly, folding her hands and resting them in her lap. "I may be warrior caste, but that doesn't mean I always follow orders."

"Like laying with some strange man who you saved from ruthless robbers?"

"Rules are meant to be broken, right?"

"Only the unfair ones."

She shrugged, nonchalantly. "I have a hard time following rules if I find them lacking in substance or usefulness."

"What rule did you break?"

"Probably the dumbest one I could have. One that carried consequences that took away titles and privileges. But there's no changing the past, is there?"

"Tell me why you got demoted."

"Not really important," she responded, nuzzling his neck. "It happened. But there's a reason why I am called a nitwit."

He gave her a moment, knowing that her nonchalant tone hid her pain. But he wanted to know, he needed to know, because it seemed to color her opinion of the world. He asked, almost sternly, "What happened?"

He felt her jaw clench against his shoulder and she sighed. "Why does it matter?"

"Because I feel like I'm the one who does all the talking. I want to know you better. The only way I can do that is if you tell me the hardest parts of your life just like I have told you."

She shifted back, resigned, staring into his hickory brown eyes. "We had gotten information that when Elixin came to the throne, he was planning to conquer and dominate those who were not human. Us, the gargoyles, Riders, you name it. Because he had figured out how to trap them, he was starting with the gargoyles first. Our kith leader and theirs had a rather public falling out prior to Elixin's ascension, so we were not speaking to each other at all. I and one of the gargoyles," she stammered, then sighed, "well we had fallen for each other and had carried on a relationship for a while even though our two groups weren't on speaking terms. We had promised not to let our leaders' issues color our relationship."

She glanced away for a moment, taking a deep breath.

"At first, I tried talking my leader into telling the gargoyles, but he refused and he ordered all of us to keep quiet. I took the information to the gargoyles anyway. I thought because of my relationship, they would listen."

She paused again, remembering the look on her lover's angry face.

"Their leader, Nicholaus, told me that I was only there to provide misinformation on behalf of Medruano, to make them paranoid, dependent on us elves. I didn't have any support, even from my lover, who told me that I was just a pawn and to leave and never come back."

Gwendin hugged her closer, watching her face intently. She grasped one of his arms and smiled sadly.

"Medruano found out because Nicholaus sent a scathing communication to him about my involvement in his nefarious plans to trick them. I was stripped of every honor, every title. Even those I had earned during the Purge."

Gwendin stared at her, mouth gaping open. "You... you fought...?"

"Yes, of course I did," she answered, drolly. "I had been trained for battle since I was a child. And I have fought in several battles throughout the decades, including the Purge."

"But that makes you..." and he stammered as he struggled to find the right words.

"Old. The word is old."

"No, not... I just thought..."

"That I was your age? Compared to others in my kith, I am actually quite young. But to you? Hm, no, I am quite older than you. We elves have very long lives."

"I imagined you could have been older but not by that much."

"Does that change your mind about me?"

"Absolutely not." Then a sly smile started to brighten his face. "I like that you have more years than me. Explains how you know some of your little tricks that I like."

She kissed him passionately as she laughed. Then he watched as that cheerful moment faded from her eyes.

"None of it mattered really," she continued, looking down at her hands again. "Very few perks came with the accolades. So, I was demoted to sentry. My only luck was that I took the hut no one else wanted so that was the only thing I didn't lose. My closest friend even got punished even though he had nothing to do with any of it. Medruano thought we both colluded. After all, where there's one, there's the other." She caught herself wringing her hands a little too tightly. "When Elixin invaded the gargoyles' territory and imprisoned them in his castle, my heart broke. Not long after, I had a run-in with them. They blamed me for letting them fall. They didn't care that I tried to help them and, in turn, lost everything that mattered at that time. And with nothing left, I decided to accept my fate."

"And yet you continue to break rules and ignore orders?"

"Why not?" she asked, flippantly. "What else do I have to lose?"

His concern about the situation, even though it was long before they ever met, touched her more than she expected. She struggled internally, not used to expressing her pain or having someone care about her feelings. Especially how she felt about her demotion. She had been going through the motions, burying everything deep. Tears threatened and she looked away from him, confusion strangling her. She sniffled, surprised at her own reaction.

"I'm sorry. I didn't realize it still hurt so much."

"Don't apologize. Come here. You've comforted me in my time of need," and he pulled her into a warm embrace, kissing her forehead, "the least I can do is return the favor."

With Gwendin's arms around her, she realized how much she had truly lost… and all that she could still lose. She found someone, even if by accident, who cared. And he was someone who wanted to care, who appreciated her time and attention. Someone she never thought she would ever find.

~   ~   ~

They carried on foolishly for a while, thinking no one paid attention.

~   ~   ~

They were wrong.

CHAPTER 8

One night, as Zawn sat watching the road, the wind whipped around her. Startled, since the night had been still, she glanced around to find a large shadow descending from the sky and landing nearby.

The gargoyle's massive wingspan was double her height, blocking out all light coming from the moons and stars. Her dark charcoal gray skin mimicked the stones of the Mehdehran castle, a chameleon-like adaptation that allowed gargoyles to blend into whatever rocky surface they resided on. Her face, arms, and wings were smooth as flesh, but the joints, torso, tail, and legs were rough as uncut stone. She wore a leather body suit that hugged her torso, with thin straps that secured it over her shoulders, along with fitted pants and gauntlets on her wrists. She wore no shoes, since her crow-like feet helped her cling to trees and uneven surfaces. Her hands and the tips of her wings had clawed features, providing another option to grasp onto things.

The gargoyle folded her wings against her back, which sounded like several birds flapping in unison, as she settled into a crouch on the same boulder Zawn sat on. Zawn didn't move, even though the visit surprised her. She hadn't spoken to the gargoyle in the years after their fallout. They didn't greet each other and Zawn waited for the other to speak. Her stomach turned at the thought that her former friend and lover wanted something out of her. Why else would she be there?

"I was ordered by the King of Mehdehra to follow his theurgist during one of his trips into the forest," the gargoyle finally admitted. "I thought it would be a boring assignment, just watching some human dig in the dirt and scratch himself. Imagine my surprise when I saw you two together. In quite an imaginative position."

"Did you enjoy being a voyeur?" Zawn snapped, bitterness coloring her tone.

"You know that I didn't."

The elf scoffed.

"Only reason I caught you is because King Elixin questioned why the man had requested to spend the night out in the forest instead of coming home the same day like he has done in these past few months. When the theurgist answered him, the King didn't like his response and told him he would think on it. He dispatched me and now awaits my report."

Zawn bit her tongue.

"I don't care who you lay with, Zawnie. No, that's a lie. I do care. You mean too much to me."

"You can't still fancy me, like you did when we were younger."

"Fancy isn't the correct term and you know it." Marassa grimaced and sighed. "Foolish of me to think that you'd cherish our time together."

"Why does it matter how I remember it? After what you and Nicholaus did and said to me… Your actions stained what was good between us. We made our own paths. You chose your clan. And I learned a valuable lesson."

They bristled in the uncomfortable silence.

"I don't want you executed because of some frivolous fun."

"Well, then, I guess you have a choice to make. Keep our secret or sell me out to your master."

"He's his master too." Marassa unfurled her wings, stretching them out before folding them again. She always did that when she was irritated. "I have to report to him what I've seen."

"So, you'd sell him out instead? Not drag me back as the culprit that manipulated him, to be sacrificed to the malevolent king?"

"I have a job to do, orders to follow."

"Even if it is sentencing someone to death?"

"He wants to find something to punish him with because the theurgist is insolent."

"Then you might as well march both of us to the King and let him execute us together."

Zawn saw the determination in Marassa's eyes to follow through with her duty. That she would tell the King that his theurgist was laying with an elf. No matter the consequences for either of them. She felt her heart sink. Zawn and Gwendin knew there were ramifications to their affair, but they carried on naively thinking they had everyone fooled. But now the life-or-death moment arrived and it was up to Marassa to decide their fate.

"What options do I have?" Zawn asked, after swallowing hard against her pride.

"End it immediately or I will have to report my findings. In great detail."

"You would give me the opportunity to put an end to our frivolous fun? Why?" Zawn searched the gargoyle's face. "So you can avoid being our executioner?"

"If you end it, I will make no mention of you at all."

Not waiting for Zawn to respond, Marassa stood, unfurling her wings again then leapt off of the outcrop and flew away.

CHAPTER 9

She thought it would be easy. She would keep her distance, end their affair, then run home. And she would never see him again. Simple. Final. After all, he was nothing more than a distraction, someone to burn off her energy. They had gotten to the point in their affair that it was repetitive. Yes, that was a good reason. She had grown tired of him. If she told him that she was bored, and that she found someone else to excite her, he would then do the same. Maybe a sweet maiden would be amenable to his need to fill the void. They could both turn to another and forget about each other. Easy.

She slowly walked out of the tree line and stumbled to a halt. She stood at the edge of the clearing, her heart shattering at the scene laid out before her. There was a fire, with a pot hanging over it from a tripod, cooking something that smelled delicious. A small tent covered their usual nook of roots and limbs. It was a true campsite, something that she had fantasized about in her private musings. Here he was, providing her a dream come true. Some place they could pretend to be normal.

But they weren't normal. They were an abomination in others' eyes. They were actually under the real threat of punishment.

And someone else was watching them.

"What is this?" she demanded.

Gwendin glanced up at her and smiled, then returned to tending the small fire. "Thought maybe we'd try something a little different. I told the King that the traveling back and forth in one evening was tiresome and it was best to forage in the early mornings. He agreed to allow me one trial night to camp out instead of wandering around for a few hours." He approached her and held out his hand. "Come sit with me."

She didn't move, still frowning. "No."

"What? Why not?"

"Because…" and she stammered for a moment, "this is courting stuff. Normal couple stuff. We're not courting, we're not normal. We are just using

34

each other. If we try this stuff, if we like it and like each other, then we'd ultimately end up heartbroken."

"You divined all that from a dinner?"

"I should go."

"Wait, don't go," he begged as he closed the distance between them. "I… yes, I hoped we could do more than just use each other. I have really liked spending time with you and wanted to…"

"I'm sorry, Gwendin, but no, this isn't what we agreed to." Her heart felt a stabbing pain as she added, "This isn't what I want."

She watched as his shoulders slumped. "I'm sorry, I just thought…"

"It's obvious that we want different things. I can't give you this…" and she waved her trembling hand, "whatever this is that you were hoping for. Goodbye, Gwendin."

"Wait, Zawn."

And he grabbed her arm before she could escape.

"Don't come back, Gwendin."

"What…?"

"Just don't come back. I won't be here to protect you."

With that she wrenched her arm free and ran off into the forest. She climbed up a tree and hid from him as he tried to follow her. He gave up after a few attempts to discern which way she ran and returned deflated to his campsite. As she watched him disappear, she felt her heart break into pieces.

Tears began to stream down her cheeks and she forced herself to leave the area, swearing never to return. As she made her way home, she repeatedly told herself it was necessary. His life was saved and he would move on now that she wasn't in his life.

She could only hope that the scene was enough for their audience and Marassa would keep her word.

Zawn entered her kith from the back, making sure no one noticed her. She ducked into her hut, secured the door, collapsed in front of her fireplace, and cried herself to sleep.

CHAPTER 10

Zawn finally got used to finishing her shift and returning home. She would eat a simple meal then rest, before she tackled other tasks assigned to her. Her schedule hadn't changed in years. She was always on duty during dinner and toward the middle of the night. Medruano had always seemed determined to keep her away from the group as a whole and ensured she had no friendships other than Taylor. She had never argued, considering the kith's opinion about her, and no one noticed when she arrived or left.

Thinking she was protecting herself, she avoided too many conversations. She didn't even react when Medruano gave her another assignment, the first in ages, this time cleaning the milking goats' stalls. She only nodded and went about her business.

~   ~   ~

She did hover one morning near the kith square, busying herself to keep anyone from asking her any questions. She waited until the messenger from the College of Theurgy arrived, delivering the tithe as expected. She felt a deep relief, knowing that if Gwendin had been executed the tithe would have ended. But with the delivery… she finished her fake task and darted into the goats' stall.

~   ~   ~

A few weeks after she left Gwendin standing in their spot, she accidentally had a free day from chores other than her sentry duty. Instead of making it obvious, she hid in her hut with a plan to drink herself stupid. She sat on the floor, on the side of her bed near the bathing room and hidden from windows and doors. She stole a rather large bottle of apple wine from the cold storage and popped it open as quietly as she could. She poured about half a glass and took a sip. Tasting the fruity spirits made her flashback to their first kiss and she immediately downed the remaining liquid.

She wanted to forget but the burn of the alcohol only made her remember. Her eyes closed and she gave in, losing herself in the memories. The feel of his lips, that sweet taste of his. The feel of his body connecting with hers. Even how his stomach hair tickled her bark. The way he laughed, his breath tickling her neck when he kissed it… his warmth, his joy, his sense of humor. The look in his eyes every time she arrived at their meeting place, every time he glanced over at her, every time they were intimately entangled.

She didn't realize how much he meant to her… until now. She had foolishly fallen for the man. This was only supposed to be an arrangement for physical release, not any kind of relationship. Definitely not love.

How did she let this happen? She had sworn off love ages ago.

Maybe when he called her beautiful? Did her heart betray her then? Or was it the way he pulled her against him and kissed her so passionately? Or held her so reverently after they satisfied each other? Or maybe it was the way he caressed her? Was it his attentiveness to her climax, to her comfort? Or was it when he consoled her after telling him about her demotion? She cursed her quivering heart.

More wine poured into her glass. She had sworn never to fall in love again. She was so young when she had been ready to share her life and take Marassa as her mate… She took another drink. That betrayal had destroyed her faith in love. Her first heartbreak was enough for a lifetime. But with Gwendin, she broke that oath unwittingly. How and when eluded her, but the culmination of moments seemed to have led up to her breaking her oath.

Then the image of him being found guilty of treason and being executed by the King intruded… she suddenly regretted only grabbing one bottle, even though she knew two would be noticed. Her chest hurting, she didn't even bother with the glass, drinking straight from the bottle. She took a long swig, until she had to catch her breath, as she drowned in her grief.

Now, as the anguish overtook her again, she felt the tears pour down her cheeks.

She never wanted much in life. Even before her heartbreak and demotion, she had led a simple life guided by the lessons she learned from her mentor. Eat, breathe, fight, win. She had been born to die as a warrior and that was all she knew.

Until Gwen. He showed her there was more to life, to the world. She found herself learning more and eventually wanting more for herself. When their affair started, she knew she had little chance of keeping him, but deep down, she had really hoped she could.

She promised herself this would be the last time. Love was a waste of time. Hope and faith were for fools. And after all this time, this one incident felt like the one to finally break her. She followed an order she didn't like and she did what was required of her. No matter what that did to her.

Having consumed the rather large bottle on an empty stomach, and within less than an hour, the lethargy suddenly hit her. Her muscles gave into the alcohol, her arms going numb and her eyes falling heavy. She leaned against the bed and her vision started to darken…

~   ~   ~

It had poured rain all night. He hid away in his tent, keeping a hopeful eye out. However, there was zero movement in the forest. All of the critters hid from the downpour, so if there had been any arrival to their nook, he would have caught sight of foliage moving. But there was nothing. No movement. No visitor.

Soggy and devastated, Gwendin walked back to the castle. The castle staff hadn't started to circulate, which saved him from any embarrassment. He returned to his chambers, laid all of his camping equipment to dry out, and stoked the fire a little higher to help quicken his own drying. He caught himself staring at the flames, feeling his own heart flash into ashes.

She wasn't coming back.

He would never see her again.

Turning and walking to his bathing room, he changed out of his wet clothing and used a towel to dry his hair. He caught his reflection in the looking glass and saw what the tears had done to his face. Puffy, red, pained. He stormed out of the bathing room and found himself standing at his table of herbs and potions. Shaking, he reached past the different bottles until his hand grasped a larger bottle. The spirits had to be ready, it had fermented long enough. He popped the lid and inhaled the mixture. It was ready. And there was enough for him to drink himself into oblivion. He grabbed the jug and a somewhat clean cup, flopped down in the chair by the fireplace and poured the liquid to the rim of the cup. His first gulp made him gag, however that did not deter him. Cup after cup, he threw the brew back until he didn't even notice how many gulps he swallowed.

His heavy, lethargic head rolled along his shoulder, until his eyes fell on his work desk. There were so many bottles, beakers, and plants that his blurred vision couldn't discern each. But he knew what they were good for. He could call her back to him. He could make her come back. Through the fog, he heard his mentor's voice chide him for such selfish thoughts. Hot tears poured down his cheeks. Why couldn't he be selfish this time? Never once had he gotten a voice in his life, not until now, but even that had been taken from him after she disappeared into the trees.

He stumbled toward the table and picked up one beaker… then a bottle…

~   ~   ~

When he woke up later that morning, he wasn't in his chambers. Confused,

38

he sat up a little too quickly and slipped off whatever he was laying on. A thump and a grunt echoed through the air. He glanced around and realized, somehow, he had teleported himself into the forest. And he had ended up on a tree limb. Then he felt something wriggle on his chest, before two very big black eyes met his. The squirrel chittered, almost lovingly at him, and rubbed his face with its nose. Startled, he didn't know how to respond to the affection. He watched as the critter blinked then darted off into the trees.

Head throbbing from the fall and the hangover, Gwendin tried to figure out where exactly he was and how the hell he was going to sneak back into the castle.

CHAPTER 11

Taylor sat next to the fireplace, honing his khukuri while Chaelene worked nearby in the kitchen. Chaen and Talor were outside working on their fighting exercises while Minee laid in her crib taking a nap after draining her bottle dry.

He used the time to worry privately about his friend. Zawn had started acting differently, but she wouldn't speak about what was on her mind. That was her way, he knew that from growing up with her. Since his mother raised them both together, she was the closest thing to a sister he could have and they knew each other inside and out.

Zawn had always found it difficult to share things, especially emotions and mistakes. However, her antisocial behavior extending to Taylor and Chaelene was new. They always tried to include her, even in dinner, but she had started turning down their offers to join them. She didn't spend any free time with them or the children. Her sudden disinterest in everything bothered him, even though he knew her well enough that they had to give her time and space.

He feared that it had something to do with her lover or whatever the person was to her. When it all started, she had changed for the better. She smiled, she joked, she laughed, all the things that she didn't do so easily before. She reminded him of her younger self, before the stresses of life took her joy. Then unexpectedly, she shut down again, very similar to how she reacted when her first love shunned her. If this idiot broke her heart or was in any way cruel to her...

"Tay?" Chae inquired, her voice snapping him out of his thoughts. "Can you help me, my love?"

"Of course," he responded, sheathing his blade and joining her.

"Cut these vegetables for the stew, please. I don't have enough hands."

He chuckled, taking the knife from her and starting in on the various vegetables on the cutting board. "You should ask Zawnie. Her chopping skills are more impressive than mine."

"She turned down dinner."

40

"Again?"

"She comes straight home now," Chaelene added softly.

"I know, I've watched her. For the last few weeks, every night, she walks this way."

"She's not her usual self."

"I've noticed, too." Finished with chopping the carrots, he slid the pieces over to her. "I don't know what to say to her."

"Do we know anything about this person she was involved with?"

"No." He started slicing the skinny squash. "Honestly, I didn't want to know. I didn't want to find out she was involved with someone she wasn't allowed to be with."

"You think she would? Even, possibly, a m…"

Taylor waved his hand to stop her from completing that sentence.

"We both know her well, Chae. Rules are only challenges for her. If she can't skirt them, she will break them. Why should she care about the consequences? But she always forgets that eventually it bites her in the ass."

"She needs to talk to someone, though," his mate responded, scooping up the vegetables and dropping them into the stew. "You're the only one she'd trust. And the only one that won't judge her."

"I will talk to her."

"Thank you. Now please, cut the meat in small bits and don't chop off a finger."

~   ~   ~

The next evening, he decided to leave early for his shift. Away from their kith, he could speak with Zawn in private, guaranteeing they wouldn't be overheard. Taylor watched his friend as she honed her short sword instead of watching the road, proving to him that she was distracted, more than usual anyway. She always sensed his approach and greeted him immediately. Tonight however, she hadn't even stopped the slow sliding of her blade against the stone. He sighed as he plopped down next to her, making her glance up and furrow her eyebrows.

"Who are they and what did they do?" Taylor inquired.

Zawn scoffed. "It doesn't matter, my friend." Then she looked back down at her blade. "It's over."

"Is it?"

She stayed silent, honing her blade carefully.

"You're a nitwit but you're my friend, Zawnie. My family. If you need to talk to anyone…"

She frowned slightly, testing the blade with her fingernail. "I gave him up."

"Why?"

"I ended it to save his life," she admitted, softly.

Realizing that he had guessed right, that she had gotten involved with someone she wasn't allowed to, made his expression darken. "Who was he?"

"The Mehdehran King's theurgist."

He furrowed his eyebrows, confused. "Wait. The same…?"

Zawn didn't respond.

"And how on this side of the canopy did you meet him?" he demanded, exasperated by her admission.

"I saved his life from some kithless thugs. He wanted to thank me with a drink. We got on and then got naked." She shrugged, sheathing her weapon. "It was only supposed to be a flight of fancy, you know. Like you said, to burn off my energy. But I let him be more than some distraction." She had to swallow hard to stop the tears from surfacing. "Then I found out that we had been caught by an agent of the King and it was his life in the balance. Because we are a crime. I was able to negotiate to save his life by ending of our… whatever it was."

"Who caught you?"

"Marassa."

"Oh, fuck."

She nodded, slowly. "She um told me to give him up or watch him be executed."

"She gave you a choice?"

"Surprised me, too."

He watched as a tear finally broke free and ran down her cheek. Then a few more followed. It was only the rarest of times that she let him see her heartache. The last time he saw her grieve was when his mother died. He wanted to hug her, but he was afraid that it could set her off into a moment of weakness she would never forgive.

"I am sorry to hear that. I really am, Zawnie."

"Why?" she demanded, her throat tight. It was bad enough that she had to give Gwendin up but now to hear Taylor's sympathy? "It wasn't like we were courting."

"No, but he was more than a distraction."

She grimaced, sighing hard. "It doesn't matter now." She grabbed her dagger, sliding it along the stone. It slipped off, her hand unsure as her emotions tore at her. "Especially since things like that don't last. He would have found someone else eventually, someone who was his own kind and we would have gone our separate ways. That's how it's supposed to go, right? At least this way, with me out of the picture, he can find someone new a lot sooner." She finally wiped her face with a shaking hand. "He'll be happier."

"What about you, Zawnie? You have spent so much time alone, without a mate…"

"Yes, but that's a good thing," she replied, with a fake smirk, "I am very difficult to live with."

He chuckled, mirthlessly. "You certainly are. But you deserve to be happy, too."

"For me, happiness is only a fairy tale. Happiness is for you and Chae, for everyone else in this world. It is not for me." Silence held them, until she shrugged. "I did what I had to," she said, voice soft. "After all, that's what we do, right? Make sacrifices for the greater good?"

"Or for those we care about?"

She didn't respond, but he knew that her comments meant more than just her affair with the theurgist. She had been through so much turmoil, especially in her love life, that he feared this could be the final blow. That she would never search out love, or any kind of companionship, again.

"Will you be all right?" he asked, watching her carefully.

She lowered her eyes, then scoffed. "I have to be."

"Go home, my friend. Try to get some sleep."

"Thank you. Stay safe."

CHAPTER 12

Evening arrived and blanketed the forest with a chill that caused the unprepared to shiver and for all creatures' breath to materialize with each exhalation. The rainy season was just starting, which meant days of rain and nights of frostiness. It could settle deep into one's soul, with the lack of sun and the dreariness of the persistent cloud cover.

It definitely affected Zawn.

She sat on the rock edge, eyes on the road below. Her thick coat kept her warm while she sat watch, but she still felt a coldness in her heart. Her thoughts had been dreadful lately, but as the clouds hid the sun and stars, it seemed to have gotten worse. She had nothing. She had less than nothing, she had emptiness. Was it worth getting up in the morning and doing the same thing over and over? What did she have to look forward to anymore?

If there was nothing here for her anymore, why did she stay? Suddenly, she wondered if leaving wouldn't be best, for her and for her kith. After all, she was just a sentry and even that she did half-assed. She could put as much distance between her, the kith, the castle... her past. Just by heading west.

The thought startled her. She had never considered that option before. Usually if an elf wanted to leave their kith, they would appeal to another for acceptance. The few who were kithless had been banished due to crimes or other issues, but even those troublemakers stayed in the forest near their own kind.

Maybe the tales Gwendin had told her about theurgists traveling to and through other kingdoms ignited her fanciful thinking? But... was it just whimsy? Or could she actually do it? Nothing held her here. Well, Taylor and Chae and their children, but they didn't count on her. She was just as much a burden on them as she was to the rest of the kith. No one actually depended on her.

She didn't have much. She could pack her satchel, hide it before her shift, then after Taylor relieved her, she could throw it over her shoulder and start walking.

She sighed, returning her attention back to the empty road below.

What a lovely fantasy.

~　　　~　　　~

One night, the thoughts still fresh, she pulled out her satchel and set it on her table.

Another night, she packed her few keepsakes.

The following week, she started folding clothes, slipping them in like pieces of a puzzle.

Slowly, her hut began to look more bare than usual.

And she finally felt something: confident, even exhilarated, in her decision.

Now, she only needed to pick a day.

Her plans were set.

CHAPTER 13

Or so she thought.

CHAPTER 14

It was late one night, when Marassa landed next to Zawn as she sat on her favorite rock outcropping. The wind from her wings whipped the elf's hair across her face, however, she didn't move. She felt the gargoyle glance over at her, timidly, but Zawn didn't bother acknowledging her. There was nothing left to say between the two former lovers. The elf continued to watch over the sector for trespassers, nibbling on sunflower seeds, a trick she used to stay awake.

"He still goes," Marassa said, soberly, "every week, no matter the weather. Without fail."

Zawn didn't respond. She kept her fully dilated eyes focused intently on the road below, while taking a drink from her hip flask.

"He sets up his campsite," the gargoyle continued, "cooks his food, eats it like it's tasteless, then retires to his tent. Alone. He is back at the castle before breakfast and doesn't say a word to anyone other than the Queen, who he attends. Even she commented on how withdrawn and quiet he had become."

"Is that what you told your master?"

"More or less. Frivolity never came up."

Zawn tried to keep her expression blank and tone indifferent. "Now you know his excursions had everything to do with his actual job. He goes there to do whatever he needs to as the King's theurgist. I was just an amenity."

Silence fell between them. Marassa didn't move, even as she breathed, reminding Zawn of how much the gargoyle resembled a statue of stone.

"Leave me alone," Zawn commanded her. "I kept my word."

"You did. I followed you too, to see if you would break it by returning to him." Marassa tapped her claws against the rock. "But after watching him these last few weeks... now I fear I made a mistake in my judgement. That I let my jealousy guide my actions."

"Hindsight has an inevitable clarity," the elf retorted, bitterly.

"I know that now. You were not an amenity to him, as he was not one to you. If you care to see him again, just know that the King is satisfied with my report and I will no longer be following the theurgist."

Zawn scoffed, shaking her head. "There's no going back. I've moved on."

"He hasn't."

"I don't care," she snapped back. Then Zawn saw movement in the trees and recognized Taylor's bulky shadow. "Goodbye, Marassa."

~   ~   ~

The next week, she started back toward the kith but halfway there, she stopped. She stood in between the trees, listening to the wind rustle their leaves. She closed her eyes, arguing with herself. She should go home. Return to her hut and get some rest. After all, she had the goat stalls and weeding to do after her nap. But Marassa's words had haunted her that night as she watched her sector.

Marassa could have been lying to her.

What if it was a trap?

What if it wasn't?

~   ~   ~

He sat in front of the fire, legs crossed, bowl in one hand while the other held a spoon. He sighed, hard, before scooping up some stew and shoving it into his mouth. The chill of a curved blade sliding under his chin made him freeze, the spoon trapped in his mouth.

"I keep getting reports of some man camping out in our territory," she admonished, in her familiarly haughty tone. "You were supposed to stop coming here."

Gwendin carefully removed the spoon and swallowed his food, his skin scraping against the blade. "It's difficult to find the herbs I need anywhere else," he responded, keeping his tone casual. "I still pay a tithe to the kith that owns these lands, which permits me to gather."

The cold metal left his skin as Zawn withdrew her khukuri.

"As long as you are a welcomed visitor, I will leave you be."

Sheathing her blade, she began to walk away when she saw him stand up, out of the corner of her eye.

"Are you, um, hungry?"

She disappeared into the tree line, her voice echoing back, "Have a good evening, theurgist."

~   ~   ~

She reprimanded herself as she stormed into her hut. What a foolish act, not only returning to see him but letting him know she was there. However, she felt it necessary to remind him how vulnerable he was… and she wasn't there to protect him. Did he not learn anything from their first meeting?

She glowered at her quiet fireplace, trembling slightly. She had expected him to dismiss her, turn her away, or yell at her. But when he asked if she was hungry, there was hope in his voice. A hope she didn't want to hear.

She growled a curse and stomped into her bathing room. She undressed, bathed, then climbed into her small bed after slipping on her sleeping gown. She glanced over at her table, where her packed satchel sat, ready when she was, and she debated taking off that night. Then she laid down in resignation. Her annoyance made falling asleep more of a chore than she expected, but eventually her eyes grew heavy and she drifted into unconsciousness.

Only to find him waiting for her, in her dreams.

CHAPTER 15

She couldn't help herself. The following week, she snuck back to their meeting place, just to see him. It would be a brief glance and she would leave. He didn't need to know she was there this time.

She refused to admit that he had invaded her dreams, leaving her with a warmth she hadn't felt in a very long time. That first time, she let it comfort her, thinking it was a one off because of seeing him. But the dreams didn't stop. They made sleeping each night torturous, because she woke from those dreams to find herself alone, yearning for him. They made her daydream through her chores and wish the day would end quickly so she could return to his arms in dreamland.

She hoped a quick glance would quell her fantasies.

She crouched behind a large oak tree, checking for any watchers. But just like the last time, she didn't hear, smell, or see any trace of the gargoyle. The trees also promised that she was alone in her spying. Reassured her visit wouldn't be reported, she peeked around the tree trunk to look for him in his camp.

He had it set up like the last time, the tent erected in the nook of the tree's roots, with something that smelled delicious brewing in the small pot over a modest fire. But he was nowhere to be seen. She straightened up, grousing. Then she felt one arm wrap around her shoulders and another around her waist.

"Got you!"

Instinctively, she grabbed the arm around her upper half and flipped her attacker over her shoulder. He cried out when he landed. Gwen laid there, staring up at her, startled. She started to apologize but her giggling stole her voice.

She stifled her laughter as he glowered up at her, then responded, "You deserved that."

He sat up, shaking his head. She offered her hand to help him up and he grasped it. But instead of standing, he yanked and caused her to fall into his lap.

As he trapped her in his arms, she pretended to struggle until he squeezed her.

They stared at each other, not having been this close since their last intimate night together several weeks ago. She couldn't help but savor the moment. Surrounded by the warmth of his presence, she relaxed as she laid cradled in his arms. Those same arms that held her during their most cherished moments. She inhaled his scent, which was always some sort of herbal mixture that she could never completely dissect into its separate ingredients.

Seeing the adoration in his eyes, even if it was shadowed by confusion and heartache, reminded her how entangled they had become. Confusion drowned her. Why did he look at her like that? Wasn't he angry with her? It all tore at her determination not to give into her feelings.

She caressed his cheek, her thumb lightly brushing his lower lip. She hated seeing those lips of his drawn down in a frown. She remembered how they felt against hers, how sweet he tasted, then her willpower collapsed and she kissed him. He stiffened at first, as if unsure, then he melted into the tender embrace while pulling her closer against him. They lost themselves, until a rattling noise caught his attention.

"My stew. Damn it. Can you stay? Are you hungry?"

She slipped off of his lap, making him let go of her. She floundered in uncertainty, but after a brief pause, she nodded. He smiled, as if relieved, then stood, grabbed her hand, and helped to her feet. Hand in hand, he led her into the campsite. He motioned for her to sit down next to the fire, while he tended to the food in the small pot. She loosened and removed her breastplate and gauntlets so she could sit comfortably on the ground, then watched him quietly. But when he looked over at her, she avoided his gaze as much as possible, afraid she would have another moment of weakness.

He dug into his duffel and pulled out two bowls and two spoons. Knowing that he still brought two of everything and the tent, which was big enough for the both of them, twisted her heart. He served her first, handing the bowl and utensil over, then served himself. He sat next to her, his shoulder barely touching hers. They ate in awkward silence, spending most of the time staring into their bowls.

"I'm not a great cook," he admitted, sheepishly, "but it's edible."

"It could use a bit of salt," she replied, nonchalantly, with a shrug.

That made him grouse, amusing her. Begrudgingly, he reached into his bag and retrieved a small canister with a twisting lid. He opened it then offered it to her. She grabbed a pinch, sprinkled it in the stew, and tasted it.

"Better."

He scoffed, as if offended, but she caught him pinch some salt into his bowl as well before putting the container away. She tried to hide her smile, but it cracked her stoic face before she realized it. She caught him glancing over at her right at that moment, a humored glimmer in his eye. Then the uneasiness settled over them again.

When they were done, he took the bowl from her and she thanked him. He set them next to his duffel, then took a swig from his flask. He handed it over to Zawn, who took her own gulp, then she handed it back. They touched, his fingertips brushing her knuckles gently. That touch, as small as it was, made her breath catch. She met his gaze and she knew he could see the pain that haunted her eyes. It reflected back in his. He reached over to caress her cheek, making her eyes close, before he kissed her tenderly. And one kiss led to another... then another...

They cherished every touch, moving closer with each one. It wasn't enough, not for her. She grabbed one of his hands and placed it on her boot, then moved hers to her other one. They untied and loosened a boot each, slipping them off before kissing again.

Without a word, he stood and offered his hands. She grasped them, using his strength to stand up, then he led her to the tent. At the opening, he let go and took a step back. She looked at him, worried, until he pulled his tunic off. Then he unbuckled his belt. She watched his muscles move under his pale skin as he removed his slacks and undershorts. When he stood up straight again, they stared at each other wordlessly, Gwen not shying away from her gaze. The lump in her throat made it hard to breathe, seeing that he offered himself up for inspection, waiting for her to decide if she found him strong enough.

She thought of everything she had listed the night she got drunk. He wasn't muscular like a warrior, but that wasn't what had captured her attention. His smile, the way he told stories, and how he regarded her like an equal meant more to her. However, when it came to the physical, the little nuances of his body drew her to him. The way his hair thickened around his nipples, converging along the middle of his chest and running down his belly to his more private parts. His pale skin that reddened when he feverishly devoted himself to her. The small calluses on his hands from digging and gathering that would roughly brush her as he caressed and held her. And those lips. They held that sweet taste that she became addicted to their first night together.

She stepped closer to him, reaching again for his hands. A mere breath between their bodies, she felt his fear fading as she brought his hands to the bottom edge of her tunic. Understanding her cue, he grasped it gently and lifted it. She raised her arms up and suddenly her shirt fluttered to the ground. Unbuckling her belt, he laid it inside, next to the opening, keeping her weapons within reach. When he straightened, her hands fell gently onto his chest, fingers lingering in the soft hair that swirled there.

Relieved that she had accepted him as strong enough, he cupped her shoulders, pulling her in closer. He ran light fingertips down her back until they encountered her pants. Slowly, he gently kissed her body as he lowered down onto his knees. Each touch released a bloom of warmth in her abdomen. He unhooked her pants and pushed them just past her hips. They slid down, while he caressed her hips, buttocks, then legs. Her breath caught in her throat as his lips instinctively traced the warmth that she thought died the night she ran away.

Making his way to her feet, he held the pants so she could slip her feet out.

He ducked into the tent and offered one hand to guide her inside as well. She straddled him and he freed her unbraided hair from the crooked bun, smiling when it tumbled around her shoulders. She shivered when the wind whipped through the opening. He grabbed his thick blanket, wrapping it around them to warm her up. His arms held her against him as their lips and their bodies connected…

Afterwards, they laid together under the shelter of the tent as rain sprinkled lightly. She laid with her back against his chest, using his bundled-up shirt as a pillow. He had both arms wrapped around her, holding her tightly to him, making sure as much of their naked flesh touched as possible. The blanket covered their nude bodies, keeping them warm against the chilly night.

She ran fingertips lightly over the one that held her around her shoulders as she listened to his soft snore, wrestling with her confusion. She had spent so much time convincing herself that he had forgotten about her and had found another lover that when he had caught her, she had expected him to turn her away. However, he looked relieved that she had returned to him and he didn't hesitate taking her to bed.

Fear gripped her as she realized that they had moved beyond just physical satisfaction. She knew that it had felt that way for her, but in the still of the night, she started to doubt if he truly felt the same way. How could he not, though? With the way he touched her, how he moved with her, how they barely took their eyes off of each other? It was unlike their dalliances before. It wasn't fervent or playful. Their physical and emotional connection felt stronger, deeper than their previous sexual encounters.

He had surprised her with how he presented himself and how reverently he removed each piece of her clothing. His tenderness, sincerity, and attentiveness strengthened his hold on her. And she knew, no matter what happened next, she would leave her heart with him.

He stirred finally after his brief doze, then kissed her shoulder gently.

Fearing an altercation now that he was awake, she murmured, "I like this," touching the tent's material as it protected them. "Feels like I'm in a dream."

"Then let's stay lost in this dream," he responded, his voice low with sleep.

"Hm, the sun will shatter the dream."

Another kiss, this time in the crook of her neck, and a heavy sigh. "If it comes out. I haven't seen it much these last few days through the weather. They had told me that we were going into the rainy season, so it made sense to pitch a tent to keep dry."

"It is a good idea. Kinda big though. I'm surprised you didn't shrink it to fit one, instead."

"I am a foolish man with foolish thoughts," he replied. "I held out hope that you'd come back."

She squeezed her eyes shut for a moment, her heart thumping. "Gwen…"

"I am willing to let you use me for as long as you want," he whispered against her ear.

She shifted her body, making him loosen his hold, and laid on her back so she could look over at him. "I don't know what I want."

"Whatever you decide, I will honor it. But know that I will always feel this way."

"What way?"

He hesitated, a worried expression on his face. "I don't want to scare you off again."

"Tell me anyway."

He searched her eyes and found proof that she wouldn't run away if he told her the truth. "I think of you all day. When something happens, I tell myself that I need to remember to tell you." He blushed, a self-deprecating smile twitching his lips up. "I usually forget most of it the moment we get naked but..." The smile faded, making her reach up and caress his lips gently. He realized in that precious moment that he might not have another chance telling her how he truly felt and let it tumble out. "I dream of you. Every night. I dream of you by my side, in my bed, in my arms. I-I dream of us being more. Not just using each other. More than allies. Lovers, friends, everything. That's why I did everything here. There have been nights where I even fancied the idea of just holding your hand while we talked."

"You have wonderful dreams," she responded, her voice faint. "But we do not live in a world that would let that dream come true."

"I am a foolish man, remember? I want to make a world where that dream could be true. I want you to be in every part of my life. Someday." His hand traced down her arm until he could slip it behind her back, pulling her against him tightly. "But tonight? I just want to keep you close."

"What else?" she inquired, when he hesitated again.

"I don't know how much more I should say."

"Tell me everything." Faint wisps of tears rimmed her eyes. "I need to hear it."

He caressed her cheek, his fingertips tracing the hair that framed her face. "You're the reason I get out of bed in the morning. The reason I close my eyes at night and dream. Every day, every night, you are my reason. Tell me you can stay longer?"

"Until predawn light."

He kissed her, passionately, persuading her into another intimate entanglement.

~　　　~　　　~

He woke to find her standing by the dying fire, struggling with her boots as she tried to put them on quietly. He sat up, watching her through the opening of the tent. She was dressed again, even her armor, with her loose hair hanging down and hiding her face. He felt his heart thump a little harder suddenly, fearing that she had decided to sneak off before he roused.

Or worse, leave and not come back.

But deep down, he held onto his hope that she would have kissed him awake and that she would promise to return to his side. After all, she did stay the whole night, she did agree to each of his requests for intimacy… she even made a few requests of her own.

He had thrilled being able to make love to her, throughout the night, but feared he had given the remainder of his heart away a little too quickly. After all, he didn't know if she meant to rekindle their connection or not. She never told him that his words had been persuasive either. He didn't know if telling her everything had been a good idea.

Once she succeeded with her boots, she glanced over her shoulder and saw that he was awake. She straightened, smiling sincerely, trying to settle her left heel in its boot. He exited the tent, wrapping the blanket around him to fend off the morning chill. When he got close enough, he grabbed her into his arms. Her armor felt cool against his skin, but her body reacted warmly. He kissed her ardently, her reciprocation confirming some of his hopes.

She frowned, apologetic. "I have to go."

"Will I see you again?" he asked, with some trepidation.

Zawn stammered, then sighed. "I want to see you."

"Then come back tonight. I'll be here."

She hesitated, debating on what to say, before she kissed him one more time. "Just make sure you're not followed." She slipped out of his arms then she disappeared into the woods.

Her words finally made sense as to why she ran, why she worried. The King was keeping an eye on his theurgist. That needed to end, immediately.

CHAPTER 16

Upon his return that morning, Gwendin dropped off his satchel and duffel in his chambers, then strode into the dining room, where the King and Queen quietly ate breakfast. They sat on opposite ends of the massive table, as if they were worlds apart and not husband and wife. Since his arrival, Gwendin had watched their rift grow deeper and deeper every day, but neither spouse acted as if it were a bad thing. The theurgist gave a quick nod to the Queen before settling angry eyes on the King.

"Ah, sorcerer, what brings you to our audience?" Elixin demanded, not bothering to look at Gwendin or swallow the food in his mouth. The King was obviously annoyed with the theurgist's abrupt arrival. "Another request to stay away from the castle longer? Maybe two nights in a row? Why not ask for a fortnight?"

Gwendin regarded him with distaste, but knew he had to choose his words wisely. "I came to question your decision to have me followed during my excursions outside the castle." Out of the corner of his eye, Gwen saw the Queen stop eating.

"You do not question your King," Elixin snapped.

"You are not my King," Gwendin retorted, causing Elixin to glare at him. "You are just my client. I am only here at the whim of the College of Theurgy. And the College dictates what I can and cannot do, as well as what rules I am to follow. Not you."

The silence was electrified with both men's anger.

"And as a contracted employee, I can question you if I am being treated unfairly. The College frowns upon such behavior toward their members."

"Then complain," Elixin replied, dismissively, returning to his meal. "They will not remove you, the College has too much invested in this part of the continent."

"They will recall me upon my request. And where will that leave you?" Silence. Gwendin pulled out a handful of roots from his belt purse. "Do you know what these are, Your Majesty?"

Elixin didn't even bother to look at him. "No."

"These stop your wife from throwing up on your shoes every morning. I forage through poison ivy and get attacked by massive mosquitos to harvest these roots, which I can only find in one certain hollow that is within the elven borders. That's why the College of Theurgy sends a healthy tithe to them."

Elixin glowered.

"I'd appreciate some respect, considering why I leave the castle grounds once a week. It is because I know what's best for your wife. Unless you want your Queen vomiting on other heads of state during her pregnancy?"

The King huffed, indignant, leaning back in his chair.

"No more trackers, Your Majesty," Gwendin warned. "Or the next conversation will occur in the presence of the College. Also, I will come and go as I wish, whatever day or night, since asking your permission was a courtesy and not a requirement on my part. Leave me to my work as I leave you to yours."

Gwendin bowed to the Queen, then exited the dining room without dismissal.

~   ~   ~

His apothecary took up most of his room. The fireplace doubled as an oven when needed, but he had managed a small fire off to the side so he could work on his potions with ease. The smoke still swirled up the flue and out the chimney, which kept him from suffocating. The mantle housed glass bottles that varied in size, shape, and color. A long table ran perpendicular to the fireplace, giving him space to mix, treat, and invent his different concoctions. A row of table top apothecary cabinets lined the side against the other wall, while the rest of the table held bowls, plates, utensils, as well as mortars and pestles. The only thing not related to his theurgy was his bed, which butted up against the wall with the large window, and a cedar chest that doubled as a night stand.

His annoyance made it hard to concentrate. Gwendin ground up the roots he had shown Elixin, then tossed the powder into the pot. He adjusted the angle of the tripod over the smaller hearth, making sure the water didn't boil any longer than necessary. He waited until he was satisfied, then moved it again to let the concoction reduce.

From behind him, he heard the secret door on the other side of the fireplace open and heeled slippers clack along the stone floor.

"You shouldn't provoke him," Queen Kemberly admonished as she approached his table. "He could easily have you beheaded."

Gwendin scoffed, resecuring the lid to one of his glass canisters. "No, actually he can't. He knows the confines of his power. He is quite limited in his choice of punishments. I made sure the College outlined the rules very clearly, in writing, before I arrived. A contract he had to sign and held by the college. A step I ensured, since I knew Elixin's reputation."

"Would you really have them recall you?"

"If needed. I only came here because you asked, not because I had any respect for him."

She hesitated a moment, straightening some of the bottles. "Does the College know of our relation?"

"The councilors do," he replied, handing her the canister which she set down in the empty space between two taller ones. "They fought me accepting your request, but when they realized no one else would take this assignment, they gave up arguing." Gwendin grabbed Kemberly and hugged her. "And how could they deny siblings, anyway?"

She sighed against his neck, then wrapped her arms around him. "I'm glad you're here."

"Even if I anger your husband?"

"You keep him on his toes. He doesn't like that."

"How are you feeling today?" he asked, rubbing her back.

"Fat."

He chuckled at her annoyed tone, then released her. He reached down and rubbed her small round belly that still hid under the layers of her dress. "Dizziness? Nausea?"

"Nothing since before breakfast, which I am thankful for."

"Keep drinking the tea with each meal since it's helping." He turned back to his pot. "I am making more as we speak. I can't forage it in great quantities because it loses strength in storage. The fresher, the better."

"Is that really the only reason why you escape the castle once a week?"

"Why else would I go torture myself?"

"You spend all that outside time alone?" she inquired, her tone lightly teasing.

Gwendin scoffed, then recited, "The College of Theurgy frowns upon their members being untoward to those they are meant to help."

"They're not here to keep an eye on you. And I know you better than you do sometimes."

He shook his head, stirring his concoction. "Getting away helps me from going stir crazy, in all honesty. I don't know how you can stand these stone walls."

"You can't tell me that there isn't a young shepherdess or someone in town to keep you company?"

"I can't believe that rumor is still running around this horrible place. You would think the kitchen staff would find something else to obsess about. Especially after they agreed that not even a blind shepherdess would find me attractive."

"They are a cruel bunch, aren't they? I have to admit, it is amusing to hear them suffer through their conspiracies without having a way to prove or disprove them." She shrugged nonchalantly. "You keep them on their toes, too. I think everyone in this castle, besides me, just doesn't understand you. You like it that way, don't you? That's also why you take off." He didn't respond to her needling. "Fine, keep your secret," she retorted, tweaking his sleeve to unwrinkle it. "But as your sister, I only hope that you find happiness. One of us should be happy. I knew that my marriage to Elixin was another cage for me to inhabit while escaping the one we grew up in. At least here, I can spend my days with my daughter and have some peace. He only bothers me when he wants something."

"Like a male heir?"

"The tribulations of a wife. Bear children and look pretty."

Gwendin hung his head, feeling his heart break again for her. He felt her hand on his arm, squeezing it gently.

"Our parents made their decisions based on their needs, my dear brother. Me and my marriage, you and your schooling. It is a shame they are not here to see what they made us become. At least now we can be together, even if it's just a brief greeting each morning." She sighed, resting her hands on her belly out of habit. "Time for me to check on Valena. Have a good day and let me know when to retrieve more of that tea from you. The midwife is always nagging at me to walk more."

~   ~   ~

That night, Zawn waited. When she had arrived, he wasn't there and she felt a rock in her stomach from despair. Maybe he had found out the truth and hated her for not telling him. She even feared an altercation between him and the King leading to his execution. However, the one possibility that struck truer than all the others... he had truly found someone else and would rather spend his evening with them. Her doubts created the same scenarios in her head that she had imagined before. Yet she had to hope for the best. Especially after last night.

She cleared the area of any branches and rocks where the tent would be set up, then sat near the fire she had already started, stoking the flames nervously. She would stay as long as she could. Either until the predawn light or until her nerves gave out. If he didn't show up...

She glanced up hopefully at the sound of footsteps and stood to greet whoever approached. Gwendin stepped out of the foliage, bags on his shoulder. His face didn't give her any hints as to why he was late or how he felt about seeing her again. She tried to hide her concerns, watching him wordlessly, letting him speak first.

"I apologize for being late," Gwen said, as he set his satchel and duffle bags down. "Thanks for starting the fire." He pulled out the tent and handed it to her. While she pitched the tent, he took out the tripod and pot, setting them over the fire. "It's been a busy day. I had to make sure that in the future, I would no longer have a tracker."

Zawn stayed silent, busying herself by tweaking the tent's sides.

"I think it's safe to say," he continued, before dumping in his bag of ingredients and some water from his flask, "that we don't have to worry about me being followed anymore."

She didn't respond, keeping her distance. She had wanted to avoid a fight, but she could hear the anguish building in his tone. He turned around finally to face her and for the first time, she could see that he was angry.

"Why didn't you just tell me that night?" he demanded, frustration in his voice.

"Because we were being watched," she admitted, walking towards him cautiously. "If I had warned you, if I didn't end it that night, you would have been executed once you returned to the castle. It was the only way."

"So you just left me here, thinking I had done something wrong? That I had hurt you? Or offended you?"

"I thought it'd be easier for both of us if you hated me."

He regarded her, torn between anger and hurt.

"What made you come back to me?" he asked.

"Your tracker told me that they had a change of heart."

He glowered, not persuaded by her answer. "And?"

"I wanted to make sure you were safe."

"That explains the night you held your blade to my throat. What about last night?" he demanded. "Zawn, why did you come back last night? Why did you lay with me?" He watched as her usually droll expression turned anxious. "Why are you here now?"

She realized that she had been successful in infuriating him. She had made a mistake coming back to him. She strode past him to leave. "You're right. I shouldn't've come back. I shouldn't be here."

He caught her by the arm, making her halt. He pulled her against him and stared straight into her eyes.

"Why did you come back to me?" he begged, the fury in his eyes morphing into something else. It was a mixture of anger and pain, frustration and... love.

She swallowed hard against the emotions that tried to break her. "I think of you every day. I even dream of you. I wanted more, too."

He wrapped his arms around her, holding her close but not saying anything. Even though he wanted to shake the truth out of her, he knew he had to give her the time to find the words.

"Please know that I didn't want to part ways with you," she admitted, laying her hands against his chest. The feel of his heartbeat steadied her. "I would have given anything to be with you that night, in that tent, for however long we wanted. But I had to make a choice that I hated. I couldn't live with myself if you were killed because of me, because the King found out about us. I hated being apart but I had to give you up."

"We don't have to be apart again."

"You can't promise that."

"Maybe not," he responded, melting away into a warm softness, "but I can promise tonight. And every night we meet, I'll make that same promise. In every kiss, every embrace, every word."

They stared into each other's eyes, still darkened by the pain of their separation and the brutal truth as to why it had occurred. But underneath that torment, their unspoken love for each other fought its way through.

Zawn wrapped her arms around his neck, pulling him closer. "So, we're safe? We're really all alone?"

"Just us and whatever critters nearby."

"I missed you," she admitted, her voice cracking under the emotions she had tried to hide from him.

"I missed you, too." He nuzzled her temple, inhaling deeply her woodlen scent. "I wished on every star, every night, that I would see you again."

Those words made her heart thump harder. "Every star?"

"Every single one."

She pressed up against him, suggestively, making him smile. He used one hand to set the tripod off to the side of the fire while the other held her closely against him.

"Let's leave that on low, shall we?"

~   ~   ~

The seasonal rains gave way to a cool, cloudy night. The critters who would forage and fuss throughout the woods hid away in their dreys, nests, and burrows. Tucked inside a realm of roots and leaves, a coverlet of light brown aragonite canvas was erected. The tent rippled here and there in the wind, but the weather remained pleasant that evening, leading the rain to other areas of the forest.

They laid together, facing each other. He caressed her face, following the path of her cheek down to her neck where the skin blended into bark. He was always astounded at how soft she was no matter where he touched her. He had never asked if that was normal or if she did something special just for him, because he had been afraid that would indicate his hopes for more. He had feared ever admitting how he felt about her. He had thanked his lucky stars that she even considered spending time with him at all.

But now, as they shared yet another intimate evening together, he wondered if she had shared all of the same hopes. If she had considered what the future could hold for them. If she could ever feel the same for him as he did for her.

His hand made its way along her shoulder, down her arm, until their hands found each other. He lifted hers up until they could both see them, then he intertwined his fingers with hers. Their differing colors made a zigzag along the knuckles, her gray-green bark, then his pale skin, and so on, while their thumbs caressed thoughtfully. A small smile turned her lips up, her beauty heightened by the modest expression. His heart beat harder and he kissed her forehead, closing his eyes briefly and cherishing the moment.

Then his stomach growled, making him sigh. "As much as I love laying here, I'm starving," he admitted with a chuckle. "I didn't get much done due to my argument with the King. Including eating dinner."

"Did you put enough salt in it?" she inquired, raising an eyebrow.

He shook his head, exasperated, then kissed her. "Let's find out."

He grabbed his trousers and slipped them on, then grabbed his tunic and pulled it over her head. Barefoot and half naked, they carefully made their way back to the fire. She sat down nearby, almost lost in his oversized tunic. He grabbed one bowl, two spoons, and checked the food. It appeared done, so he transferred a good portion into the bowl, then handed it to her with the spoons sticking out. He sat behind her, leaning against the massive root that seemed to rise out of nowhere, his legs sprawled around her. The angle was uncomfortable so he turned her until her left shoulder rested against his chest. He flopped her legs over his left one, then took one spoon. They ate quietly, enjoying their first real feeling of privacy in a long time. The stew wasn't extravagant, but warm and filled with carrots and potatoes.

"How did you contend with the King?" she asked, between bites.

"I just reminded him," he responded, scooping up a small spoonful, "that I am the theurgist, not him. I know what I'm doing and if he wanted to keep his pregnant wife from retching on everyone's feet, he'd best leave me alone."

Zawn watched him shove the spoon into his mouth and chew. "She's pregnant again?"

"Yes. She thinks it's a boy with all of her sickness. She said she had none of this with the princess, but it's similar to when she carried their first son."

"I'm surprised they chose to have another child after their son's death."

"It is a patriarchy," he replied, saying the word with some distaste. "They need a male heir or the bloodline is decided by who the princess marries. No King in his right mind would allow that. I do worry though, she's not very far along. Anything could happen."

Gwendin stopped eating and hugged her tightly with his one arm. His expression became extremely serious, concerning her.

"I need to tell you something, Zee. Before we go any further with, well whatever we decide. It could," and he took a deep breath, "it could be a deal breaker, I think."

He hesitated, making her reach up and touch his chin gently. Their eyes met and she could see his fear. "Gwen, tell me."

"I didn't just get assigned here because I was a mediocre theurgist or someone who irked the council. I was asked to come here, specifically by my sister."

Her eyebrows were furrowed together, confused. "Sister?"

"Kemberly's my sister."

She didn't respond immediately, wrestling internally with that information.

"You told me that the castle was lonely. But your sister is there?"

"Yes, but she is still queen and I am only a theurgist. Elixin is very much a separatist when it comes to servants and royalty. No friendships, no romances. No family relations. I only see her when I am treating her. I don't even get to spend any time with the princess and I only had access to my nephew before he died because I helped treat him."

Zawn had been frowning the entire time, first because of his admission then because of his situation. "I'm sorry. It sounds like you would see your sister just as much had you taken a different assignment."

"That's how it feels. But I think just being in the same building, even the same kingdom, brings her some comfort. Especially with such a delicate pregnancy."

"Does she know about me?" Zawn asked, concerned. "About us?"

"No. As much as I love her, and she me, I doubt she'd understand. I know she'd be happy that I found someone but…"

"But someone like me?"

"I didn't want to endanger us. And knowing about everything that had happened because of Elixin and his meddling, it's not safe even if she accepted us."

"You didn't defend them," she whispered, suddenly.

"What?"

"When we first met. I had some choice words to say about your family."

Gwendin chuckled. "Well, you weren't wrong. So, nothing to defend." He stared at her for a moment, his guilt still weighing heavily on him. "I'm sorry I didn't tell you sooner. I just didn't know how and I thought it would turn you off from seeing me anymore."

"Before? It could have," she admitted, twirling her spoon in the bowl. "But, now?" And she met his eyes again. "I'm glad you told me. I can understand now why you stay in a place that makes you unhappy, when you could just appeal to the College for another assignment."

"There's more than just my sister that keeps me here, Zee, you know that right?"

She didn't respond immediately, then asked, "If we… Would you have stayed, if it wasn't for your sister?"

He inhaled deeply, eyebrows jumping up. "I don't know. I didn't even think about that." Then he watched her, realizing her question hinted at her own thoughts. "If we couldn't be together again, what would you have done?"

"I had planned to leave. I-I already had my satchel packed."

"Leave? Like move to another kith?"

She blinked a few times, her heart warming at the fact that he had listened to her explain elven ways. But the reality of what she meant made her stammer. "No. Leave this forest," she whispered, unable to meet his eyes. "I was going to just start walking and not look back."

"Zee…"

She set her spoon down in the bowl. "I couldn't stand the thought of being so close to you and knowing that you had moved on. And I had feared seeing you again, by accident. After all, you still had permission to be here. I, um, got drunk one day, something I never do, and I knew I had to make some sort of change. There was nothing holding me here, after all. Leaving was the easiest decision for me. But being told that it was safe to see you again derailed my plans. I was ready to take off in a few days."

"But now? Have you chosen to stay?"

She stuttered, setting down the bowl and folding her hands together. "I haven't decided yet."

Heartbroken silence settled between them. He had known there was a good chance that he'd never see her again after she took off, but the thought of her leaving completely shattered his heart. But they found each other again, they were there in each other's arms. It hit him suddenly that she took their ending harder than he could have ever expected. If she knew how much he suffered in her absence...

"So, you, uh got drunk too?"

Hearing some embarrassment in his tone, she asked, "Did you?"

"I really thought I had done something wrong, read everything between us wrong. I thought you hated me. And I had no way to talk to you. It's not like I could walk into your kith looking for you. One night after you didn't show up again, I walked back to the castle and locked myself away with a nice new brew. I hated myself in the morning, but I just didn't want to feel anything. Even if only for one night."

"I can understand that."

"If you think that we can't keep this up, will you tell me?" he requested. "At least tell me."

"I will. I-I know I owe you that much."

"As much as..." then he cleared his throat, trying to banish the tears that threatened. "I will respect whatever you decide." He had to change the subject, to avoid breaking down in front of her. "How did you know that our watcher didn't report me? That I wasn't executed? I'm sure you didn't take them at their word."

"I kept an eye out for your weekly tithe to arrive. I knew if you had been executed, the College would have stopped sending money."

His eyebrows popped up. "That's actually true." He cleared his throat, nervous. "Will you stay tonight?"

"I had planned to."

He nuzzled her cheek, smiling in relief. "Good. We have a lot of catching up to do." He nudged her, making her move her legs, then stood and offered his hands.

~ ~ ~

Hiding in their tent, listening to the nocturnal creatures chitter and forage, the two lovers faced each other. After being apart for so long, they found themselves embracing, touching, remaining close at all times. It was as if they both feared the other would disappear if they didn't hang on tight.

"I hate how quiet you've become," he whispered, missing their varied conversations and her beautiful laughter.

She frowned. "I'm afraid to say anything more. That it will come out wrong or hurtful."

"Zee, please, I want us to find our way back. Only way we can is by being honest with each other."

She sniffled, pulling away and sitting up. "I feel so foolish."

"Why?" he asked, propping himself up on his arm.

"I shouldn't have let you become more than a distraction," she replied, pulling the blanket up around her chest. "I-I didn't even know that I could ever care for someone like this again. I swore I wouldn't. I never wanted to get hurt again."

His heart almost skipped a beat when she admitted her feelings for him... and her fears. "I don't plan on hurting you, Zee. And I'm sorry that someone who you had loved hurt you so."

"She's the one who caught us," she responded, glancing sheepishly over at him.

His eyes widened. "Now it makes so much more sense. The gargoyle, I can't recall her name, but she shot daggers with her eyes at me for weeks. I didn't know why at that time. She's your former lover."

She scoffed. "I don't know if she was angrier because I chose a human or because you were male." She shook her head, her hair falling over her shoulder and hiding her face. "She and I were such fools to think we'd stand up against our leaders."

"You think us fools too? Thinking we can stand up to the laws of elf and man?"

"I don't know."

Silence settled.

"Can I ask something?" she inquired, from behind the curtain of hair.

"Of course."

"Is it a rule that you don't mention your relation to the Queen?"

He stared at her for a few moments, realizing that his family connection to the wife of his lover's enemy had made some things awkward. "We don't announce it because it can make me a target for their enemies."

"Does that mean you have a title?"

"Why would you ask that?"

"I doubt Elixin would marry a nobody."

He grimaced, finally sitting up. His shoulder touched hers as he took a deep breath. "I am a count."

"You're royalty?" she asked, brushing back her hair and meeting his eyes.

"No, my sister is. I am just what's left of a dishonored royal family from Maroe. The family had to leave one continent for another to survive. Ask anyone and they will tell you the dishonor is well-earned by my great-grandparents. There's nothing attached to the titles but shame."

"Is that why you went to the College so young?"

"It was financially better for my parents to groom my sister for marriage and send me off to the College on scholarship. My mentor, when he tested me, told my parents the earlier the better. They took him up on that offer, even though he knew I would be a late bloomer. I think it was beneficial for both, because they wouldn't have to care for me and he wouldn't lose track of me."

"But it's a patriarchy," she replied, drolly.

He laughed, mirthlessly. "My family had nothing to offer a woman of royal standing. Marrying my sister into a wealthy family brought our family something."

"Why do you not introduce yourself as a count?"

"I am a theurgist first and foremost," he answered. "Anything beyond that, well, it gets complicated on how to address me, as a count and as brother to a Queen. And it's not who I am. Not how I want to be addressed."

"How should you be addressed?"

"Gwen," he responded, with a wry smile. "That's what I want to hear when you call me. That's what I want to hear when you scream."

"Is that so?" she inquired, the Zawn he loved peeking through her distress. "I don't think I've agreed to follow that rule."

"No? Well, I guess we'll just have to keep at it until you do."

He moved one arm behind her, making her drop her shoulder so he could lean in. He kissed her, ardently and whole-heartedly, then pulled her closer while they giggled. In that moment, they were back to how they had been, even if briefly. He nuzzled her cheek, loving the interaction and loving her.

He took a deep breath. "My life before the College doesn't matter," he said. "Who I am related to doesn't matter. I am not that person. And I am not just some theurgist. You've made me into someone... more."

What amusement she felt faded from her face.

"What is it?" he asked.

"What if I'm not enough?"

"Not enough? Zee..."

"You could change your mind. Maybe someone of royal standing will take a shine to you and that could help your family? I have nothing to offer you, not in that way. We've nothing to lose, do we, with walking away?"

He caressed her cheek, staring seriously into her eyes. "Hasn't any of this changed your mind? Don't you think you have something to lose now?"

"I guess I haven't even thought of us like that. Maybe because I still think I've lost you. This," and she glanced around them, "is only temporary."

"Why would you think that?"

"I had to accept that you hated me, and you had moved on, because the alternative… Every night we were apart, I just kept telling myself you turned to someone else. That you forgot about me and you had moved on. When I saw you again, I didn't think you'd want to be with me anymore."

He noticed her hesitation, but he knew something else was on her mind. "What is it?"

"There's still nothing stopping that from happening."

"Zee, don't you get it? You never lost me. I came here every week waiting for you. Didn't my tracker tell you that? I'm sure they watched me for quite a while. I never missed a rendezvous. No matter the weather, I was here. Hoping to see you again. I would have continued to do so until the day I died, even if I was reassigned, always in the hope of seeing you again. And I never turned to another. There could never be another, not for me. You talk like you don't think anyone would catch your eye instead. I'm sure there are plenty of choices among your group." Then he cautiously asked, "Did you turn to another? Did you…" and he paused.

"I didn't. I couldn't." She scoffed. "Not like anyone'd want me. I'm the nitwit of my kith. An embarrassment. No one even looks at me."

Gwen frowned, his heart hurting for her. He remembered their one conversation, where he called her beautiful and how she reacted. Now he truly understood why she acted so surprised and couldn't understand why he thought of her as pretty. He hated that deeply, knowing that she was amazing both in physicality and in personality.

"Good," he responded, making her glance up in surprise. "I don't like to share."

She kissed him, passionately, making him wrap his arms around her and pulling her back down to the ground.

CHAPTER 17

Gwen told her to come back the next night. She thought it odd that he would be free to stay overnight more than twice in a row, but as she walked back home, she recognized that he was proving his point to Elixin. He could do whatever he wanted and the King had no say. She wondered if it was wise to taunt the King, considering the animosity he already held for Gwen, but she had to trust her lover's actions.

Lover. She stopped mid-step, almost startled by the word. Was he? Could she call him that? He had her heart, she left that with him when they reunited, and there was no getting it back. She started walking again, a little slower than before. Realizing how much he had meant to her while they were apart kept her tethered to him. She still feared him leaving her, either for someone else or because their relationship was too difficult, however he didn't act like that was what he wanted. He wanted them to find their way back to each other and themselves.

He wanted to see her.

She wanted to see him.

~ ~ ~

She made her way to him that next night, without hesitation. He waited for her, with the campsite set up just like the other nights. They embraced, sharing a loving kiss. Then he pulled her over to the fire. They sat down in front of it, Gwen holding her tight, while she laid her head on his chest. Together again, they let the fire serenade them.

"Sorry dinner wasn't done already," Gwen said, with a grimace. "I wanted everything to be perfect… almost forgot to put it on."

"It's fine. I like sitting here, with you, like this."

"Me, too."

"How do we know that we are not still just using each other?" she asked, cautiously.

The question surprised him, making his eyebrows rise. "I don't know, to be honest. But if that is the case, then I wouldn't want to do this with anyone else. I'm just glad we found each other," he admitted, before kissing her head. "Our spirits are more kindred than we thought. We were starved for attention as well as affection."

"I'm glad we can give each other both."

"Me too."

Silence settled over the lovers, their bond growing stronger with every passing moment. They spent the rest of the night eating, loving, and making small talk, like they used to. Their familiarity and connection began to override any fears or heartache. With each touch, each word, they followed the path back to each other.

~   ~   ~

The next morning, she helped pack up their campsite before departing. Something fell out of his duffel when he started packing the tent. She bent over and picked it up.

"What's this?" she asked, cradling the metal object in her palm.

Gwen grabbed it from her, stammering through excuses, before sighing hard. "I found the stone a few weeks after you stopped... I was foraging one night and I heard it fall. Something had knocked it loose from a short rock wall. It made me think of you. I decided to clean it up and the castle blacksmith made the shank and head for me. I set it. I told him I thought of selling trinkets on the side but... I made this ring for you. If I ever saw you again. I didn't know if you'd like it or not. But I just didn't want to scare you or make you uncomfortable by..."

"Put it on," she requested, holding her hand out.

"I don't know if it'll fit. I guessed the size."

She wiggled her fingers, impatiently.

Fumbling for a moment, he finally slipped it over her middle finger. The metal glistened in the predawn light, while the large flat stone, a moss and chocolate jasper, felt cool against her skin. She grabbed his collar and pulled him into a passionate kiss. He wrapped his arms around her, thrilled that she had accepted his gift without a second thought.

"Thank you," she whispered against his lips. "I love it, it's beautiful."

"I hope it doesn't interfere with your fighting."

She smiled, flattered that he worried about such things. "It will not. I am sure of it."

~   ~   ~

They agreed to take a few days to lay low, even though both wanted to spend as much time as they could with the other.

CHAPTER 18

She waited for Taylor to relieve her, so she could go home and rest. She kept hearing Gwendin's words, about how he felt about her, and how she never lost him. They were now in a different place. They were safe from prying eyes, at least those from the castle, and they were aware of how they felt about each other. At least an idea. She still had a hard time letting him get too close to her, after her previous relationship turned so deeply sour, but she felt her connection to Gwendin was different. If she could love someone whole-heartedly, there was a very good possibility it would be him.

She felt the air shift and knew Taylor was approaching. She turned and smiled a greeting, waiting for him to sit down so she could catch him up with border details. He plopped down and listened, nodding. Before she could stand up to leave, he grabbed her arm.

"You're not coming home straight away," Taylor stated. "You have stayed out all night, not at random, but several in a row. Chae saw you sneaking in at daybreak. You have that stupid smile on your face when you think no one is looking."

Zawn lowered her eyes, fiddling with a ring on her finger. Taylor didn't recognize it, since she didn't wear any jewelry, but noticed its simplicity. The piece of stone wasn't some shiny gem of great wealth, but something earthy, tumbled in a natural way, something that he knew she would love. Had this theurgist figured out the same thing about her?

"Do you know what you're doing, Zawnie?"

"I, uh, no I don't."

"Is he that important to you? Is he really worth your life?"

Zawn raised her eyes and met his gaze. "Yes, he is."

Her friend stared into her eyes, reading her honesty. He couldn't ever remember a time where she expressed such adoration for someone., not even Marassa His heart warmed at the thought that she finally found someone she would consider that important, but he still worried about the ramifications. She knew the dangers and he was sure the theurgist did as well. He sighed, accepting her decision.

"Then we will keep your secret and make sure if someone has any suspicions, we will bring them to your attention."

"We?"

"If Chae finds out I kept this from her, you know she will kill me swiftly. And then take you out."

Zawn chuckled. "You have a point." Then her smile faded. "Thank you."

Taylor grunted, dismissive, then patted her on the shoulder. "You are my friend and my family, even if you are a nitwit."

"Have a good night, Tay."

"You better come to breakfast soon. The children miss you."

~   ~   ~

Zawn stared at the hut's door, her stomach twisted. It had been a while. Weeks actually. She closed her eyes for a moment, took a deep breath, then knocked. A familiar voice granted her permission and she opened the door carefully. She stepped inside, closed the door behind her. She could see her friend in the kitchen, the fireplace flickering low, and the bassinet next to the couch. Suddenly, two heavy bodies landed against her.

"Auntie!" both boys shouted, but their voices were muffled against her body. "We missed you!"

"I'm sorry," she stammered as their arms held her tight, "that I haven't been visiting."

Chaen looked up at her. "Momma said you lost someone."

"And that you were sad," Talor added.

"Did you find them?"

"I did," she replied, trying to fight back her tears. "They are safe and sound."

Talor frowned. "We would have helped you look."

"You just had to ask," Chaen pointed out.

Their love for her made her tremble.

"I wasn't quite myself," she responded, "so I didn't know how to ask for help. But I know how to ask now. And next time, you will be the first ones I ask. I promise."

"Come sit with us! We have so much to tell you!" Talor announced as he grabbed her hand and pulled her to the couch.

Chaen pushed her from behind, neither willing to let her get away. Talor sat on one side while his brother sat on her other side.

Then Chaen lamented, "You look tired, Auntie."

~   ~   ~

Chae had been distracted with cooking breakfast that she hadn't immediately realized how quiet it had gotten. Startled, she stepped out of the kitchen area to figure out why. The two boys and Zawn had fallen asleep on the couch. Zawn was on her side, with her boots hanging off, while Chaen had pressed his back up against her chest. Talor laid on top of her, like a feline would on the back of a couch, with a blanket in between them. Chaelene groused, considering what it took to get the boys out of bed every morning, but felt the warmth in her heart. She knew it was important that their bond was renewed and she was reassured now, seeing her friend back with her family.

Taylor entered, loud as usual, then stopped to take in the scene on the couch. Chae could see the well of emotions that threatened to break his usually stoic face. He made his way quietly through the hut without disturbing the sleeping trio, until he reached his mate. He hugged her, a sigh of relief escaping.

"How is she?" he asked softly.

"I've never seen her this emotional. But I take her return to us as a good sign."

"They've reunited."

"So that is why she returns after predawn light?"

He nodded.

"I need to tell their instructor that they will miss today," Chae admitted, pulling free from her mate's embrace.

Chae exited the hut and Taylor started to remove his armor in their bedroom. When she returned after a few moments, she was shaking her head.

"What's wrong?"

"I told Darend they were not feeling well and he wouldn't accept that as an excuse to miss today. Until I told him I wasn't feeling well either and feared they could be contagious. Then he dismissed me with a grunt. He is a piece of work."

"He answers to the same leader as we do, Chae. Who knows what ultimatums he has to deal with."

She wrapped her arms around Taylor, glancing through the doorway at Zawn. "Do we think they will work through this?"

"I hope so. When she started seeing him, I hadn't seen her that happy since Marassa. Actually, happier."

"And we hadn't seen her this sad since then, either."

"This was… worse, to be honest. She said he was worth the consequences though." He rubbed her back. "Is her satchel still on the table?"

"It is. I peeked in this morning before everyone else was awake. Her shelves are still empty. Nothing has been put back."

"We will give her the time she needs to figure out what is right for her. And hopefully he will be the right thing."

"Come, I made pancakes and bacon. We will eat and chill the rest for them later."

~   ~   ~

Zawn and the boys got a good nap in before rousing later that morning. As they ate their breakfast, the boys chattered away about the many topics that ran through their minds. Finished and happily full, Zawn took all of their dishes into the kitchen. The boys headed to their rooms to study, while Zawn and Chae cleaned up.

"Chae, do you think you could show me how to weave a bracelet?" Zawn requested.

"I could just make it for you," her friend offered, absent-mindedly, as she scrubbed a plate.

"No, I… I want to be the one who makes it."

Chae stared at her for a moment. Zawn didn't have much talent for weaving, let alone the patience for that kind of work, but her tone made it evident that she was determined to create a piece of jewelry for someone with her own hand. She wondered if it would be for her lover, however Chae hesitated teasing her about it. After all, Chae and Taylor had agreed not to mention his name or their situation if she didn't. Especially within earshot of other kithlin.

"I'd be happy to show you," Chae responded. "Pick the colors and we'll talk design?"

Zawn smiled, a loving expression. "Thank you."

~   ~   ~

King Elixin and Queen Kemberly, along with their daughter Princess Valena, stood at the top of the stairs that led into the castle. They were dressed in their finery, patiently awaiting whoever visited.

Suddenly, sounds echoed throughout the outer bailey and inner courtyard. The King's brother arrived with flair, trumpets and regalia heralding his gelding's clopping hooves.

The page cleared his throat and announced for all to hear. "Crenast of Garadni, to see the King of Mehdehra!"

"Crenast, my brother!" Elixin shouted, grinning widely. "Welcome to Mehdehra!"

The man on the horse, who had similar facial features as the King, dismounted at the steps and flung his arms wide. Elixin trotted down the stairs without the usual pompousness suited to his status. The men embraced heartily, showing that the visitor was at least a foot shorter than his brother. They laughed and talked excitedly, making their way into the castle. Kemberly and Valena curtsied as the two men passed by but were not even recognized. They followed quietly behind the raucous pair and the guards closed the large wooden doors behind them.

From his window, Gwen scoffed, returning to his brewing of tea and other medicinals.

~   ~   ~

The next few days revolved around the visitor. He was given the best guest quarters, the best valet, and best maids. He spent most of his time in revelry with his brother, their voices and laughter shattering the usual dour silence that haunted the halls.

And because of Elixin's brother, everyone had been pulled to work in the kitchen as large dishes were prepared and served at each meal. Kemberly spent most of her time managing the staff to keep her husband and his guest happy, which meant Gwendin had to deliver her teas instead of her retrieving them. Gwen enjoyed the dead spaces in the castle, not having to deal with the rude house staff and leaving him alone with his thoughts of Zawn. Wishing it was like this every day, he dropped off two canisters of tea for his sister in her bedchambers, then strolled down the empty hallway. Voices caught his attention and he walked toward the hallway concourse, but stopped short of entering the next passageway.

Near the guest bedchambers stood two figures, awfully close to each other. Gwen watched from the archway, hidden from sight, as Crenast caressed Kemberly's cheek gently. For the first time, Gwen saw his sister blush and look at a man… like she was fond of him.

Gwen frowned but refused to make a scene. After all, what would Elixin do if he found them like this? As Crenast leaned toward Kemberly, the theurgist knew the man's intentions. Gwen turned away and headed back to his chambers.

His mind ran with concerns. Was his sister having an affair with her husband's brother? How long had this been going on? And the most concerning thought… what if the child his sister carried wasn't her husband's?

He stared at the empty kettle, which he had used to make her antinausea tea. A dark thought crossed his mind, but he made himself cool his temper. It was his sister's life, she could take whatever lover she wanted. Even though she had to take the consequences along with those decisions. Did she understand that?

~   ~   ~

The next morning, Kemberly made her way through the secret passages to see her brother. She preferred to make her way along the hidden hallways because it gave her some much needed privacy and allowed her to visit her brother without every movement being reported back to her husband. She didn't even tell her own daughter about the passageways, keeping it between her and Gwendin only.

She had been so tied up with their visitor that she hadn't seen Gwendin for a few days. Now that he was gone, she headed off to see her brother. She pushed open the secret door, slipping into his chambers. He was at his table, as usual, fussing with whatever concoction he was working on. She walked up to his side, knowing he could hear her slipper clad feet pad along the flooring, but he didn't acknowledge her immediately.

"Everything all right, brother?" she asked after she saw the displeasure on his face.

He stopped what he had been mixing and leaned against the table. "Do you know what you are doing?" Gwen demanded, softly but darkly, causing his sister to take a step back.

"What are you talking about?"

He turned toward her, folding his arms across his chest. "I saw you in the passageway. With him."

The color drained from Kemberly's face.

"Were you alone?" she finally croaked out.

"This is me, sister, of course I was alone. And no, I haven't said anything to anyone. It is your secret, not mine. But…"

"He treats me kindly," she whispered, touching her cheek as if remembering the gentle caress Gwen witnessed. "Something Elixin has never done."

"Just be careful, Kem."

"Gwen, I-I…"

"I will never deny you happiness or love, Kem," he reassured. "But I know the man you married. He was willing to go after me for just spending the night outside the castle. Now imagine what he would do if he even had some suspicions about you. You can have your time with him as long as you both make sure secrecy is paramount. Keep to the secret passageways and stay away from the watchful eyes of the staff."

Kemberly nodded, solemnly.

~   ~   ~

Every night they met, Zawn checked the perimeter. She relied on her knowledge and paranoia to keep them safe. She asked the trees a little further out from their hideout to protect them and they agreed. With that extra layer of protection, since Zawn calculated how close Marassa had to be to see them without being detected, Zawn could enjoy her time with Gwendin.

Each night, they grew closer. Each kiss tasted sweeter. Each intimate connection strengthened their bound. And each conversation, they learned more about each other.

One night, as they reclined by the fire, their stomachs full and bodies satisfied, they spoke softly about trivial things that made them laugh. Gwen didn't want to think of his sister's affair or what Elixin would do if he found out. Gwen only wanted to lose himself in the beauty of Zawn.

"There is one thing I am thankful for at the castle," Gwen admitted, as he entwined their fingers. "I have a window in my room. I can look at the stars all evening if I wish. The forest's canopy does eliminate a wonderful view. And there's supposed to be an amazing celestial shower tonight."

"You should have said something."

Zawn reached behind him, touching the tree's trunk while he frowned, confused. She closed her eyes and whispered something he couldn't understand. The tree shivered in response, then above them, the limbs started to move. Some leaves fell as they did so, showering them gently, until the tree stopped moving. Gwen looked up and saw the stars through a lovely opening.

"Is that a big enough window?" she asked.

"I didn't know you could do... that."

"Don't they teach you anything at the College?" she chided, wry smile lighting up her face.

"Does your kind give away all your secrets?" he retorted, squeezing her teasingly.

She chuckled. "All I did was ask grandfather here to give us some sky. He was amenable."

He looked over his shoulder at the trunk he leaned against. "Thank you, grandfather."

"He says that you're welcome."

He kissed her ardently. "Thank you."

"Next time, just ask."

They sat there, together, as the stars shimmered and the celestial shower began.

CHAPTER 19

When she reached their spot, Gwendin was nowhere to be found. No tent, no fire, nothing indicating his arrival. She could only think the worst.

Then something white caught her eye. Amongst the roots that they nestled in under their tent laid three tulips: one white, one red, and one yellow. There was nothing else around them and they weren't bound. Tulips didn't grow in her forest, they were something that existed only in the higher plains. But they laid there as a sign. A message letting her know that he wasn't there because of something that was out of his control. To have courage, to know his love, and to keep her faith.

She retrieved them and held them to her chest, her heart shaken, then she headed back to her kith.

CHAPTER 20

She returned the next day, and the next after that, but Gwen never showed.

CHAPTER 21

It had been a fortnight since she had last seen Gwendin. She diligently headed to their meeting place at the end of every shift. There were no flowers or any other signs to reassure her since she found the tulips and hope was fading fast. She knew he was still alive, since the tulips still looked the same as the day she found them and he must have been sustaining them with his magic. But she was about to give up seeing him again... until she arrived to find him waiting for her.

She stopped at the large oak, the tightness in her chest releasing as she saw the campsite set up. The fire glowed, the food cooked, the tent pitched. And Gwendin stood at the fire, watching the food simmer. He caught movement in the corner of his eye and he looked up, seeing her hesitating.

"I feel like I'm hallucinating," she admitted, not moving.

He set down the spoon on the mat nearby, then held out his arms. Seeing that it was truly him, she rushed into his embrace. She threw her arms around his neck and felt him nuzzle into her hair, both breathing each other in.

"Did you get them?" he asked, his voice shaky.

She nodded.

"I'm glad. It took everything in me to manifest them with everything going on."

"What happened?"

"The Queen miscarried," he replied, his nerves still uneasy. "The King blamed me, blamed the healers and midwives. It was everyone's fault. Even the Queen's. It's been hell. He refused to let any of us to leave for several days. This is the first time he didn't stop me. Some of the staff hadn't seen their families in two weeks because of his anger."

She leaned back to look him in the eyes, seeing his pain. "I am sorry to hear about the miscarriage. That's a lot of loss in such a short time for your sister."

"I don't know which one hit her harder."

"A loss of any child is a tragedy," she agreed, cupping his face. "How are you?"

"What do you mean?"

"Your sister lost her child, but you also lost a nephew. The second nephew in what? Less than a year? And then to be blamed for the loss?"

A tear surfaced then ran down his cheek. "I hadn't even thought about it that way."

She pulled him into a tender embrace as more tears followed.

Later that night, they sat together by the fire. Zawn had her arms wrapped around Gwendin, running loving fingers through his hair. He had his head against her chest, listening to her strong heartbeat. She hurt because of his grief, but knowing that Elixin had the gall to blame Gwendin and Kemberly for the miscarriage, that angered her. It fueled her ability to stay strong for Gwen, even though she wanted to cry with him.

He stirred against her, moving into a more comfortable position. "Both deaths have changed my sister. I see it in her eyes."

"Death usually does. I cannot even imagine losing a child."

"Who have you lost?" he asked, having noticed something in her tone.

She took a deep breath, chest tightening at the thought. "Oh, um. Both of my parents. My father was killed in a border skirmish a few months before I was born. My mother died giving birth to me. I almost died then as well. But one of the older women reached in, yanked me free, and smacked me hard enough to bring breath into my lungs. I had no other family. Taylor's mother, Inari, took me in, raised me. That's why he and I are so close. During the Purge, we lost our mentor Brennan and then not long after that, we lost Inari." She shrugged slightly, trying not to disturb Gwen too much. "Taylor's the only family I have. He's my brother. When they were dividing us into castes, the elders and our leader had already determined that I was a fighter so I was immediately placed in the warrior caste. Taylor joined me in those ranks too because, well, where's there one, there's the other."

"I didn't know that you had lost so much."

"And yet, look at all that I have gained," she responded, kissing his head. "I'm lucky to have family that may not be made of blood, but one that was brought together by love. I have Taylor and his family, and now I have you. Can you stay long?"

"Till predawn light."

They tightened their embrace, holding each other close, and let the night and the forest comfort them.

~   ~   ~

Spending the night with Zawn helped Gwendin think straight. Because he had been running on the smoke from a wasted candle for the last few weeks, he hadn't realized his own emotional turmoil. She took care of him, fed him, and held him while he finally got some sleep. When he woke, she greeted him with care and affection. Zawn reminded him who he was and that he wasn't to blame. He loved her even more for her ability to ground him and support him through everything.

He made his way to his room to drop off his stuff, then he headed to the royal bedchambers. He cautiously glanced inside, only to find Kemberly alone. Even the maids had gone, probably to complete their other chores before more yelling shook the dreary silence. He slipped through the door, shutting it behind him as quietly as possible.

Kemberly laid in bed, her back to the door. She hadn't moved, apparently not hearing his entrance. She was curled up, knees almost to her chest. The only thing stopping her body from completely balling up was the pillow Gwendin had pressed into her arms before he left. Her hair was still pulled back and up into a messy bun and he could hear her sniffling.

His shoulders dropped in disappointment. Had Elixin attacked his wife again with another barrage of abusive words once her brother escaped for the night? He walked around the bed, carefully entering her peripheral, not wanting to startle her. However, her eyes were closed and her most recent tears had left their tracks on her cheeks.

"Kemberly?"

Her eyes fluttered open, at first confused, then her expression softened when she saw her brother. She reached out a shaking hand, which he grabbed instantly and sat down next to her on the bed.

"Did he attack you?" he demanded.

"No, I haven't seen him since yesterday morning," she responded, her voice hoarse from crying. "I'm just sad."

Gwendin reached out with his free hand, brushing away the loose hair that attached to the saline streaks. "At least let me give you something to stop conceiving. Your body, your soul, and your heart need to rest."

Kemberly hesitated, but after careful consideration, nodded finally.

"We will not mention this to him, agreed?" he asked.

"He wouldn't understand."

"No, he wouldn't."

~   ~   ~

Gwen headed down the hallway after not just medicating his sister against pregnancy but also adding something to help her sleep. As he strode back to his chambers, he turned a corner and almost ran over a young child. He avoided the collision, then realized that it wasn't just any child. It was his niece, the princess.

"Princess Valena," he greeted, with a quick bow of his head. "Apologies. I didn't realize you were out of your room."

"I wanted to get something from the library," she responded, curtly.

"Oh?" He glanced at the large book in her arms, reading the spine. "Magical creatures? That's a rather complicated topic."

"I like the pictures," she admitted, with a small smile.

"The artwork is excellent in that tome." He bowed his head, again. "Enjoy, Your Majesty, and have a good day."

They parted ways, heading to their own chambers, without another glance.

~ ~ ~

As Valena entered her room, a voice whispered to her. A gentle call of her name. She looked over at the reflecting glass, where swirls slowly manifested.

Valena set her book down, before approaching her vanity with a smile...

~ ~ ~

Zawn returned to her hut later than usual, slipping in through the back way to avoid any kithlin who could be awake. She shut the door behind her, then started to strip off her breastplate and boots. As she moved to set them on the chair next to the table, her satchel stared back at her.

She had removed the clothing as needed, but most of her personal items were still packed away inside. She reached in and pulled out one item, a small journal, and stared at it thoughtfully. She turned and set it back on the shelving that ran next to her fireplace. Then she reached into the bag again. Before she knew it, all of her things were returned to their former homes and the satchel laid limp with emptiness.

She blinked a few times, realizing that she had decided to stay. She hadn't even thought about weighing the pros and cons. But emptying the satchel and now sliding it back under her bed felt right, no debate needed.

With that, she walked into her bathing room to clean up and rest before starting the second part of her day.

CHAPTER 22

They sat, entangled, in front of the fire. They couldn't bring themselves to hide in the tent yet, enjoying the warm wind that cascaded through the leaves and limbs. Their clothes were piled nearby, while they wrapped themselves up in his blanket. She sat between his legs, leaning against his chest, hands hooked over his arms. To keep the blanket firmly against them, he wrapped his arms around her with the blanket edges grasped in his hands. He nuzzled her left temple, sharing kisses without shifting their positions.

Then he said the words he had tried to avoid all evening. "I have to travel back to the College."

"For how long?" she asked, worried.

"I will be gone for a few weeks."

He felt her demeanor shift, the relaxation that had made her pliable draining away. "Weeks?"

"I know. I tried to get out of it, but as part of my contract, I'm required to return with updates and for training throughout my assignment. I tried telling them that with everything going on here, I shouldn't leave. But the council believes I need a break from the turmoil. I think they want to reevaluate the need for me to be here, other than being here as my sister's brother."

Zawn nodded, her shoulders slumping. She dreaded the thought of him being reassigned. He could leave and not be allowed to return. And after making their way back to each other...

"I already have the evidence that proves I'm more useful here than anywhere else. I keep them updated with all of the politics in the area by sending letters weekly. And considering the agreement I've drafted with the local kith, there are herbs and roots here they can't get anywhere else. I'm useful here. I think they already know that but I will remind them."

She didn't respond, but he could still feel her discomfort.

"Will you wait for me to return?"

She looked at him confused. "What do you mean?"

"Well, me being gone that long, you might find someone better."

Her expression turned droll as she chuckled. "I doubt there could be anyone else who would put up with me."

"Oh, is that so?" he inquired, dryly, tightening his hold on her. "Does that mean I have your devotion?"

"No, it means I don't have the energy to rope in another nitwit to be my lover."

He started to laugh. "I wasn't that difficult of a campaign to begin with."

She didn't answer immediately. He watched her face, his smile fading, as her eyes darkened with whatever doubts still weighed on her.

"But keeping you has been," she finally admitted.

"You think I'm getting bored with you?" he asked, disappointed that she would feel that way, especially after everything they had already been through.

"No, but… Maybe no one at the castle or nearby townships interest you, but now you're going back to the College, the one place you call home. There have to be very beautiful women there. Maybe someone new or someone you've known a while will make their feelings known? How can you decline that kind of offer? One that means you can be free with your affection and announce it to your friends and family. And maybe one day, marry."

"I haven't even thought about looking at anyone else. Why waste my time? Because none of them could compare to you, Zee. Will you wait for me?"

"As long as you promise to come back to me, unsullied."

He smiled at that, then whispered, "You hold my heart and have my absolute devotion."

"And you have mine."

He leaned in and kissed her, at first gently then ardently as their hearts demanded their lips to confirm their commitment. He nuzzled her cheek once they parted and he could see her thinking carefully about something. Then she shifted in her position, making him loosen his hold on her.

She reached for her pants, then hesitated opening her belt purse. He waited for her to decide, watching the conflict alter her face until she surrendered with a grimace. She pulled something out that appeared to be woven threads. Leaning back against him and feeling his arms wrap around her again seemed to reassure her. She grasped one of his hands and placed the trinket in his palm.

He moved his arm to see what it was, hooking his chin over her shoulder. The threads wove through each other in a uniformed twill pattern. There were shades of violet, amethyst, and juniper. It appeared about as thick as his thumb was long. In the middle of the design were beads of fluorite and aventurine, simple in ornament but dynamic in colors. There was a clasp made out of matte pewter on each end to secure it. The length perfectly mirrored the diameter of his wrist.

"Did you make this?" he asked.

"It took longer than I expected. I'm not very good at these kinds of things."

"Put it on?" he requested, placing it back into her hand and holding his left arm out in front of them.

She wrapped it around his wrist and latched it, the bracelet fitting snuggly. The beads were cushioned by a secondary weave, making sure they wouldn't chafe. The purples and greens were bright against his pale skin. He fell in love with it, and with her even more, as it glinted in the firelight.

"I'm sorry," she whispered, solemnly.

"Why?"

She traced her fingers along the uneven borders. "It's not perfect."

"It isn't? You spent your free time making this. Your intention was to give me something that showed me how you felt. I can feel how much you care about me. I can feel how special I am to you. That makes this the most perfect thing in all the Kingdoms."

She laid her hand next to it, the one that wore his ring. "I hope it won't interfere with your work."

"It won't." He turned her face toward him with his free hand and kissed her deeply. "It's beautiful. I love it."

She finally relaxed in his embrace, returning to her previous position. He kissed her temple while his bracelet and her ring seemed to glow in the light of their small fire. He wanted to say more to her, but they were both still skittish. He refrained from saying those specific words… for now.

"So, does this mean that we're courting?" he inquired.

Zawn stared at the fire, dumbfounded. "Honestly, I don't know."

"Let's say we are and leave it at that."

Those words. Devotion, courting, having his heart. She thrilled at the sound they made and the explosion of emotions they set off inside of her. She quivered at the prospect of the reality of those words. He was her lover, no longer any doubt about that. They were courting and they promised their devotion to another. "I'd like that," she replied after a moment of letting it sink in.

"Good. Now, let's retire to the tent," then he whispered close to her ear, "so I can thank you properly."

~   ~   ~

After he'd left for the college, she missed him. Every day seemed tedious without him. But she dreamt of him every night.

CHAPTER 23

The College of Theurgy looked exactly like it had the day he left. The centuries old institution stood proudly over the beautiful valley below that led into the Kingdom of Saria. It was a stone keep, not really a castle like the one in Mehdehra. Several turrets lined the outer wall where the guards kept the College and its students safe from invaders and marauders. The actual keep, which housed the bedchambers for students and councilors, was chiseled directly out of the dark-veined green and yellow swakane gneiss mountain in the back of the bailey. Against the east wall was a great hall, where students learned and ate. The bailey was filled with bustling bodies, either off to class or off to formulate.

Gwendin didn't realize how homesick he had been until he saw the life he left behind. Then he heard his name called out over the familiar chaos. He glanced around until he saw the tall man with howlite hair. The other man's gray eyes glittered with joy at the sight of his student and he gestured for Gwen to join him. Gwen strode across the yard, dodging students and teachers alike, to embrace his mentor.

"Welcome home, lad," the older man greeted, thumping Gwen hard on the back.

"Good to be home, Master Yunji."

"You've been gone too long."

Gwen chuckled. "Don't tell me you haven't enjoyed the peace and quiet? I'm sure things have been lovely since I was assigned."

"You haven't met the newest class. They have been a, well, a challenge. Come, I cannot wait to catch up on all the things you couldn't put in writing."

~   ~   ~

Yunji stared at his glass, swirling the brew he had made for Gwen's return. The younger theurgist had detailed his experiences in Mehdehra, not just as a theurgist but as someone living within the walls of the castle. The older man had known about his student's frustrations with Elixin, but never knew the threat to Gwendin's life.

"I should recall you immediately," Yunji responded, finally.

"What good would that do?" Gwendin asked, his patience evident. "I've managed his issues with me, putting fear of the College into him. Staying lets me provide for the College, all the while keeping you involved with the local news and annoying him with our support of the neighboring kith."

"Is that the only reason?"

"What do you mean?"

Yunji gestured at Gwen's wrist. "What's their name?"

Confused, Gwen followed his mentor's gaze and saw that he had noticed the bracelet on his wrist. Gwen covered it with his other hand, stammering. "Zawn," he admitted, softly. "Her name is Zawn."

"And is she a member of the kith we pay tithe to?"

The young man blushed. "She's the one who told me what to do, yes."

"It must be something special between the two of you, if she made you that bracelet."

"She is special. She's... incredible."

"And did you give a gift in return?"

"I made a ring. We both have something from the other."

"Good. I'm glad you found someone."

Gwendin's eyebrows raised up in surprise. "You're not going to chastise me?"

"Why should I?" Yunji asked, with a wry smile. "No matter the rules, life happens. And it is every theurgist's prerogative to make their way in the world, be it alone or with someone special by their side. However, not every theurgist is as lucky as you."

"Then can I ask a favor, Yunji?"

"Of course."

"If anything happens to me, make sure she's taken care of?"

His mentor frowned, worried. "Do you think something is going to happen to you?"

"Well, seeing that I just told you how bad things have been lately in Mehdehra and your instant reaction is to recall me? That's just what I've witnessed, I'm sure there are things that happen outside my purview. And if I'm being honest, I don't trust Elixin. It matters little to him that I am his brother by marriage. And I don't trust any of his allies. They turn like snakes in the grass when they see something that fits their goals."

"I will respect your wishes, Gwendin. If anything happens, I will personally ensure she is well taken care of."

"Thank you. Just, uh, don't make it sound like charity. She will rebuff you quickly." Gwen paused then admitted, "But she's my everything."

"Does she know everything?"

"Almost. She knows who my sister is, who my family was."

"Does your sister know about her?"

"No, no one does. Well other than you now and Zawn's closest family. We know the consequences of our… well our… courting."

"Then I will also respect your wish for secrecy. It is just another form of privacy, isn't it?" Yunji sighed, staring meaningfully at his apprentice. "There are no guarantees when it comes to reversal spells, they usually fail epically more often than they work, but if the time comes, I would be willing to try. For you."

Gwen blinked at his master, surprised by the strange comment, until the meaning sunk in. His mouth fell open and he struggled to find the right words. He was shocked, but also flattered. To think his mentor and master would be willing to undo a magical binding just for Gwendin, to let him start a family with Zawn, meant the world to him.

"Thank you," Gwen finally responded, most of his voice missing. "That means a lot to me, Yunji."

"As does your romance, dear boy. I am beyond happy, for the both of you, and hope one day to meet this special person." Comfortable silence settled, both men smiling and enjoying a sip of their brew. "But for now, while you're here, maybe you can help with the new class? They need a speech from someone who has been in the real world for a while."

Gwen laughed. "Fine, lead the way."

~   ~   ~

Gwen walked at Yunji's elbow, still ever the student. He knew he would never be his master's equal, and even though they had a very close relationship in private, in front of the other students he would remain one step behind. It didn't bother him like it would most of the senior theurgists, because he never felt less than Yunji. He walked a step behind out of respect for the man who raised and taught him everything he knew.

They entered a massive study hall, where rows and rows of counters and tables ran the length of the room. There were dividers for each station, allowing a student some privacy but also helped protect the others if one's concoction ended up being dangerous. The light swakane walls made the building feel warm and welcoming, while the dark veins gave it depth and regalness. The furniture utilized that lighter wood from Saria to keep the area from feeling like a dungeon.

There were students working with crystals, either causing them to glow or testing their quality compared to other crystals. Some students had beakers lined up in front of them, testing the properties against simple things like twigs up to complex things like crystals. A few were levitating objects, which Gwen had never mastered, while others manipulated elements like water or fire.

A smirk flashed across Gwen's face briefly, as he remembered his fellow students causing chaos and damage when they didn't follow instructions word for word. He also felt pride because he never had a potion go haywire or been reprimanded for poor work.

Past the line of workspaces arched a large doorway, which led into the College's extensive library. He remembered so many nights studying away in the vast shelves of the library, even falling asleep in a few aisles out of sheet exhaustion. But he loved the smell of the books surrounding him and waking up on the floor never felt embarrassing. Most of his fellow students would step over him and apologize for waking him up.

The contrast between the College and castle was nerve rattling.

Yunji led Gwen further across the campus, until they entered a classroom. Lined up in small chair-and-table combos were young students, not quite teenagers. He could tell they were faking their attention, the boredom obvious in their posture. Gwen felt for the kids. Their instructor, Olivien, had been droning on about the difference between conjuring and manifesting, something he did every semester. When he saw Yunji and Gwen though, he perked up with what was his version of a smile.

"Well, don't we have a pair of special guests," Olivien exclaimed, causing his students to startle and glance around. "And what do we owe for the honor?"

"Nothing owed, just glad to get out of the office every once in a while," Yunji responded with a chuckle.

"And Gwendin Graywhim, welcome home."

"Thank you, Master Olivien. It's quite lovely coming home."

Yunji gestured to Gwen. "I asked Gwendin if he'd mind speaking to some of our new students about the real-world theurgists face when they leave the safety of our College."

"Oh! Yes, please come up here. Speak away!"

~   ~   ~

They watched as the students filed out, chatting excitedly about Gwendin's stories. His concern must have been written all over his face because Olivien shook his head while Yunji laughed.

"You did a good thing, youngster," Olivien chided. "These children will want to work toward similar goals."

"I didn't think my life at the castle was so exciting."

"Brokering a peace with the local kith and standing up to a bastard like Elixin?" Olivien chuckled. "That is no more than miraculous."

"It was meant more as a warning."

Yunji patted Gwen on the shoulder. "Either way, you have inspired the youngsters. Come, dinner should be served soon."

~   ~   ~

Gwen opened his eyes, greeted by the morning sun. He blinked against the harsh bright light, head aching. It took him a moment to remember where he was and why his head throbbed relentlessly.

He grinned when he realized that he was at the College and he had tried to keep up drinking all night with his fellow theurgists, only to find out that he was out of practice. Dinner started out innocently enough, but the moment one theurgist announced his brew was the best, a contest ensued. He had been ill equipped to drink so much however he had enjoyed the different styles and flavors that were passed his way.

Hungover, but pleased with the joyful memories of the night before, he rolled up into a sitting position and inhaled deeply. The early morning sun caught on his bracelet, reflecting hues of lavender and shamrock onto his face. He lifted his wrist, kissing the beads tenderly, wishing they were her lips instead. He wondered what Zee would have thought of the College. He wanted to show her the place where he grew up someday, where he called home. At least the place he had called home before finding it with her.

He sat for a moment, lost in his musings. At first, he thought he saw her lying there beside him when he stirred in the middle of the night, but it had only been a dream. He felt his emotions well up in his chest. He felt lucky – no, blessed - that they had met. Now, alone in bed, he missed her, her smell, her laugh, her touch.

Yunji offering to undo the magical sterilization also gave him food for thought. He knew they weren't there yet in their relationship, so he wouldn't bring it up to her until the time was right. However, knowing that he had a choice, he could let himself dream of a few different futures with her. He let his imagination play scenes in his mind. Living together, maybe even having children. What would their children look like? Would they have magic like him or would her elven nature deter that? And he knew they would raise their children differently than they had been. The only question he had was where would they live and raise their family?

He shook his head laughing at himself then groaned when the movement reminded him of his hangover. One thing that was good about being a theurgist, they had some fantastic cures for self-inflicted pain. With a deep sigh, he left the bed to mix his remedy and to start his day at Yunji's side.

CHAPTER 24

It started one morning as Zawn entered the goats' stalls, when her kithlin readied for their chores. The kith leader, Medruano, notified them that changes would be made and certain groups would be required to make sacrifices for the good of the kith.

He started with the children. One morning, he had the boys line up for him. He made notes in a ledger, then dismissed them. The next morning, he did the same thing with the girls. The following week he called upon the unmatched. First, the men, then the next day, the women. Including Zawn.

As Medruano looked the women over, the one he gave Zawn disturbed her. It was the first time his gaze made her feel... dirty. She could usually think one step ahead of him but this time... Anxiety filled her when she couldn't surmise his plans.

That was never a good thing.

~   ~   ~

Medruano didn't waste time in relaying his plans. He called a meeting of the kith in the square a week later, before dinnertime. He glowered at everyone, as if they had all committed some horrible crime, before speaking in an intolerant tone.

"After years of disappointment, we are now at a breaking point. We have no money. What we have spent it on have been absolute failures. We are supposed to be farmers, metal smiths, masons. Yet we sit on the brink of starvation because of your incompetence. There are too many mouths to feed and not enough food to spare. I have no choice. There has been interest by the men in nearby towns about buying servants to work their households and businesses. They have asked for younger ones, children, so they can be trained and can work for a long time. I have made a list of who will be auctioned off first."

Anger, fear, and confusion echoed through the crowd. Mothers and fathers grabbed their children and held them close, incredulous and terrified.

"Do not worry, once the kith is back on its feet, I will permit you to have more. We also have the opportunity to share our unmatched with the bordellos. Elves can fetch a higher price than humans because we are a novelty. I also have made a list of those who will be tendered first."

Beside her, Zawn felt Ehdzia tremble and Mahij grabbed Zawn's upper arm so tight that nails entered flesh. Both women, who Zawn knew since they were infants and had watched them grow up into talented archers, were not only unmatched but also chaste. The thought of being sold to bordellos ran by men, to be used for sex by men...

Before she could stop herself, Zawn demanded, "Auctioned? Tendered?" She heard her kithlin whisper her name, panic evident as she voiced their collective thoughts, but her own anger got the best of her. "What are we, your possessions?"

"Yes," Medruano responded. "I am leader of this kith and I own you."

"We are not cattle. And we are not the failures. It is you who has failed us. We have naively followed your leadership. We have worked jobs, we have received tithes, we have sold goods. If all the money is gone, that is *your* fault as leader."

"Are you challenging me, nitwit?"

"I am."

She felt the gasps more than she heard them.

Medruano drew his sword, grinning sadistically. "I cannot wait to thrash you until you exhale your last breath."

As Zawn reached for her own weapon, "Stop!" someone shouted.

They all turned to the kith historian and elder, a crippled old man with white hair, who sat near the fire.

"Are you trying to deny me my rights, Jheferin?" boomed Medruano.

"No, you will answer the challenge in due time. But we have had an emotional and terrifying evening already. Neither of you are at your best. It is only fair that both of you have time to take care of your affairs and ready yourselves properly. You have not answered a challenge in a very long time. She has never challenged before. We need to make sure that all of the rules are recognized properly."

Medruano glared at the older elf, then flashed baleful eyes at Zawn. "Fine. Teach her the rules. What little good they will do her because she will be dead." With that, he stormed off toward his work hut, leaving all of the kithlin shocked, terrified, and only having the kith nitwit as their one last breath of hope.

~　　~　　~

After dinner, she was summoned to a quaint hut on the other side of the kith. Inside sat the kith historian and elder, Jheferin. His great-great grandson

Sileas gestured for her to sit down across from the blind elf, then he closed the door and guarded it as if they expected to be disturbed.

The elder's face had wrinkled heavily due to his age, his skin turning dark with time and weather. The heaviest wrinkles scrunched above his cheeks, hiding his almost blind eyes. He could still see light and shadows, and make out certain colors only on good days, which meant Sileas had to guide him everywhere, describe what was in front of him, and help with the requirements expected of a historian.

A body-withering disease that came with age caused his left shoulder to hunch forward, making him look as if he had a massive tumor on his neck. His long, white-as-the-moons hair ran down his back in long locks, covering his shoulders almost like a cloak. Because of his deformity, he had been relegated to wearing robes and other outfits that were easy to slip on and didn't require too many steps. He also wore slip-on sandals, which saved Sileas from having to lace and unlace boots every day.

The old elf looked like he was regressing into an old tree. He personified the tales of how they had always imagined their ancestors. He reminded her suddenly of the deaf grandfather birch who tolerated her meetings with Gwen.

The only reason why Medruano couldn't retire the elder from his job was thanks to Sileas, who made sure none of the tasks assigned to such a prestigious position were ever left unfinished. He would be a fantastic replacement for Jheferin once the elder decided to resign, but she knew the elder didn't want to give Medruano the satisfaction of naming someone else as his heir out of spite.

Zawn sat, suffering in silence, while Jheferin tapped his finger against the top of his walking stick. The old elf's staff not only helped hold him up as he shuffled from one place to another, but he wielded it as a hefty weapon when he found someone too close or too annoying. For a mostly blind man, he always knew precisely where to strike to cause the most discomfort. She had been on the receiving end of a few of those whacks and she braced herself for another.

"You are an idiot, child," the old one complained, thumping her hard with the staff.

She tried to muffle her yelp, then took a deep breath. "I didn't have a choice, Jheferin. Selling our children? Whoring out our unmatched?"

"Including you."

"Including those who are chaste and young and naïve. They haven't even had a chance to fall in love yet. I don't matter, they do. We are not like men, we do not treat each other in such a horrendous manner."

"Do you understand the consequences if you win?"

She scoffed, shrugging dismissively. "I understand the consequences when I lose."

"It is true, he will more than likely kill you. And for what?"

"To show that we are better than this and that we don't have to follow him blindly. And if I can challenge him, others can too. If they want to protect their loved ones, they can see that standing up is not wrong."

"And if you win? Compared to his allies, you are a baby. You will be challenged daily."

"Let them. At least some good will come of that. I won't need training if I'm fighting all day." She lowered her eyes to the ground, kicking her toe in the rug. "But win? You have such high hopes, my friend. No, I will not survive this. I am nothing but an unqualified soldier who isn't even good at being a subpar border sentry."

She felt his hand clasp hers, in sympathy and maybe in reassurance, she wasn't really sure. She grasped it in return, appreciating whatever sentiment he meant.

"If you are to move on to the other side of the canopy, know this." And his aggravation melted into empathy as he spoke. "You will never be documented as the nitwit of this kith. You are Zawn, our daydreamer, a hero of the Purge. Even if you are an idiot. Your passion drives you too hard sometimes. But also know this. All of those here are placing every ounce of hope into you. Let that be your strength when you face Medruano."

Her voice stolen by his sincerity, she could only nod. She glanced up at Sileas for a moment and she could see sadness in his eyes. He, too, was young and unmatched. He would be another victim of Medruano's decisions. The weight of her challenge and everyone suddenly counting on her, it all made her heart shatter.

"Please, outline the rules," she requested, her voice strangling under her emotions. "I have somewhere to be tonight."

"He doesn't have you working your sector?" Jheferin demanded, indignant.

"No, of course not. He's even banished me from my own home. No, I have other affairs I must put in order before I die."

~   ~   ~

Her heart thumped harder with each step. She hated it. She hated the fact that this would be her last night with the man she loved. She had been so excited to see him after their long separation. But after Medruano's announcement and her challenge, she was left with trying to explain to Gwen why he would never see her again. She didn't want him to know what she and her kith were enduring, especially because there was nothing he could do to change it.

After three weeks of separation, she could blame that span of time for the dissolution of their courtship. She would anger him, mistreat him. Whatever it took. He was better off hating her.

She made it to the edge of their campsite, where he stood waiting. The tent was up and a small fire flickered, but no food was cooking. She knew what his expectations were the moment they touched and it wasn't sharing dinner.

She jumped down, after briefly hesitating, then felt his hands grasping, arms embracing, and lips kissing her. He felt so good. She fell into his mindset, wanting every bit of his energy to protect her, inspire her, and distract her. But she had to tell him… He started kissing her neck passionately, making it difficult for her to talk.

"I need to talk to you about something," she finally got out.

"Can it wait?" he inquired, as his hands pulled her tunic over her head. "I haven't seen you in weeks."

She gave into his desire, especially as his hand slipped into her pants. She moaned against his lips. Her eyes closed as he caressed her before removing the rest of her clothing. She started helping him out of his own clothes and once they were both naked, he scooped her up and took her into the tent. She allowed their passion to insulate her, wanting to feel him one last time. She wanted to remember everything about him, his warmth, his taste, his expressions, all those small things that she loved about him. She wanted mementos to take with her to the other side of the canopy, hoping to keep them in her heart forever.

Afterwards, they cuddled and tried to catch their breaths, the work they put into satisfying each other leaving them exhausted. Their passionate reunion had knocked the tent down and it laid limply around them. He sat leaning back against the tree, with her straddling his lap and resting against his chest. He had his arms wrapped around her, his warmth briefly melting her dread away.

"What did you want to talk about?" he asked, his panting finally easing.

She laid her head against his chest, losing herself in the rhythm of his heart for a moment. Then she resigned herself to her decision and sat up, looking into his eyes with a strictness she had never used on him before.

He didn't like the look on her face.

"We can no longer meet like this," she stated, pulling away and escaping his embrace. "I'm sorry, Gwendin."

She stumbled out of their disheveled bedding, then stood and started gathering her clothing. He watched her from their deconstructed love nest, frozen with shock, then blinked and cleared his throat.

"Tonight or…?"

"My responsibilities have been falling to the wayside. It became evident while you were gone that I need to focus. I don't have time for frivolous fun anymore. I can't say I haven't enjoyed it but it's becoming an inconvenience."

"Friv… fun? Inconven…?" He stammered as his eyes narrowed. "Now that's horseshit." He jumped to his feet, grabbed her pants out of her hands and tossed them to the side. Grasping her by the shoulders, he gave her a shake but she wouldn't meet his eyes again. "What is really going on, Zee?"

"You said you would let me use you until I wanted to stop. I want to stop. And I'm leaving. I decided I don't want to stay here anymore."

Then he called her by her full birth name. "Zawn, heir of the Haley family, daydreamer of the Whispering Hornbeam Kith."

Hearing him say it in such a stern tone, she became speechless.

"Talk to me," he ordered.

She struggled for a moment to find her voice. "I um, I made a mistake."

"With me?"

"No," she replied, heartbroken. She cupped his face with her hands and she finally met his eyes. "You've never been a mistake."

"Then what's going on?"

Reality twisted her stomach as she answered, "I will be dead by the end of the week."

"Dead? What do you mean?"

"I challenged the leader of our kith. I um… He will best me. And considering what I said to him, he will have no mercy and will end my life for my insolence."

He drew her into a hug, sighing heavily. "So, you'd rather have me mourn our relationship than your death? You are such a nitwit. I love a nitwit."

She finally wrapped her arms around him after hearing the word love.

"Why did you challenge him if you knew he'd kill you?"

Everything tumbled out. "We're on the brink of starving. We haven't been able to work the land like we used to but, when we try, it never turns out right. Crops die or produce very little. We do odd jobs for the towns nearby but the money never seems to be enough. Every time we turn around, there's something wrong or ruined."

Gwendin felt sick hearing that. He knew the very King he worked for was the reason for all of this. The King had strangled their kith with his laws and his hatred.

"He had decided to sell some of us off, so we could afford food. He's starting with our children and our unmatched. The unmatched can be sold to the bordellos and the children would fetch a big price as servants and, why not," and the bitterness darkened her voice, "we can always have more."

"Unmatched?" He leaned back to look into her eyes. "Including you?"

"I don't matter," she automatically responded.

"You matter to me, Zee."

"Had I not spoken up," and she squeezed her eyes shut for a moment, "I'm sure I would've been the first one sold off."

He wanted to tell her to run. To escape and hide, until the worst blew over. However, with all of their conversations, he knew honor was integral to the soul of an elf. Avoiding a conflict after challenging someone would be seen as dishonorable. Any elf with integrity wouldn't survive that and they would have no standing in any kith.

"What would happen if you best him?"

She laughed, mirthlessly. "I am nowhere near the warrior he is. But if I did best him, then I'd be leader and I'd inherit all of the problems. Honestly, I can only hope my death will spur the rest of my kith to stand up to him and cause them to leave the kith for another."

"You've faced death before."

"I don't fear death," she snapped, defensively.

"I didn't say that."

"I was born to die."

Those words hurt him. "Zee, no, you were born to live."

"I never thought of..." She stared at him, baffled. She inhaled deeply, but he could hear the heartbreak in her voice as she continued. "I am not afraid to die. But I hate to leave you so soon after finally finding you."

"I don't want you to leave me either." He pulled her against him again, nuzzling her hair. "Is there anything I can do?"

She sniffled, unable to hide her fear and regret any longer. "Just hold me?"

"Come, we'll fix the tent and I will hold you all night. And do me a favor? Will you stop breaking up with me? I don't want to have to undress for you every time something bad happens."

That elicited a strangled laugh from her.

He leaned back to meet her eyes again. "I'm with you, to the end. I mean it. All the way."

~　　　~　　　~

The sun hadn't risen yet, but they were awake. They couldn't sleep after they fixed the tent nor could they find the right words to say. They were unsure what their future held, knowing that she would have to fight for not just her life but for those in her kith. The song birds started heralding sunrise and she sat up, making him let her go despite himself. She didn't leave immediately, allowing him to rub his hand along her lower back. He watched as her eyes closed at his touch, then he sat up and cupped her face.

Kissing her long and deep, he cherished every second. After they pulled away, he leaned his forehead against hers and touched noses. He closed his eyes for a moment. "I know you believe that you matter little in this world. The time apart made me realize how much you mean to me. You are everything to me, Zawn, heir of the Haley family, daydreamer of the Whispering Hornbeam Kith. My heart, my breath, my home, my life. My everything."

Zawn leaned back, staring at him with such a serious expression. Gwen was unsure of her thoughts. Then she moved to straddle his lap. She tenderly cupped his ears, tracing light fingertips from the tragus up along the outer cartilage down to the earlobe. Next, she took his hands, resting them against her ears. Taking her cue that it was his turn, he just as lovingly caressed her ears, starting at each tragus, moving up the tip of her ears, then down to her earlobe where it connected to her jawline. As he did so, her eyes closed slowly and when he reached the end, tears ran down her cheeks. Concerned, he cupped her face, making her open her eyes again.

"You've never let me touch your ears," he whispered. "Not like that."

"No one ever has."

"Never?"

"That's how we express love to each other. It's a... very intimate expression."

"Had I known that, I would have done that sooner."

She scoffed and he responded by kissing her.

"I want you to listen to me, Zee. Don't just fight for your people, win for them. Claim victory in their names. And come back to me. Do you hear me? Come back to me."

CHAPTER 25

Zawn stood in her hut, Chaelene moving carefully around her. She made sure the armor was fastened tightly and double-checked Zawn's weapons. She confirmed that Zawn could move but paid close attention to any weaknesses like that would expose her to a fatal blow.

"I wish you still had your armor from the Purge," Chae said, softly. "It was sturdier, thicker." As she moved behind her friend, Zawn could hear her sniffling.

"I'm sure Medruano destroyed it after he demoted me." Zawn glanced over at Taylor, who leaned against the closed door. "Remember what they told us when we were sent to the warrior caste to train?"

"We were born to die," he answered.

"Finally meeting that expectation."

He frowned at her after watching his mate for a moment. "Chae is trying very hard to be strong, Zawnie."

"I know, but she doesn't need to be," Zawn responded, turning and embracing her friend. Chae started to sob, which tore at Zawn's resolve to be stoic. "I know my death means I will leave you all behind. My only hope is that I earn an honorable death so I can meet my parents proudly when I move onto the other side of the canopy."

"They're already proud of you," Taylor replied. "So are Momma and Brennan."

Sighing, Zawn looked back over at Taylor. "When I lose, don't stay. Go to Taikin."

"How do we know he would take us?"

"I already asked. He said he would accept you. You can thrive in his kith."

"How can we leave our home?" Chae demanded, pulling away and wiping her face dry.

"Is this a home? No, it's not. Medruano turned this kith into a prison and a death sentence. You deserve better. You all do. He can't stop you from leaving.

Honestly, he can't stop you all from leaving."

"We will go to Taikin," Taylor assured.

"Good, he is expecting you. You know the place the messenger picks up my letters? He will honor our agreement for a few months after I…" She swallowed hard. She adjusted her archer gauntlets and caught sight of herself in the window. She looked half the warrior that Medruano was and ill equipped for the battle. But there was one other thing she had to discuss with Taylor. "Jheferin said that if I somehow win, that I need someone to be my second when I take the mantle of leader. Medruano hasn't had one in decades, which has been frowned upon by the other kiths. But if I succeed…"

Taylor crossed the room and stood in front of Zawn. Towering over her, he remained silent as he stared into her eyes. Then he reached out and grabbed both of her hands. "I will proudly stand by you as your second. If you win, we will both work together, whatever it takes, to save our kith."

~ ~ ~

The fight was set to occur mid-morning. The kithlin spent their morning hidden away in their huts, afraid to mingle and gossip. They feared provoking Medruano's anger and making them first on his list for sale.

Zawn knew there were plenty of bets against her by his staunch allies, but most of the kithlin were unwilling to lay down anything worth noting. Probably a swap of errands or tasks, since money was scarce amongst them. She stood to the east, with Taylor and Chaelene behind her. They had Meagan stay inside their hut, which was far from the kith's center, with both her children and theirs, unwilling to have the youngsters witness the brutal battle. To the west stood Medruano, kitted fully in his extravagant armor. Zawn felt underdressed again, having been left only her breastplate and archer gauntlets to protect her.

"It will be a moment of pride to spill your blood," Medruano shouted, his voice dripping with distaste.

"Ignore him," Taylor whispered.

"He sounds like the generals during the Purge," she responded to her friend, softly. "They spoke viciously and yet died quickly."

Chaelene scoffed. "Think of him however you wish, Zawnie, if it will help you defeat him."

"I won't defeat him," she replied, with a shrug. "But he will have to work very hard for the killing blow."

Jheferin shuffled into the kith square, with help from Sileas, and glanced from east to west. "You both have been given the rules of challenging. Now for the crowd who gather. No one is permitted to interfere, no one is allowed to take their place. This is to submission or death, whichever comes first."

"Do not surrender, pest," Medruano said. "There will be no mercy."

Zawn raised an eyebrow in disapproval.

"Any questions?"

The kith was deathly silent.

"Then let the challenge begin."

Medruano and Zawn lifted their haladies up, handle over their hearts, then bowed their heads. They both adjusted their stances, readying for the coming battle.

Medruano raised his haladie as if it were a spear, then charged Zawn. She held her ground until he was close enough, then darted away while he tried to plunge his blade into her torso. He spun quickly, trying to grab her arm, but she dropped into a somersault and gave herself some distance from him. She jumped back onto her feet, only to find him gaging his next move. She could only keep away from him for so long. They had to cross blades eventually. But her mentor, Brennan, had taught her one thing that she always utilized: don't strike the first blow.

"Let the other open themselves up to you when they attack," Brennan had warned. "You only get one chance to find their weakness and that first blow always exposes it."

She took a deep breath, then figured his next attack would allow them to clash and for her to take notes. And with that, he rushed her again. She watched as he held his haladie over his head like an ax. At that moment, his armor lifted up and exposed a very slight portion of his belly. Then she slid into a bracing stance and felt the power of his blow as it bashed her a few inches into the ground. She twisted her arm against his weight, making him spin to the side while she jumped back away from him again.

Medruano didn't hesitate this time. He slammed into her again, the bashing of their haladies causing their audience to flinch at the loud cacophony. As he slashed at her, Zawn blocked each blow quickly and efficiently, avoiding the injury he planned to cause. Every strike made her arms weaken by degrees, eventually making them become wobbly. She started to avoid as many collisions as she could, shaking her arms to regain feeling in them as she did so.

"Give up, pest. Just die."

"You're welcome to surrender instead," she retorted. "Save us both some sweat."

He growled and advanced again. Instead of blocking with her blade, she charged him before dropping to the ground and tripping him with a sweeping, outstretched leg. He sprawled on the ground behind her. She rolled back to her feet, then started her own advance. She landed her blade onto his as he blocked her. He tried to grab her leg, to pull her onto the ground too, but she danced away before he could get a strong enough hold. Before he could move his arm under him to lift himself up, she stomped on it, making him cry out and roll onto his side. Then she delivered a swift kick straight into his gut, where his armor exposed him.

He cursed and coughed, but grabbed her leg when she tried to kick him again. She felt him grasp her lower calf then yank, pulling her so hard that she crashed back onto the ground. Her haladie flew out of her hand as she landed.

Groaning in pain and trying to regain her breath, she laid there on her back for a moment. Medruano used that brief pause to crawl over to her and straddle her pelvis. He struck the left side of her abdomen before landing a blow straight into her jaw. She cried out in agony, then turned her face to the side and coughed out blood and teeth.

Medruano leaned in, his hot breath crashing against her cheek as he chuckled. "This kith will never remember you for anything other than being an embarrassment. They will all be relieved that you are dead and gone." Then he straightened his back, lifting his haladie over his head again, this time for the death blow.

Even through the pain and the ringing in her head, she could hear her name being whispered, screamed, and shouted from different directions. Voices begging for her to get up. Not to give in. It wasn't just Taylor and Chaelene, but several voices. Warriors, archers, friends, and even critics. Because beyond those titles, they were mothers, fathers, siblings, unmatched but beloved... They all pleaded for her not to give up.

As did Gwen's voice. Amongst the others', she could hear him whispering, "Win for them."

When Medruano recognized that the kith wanted her to keep fighting back, he growled obscenities and glared at the audience. "Silence! She has lost. She will now die for her insolence. And you will remember this the next time you decide to question my orders!"

Zawn tried to say something, but it came out too softly to be heard over the other voices.

Startled, Medruano stared down at her. "What did you say?"

"I said..." and she gasped, "surrender."

Medruano laughed in her face.

"No?" she replied, gurgling. She spit out another tooth, straight into his face, which made him grunt in disgust. "Then fuck off."

In one quick move, Zawn grabbed his hand and pinched the nerve in the wrist, making him drop his weapon. As it came free from his fingers, it landed in her other hand and she didn't hesitate. She drove one blade straight into his stomach, right where the skin showed. Buried deep, she twisted and yanked, essentially gutting him. He jerked, in shock, then slid off of her and collapsed onto the ground. His blood gushed violently from the wound, the weapon still grasped in her hand, doing nothing to quell the spewing liquid.

The gasps around her barely registered. There was shock, surprise, elation... among other emotions that she couldn't define at the moment. The pain in her face, as well as other parts of her body, kept her from realizing that she had won. It did not prevent her from remembering the fact that she was now fair game for any other challengers and this time, there would be no mercy of preparation. She gasped, trying to inhale a deep breath but it kept evading her. She heard Jheferin say something, then Chaelene and Taylor were at her side. Her friends asked her questions, but she was still stunned from the events. She only asked softly for help to stand up.

They got her on her feet while Taylor tried to hide the fact that he had to support her upright position. Jheferin said something again, then Sileas appeared in front of her. She felt him loop something over her head and it took a moment for her to recognize the large pendant that Medruano wore as the sign of his leadership.

It was now hers.

"Zawn, heir of the Haley family, our daydreamer is now also our leader," Jheferin announced. "Leader Haley, have you picked your second?"

She tried to reply, but her jaw protested.

She saw Taylor straighten out of the corner of her eye as he stood proudly next to his friend. "Taylor," he answered, "patriarch of the Grayheart family, our protector."

She spit out a gob of blood and saliva that threatened to choke her. "Are there any other challengers today?" she demanded, shaking off her shock. No one stepped forward. "Good. We have a lot of work to do and I need every single one of you to help me bring this kith back to its glory." She was thankful the words only came out slightly slurred. "But first, we mourn the death of our former leader. Please allow his family to come forward and claim the body."

A young man stepped into the circle, who was Medruano's grandson, then he glanced around at a couple other elves around his age. They didn't move, all staring at Zawn, fearful. She waved them over, permitting them to help the grandson pick up Medruano's body and carry it away for funerary.

She turned her attention back to the rest of her kithlin. "Please assist his family with his funerary if they ask. We will bid him a hero's farewell, thanking him for his service to the kith."

The group started to break up, most still in shock that Zawn had bested Medruano in the first place. She knew she needed to let them all process the situation before asking too much of them too quickly. Their participation with the funeral would keep idle hands busy for now. When everyone was far enough away from the area, Zawn's knees buckled and her friends half-carried her over to one of the benches.

"What do we do first?" Taylor asked, while Chaelene checked her injuries.

"Figure out what happened to all of the money," Zawn responded.

"We need to tend to your wounds first," Chae admonished. "You're drooling blood."

"I'll be fine, just shove some cloth in my mouth."

Chae groused. "Tay, help me…"

"She has a point, Chae. If his allies realize she is in this bad of shape, they will challenge her immediately."

"Fine, at least let me get a kit and I'll patch you up while they're distracted."

"First get me into the work hut, Tay," Zawn requested, another glob of blood and saliva escaping.

"I'll meet you inside," Chae responded.

Taylor tried to discreetly help her back to her feet and assist her in walking. They entered the Leader's work hut and he grabbed a chair with his one hand while keeping hold of her with the other. Once in the bathing room, he had her sit down. It didn't take Chae long to grab a kit and slip inside too. Then she ordered Taylor to get some ice in a pouch and a change of clothes for their friend. Chae made Zawn swish water in her mouth a few times to clear out any debris and blood. She stopped the bleeding from the bashed-out teeth, then rubbed a light coat of pain relief cream on Zawn's jaw. She also discovered a large laceration on the new leader's lip and applied some antiseptic salve.

When Taylor returned with the ice, and a clean shirt, Chaelene held the cold pack against her friend's face. "Alternate between your jaw and your side. Take it slow. Let Tay do any heavy lifting. I don't know the full extent of the damage to your jaw but I can see at least three teeth missing. And I think Medruano broke a few of your ribs. You might want to change your shirt too. It's mostly blood colored now."

Zawn glanced down, finding herself rather a mess. "Agreed. Can you help me?"

Chae and Taylor helped her out of her armor. Chae pulled off her blood-soaked shirt then hissed when she saw the blooming of a bruise on her friend's abdomen. She carefully rubbed more pain relief cream on the area which caused Zawn to curse colorfully. Once done, Taylor slipped the clean shirt over her head. She left the breast plate off, but slipped her gauntlets back on.

"Chae, can you keep an eye on things out there while we work? Make sure Medruano's family and allies behave?"

Chae nodded as she returned the supplies to the kit. "Of course."

"Thank you. Come, Tay, let's take a look around."

They started searching every inch of the place. Nothing. Even the books were blank, with evidence of pages being torn out. The fireplace looked suspiciously full of ash, making Zawn believe that Medruano burned everything that incriminated him. She felt bitter allowing him an honorable funeral, but she reminded herself that it was the only way to keep the peace. At least for now.

"All the money?" Taylor cursed. "All of it really gone?"

"Even Gwen's tithe, which I know was paid yesterday. They're never late."

"That job we did for the Crintsons was lucrative."

Tears threatened as her heart deflated. "It's all gone."

"What could have happened to all that money?"

"If I am to guess, I'd say gambling." Her mind rolled over other places that money could hide. "Come, I want to search his family home. Maybe I'm wrong."

"We can't. They'll be there dressing the body."

She grimaced, then slowly lowered herself down into one of the chairs. "Then we'll sneak in during the pyre. I doubt anyone will notice our absence." She leaned her jaw against the ice pouch.

"Why give him such an honor?" he finally demanded, flopping down into the other chair. "He had nothing but contempt for you. Had he killed you, he would have left your body in the woods for the carrions to feast on. Then he would sell off our children and unmatched. He would have sold you off first if you hadn't challenged him."

"I know. But I thought this was the only way to avoid a civil war. At least for today. His allies and that grandson of his could have pulled together and challenged me. I wouldn't have been able to survive another round. At least this way, they mourn and think me honorable even though I despised Medruano with every fiber of my being."

"Will you rest for now? At least until the funeral?"

"And show weakness? No, I have to pretend as long as I can. Maybe at bedtime I can finally give in to the day. But right now, there is one other place I want to check, for something else."

~   ~   ~

Zawn carefully opened the armory's door, seeing shelving full of armor and other kits. She didn't see anything familiar, but spurred on by sheer curiosity, peeked into one of the chests shoved toward the back. As she lifted the lid, she saw a flash of a dagger as it laid on top. Her breath caught. She reached in reverently, touching leather and metal. All of her weaponry and armor, from her days as a fighter in the Purge, remained encased safely in the chest. She felt pride filling her.

She flipped open another chest nearby and recognized the items inside that one as well, a smile breaking through her injured face.

Then she shouted for Taylor.

CHAPTER 26

The next day, Zawn felt every blow, every ache. She never thought she could feel worse than the day she suffered through her wine-induced hangover. It took everything in her to get up, clean up and start her day. Taylor had helped her search Medruano's personal hut while everyone attended the funeral pyre, but they hadn't found a trace of any money or ledgers.

She had returned to the work hut, which was now hers as leader, and rifled through what little remained. Finding that hopeless, she decided to organize herself and the kith. She spent the rest of the morning walking slowly around the kith, taking stock of what they had and what they didn't. What she found was heartbreaking.

All they had left of livestock were a few old chickens and the goats whose stalls she had been ordered to clean. When she had checked in on the goats that morning, they had moved toward her for the affection she always showed them during her chores. They had begged for food and happily followed her across the path to the barn. When they entered, her heart sank. She hadn't realized how low they were on hay. She ended up leading the trotting and bouncing creatures to the pasture to wander and nibble. She checked the corn crib and found that it too was almost empty. What little remained looked moldy. Zawn tried to remember the last time they planted and gathered any corn.

She returned to the work hut and started a list. Exhausted, she held another ice pouch against her cheek. She sat alone at the desk reviewing her notes, sullen. She had been mistreated by Medruano for so long that she didn't bother paying attention to any daily activities. Becoming responsible for the day to day as well as the kith's future, she realized that she had won the fight, but she wondered if she had lost the battle that was supposed to save the kith.

Then someone shouted her name, making her drop the icepack onto the desk and exit the work hut. She glanced up the main road, where a young man in white clothing jogged into the kith. It was the messenger from the College of Theurgy, looking rather rattled. He recognized Zawn, rushing up to her and bowing. When he straightened, his eyes widened at the injuries to her face.

"The College apologizes for the delay in our tithe," he said, panting. "Circumstances that were beyond our control stopped us from traveling."

"And what circumstances could that be?" she demanded, her tone stern.

The messenger blushed. "The new first-year students learned the danger of not reading labels fully. We are lucky that no one was injured in the explosion."

"Oh." She accepted the purse from the messenger. "I am sorry for snapping at you. I'm glad no one was hurt."

He bowed. "Thank you, milady. The College added a bonus in apology. And we will be punctual next time, no matter the circumstances."

"Safe journey." A sudden thought crossed her mind and Zawn called out, "Wait."

"Yes, milady?"

"Are you headed to the Mehdehran Castle?"

"Yes, I am to drop off a letter to the King." The young man flashed a devilish smile, reminding her how much theurgists loved good gossip. "Do you wish something shared?"

"Would you mind casually mentioning that Medruano is no longer leader of our kith?"

"I will casually mention it, milady."

Then he bowed again and turned on his heel, returning to the road with almost a skip in his step. Taylor approached her as the young man jogged back out of their kith. He stared at the purse in her hands.

"Money?" he asked.

"Gwen's tithe. Late but timely." She laughed, with relief and exhaustion, grasping the purse tightly. "Where's Chae?"

"With the other archers, taking stock of our supplies in the food storage as you asked."

"I need to speak with them. Right now."

~   ~   ~

Zawn entered the storage unit, only to be met with saddened eyes. That was enough to tell her their news was not good. But she motioned for Chaelene to hold out her hand. After Zawn opened the small bag and let the contents tumble out into her friend's hand, Chae stared at the coins that glittered there. "Where did this come from?" she demanded.

"It's the theurgist's tithe," Zawn answered. "Do you think that's enough to buy supplies for bread and other food?"

"Meagan is a ruthless negotiator," Chae replied, with pride. "I think she can get a lot with this."

"Do you think we can turn it into more coin?"

Chae's eyebrows furrowed. "What do you mean?"

"If we bake breads, treats, things like that and then sell them, do you think we could make a profit?"

"Families like the Crintsons love our goods. They complained this last time we worked their fields that they missed eating our treats. I doubt they are the only ones." Chaelene bit her lower lip, thinking quickly. "Yes, I think we can turn a profit."

"Then do it. Get Meagan to barter and get baking. Some for us, some for sale. Get some more chickens, too. We never replaced the ones that died. That way we can have our own eggs. Have the hunters returned yet?"

"No," Taylor responded, "they were determined not to come back empty-handed."

Zawn nodded, but her thoughts were running faster than she could express. "I need to find Gaylon. We've a growing season fast approaching and I know we need seed."

"He was tilling some fields to the east," Saronin told them, as she consolidated two baskets into one. "He took his children with him to help."

"Thank you, Saronin. And Chae, thank you and thank Meagan."

~   ~   ~

Some of the money was used to buy food already made, to fuel the kithlin. Ingredients were also purchased and baking began in earnest. Measurements and chatter, clacking and clanking started ringing through the kith. Each household offered up pots, pans, ovens, and other utensils for the large baking experiment. Smells of breads and treats started wafting through the air, bringing the energy of the kith up, making it vibrate with excitement.

The hunters returned the next day with a few large bucks and were greeted by cheers. Each member of the kith touched the animals and whispered thanks for their gift before the next steps were taken. Zawn approached Eddard, who frowned.

"I'm sorry it took us so long," he said.

"No apologies necessary. You needed the time to be successful. Most importantly? You are all home, safe."

Eddard nodded, then gestured to the others behind that carried heavy satchels. "We also foraged nuts and berries in the wild, while we hunted."

Duard and Iloran opened their satchels, making Zawn's eyes widen and smile broaden.

"Please, get those to Meagan," she instructed and the two elves headed directly to Meagan's hut. Then she glanced at the tall elf next to her, knowing he was torn between pride and disappointment. "Thank you, Eddard, and everyone who hunted with you. You have added to our options. Now rest, you all look exhausted."

"Thank you, Zawnie, uh, Leader Haley, but… the work isn't done yet."

And with that, Eddard followed the other hunters and worked alongside the novice fighters to skin, portion, and dry the meat. One portion was set aside for the stew that evening, for the entire kith to enjoy. The fur was handed to the older women, who started to work on fashioning blankets and cushion covers that could be sold for a profit. Hopeful chattering filled the air, and without Medruano there to glower them into silence, the kith began to act and feel differently.

Zawn wasn't very talented in cooking or crafting, so she focused her time on the fields. Gaylon had explained to her, in painful detail, the issues plaguing their tillable ground. Between the soil not being renewed using manure and other nutrient-filled crops and the irrigation system not working properly, Zawn had to learn quickly what was needed and how soon.

Crops like lucerne were coming into season and they had purchased enough to energize the soil. Manure on the other hand... When she had realized that Medruano had sold off most of their livestock, she reached out to the neighboring kith for help. As she waited to hear back, she started figuring out the irrigation system, with Gaylon and his three children right beside her.

It didn't seem difficult to fix but it would be time consuming. Years of Medruano's disrespect for Gaylon's knowledge and refusal to fund efficient maintenance left the system limping.

Gaylon frowned. "I swear I tried my best with what little I had to work with."

"My friend, based on what I see," Zawn replied, looking at the pieces that had crumbled in her hand. "I have no doubts you did. And I am quite sure that Medruano was the culprit for your lack of resources."

"What are we to do?"

"Well, I learned some things during the Purge about mechanics, mostly stuff that pertained to mechanical weapons," she responded, grasping his shoulder. "This isn't terribly different from catapults and the like. We've bits and pieces somewhere. Keep tilling, I'll start looking around."

And with that, she spent most of the afternoon digging through storage buildings for pieces and parts that could be altered to replace the broken parts.

Days blurred together. With her plans in motion, an exhausted Zawn sat down at dinner and sighed. Her adventures in the irrigation ditch did nothing for her pain or patience. But as she fought off the self-pity, she watched her kithlin as they put her orders into motion, working together instead of being separated as they had been for so long. She hadn't realized just how divided Medruano had kept them. However, eating food they made, keeping families together, and proving they were as resourceful as their former leader was negligent, seemed to be the fuel needed to push forward. Even through her exhaustion and pain, she felt pride.

Then she realized what day it was and she needed to leave for the night. She tried to walk as casually as possible to her personal hut, even though her aches and pains slowed her stride. She closed her door behind and hissed a curse. She had tried to hide her pain from her kithlin, but she knew they caught an unintentional flinch here and there. Now in the privacy of her hut, she let her guard down and hobbled toward the bathing room.

After bathing and dressing in clean clothing, she approached Taylor near the armory hut. He and a few other fighters were taking account of the weapons, to see what had been sold or traded and what remained. A list nailed to the wall kept them organized, with scribbled descriptions and ticks marking amounts. The lack of arrows caught her eye, but she knew she had to wait for the full report.

"I have to be somewhere," she said, keeping her voice low. "Can you keep an eye on things?"

Taylor stared at her for a moment, frowning. "Zawnie, I…"

"I know, Tay, but I promised him. That's why I have to go. And now, with everything changing, I have to figure things out with him."

"I understand."

"You know where the grandfather tree is? The one with the roots that twist up about three feet and wrap around into a nook? That's where I'll be. If anything happens while I'm away tonight, come get me."

"We'll try not to disturb you," he responded, gripping her shoulder gently. "I hope you can work something out. Just be safe."

CHAPTER 27

She stood at the edge of their meeting place, waiting for him to walk into the clearing, and he could tell so much had changed about her. Even her clothing. She still wore her topaz-colored tunic and suede pants, but her leather breastplate had buckles instead of lacing and the skirt was four large panels instead of smaller petals. A chunky necklace made of some matte blue stone now adorned her neck and a black leather band wrapped around her left upper arm, with matching stones tied off at the end.

What really differed was her face. Under the massive bruising and cut on her lip, she looked like she had aged decades in the few days they had been apart and her expression was a mixture of exhaustion, worry, unsurety.

He dropped everything onto the ground and held out his arms. A few heartbeats passed then she strode across the space between them and landed in his embrace. He held her tight, kissing her temple and hair. Even though everything hurt, the feel of his arms around her made it all bearable.

"You came back to me," he whispered, his voice shaking with relief.

He wanted nothing more than to crush her against him and kiss her until she was breathless, but he could feel tension in her body as he held her close. He leaned back and he saw that her eyes were dark with something he couldn't put his finger on.

"Come, sit with me."

He led her toward their little area where he usually put up the tent. He tried to unfasten her armor, but being unfamiliar with it, failed miserably. She smiled mirthlessly and removed it for him. She laid it down nearby, as well as her belt that kept her haladie and khukuri sheathed. He sat down and pulled her close, wrapping his arms around her carefully. She wasn't as pliant as usual and by the way she guarded her left side, he knew she was in pain.

"What hurts?"

"Besides everything?" She chuckled with little humor, then sighed. "My face. My left ribcage. The breastplate kept pressure on it so it didn't hurt much when

I walked."

He patted the root behind them. She raised herself carefully and sat on it, flinching. He dug through his bag and pulled out a stone that had dark blue hues with chips of red.

"What is that?"

"Bloodstone. It'll help me see."

Kneeling next to her, he lifted her tunic and saw the sprawling bruise all along her left side. Gwen laid a warm hand against her cool skin, with the stone cupped in his palm, murmuring something as he closed his eyes. He hissed in sympathy, then grabbed his theurgist bag.

"Definitely broken ribs. I think it's just those three ribs at the bottom."

"The whole side hurts."

"I can give you something for the pain."

"Already done."

"Ah, but I have stronger stuff." He dug into his satchel, pulling out a glass jar with a twist lid. "We'll mix this in some water and have you drink it. Then I can mend the bones."

She stared at him oddly. "I didn't know you could heal."

"I can heal bones to a certain extent," he explained as he poured the powder into his flask and shook it, "but nothing beyond that. I can't do much about the bruising. Even magic has its limits."

"I can handle the bruising. It proves I survived the fight."

"It does. Drink this, slowly."

She took his flask, then frowned. "Will it interact with what I've already taken?"

"What was it?"

"Mature winter cloves."

"No, you should be fine. But this should slowly enter your system, so don't chug it."

She followed his instructions, sipping at the flask occasionally. He pulled out two more crystals from his satchel which she recognized as selenite and amber. When she had consumed enough of the painkilling brew, Gwen repositioned himself in front of her.

"Now, let me check your face." He murmured again as he cupped her face. His eyes widened as he exclaimed, "How are you able to talk? He shattered part of your jaw, here, near the chin."

"Pain relief mostly. And talking much slower than usual. He knocked out three molars, I think. Been on a liquid diet since the fight."

"I can heal that as well. If you permit me?"

"Thank you, but just focus on my jaw. The ribs will figure themselves out."

"I can manage both. But I agree, your jaw should be first. How is your pain level?"

"I'm comfortable."

"Good. It will help numb you for a while. But healing, well, this is gonna hurt. Stinging more than stabbing. Ready?"

She took a deep breath, set down his flask, and nodded.

Whispering an incantation she didn't recognize, Gwendin closed his eyes and furrowed his eyebrows as he concentrated on her jaw. The air around them felt dead suddenly, then a light seemed to draw from the ground, into his knees, up through his body, and into the stones. The aura brightened to the point where she had to close her eyes. She could feel the fractured pieces of bone move and heard them clicking together, like a puzzle, the healing magic performing as the glue keeping it together. His hands went from warm to scalding, the swarm of bee stings focused on her making her cry out. The heat finally faded and they were both left panting, her from the surge of pain and him in exhaustion. With all his energy drained, he slumped against her.

"Gwen? Are you hurt?" she asked, worried.

"No, not hurt. It just takes a lot out of me. We'll have to wait on the ribs. Can you stay?"

"I can."

"Good, that'll give me time to recharge and time for you to tell me everything." He sat back down, resting against her legs then chuckled. "What a pair we make tonight."

Laughing, she nudged him, making him move so she could lower herself back onto the ground next to him. He weakly pulled her close, trying to be mindful of her broken ribs. They wrapped loving arms around each other and let the silence lull them for a while. As she laid her head against his chest, she found reassurance in the feel and sound of his heartbeat.

"Did you tell the College to deliver the tithe late?" she asked, already knowing the answer.

He stammered for a moment then shrugged. "I may have warned them there could be a change in leadership. But I didn't expect that someone would mix the wrong chemicals and blow out a wall. It turned out to be a good excuse for your leader if he had won and didn't get the funds on time."

"And if I won, then you knew the money would be there for me to use?"

"A foolish hope, but it was all I had left to me to help you."

She kissed him. "Thank you. You don't know how much that has helped."

"I'm glad it wasn't in vain." He caressed her cheek gently. "Can you tell me what happened?"

She laid her head on his shoulder, sighing. "We fought. He was formidable but I guess I handled my weapon better than he expected. But he overtook me, punching me in my stomach and face. I tried to get him to surrender. He went for the final blow but I disarmed him and killed him with his own blade. I had to kill him," she admitted, solemnly. "I had no choice. I hate that I had to kill another elf. But he wouldn't relent. He didn't give me a choice. I know that. But still..." She paused, then looked up into his eyes. "When he had me pinned... I heard everyone around me. Voices, words... I heard you too. Telling me to get up, to win. It was so clear."

He stared at her, confused by her comment. Then his eyebrows relaxed when he realized what she meant. "I tried to keep myself busy that day. I didn't want to sit there and dwell on all the bad outcomes. But there was a moment where I felt just absolute dread. I couldn't figure out why I felt that way immediately, but, well, then I realized it had to be the time of the fight. Nothing else made sense. So I just, I lit a white candle and I concentrated on my love for you and tried to send that to you."

"I felt it."

He caressed her cheek. "I guess we're more connected than we've ever realized."

She stared into his eyes, hers filling with tears and making him squeezed her gently.

"There's… something else. I'm leader now. I can't just disappear for hours and not explain where I am or what I've been doing. I don't know when I will see you again, or how often."

"What did I tell you about breaking up with me?" he chided, disliking the tone of her voice.

She rolled her eyes, in frustration. "I'm not breaking up with you. It's just… I know none of this is fair to you."

"If we love each other as much as I believe we do, we will make it work."

Doubt fell like a shadow across her face.

"Do you love me?" he asked.

Her eyes widened. That question made her heart clench. How could he ask that? Of course she did. She had permitted him to touch her ears. She reached up and caressed one of his ears, reverently. "Forever."

He ran loving fingers along her ear as well, watching her adoration for him chase away her worries. "Then we'll make this work, Zee. We always knew it wasn't going to be easy. But we've come this far, together, and we'll find our way from here. And it'll be on our terms."

She nodded, kissing him again.

"Let's get the tent up and eat dinner. You have to be hungry for something other than soup."

She chuckled, her eyes brightening. "You have no idea."

They settled into their usual routine by setting up camp and sharing a meal. They ate cold meat sandwiches and vegetables, Zawn making happy sounds because she could chew solid food for the first time since her fight, even if it was only on one side of her mouth. Then they cuddled up underneath the protection of their tent, facing each other and sharing undemanding kisses. But before they resigned themselves to sleep instead of fooling around, Gwen healed her ribs. Exhausted yet content, they both fell asleep in each other's arms.

~   ~   ~

The next morning, as she readied to part ways with Gwen, she removed something from her belt. As he walked up behind her and wrapped his arms around her waist, he noticed the metal glinting in the pre-dawn light. The weapon wasn't fancy or bejeweled, but when she pulled it from its leather sheath, it had a wicked wink.

"A dagger?" he inquired, surprised.

"You should have something to protect yourself, when I can't be here."

"You'll have to show me how to use it," he replied, resting his chin on her shoulder. "I was never trained to fight. Although, I did punch a classmate when he insulted me. Broke his nose when he called my fire spell feeble."

She chuckled. "Well, then, there's hope for you." Then she held it over her shoulder, making him reach for it. "Keep it on your belt, where you can grab it easily. Sometimes just flashing it will spook an intruder."

"Where did you get it?" he asked, taking it reverently.

"It was mine. I carried it during the Purge, as well as a few other campaigns. I found it again after I took leadership. It has been a good ally. I know it will treat you well."

He kissed her cheek. "Thank you."

"Here, let me show you how to handle it," she replied, turning around in his arms. "I can't stand the thought of you cutting off a finger."

He laughed. "I would appreciate it."

She unsheathed the blade and placed the hilt in his hand, positioning his fingers correctly. "My sentries will also be told to keep an eye on you."

"I don't expect you to change the agreement, Zee," he responded, squeezing her with his arm that still encircled her waist.

"I know, but I will." Then a wry smile stretched across her face. "I have to keep our visitor safe considering we need your tithe to keep moving forward."

"Is that all I am now, a tithe?" he lamented.

She wrapped her arms around his neck, pulling him close. "Of course not. You forget that you are also someone that helps me burn off all my extra energy."

He groaned playfully, making her kiss him ardently.

"To everyone else, you are a tithe," she whispered against his lips. "But to me? You are my everything, Gwen. I don't want anything to happen to you."

"Between your kith and this dagger, I think I am well protected."

Then, she responded, her voice faint, "You said something. Something I… That I was born to live. I don't think I could ever believe that before. Not until I met you." She tried to say something else, but her emotions stole her voice. Even with her round pupils searching his for the strength to speak, she could only stammer breathlessly.

He smiled, knowing exactly what words laid on her lips. "I love you too, Zee."

CHAPTER 28

First thing after she arrived home, she wrangled the goats. Her kithlin had a hard time managing the bouncing creatures but for whatever reason, they followed Zawn. She made them her priority in the morning, letting them out and leading them to the pasture. Then before dinner time, she would lead them back to their stalls in the stables. If they needed to be milked, she led them back no matter the time of day. She thought originally it was because she had been kind to them, but she remembered how they would headbutt her and she didn't hesitate to return the favor. Maybe she had proven herself dominant? She chuckled at that.

She spent the later part of the morning with Meagan and Chaelene, taking stock of their new goods. Each woman held a dark red chicken, while they walked amongst the baskets and boxes.

"I tried to take the most mild-mannered hens," Meagan informed her leader. "Ones who would care less about us moving them around and would not bother the older ones we still have."

Zawn glanced between the hen Meagan held and the one she had in her arms. Meagan's was asleep while Zawn's pulled and pecked at her braid.

"I think mine is defective," Zawn complained.

Meagan grimaced. "She slept the whole way here."

"It must be you, Zawnie," Chae teased.

"Not a smart chicken to pick on the kith leader," Zawn retorted, making the other two women laugh. "Guess egg gathering will not be on my chore list. How much did these cost us?"

Meagan frowned, as if she believed she had made a mistake. "We didn't pay any coin to the Milluns because we didn't have enough for any chickens. I had to promise a large batch of our goat cheese as payment for these three."

"Bartering is better than just spending coin," Zawn responded, with pride. "You did amazing for what little you had to work with. These chickens will produce eggs and give us options. Either using the eggs ourselves, for our food or for food to sell, or even selling the eggs themselves. Maybe we can even breed them. We'll think about roosters next time."

"Wish I could have done more." Meagan stared down at the sleeping chicken in her arms. "I will accept if you want someone else to barter next time."

Zawn's eyebrow rose up while she smiled wryly. "You think your bartering days are over? You've yet to begin."

Meagan looked at her confused.

"You don't realize how successful you've been? And that this is your task now? I trust no one else, Meagan. We will get another tithe in about a week and I expect you will buy and barter to the best of your abilities." Then Zawn flinched as the hen she held secured her braid in her beak and yanked hard. "I think a nice grilled chicken breast will be my dinner tonight."

Chaelene and Meagan laughed.

"Let's get these hens acquainted with our old ones. Hopefully they will play nice with them even though this one is quite a character."

~   ~   ~

The new dark red chickens had settled in nicely with the four remaining older hens that were black, green and purple, but the coop had been left in disrepair for so long that the nest boxes were incapable of holding too many eggs. She and a few of her kithlin had been working on reframing the nests, and the hens were unbothered by their new owners, except the one that disliked Zawn. That chicken pecked at her heel as she worked.

Someone shouted her name early one afternoon, pulling her away from her work in the chicken coop. She exited to see three elves walking toward their kith, one on each side and one behind the five head of cattle that moseyed down the road. The cows were large with dark auburn fur, black eyes and noses, with long dog-like faces, and ears that folded in, like upside-down lilies. The four heifers and one proud bull made their way into the kith square, before being paraded through toward the pastures to the east. Zawn's kithlin hurried to help usher the cows toward the gate, while the two elves on the sides clicked their tongues and uttered reassurances.

Taikin, patriarch of the Browen family, sojourner and leader of the Whistling Cedar Kith brought up the rear and stopped next to Zawn. Grinning, he looked down at her as she gawked at the cows. Taikin was a little older than her, but they had known each other since the Purge. They had fought side by side in many battles, earning each other's respect, and had remained friends through letters since.

Zawn stammered.

"What?" he asked, smirking.

"We only asked for manure."

The taller elf next to her chuckled. "Five cows will give you all the manure you can shovel. One is pregnant, the others will be soon. Calves will help build your herd and the milk the heifers will produce will benefit you as well."

"We don't have the coin to pay you for cattle, Taikin."

"How long have you known me, Zawnie?" he chided. "Coin isn't the only thing useful in this world. And you know I love a good barter. But we'll tackle that in private. For now, you can provide some cold refreshment for me and my lads. It's a hellish walk even without the cows to manage."

She watched as their kithlin escorted the cows into their pasture and locked the gate behind them. Taikin's men returned to his side while Zawn's stared at the cows in wonder and smiled with excitement.

"Please, follow me," Zawn said, gesturing toward the kith square. "Let's get you off your feet. You've all earned the respite."

~   ~   ~

Later that evening, Zawn and Taikin sat in the leader's hut. After listening to her detail the sad state her kith was in and what Medruano had planned to do in order to make up for his mistakes, Taikin didn't say a word for several moments. His face was blank, however the narrowing of his light henna-colored eyes gave away his thoughts.

"Every last coin?" he asked, finally, his voice strangled by his disgust. "Gone?"

"All I was left with was a pile of ash, empty coffers, and no hope."

"I am sorry, my friend, I didn't know. Medruano kept so much to himself. But now I understand better you challenging him and your request for me to take in Taylor and his family. And anyone else who would ask."

"We didn't know how bad it was either, to be honest. We really thought he had just gone insane."

"If you had no money, how did you manage the few supplies you have?"

"Theurgist's tithe. It had arrived late due to an incident at the College. We've had to make it work. Meagan stretched her coin until it bled and bartered for the rest."

"You've done amazing work with it, Zawnie." Taikin scoffed. "And here I thought Medruano was an idiot for agreeing to that tithe. Turned out to be a kith saver." He sighed, heavily, staring at the fire. "He had been isolating your kith more and more, ever since he drew up that damned treaty with Elixin."

"He was good at keeping us isolated and scared. Yet we were good enough to work for men when money was needed," she responded, then shook her head. "I think there are those here who still think that working for men was for the best. And some who think we should cut off all ties. Yet look at the state the kith is in. How can isolating it make it thrive?"

"Well, you are leader now, Zawnie. That will no longer be the case."

"But for how long, my friend? I wake up every morning wondering if this will be the day I am challenged until I lose."

"They'd be fools to do so. You have brought hope back to your kithlin."

"But his allies do not care about hope, Taikin. They will take the leadership out of spite and strip our kith of what little pride they've regained."

"If I hadn't already a mate, I would take you in an instant."

Zawn stared at him in shock.

"I wouldn't be averse to an affair, though," he continued. "It could give you extra protection, if your enemies believed you were laying with another kith leader."

She had to shake herself, trying to stammer out, "I'm flattered but..."

"You know, when we were younger, I honestly thought about it. Making you my mate, bringing you into my kith. I knew Medruano would never see what I saw. Never appreciate you for all that you brought to the table. And I didn't care if you were not my type. I would have even tolerated laying with you if it meant giving you all the children you wanted, if it made you happy." Then he winked. "Do not tell Darion. He would be displeased if he knew he wasn't my first choice."

She sat in stunned silence for a moment, then scoffed when she was able to regain her thoughts. "Knowing how you were back then? I imagine you would have taken us both as mates and juggled us to your benefit."

The other elf glowered at her, then guffawed. "You do know me well."

"Why didn't you?" she asked, curious as to why he didn't take the chance.

After finally catching his breath, Taikin sighed, sadly. "Brennan talked me out of it one night, right before he died. He said that me taking you from your kith would cause a rift between ours and yours. Medruano was very protective of his fighters. But he cut you all off from us anyway. Your letters were the only updates my kith ever got about yours." His smirk reemerged as he stared at her knowingly. "I'm sure you snuck them out behind Medruano's back."

"And bribed the messengers with bottles of apple wine. They agreed to leave your letters and pick mine up just outside the kith."

"How did you hide the theft?"

"I switched the bottles out with my homemade apple juice." She grinned, remembering Medruano's reaction tasting the unexpected bitterness. "Medruano thought the bottles had gone bad."

Her smile faded as she watched sadness drown Taikin.

"I regret listening to Brennan. I would have loved you even if only as a friend, but I would have honored you as my mate. Your life would have been quite different with me."

Silence settled, remorse and confusion rattling both kith leaders. Zawn took a deep breath, trying to shake off the emotions.

"So, tell me, you lunatic, what do we owe you for the cows?"

Taikin's sly personality came back out of the darkness. "There are a few things I can think of. Especially that goat cheese that you all make with the little pieces of fruit inside. Blackberry is my favorite, if you forgot."

"I haven't forgotten," she responded, shaking her head. "It seems to be a popular product. We're working on some now. I'll make sure to add your request to the list. But that isn't payment enough."

"No, it's not. I'll work on my list of demands after I get some sleep."

"And here I thought you'd have one already prepared," she retorted, then grimaced. "I'm sorry we cannot offer you more in hospitality. The guest huts aren't much and are on my endless list to update, but hopefully you and your kithlin can get some decent rest."

"I could stay in your hut for the night. Give your enemies something to think about?"

"The way you snore? They'd know no naked business had been had."

That made him laugh again.

"You are very dear to me, Taikin, and I appreciate your deviousness. But even if they make the correct assumptions, it would probably make things worse. I need respect more than I need fear. Fear is harder to break, trust me. I still have kithlin that won't even look me in the eye." She frowned, her heart hurting as she reflected on the people who hung their heads, afraid to even look at her. "But those who hate me, well, let them come at me if they wish, without any worries of consequences. I wasn't supposed to win anyway."

"But you did win, Zawnie. Do not think that everyone hates you. As you said, you heard them beg you to get up, cheered you on. There are those here who know you have their best interests at heart. And I had to offer. After all, you are very dear to me as well."

"Come, let me take you to the guest hut. We should all get some sleep."

He winked at her again, unable to resist. "Any bed sounds appealing. But if it's the guest hut, then fine," and he sighed, dramatically, "lead me there now. All of us need to rest."

"Follow me."

CHAPTER 29

A few days after Taikin's visit, Zawn sat at the firepit, eating breakfast with her kithlin. With her bones mended, she only had to be careful not to irritate the bruising. Sitting down wasn't always the most comfortable position, especially on benches that were solid wood, but she pretended in front of her people that nothing bothered her. She reserved grousing and grimacing to the private moments she had in the work or her personal hut.

Speaking of her kithlin, most were chatting softly amongst themselves about the expectations of the day, while keeping their children wrangled. She watched as the children were kept close, hushed and ordered to eat their food because they had to have their energy to work through the morning. The obvious misery on their faces struck her hard.

She bristled. "We are only as good as our next generation," she blurted out, startling Taylor and Chaelene. "I want our children to learn. I want them to learn how to read and write, just as much as I want them to learn how to fight and how to shoot an arrow."

"We haven't had a teacher in the kith since ours died," Taylor responded. "Medruano thought lessons were useless and work was necessary."

Chae whispered, "We did what we could."

"That changes now that I'm leader. We do what is best for our children."

Her friends nodded.

"I can ask the parents who they would approve of," Chae offered.

Zawn mulled something over, something that Gwen had told her about the College. "Get as many names as they are willing to give. We should have more than one teacher. Each should have a strength or a focus. That way we don't wear them out or bore the children." Then she paused, watching the children suffering in the silence. "And I want our children to play. I want them to explore. To be excited to wake up and start their day."

~   ~   ~

The kith had about thirty children who were of learning age. Zawn requested that they and their parents meet with her in the kith square one morning, after breakfast.

The parents and children all stared at her in terror. She knew it wasn't personal. The last time a leader wanted to talk to them about their children, he was telling them to ready the little ones for sale. The parents held on to their children a little tighter, either by hands, shoulders, or in their arms.

"I remember when we were young," Zawn stated, glancing around at the group. "We would get up, eat breakfast, then learn the lesson of the day before separating into our castes. The only time we worked the fields all day was during the planting and harvesting seasons, because all hands were needed. But we were not relegated to work every day. We were given a chance to learn, to grow, and to play."

The parents looked at each other, surprise eating away their fear.

"Our children should have the same opportunities, maybe more. And these important lessons should no longer be secret. After speaking with you all, we learned who you would trust with such a monumental task."

Zawn gestured to Chaelene, Lulee, and Halyn.

"They have agreed to be the daily instructors, ready to teach reading, writing, and counting, as well as hand-to-hand combat, staff and haladie fighting, and archery. Lessons our children should learn, so they can grow and be productive kithlin. Jheferin has also agreed to do a weekly lesson in history. Others have offered to pick up the more specialized lessons like herbology and some of the other sciences." She glanced over the crowd, feeling relief as shoulders and faces began to relax. "I have also decided to do a weekly lesson as kith leader, subjects to be determined later. Our first task is to figure out levels of knowledge and also keep in mind ages, so that no students are left behind or left bored."

She heard a chuckle. "Like you were bored?" Cadao inquired, then flushed when he realized he was teasing his kith leader.

"Yes, like me," Zawn retorted, with a laugh. "And we know how I turned out, don't we?"

Startled laughter erupted from the group.

"I know we are used to one style of leadership," she continued, her amusement fading. "And I want to change that. Change it for the better. Not just for our children but for us as well. You all know me. We grew up together or I watched you grow up. We should be able to talk, make decisions, together. We should give our children the life that we wanted."

"Will they be placed into castes?" Cascata asked, then paled when she realized that she had spoken.

"Castes were originally created to teach those with affinities in ways that fit their personalities or abilities. But they seemed to have divided us instead of strengthening us. So, no, no more castes."

One of the children broke from his parent's grasp and approached Zawn. She smiled, kneeling down to meet him face to face. His peridot-colored eyes were fixed on her face, trying to memorize each contour.

"And what's your name?" she asked, voice gentle.

"Meren."

"Do you have a question, Meren?"

"Can I draw?" the little boy, all of maybe six years, asked shyly.

"Can you? Hm, well, I want you to. Is that amenable?"

With his wide smile, he nodded.

"Good."

Then she tapped his nose once, making him laugh and he ran back to his father.

"Our children will learn every aspect of the kith, every aspect of life, and will thrive as well-rounded individuals. Is that amenable as well?"

The parents nodded and murmured excitedly.

"Good. For today, then, let us test the children to see where they are. And please, don't hush them at meal times. Let them laugh, run, play. It has been missing for too long. It makes us who we are."

CHAPTER 30

Months had passed since Zawn took over leadership of the kith. She still faced bitterness from Medruano's allies and family, their angry eyes trying to melt her as she doled out assignments. Determined not to flinch, she met their eyes unflinchingly as she spoke. They didn't respond with anything other than, "Yes, Leader Haley," and they completed their tasks satisfactorily. She took that as a good sign, but still kept her wits about her when she was physically close to any of them.

Each morning, the children ran around and laughed, screamed and shouted. Then they would be wrangled by their teacher of the day to learn whatever lesson was on the board. Chaelene and the other teachers found areas that fit their groups the best and they set up classrooms outside the main kith itself so the children wouldn't be distracted by the daily goings-on.

Others like Vaghide, Nealon, and Naji came forward with additional ideas to help the kith. Metal work came up, as well as stone masonry, both having been major parts of the kith before Medruano took over leadership. There were still those among their ranks, Nealon promised, that remembered how to work metal and stone and were adamant that they would benefit the kith, personally and financially. When Zawn inquired about equipment, Vaghide eagerly led her to some abandoned buildings at the very edges of the pastures. One was for smithing, one for masonry. Each building was dark and dusty, but she could tell someone had been investigating them. It was obvious that there had been minor attempts at getting the smithing shop set up. She smiled and nodded at the three elves, giving them permission to move forward but to let her know immediately if they needed anything so they could ration funds.

Even though she was leader, Zawn refused to sit back and order others around like Medruano did. She worked every day to better the lives of her people, including sludging through irrigation ditches, climbing around barns and stables, and even helping with laundry. Whatever needed to be done depended on the day. Except cooking of course, she didn't want to waste resources with her lack of talent.

But every morning, she dealt with the mischievous goats.

And she wasn't alone in working hard.

With the next tithe, Meagan was able to buy more than enough supplies to make several types of breads and treats. They sold a portion to nearby towns during festivals and celebrations, which brought in a more consistent income. The extra coin went to Gaylon, who bought seeds for the current planting season and with Zawn working so diligently on the irrigation system, crops were growing heartily.

Zawn was determined to bring joy and positivity to her kith. She had started with permitting the children to play and make noise, but it wasn't enough. When something good happened or someone succeeded in a task, she would find ways for the kith to celebrate. Treats, games, and even simply singing brought up the energy of her people and brought smiles to their faces. She thrilled with the happiness she could see in her people, especially after it had been throttled for so long.

Her visits with Gwendin suffered because of her responsibilities, but when she did get away, their reunions were sweeter than she could ever hope for.

~   ~   ~

One evening, her sentries asked to meet on the road to the castle. She made her way to the lookout point where she met up with Satria. The other elf led the way and they found Ehdzia hiding in the tree line, eyes intently watching something on the road. A quick glance provided Zawn some information: a cart and two people next to it.

"They are on our side of the road," Ehdzia explained. "What should we do?"

Zawn watched for a moment, taking in what details she could from her point of view. There was something unusual about the scene in front of them. The cart was at an odd angle. The two people nearby were a boy and an older man. The boy sat at the head of the man, who laid unmoving on the ground.

"Something's wrong," Zawn responded. "Something has happened to them. Ehdzia, stay here, keep us covered. Satria, with me."

"Leader Haley?" Satria inquired, confused. "Are we not to dispatch them immediately?"

"No, we're not. Now, follow me. And put your weapon away."

They left the protection of the tree line and approached the wagon, only to be announced by the mule's loud bray. The one person who was laying down didn't rouse, but the smaller one sitting next to him spun around. The little boy, who probably wasn't older than eight human years, stared up at them in utter terror. He had black hair and dark brown eyes, with skin almost as dark as a pine tree's bark. He was grasping the older man's shoulder and arm helplessly. The splayed-out man had the same type of hair and skin color as the boy, even though his hair had white and gray locks mixed in. There was a cloth tinged with red against the old man's forehead and he didn't react to the elves' approach as they got closer.

"Are you hurt?" Zawn asked, keeping her tone kind and soft.

The boy started to tremble, tears running down his cheeks. "My granddaddy... he fell..."

"Can you see what's wrong with the wain?" Zawn requested of Satria, who nodded and moved toward the other side of the wagon. Then she turned her attention back to the child. "May I take a look?"

He nodded, clumsily, then glanced around as if he expected the entire kith to show up.

"Here, let me kneel beside you. Oh, he has a very nasty gash on his head. Can you tell me what happened?"

"We were just riding along the road. And then we hit something and Granddaddy fell off. He hit his head and then didn't move."

"Well, by the looks of it, he saw stars, birds, and faeries when he hit his head. We'll need to wrap it to stop the bleeding. Do you have a thin blanket or something that I can use?"

Visibly shaking from head to toe, he stood and stretched into the wain. The boy reached into the duffel bag that still sat in the back, pulling out a sheet that they probably used to sleep on while they traveled. Zawn started working on wrapping the older man's head by ripping long, thin strips. As she worked, she heard Satria accounting for the damage to the cart.

"Looks like the wheel is shattered," Satria's voice explained from the other side. "They must have hit a pretty big hole. There's a spare."

"Can you change it out?" the kith leader asked Satria.

"Yes. It should be easy... oh wait, it's cracked."

The boy frowned. "We were gonna get it fixed after this job."

"I have an idea, if you trust me?"

"Of course," Zawn responded. "We should get both wain and man in better condition before sending them off to the castle."

Satria gathered sap from a nearby tree. Zawn smiled when she realized what type of tree it was and felt deep pride in the younger elf's ingenuity. Her kithlin used that sap as glue for various projects. It could hold the spare wheel together long enough to get the cart to the castle.

"We're supposed to go there," the little boy whispered. "But can they help Granddaddy?"

Zawn smiled over at him, trying to reassure him. "They have a theurgist and healers and medicine at the castle. I'm sure they will do everything they can."

The child watched quietly as Zawn fastened the dressing around the unconscious man's head. She glanced at him after each step, explaining to him what she was doing in a calm and quiet voice. She did so to show him that she took care with his grandfather's head and wound. Zawn never expected to interact with a human child in the same manner as an elf child, but the similarities were surprising. Patience and simplicity helped keep the boy calm and his attention focused on her. Involving him in the care of his grandfather made him part of the solution and not part of the problem. Once she finished, she used the remaining material to pillow the older man's head. Then she stared at the boy, who started fidgeting next to her but made sure he didn't touch her.

"Are you afraid of me?" she inquired.

"No." Then tears welled up in his eyes. "I'm just scared."

Suddenly, he leapt toward her, wrapping his short arms around her neck. She could feel him trembling against her while his sobs crashed against her hair. Unsure if it was the correct response, she hugged him back. Even through her armor, her physical warmth reassured him, as did the emotional support of her embrace. He started to breathe calmly and the shaking slowly abated.

"Feel better now?"

He nodded, his head rubbing her hair.

"Good. Now we have to figure out what to do next. We have to do what's best for your grandfather. Clear minds help make good decisions."

He slowly let her go and sat back on the ground. He touched his grandfather's shoulder, reverently. "Is he going to get better?"

"That I cannot say. But we will get him to someone who can help him. Does that sound like a good plan?"

"Yes, milady."

"Then let's work on making that happen. What's your name?"

"Chaddie."

"You said you were headed to the castle. Have you ever been there before, Chaddie?"

"A couple of times. I know which way it is. Granddaddy made sure I memorized the road, making me tell him which way each time we came this way."

"Do you know how to handle the mule and cart?"

The boy frowned. "Granddaddy tries to show me, but the mule doesn't always listen to me. I think because I'm not very good at it."

"Mules usually don't like anyone," Zawn replied with a chuckle. "Stay here with your Granddaddy and keep a good eye on him. I'm going to check on the wheel."

"Yes, milady."

Zawn stood and made her way around the cart, watching as Satria turned the wrench in one final rotation.

"How goes it?"

"It's on." She tapped it with her boot. "It'll get them to the castle at least."

Zawn stared at the cart, then glanced over at the boy who watched his loved one with such a worried expression.

"Are you comfortable driving it to the tree line leading to the castle?"

Satria frowned. "If you order it, I will do so."

"That's not what I asked."

"I do not know if I am comfortable," her kithlin responded, looking toward the boy and man on the other side of the wagon. "But the old man needs proper care. I will do what's needed."

"Thank you. We'll get the grandfather in the back and I'll have you drive while I keep an eye on him. Can you also show the boy how to handle the reins? I think he needs a lesson from someone who isn't afraid to handle a grumpy mule."

Satria rolled her eyes with a smirk, having wrangled a few mules in her time, then cleared her throat. "I will do so."

"It is appreciated," Zawn responded, smiling at the brief break in Satria's seriousness. "I will tell our kithlin the plan." Zawn strode over to the tree line where Ehdzia watched over them. "We will be taking the boy and his grandfather up to the boundary."

Her eyebrows furrowed deeply with distaste. "Why should we do any more than what we have? We are putting ourselves in unnecessary danger."

"Would you leave this child to the woods without anyone to protect him?"

Ehdzia lowered her eyes, frowning in the shame that hit her. "You are right, Leader Haley. We cannot leave a child to the predators."

"And we are the only ones here to help. I only ask that you stay here and monitor the road for us. It shouldn't take us long to deliver them to the boundary, then we will head back. But if you see anything concerning…"

"I will raise the alarm."

"Thank you, my friend. Please, can you help me and Satria lift the man into the back? I want to make sure we have him level and his head supported."

"Yes, Leader Haley."

With that settled, Zawn returned to the boy's side where he kept watch over his grandfather. Ehdzia followed and Satria joined them on the other side of the cart, but both stayed behind her as she spoke.

"Chaddie, I need you to listen very carefully. We will help you get to the castle, but we can't go past the tree line. You will have to manage the wain from there. My friend here will show you how to drive on the way there. But only if you make a very, very important promise."

"What's that, milady?"

"You cannot tell anyone, not even your granddaddy, that we helped. I don't care what story you make up, but you cannot tell anyone you saw us, let alone got help from us. Do you promise?"

"I promise, milady." Then he paused, looking torn. "But can I pray my thanks every night?"

Zawn smiled. "Yes, as long as you use your thoughts and not your voice."

"Then I promise very, very much, milady. I won't tell."

"Good. Now go sit up front and hold the reins. My friends and I will get your Granddaddy into the wain. My friend here will drive and teach you as we go. I will stay back here and keep an eye on your grandfather."

"Yes, milady."

With Chaddie holding the reins, Zawn, with the help of both Satria and Ehdzia, lifted the unconscious old man into the back of the cart. Zawn and Ehdzia had each side, while Satria supported his head. They got him settled but his feet hung over the edge, so Zawn strapped him to the sides so he wouldn't slide out. She used a thicker blanket to cushion his head and tucked two boxes under the edges to make sure his head didn't bob around. With him settled, Ehdzia returned to her perch and Zawn gave the go ahead.

They started down the road, slowly and carefully, taking into consideration the old man's head injury. The head and neck brace they created did its job, but they didn't want to take any chances. As the cart rattled and rocked, the noise echoed against the trees and their trunks along the road.

Zawn and Satria kept an eye out for any trouble that could come their way, neither wanting to frighten the boy. At the same time, Zawn listened as Satria explained to Chaddie about the sap and its adhesive qualities. The conversation between elf and boy was a pleasant experience, not just for Chaddie but for both Satria and Zawn.

Next to her, a confused moan escaped the old man's lips. The grandfather's eyes fluttered open, dark brown eyes blurry with concussion. "I must be dreaming."

"Ah, you dream of monsters, do you?" Zawn inquired, drolly, looking down at him.

"I dream of blessed helpers," he responded, voice slurring a little bit.

She stared at him for a moment, surprised.

"My Chaddie?"

"Upfront, helping with the drive."

"He's a good boy."

"He really is. He kept very diligent watch over you until we got there. Now, close your eyes. We will get you to someone who can help you. But remember, this was only a dream."

He smiled, weakly, then slipped back into unconsciousness.

~   ~   ~

The last cluster of trees lined the road and the cart slowed to a halt. Satria glanced behind her where Zawn sat, who checked the braces and secured the grandfather a little better. Then Satria handed the boy the reins and jumped down. "Chaddie, remember, keep the reins slack and the mule will follow the road and cross the bridge all on his own."

The boy nodded.

Zawn hopped out of the back of the wain, stepping up to her kithlin's side. "And what was your promise to us for our help?" Zawn asked.

"Tell no one," Chaddie responded. "And thank you in my prayers only in my head."

Zawn and Satria smiled.

"We will hold you to that, Chaddie," Zawn warned him. "Now, go, get help for your Granddaddy."

"Thank you, miladies."

As the cart started to rattle away, Zawn and Satria took to the trees. They kept watch on the wagon and saw the boy glance back one more time. When he saw they had disappeared, his shoulders slumped and he returned his attention to the road ahead. They could hear the boy shout for help as he rode past the outer courtyard walls and the bustling of people rushing toward him. Zawn glanced up at Satria, who looked torn between the pride in what they had just accomplished and whatever dissenting voices she heard in her head.

"Talk to me," Zawn urged her.

"We have always been ordered to kill any trespassers," Satria whispered. "Especially humans."

"By Medruano, yes," Zawn replied, just as softly. "But we cannot blindly move through this world guided by fear and hate anymore. Tell me, Satria," and she reached up to caress the other woman's stomach, "as this life grows inside you, can you still see yourself killing a child just because he is not an elf?"

Tears welled up in Satria's eyes as her hand covered Zawn's. "No, Leader Haley. I couldn't ever imagine killing someone's child even before I found out I was pregnant."

"Then there is hope for our kith and our people. We must be better than those before us. Yes, we are to defend our home and our kithlin. But we must be able to decide when to fight and when to help. That is who we are, who we have always been. Except now, we can be that without hesitation. Come. We know he is safe and he has better help. Let us return to our kithlin and let her know that the task is complete."

~   ~   ~

It didn't take long at an even jog for the long-legged elves to make their way back to Ehdzia. Zawn thanked them for helping Chaddie and his grandfather, but Ehdzia's face took on the same expression as Satria's had earlier.

"I understand that you feel confused by my request to help them," Zawn responded to her reaction. "We must be better than man. We have been motivated by fear, hatred, and anger for far too long. Is that what we want to teach our children? Or do we want to teach them that there is more to our life on this side of the canopy than what has driven our generation?"

"Can we move past that, Leader Haley?" Ehdzia asked. "Can we be untaught?"

Their leader's warm, hopeful smile filled them with courage. "We can adapt, I know we can. Why? Because we already are. Look at everything we have accomplished even though our previous leader doubted our abilities. We are elf-kind. If we can be taught one way, we can adjust and learn another way. What else can we do, but do what's right?"

CHAPTER 31

The boys were tucked away in bed, after begging their mother for just one more story. Chae relented with three and finally had to cut them off, blowing out the candles and pulling the door closed. Then she quietly straightened up the hut, while peeking in on Minee as she dreamed away in her crib. As she tended the fire so it would last the night, Taylor entered their home, a thoughtful frown on his face.

"What's wrong?" she asked.

"When we were eating lunch, I asked Zawnie if she was going to the grandfather tree tonight," he responded.

She chuckled, enjoying that Taylor had decided this was his code for asking Zawn if she would take off to see her lover. And no one in the kith was any the wiser.

"And?" Chaelene inquired.

"She said that she would take him on a walk somewhere else tonight. She said she wanted to do something special." Then he leaned against the table. "I didn't realize it's been a year, you know."

Chae stared at him in surprise. "They've been seeing each other for a year now?"

"I guess it's the anniversary of when they first met."

"And she... wanted to do something special? Tay, she's never been with anyone this long, let alone had any inclination to celebrate things like this."

"I know. And the fact that she's taking him to see Morai Meadow, I do believe this relationship is more serious than I ever expected."

"You sound unsure about it."

"Well, we know what his people would do if they found out. They almost did, remember? Our people, well, I don't know what they would do now that she's kith leader. But if she is this serious about him, what kind of future do they really have together?"

"It sounds like they have already decided on finding out together, Tay." She

132

wrapped her arms around her mate. "They don't have to tell us what they hope or expect. And I do not believe we have much say in it."

"No, we don't. But that doesn't mean I'm not allowed to worry."

"You can worry, but you must also support her. She is family, and in turn, so is he. We will support them both in whatever they decide to do moving forward."

"Even if it's leaving?"

Chae's stomach dropped. "Is her bag packed again?"

"No, it's not."

"Has she said something?"

"No. But she considered it before, without any discussion."

"When she thought she had nothing left for her. Now, she has the entire kith to care for. I doubt she would give it up so easily after everything she's done. And she wouldn't throw it all on you without discussing it properly with you."

"I know."

"Come, the children are asleep and you and I have had very little time together. Let Zawn have her time with her love, and let me have my time with mine!"

~   ~   ~

Zawn was waiting for him. But before he could set down his duffel bag, he noticed that she had her own on her shoulder. He hesitated, raising an eyebrow, which made her chuckle.

"I want to show you something," she stated, cocking her head to the side.

"I'm not supposed to go past the river."

"I think the new kith leader will permit you one trespass."

"I do know the new kith leader, well, intimately..."

She took a hold of his hand and smiled shyly. "Come, this way."

~   ~   ~

Zawn led Gwendin through the thick woods, ducking and dodging low hanging limbs. He tried to look around but had to concentrate on keeping his footsteps in line with hers, so he would not to trip. Roots and bushes were haphazardly layered throughout their path, but she acted as if she was following a road that he couldn't discern. Thankfully, the forest's canopy allowed the moons to light their way, especially since he could not see the same way as Zawn.

He could hear roaring and a random thumping in the distance, and as they continued to walk, the sounds got louder and he could feel vibrations under his feet. After walking for several lengths, they finally stepped out into a moonlit lea.

She watched him as he glanced around. She couldn't help smiling at his amazement and knew he was as smitten with the place as she was. It was a large meadow, surrounded by the massive oaks, birches, and other species that thrived in the area. To the left, there was a massive mountain so tall that it seemed to disappear into the night sky. And falling from its height was a beautiful waterfall that shimmered in the celestial lights. He glanced around in surprise, realizing that this was the source of the river that ran past the castle and through the kith's territory.

On either side of the glimmering and chaotic water, varying types of grass filled the open areas, reaching different heights, swaying softly in the breeze created by the crashing water. Most of the blooms that would have decorated the perimeter in springtime excitement laid dormant in the darkness of night. But a few rebels bloomed. White epiphylla, pink and purple datura, and blushing brugmansias brightened the landscape.

The sounds and smells were an inspiration to the theurgist in him. However, for the man following his love into a hidden world, his heart warmed at her invitation.

"Welcome to Morai Meadow." Then she gestured to the roaring water falling from the heavens. "This is Irem Waterfall and Irema Lake."

"This," he stammered, "it's amazing."

"Here, we can set up the tent and fire over here," she suggested, taking his duffel from him. She started unpacking the tent after gathering some wood for their fire, chuckling at his dumbfounded expression. She let him gawk while she worked, because she remembered how she felt the first time she stumbled onto this gem. "Do you want to take a swim?"

"I'd love to. Is the water cold?"

She chuckled. "Probably. That's the best part though."

As if finally freed from a spell, Gwen moved, walking up to the edge of the river. He looked into the swirls of water and he gasped.

"What's wrong?" she asked.

"I thought, well, I thought I saw a face."

She furrowed her eyebrows, making her way to his side. "A nymph? This far west?"

"I don't know, it was just a flash."

She glanced around the water, but didn't see anything. "It's rare, but we've seen them around before. Usually only when the Sedorans send them for reconnaissance, border checks and the like. They are allies to us, though. They won't harm us."

She tugged on his arm, grinning, and led him back to the small nook she had set their stuff down in. They set up their tent and started a small fire, before propping up his tripod and hanging the pot. He filled it with his pre-made stew, leaving it to cook slowly, then they started to strip off their clothes. Amused, he leaned back against a rock and waited.

She glanced over, eyebrows furrowed in confusion. "What?" she asked.

"Nothing. I just… I don't remember the last time I watched you undress."

She blushed, giggling. "Usually, you help me. But I guess you want a show this time?"

He shrugged, nonchalantly, but the look in his eyes answered her. She unbuckled her armor and laid it down before removing her boots and gauntlets. She pulled her shirt over her head, freeing her unbraided hair from its ponytail as well. Then she removed her belt and weapons, keeping them nearby, and stepped out of her pants after they fell to the ground. With each article of clothing removed, his smile grew wider.

Completely nude, Zawn crossed the distance until he captured her into his arms. A slow, tender kiss left them warm and giddy.

"Am I strong enough?" she inquired, somewhat teasing, somewhat serious.

"You are," he replied, running hands along her back. "You're incredible."

"Your turn," she whispered.

She reached down, freeing his tunic from his pants. He released her, lifting his arms up so she could remove his shirt. Then his belt and pants followed. Another kiss before she slipped away and walked toward the edge of the lake.

She dipped her toe and giggled, then slipped into the water with ease. He watched, fascinated, as she swam out and ducked under the calmer water. When she burst back up through the top of the peaceful glass, he dove in after her. He surfaced with a yelp.

"That's frigid!"

She started laughing. "You're awake at least."

He grabbed for her but she swam away, still making her jovial sounds. He chased her around until she darted under the waterfall. Trapping her behind it, he finally caught her, kissing her heartily. She led him over to a hidden set of shelves, where she could sit behind him and he could settle between her legs. She wrapped her arms around his shoulders as he leaned back against her chest. His hands lovingly caressed her calves under the water.

They sat in content silence as the waterfall thundered in front of them, distorting the landscape with its magical movement.

"Watch this," she instructed, reaching one hand out in front of them.

Like a moon peeking over the horizon, a glow grew from deep down in the water and rose up toward them. Then the single light burst into dozens, as small luminescent tadpoles surrounded them. The critters dispersed up and around then disappeared past the waterfall.

Gwen gasped, delighted. "I didn't know elves could do that."

"Elves can't," Zawn responded, making him glance over his shoulder at her. She shrugged, smiling wryly. "There's some questionable blood in my lineage. Not many know about it though. After all, an elf and an Elemental, how scandalous can you get?"

"Is that how you can talk to trees?"

She nodded, solemnly. "Elves can't do that."

"I always knew you were special," he chided.

She chuckled.

"Thank you, Zee."

"For what?" she inquired.

"For bringing me here."

"I've wanted to bring you for quite a while. But with the rules set by our previous leader… and with everything else going on in the kith… I'm glad I finally have the chance to break that rule."

"Me, too."

"I also wanted to do something special for you."

"Because I'm still with you?" he joked.

"For a whole year."

He blinked at her for a moment, then smiled. "You remembered?"

"How could I forget?" she demanded, offended.

"You've had a lot on your mind, Zee. Remembering the day you saved my life? That's not something I expected with everything going on."

"Well, I did remember," she retorted, haughtily. "And I thought since this is an important time of year for us, this would be a nice way to celebrate."

He turned around and with one quick move, he pulled her into his lap. He kissed her deeply, not letting her go until she gave into his passion.

"Thank you for making this special," he whispered against her lips. "I can't believe it's been a year already."

"Feels longer with everything we've been through."

"We knew it wouldn't be easy, not with everything against us. But I am glad that we met and that you said yes to my invitation."

"Me, too."

He sighed. "But I am now very wrinkly and hungry."

She giggled. "Fine, let's eat."

After drying off with the cloth towels that she had brought with her, they snuggled up by the fire. He grabbed his flask and smiled devilishly, before wrapping themselves up with his thick blanket.

"A new brew I put together just for tonight," he announced. "In celebration."

"Will it inebriate us as quickly as your first one?"

He laughed. "No, I went more for flavor than alcohol content." Then he blushed. "I'd rather remember tonight, to be honest."

She raised her eyebrow, suspiciously, and made him take the first swig. Seeing that he didn't flinch, she took her turn and agreed that it was more flavor than burn. They shared it while they ate, using only one bowl but two spoons. They quietly talked about everyday things, until she made a comment about things being quiet along their borders.

Gwen stared at her suspiciously.

"What?" she demanded.

"The other day, a young boy drove a cart into the courtyard with his grandfather in the back. He didn't tell us much, only that his Granddaddy got hurt and the boy had to get him to the theurgist at the castle. The old man had a nasty head injury."

Zawn feigned surprise and concern. "Poor thing. But sounds like he kept his head straight."

"The grandfather, when he came around for a moment, only mentioned blessed helpers but nothing more."

"Well, we both know head injuries can leave people confused."

"The head wrap looked familiar."

She smirked. "I have no idea why."

"Thank you, for whatever you did," he whispered, then kissed her temple.

"I don't know what you're talking about."

"Tell me what happened."

She rolled her eyes, shrugging. "One of my sentries found them. Under our previous leader, the order was kill and move on. She hesitated, unsure if I would have given the same order. I never thought about adjusting that thinking because of everything that we've been through. But seeing what had transpired, I knew helping was the right thing to do. Especially because I didn't see some random human. I saw a frightened child who had nothing and no one to protect him. I saw this child like I see our children."

Gwen could see her thoughts were unpleasant, then she shook herself.

"We have since discussed changing the orders for the sentries."

"Did you kill? Just because of someone being a human?"

"If I had followed that rule, we wouldn't have met."

"Or gotten to know each other?"

She nodded. "After the Purge, I'd had enough of that. And when I got demoted, I chose to scare trespassers, mostly to amuse myself. Or if they accidently ended up on the wrong side of the road, I didn't even bother them."

"Again, I am thankful that you liked to break the rules. How does the kith feel about the change?"

"Apparently, we all had the same philosophy even under Medruano even though we never said a thing to each other. We have all agreed that killing indiscriminately has always been against our way. We must live in the light, not the darkness. We are celebrators of life, not murderers of innocents."

"That sounds like the perfect description of your kith. Celebrators of life."

She pulled him closer, kissing him deeply. "Part of this new way is your fault."

"Mine?"

"Yes, I blame you. If we hadn't met, if you hadn't changed my mind about your kind, I don't know where my kith would be right now."

"It's not all me, Zee. Like you said, you have seen so much and have seen the world through a lot of different eyes. Your mentor's, your leader's. Now, you're seeing it through yours. For the betterment of not just your kith, or your kind, but for all that may interact with you."

He looked down at her and they kissed lovingly, letting the sounds of the waterfall and night loving critters comfort them.

"I was thinking," he said, slyly, "since this is the anniversary of our first meeting…"

"Debauchery?" she inquired with an impish gleam in her eyes.

"You are thinking what I'm thinking."

It didn't take long before their laughter and moans echoed through the lea.

CHAPTER 32

One morning, Zawn wasn't out amongst the kithlin. Worried, Taylor entered her hut to find her retching uncontrollably in the bathing room. He rushed to find Chaelene, asking her to keep an eye on Zawn while he worked out how to distract the kithlin for the day. He didn't want any panic or questions until he figured out what was wrong with his friend. Then he returned, wracked with confusion about Zawn's sudden illness. They spent the day trading off, trying to keep her comfortable and hydrated, however it felt like a momentous task.

Later that afternoon, Zawn laid in bed, delirious, murmuring incoherently in her stupor. She had finally stopped retching about an hour before, but she was very dehydrated. Anytime they tried to give her water, her gag reflex pushed it back out. Taylor didn't know what to do. Then she groaned and mumbled a name. As he watched and listened, he knew that was his only option.

~   ~   ~

Taylor leaned against the tree, waiting impatiently. He never knew exactly when they met, but he knew it was at least around dinner time. He worried the longer he waited, the less chances Zawn had to get better. His thoughts grew dreadful until he heard a noise in the trees.

A cloaked man strode through the foliage, then stumbled to a stop when he noticed the elf. He glanced around startled, only to find they were the only occupants of the area, and straightened indignantly. Even with a duffel on one shoulder and satchel on another, he was still able to reach for something under his cloak.

Taylor chuckled, mirthlessly, at the thought this human would be able to fight him. "I am not here to harm you, theurgist."

"Who are you?"

"I am Taylor."

"Why are you here?" the theurgist demanded. "Where is she?"

"Zawnie is very sick. I don't know what it is, but I fear something nefarious."

"How bad?"

"Bad enough for me to come find you," Taylor responded, frowning.

The theurgist blinked, thinking. "Can you sneak me in without anyone seeing me?"

"I can."

Readjusting his satchel with one hand, he gestured with the other for Taylor to lead the way. "Tell me everything on the way."

"Follow me."

~   ~   ~

Taylor kept an eye out for his kithlin as they approached Zawn's hut from the back of the kith. Her home butted up against thick foliage and a pair of large trees. She chose it for that reason, because it made sneaking in and out easier for her. Now, it helped Taylor sneak in her theurgist.

Taylor made Gwendin wait behind a large bush, first checking for anyone nearby then stepping into the hut and asking the person inside to distract anyone that would approach the hut. The woman left and Taylor retrieved him. He ducked and tiptoed around the front and entered the door, with Taylor right on his heels. He walked straight to the bed, kneeling next to it, setting down his bags and shedding his cloak. He touched her forehead, paused, then checked her mouth and eyes. He rested his hand on her throat next and closed his eyes briefly, his lips moving as if counting. He sighed, staring at his lover's face and chewing his bottom lip.

"She's very dehydrated," Gwen confirmed. "You said you tried to make her drink?"

"Everything we tried to give her just came right back up."

Zawn stirred, her eyes fluttering open. Her forehead scrunched in confusion and she made a puzzled sound. Gwen moved his hand from her neck to her cheek, caressing it lovingly.

"I must be dead," she said, in a frail voice that was gravely due to retching.

Gwen chuckled. "Not dead. Not even close."

"Then I'm hallucinating."

"Just make sure you listen to this hallucination when it tells you to do something."

She attempted to sit up. "But you can't be here…"

"It's fine, Zee." He pushed her back down onto the bed and she was too weak to fight him. "Stay still."

"They will hurt you."

"Like they hurt you?"

She closed her eyes and swallowed hard.

"What are you two talking about?" Taylor asked.

"Your suspicions were correct," Gwen responded. "She's been poisoned."

Taylor hissed, seething with anger, his hand resting on his sword's hilt.

"With everything you told me," Gwen continued, "and now seeing the shape she's in, I don't recognize the symptoms as an ailment that affects your kind, so it must be some sort of poison. Unfortunately, without the source, I can't identify it."

"So, this was useless?" Tay demanded. "We cannot do anything to help her?"

"I can try a few things," the theurgist replied. "I will give her some anti-venom serum that neutralizes most types that exist. Her urine and feces will smell rancid, but if it does, that means it's working. And I can give her something that will stop any further vomiting. That should help her drink some water and maybe even broth or milk, which she needs because she is quite dehydrated. That's the best I can do."

Taylor made an annoyed sound, but nodded understanding.

Gwen opened his apothecary satchel, rummaging through the bottles to find the ones he needed. He asked for some water, which Taylor provided, and he mixed a concoction. He set the mug down onto the table nearby, then helped Zawn sit up. She had to lean heavily on him, making him brace her from behind with his torso. He held the mug for her but she drank what Gwen gave her, making an offended expression after the first sip.

"I know," Gwen whispered, "I don't have time to hide the taste, I'm sorry."

She took her time, while making repulsed sounds after every sip, but she drank the entire brew. Exhausted by the exercise, she started to fall over but Gwen tightened his hold on her. He handed the mug over to Taylor, then helped her lay back down. He tucked the copious number of blankets around her, making her sigh.

"I was afraid they would try something like this," Zawn admitted.

"What, you knew?" Taylor accused Zawn. "You knew a coward would…"

"Tay, stop," she ordered, her voice coming out stronger than expected.

Taylor stood there, seething.

"She's right," Gwen responded. "We can't blame anyone without proof, especially when someone like me is now involved. And you can't just challenge someone based on suspicion."

Surprised at how eloquently the theurgist spoke about their ways, Taylor scoffed. "She's taught you well. Our ways are very… structured." He sighed, as he watched her eyelids close heavily. "But it has to be family or friend of our former leader. They would want revenge, but would be too afraid to challenge her after she already killed someone like Medruano."

"She told me she didn't want to kill him, but he wouldn't relent." Gwen shook his head, returning his medicines to his bag. "I can stay until daybreak. I'll keep an eye on her. You should rest."

Taylor started to argue, but Zawn came around long enough to wave her hand at him. "Go. Rest."

Reluctantly, the tall elf nodded, then ducked out of her cabin. Gwen held her hand and caressed her forehead, making her close her eyes again and she slowly started to doze off. Then her eyes fluttered open and she inhaled deeply.

"Come to bed," she whispered.

"Think that's wise?" he inquired. "Anyone can walk in on us."

"You would reject your dying lover?"

"So dramatic," he chided, even though worry still tainted his tone. "You'll survive. You already got through the worst thanks to all the vomiting. But we shouldn't instigate any more actions against you."

"They already tried to kill me for winning. Let them try again because of you. I don't care."

He shook his head, but realized he really couldn't deny her. Seeing her ill shattered his heart and he wanted to hold her, to comfort her as well as himself. Since he had already removed his cloak, it wouldn't take much to get undressed. He started unlacing his boots and set them off to the side of the chair. Then he stood and slipped off his pants and shirt, folding his clothes and setting them in the chair's seat. He left his undershorts and socks on, to keep some decorum. He lifted the pile of blankets and slipped into the bed with her. Too weak to move over or help, he had to adjust her position first, then he laid on his side, facing her. He wrapped his arms around her, pulling her against him as tight as he dared.

She sighed, contentedly.

"Will you sleep now?"

When she didn't answer, he knew she had already slipped back into unconsciousness. He bit his lower lip, feeling the dread seeping in. Elves fought, using physical battles to make a point. Zawn besting the previous leader wasn't enough for her own people to abandon their ways and outright poison her. On the other hand, men poisoned. And those who were going to buy kithlin from their previous leader, those men would be willing to try to kill her off in such a manner. She was a cog in the wheel that had to be removed.

Feeling her breath against his skin reminded him that, even though she was in bad shape, she was alive. She was a survivor. She had survived wars and battles, demotions and heartaches, and struggles only a leader could endure. She would come out of this stronger than before. And knowing her, she would find the culprit and avenge this. He held onto those hopes as his eyes started to slowly close...

~   ~   ~

He woke to her struggling against him. At first, he thought she was having a seizure or maybe a nightmare. When he glanced down at her, he realized she was wide awake.

"Privy," she ordered, a slight panic in her voice.

He tossed the blankets off of them, picked her up and carried her into the other room.

~   ~   ~

After cleaning her up, carrying her back to bed, and making her drink a glass of water, Gwen covered them with the pile of blankets to help warm her up then wrapped his arms around her to hold her close. Her hands and feet still felt ice cold. Her body had been shivering intermittently throughout the night. She moved against him, making him lean back slightly to find her staring up at him.

"You must really like me," she whispered.

"Why do you say that?"

"You're still here even after all that."

Gwendin chuckled. "I knew it was going to be disgusting. You're not the first person I had to use it on."

She furrowed her eyebrows, curious.

"A college story for another day," he continued, "But this tells me that the medicine did its job. It absorbed the poison from your system and expelled it."

Exhaustion and the physical trauma of the poison left her pale and listless in his arms. Yet she mustered the strength to say, "I can officially say that you are no mediocre theurgist." She lifted her hand slightly, to trace his chin with a cool finger. "Thank you for coming to my side."

"I would be nowhere else." He kissed her forehead. "Sleep, my love."

"Hmm, say that again," she whispered, sleep slowly pulling her in.

"My love."

"Hm, again," she requested, dreamily.

He chuckled, then repeated softly, "My love."

She made one more content sound before slipping back into a deep slumber.

~   ~   ~

Zawn slept soundly for the rest of the night. He woke before the sun rose and after checking her one more time, he felt comfortable leaving her in her friends' care. Gwendin slipped out of the bed carefully, reaching for his pants. Zawn mumbled something in reaction to his movement. He leaned over and caressed her forehead, then kissed it lovingly. His touches settled her down and she sighed, happily.

Smiling down at her, partly amused, partly relieved, he reluctantly turned away and started dressing. He didn't want to leave her. He wished he could just stay with her in his arms forever. Or at least until she was back to her old self. But he had to return to the castle and she could not be found with a man in her bed. They still straddled their two worlds and teetered dangerously along that fine line of the laws.

He had his pants on but hadn't gotten to his shirt by the time someone entered. A woman snuck in then froze at the sight of a half-naked man in her friend's home.

She cleared her throat, smiling. "Now I see why she likes you."

Gwen started to fluster, rushing to put his shirt on, which made the woman giggle.

"You're honorable," she continued, then her smile faded. "You risked your life to come help her."

He fixed his clothing while staring down at Zawn. "She's worth it."

"You do care a lot about her."

"We're not allowed to."

"That was an observation not a question."

He found himself speechless, grabbing and putting on his boots as a distraction.

"Keep her hydrated," he finally responded. "Milk, water, melon juices, broth. No solid food, yet. Maybe soup, but nothing too heavy. I should be able to return later tonight to check on her. If we can sneak me back in, that is."

"Taylor will take care of that. Speak with him on the way out."

He nodded. "She'll fight orders, but let her sleep as much as she allows. Rest is key."

"I understand."

"Is Taylor nearby?"

She glanced out the window. "Here he comes. Have a safe journey back home, theurgist."

"Gwendin. You can just call me Gwendin."

"It has been an honor, Gwendin."

~　　~　　~

Taylor walked the theurgist back to his and Zawn's rendezvous spot, where they agreed to meet later that evening. After Taylor returned to the kith, he made his way to Zawn's hut. Recognizing the look on his face, his mate hugged him when he entered.

"You look worried," Chae pointed out.

He wrapped his arms around her waist, keeping her close. "Just the events. Her poisoning, sneaking him in. Him staying."

"She's getting better. He helped. And he did nothing untoward that I saw. They do truly care about each other." She kissed his cheek. "You didn't see him just now. He cares more about her than he does for himself."

"Were you spying?"

"I may have peeked before coming in. I didn't want to startle them. But he was holding her, I assume all night. When he touched her, he was gentle, caring." She stared at Zawn for a moment, a small smile on her face. "They have exceeded anything I could have expected or even hoped for her."

"I have seen the same thing, but I also saw how he reacted when he heard about her ailment. He even walked faster than me to get to her. It's not them that bothers me. We both have known about him all this time. But what about the others? What will they do if they find out?"

"She's the leader, it's her rules to make and to change. She keeps forgetting that she doesn't always have to break them now. She can change the laws at least for us. And maybe it's time."

"But neither of them could fight off any challenges right now."

Zawn groaned, waking up from her deep slumber. She caressed the space in front of her and frowned, then opened her eyes. "Gwen?" she whispered.

"He had to leave," Chae responded, slipping out of Taylor's arms and moving closer to the bed. "You've slept through most of the morning."

Zawn caressed the impression where Gwendin had laid, sighing. "Did you walk him back?"

"Only to the campsite," Taylor confirmed, "since he knows his way from there. He will be back tonight to check on you."

"His main instruction is drink, drink, drink." Chae poured some broth into a mug while Taylor helped Zawn sit up in bed. "He wants you hydrated as much as he wants everything flushed out."

"What about our kithlin?" Zawn asked. "Have they noticed my absence?"

"Vergun said something," Tay replied. "I told him that you decided to work on the books for a few days, to get everything ready for the next supply purchase. He seemed to take that answer at face value."

"I can't hide for long."

"Unless you regain color and strength in a snap, they will worry at the sight of you."

She carefully sipped, thinking. "Let's tell them I've taken a trip somewhere. Or I went to check on a border concern. We'll keep the fire low and shutter the windows to make it look like I'm not here."

"Border concern is more believable. And I can say that I'm to keep an eye on things for you," Taylor agreed. "Be the excuse for me going in and out."

"Let's do that then. Keep them from worrying about me."

With their plan in place, Zawn focused on recuperating as quickly as her body would allow her.

~ ~ ~

The castle remained under the heaviness of slumber as he entered. He hurried to his rooms, relieved that he could avoid interacting with others. Locking the door behind him and setting a chair against the secret passageway's door so his sister couldn't enter without warning, he sat down hard on his bed.

His thoughts scattered and rattled in his head. She had always been the image of strength. Not just physically, but her spirit was the ray of light in the darkness. Seeing her frail, sick, weak, he felt his heart being ripped out of his chest. He couldn't imagine losing her like that. He wasn't a spiritual man, but he knew elves believed in an afterlife. But to think of her dead... After finally finding someone who not only loved him but understood him and made him feel like a whole person... hot tears started pouring down his cheeks.

CHAPTER 33

Gwendin returned that evening, Taylor sneaking him in while the kith was distracted during dinner time. The elf opened the door but closed it after him and joined Chaelene by the firepit. They ate quietly, keeping an eye on their kithlin, hoping no one saw their secret visitor.

Gwen saw that Zawn was sitting up, but she had more pillows than he ever thought possible, apparently to keep her from sinking down or sliding over. She smiled weakly at him, her pale lips thin. He dropped his bags, slipped off his cloak, and sat down on the bed next to her. He checked her pulse and coloring, murmuring to himself. Then he sighed, caressing her face tenderly.

"You've regained some color," Gwen observed, pleased. "You don't seem as dehydrated, but you've got a ways to go before you're back to normal."

"What do you think they used?" Zawn asked.

"Not sure, but it has to be something easily accessible and nearby. I thought about some animal venom that would be in the area and possibly soluble in liquid." He slipped his hand in hers, frowning. "It had to be something they knew only you would digest."

"My bitter apple juice," she replied, after thinking for a moment. "I'm the only one in the kith who enjoys it."

"Do you have any left?"

She pointed to a space behind her small table and chair. "In my chill box. It's the same batch. I haven't had any since the night I got sick."

Gwen stood and looked, then lifted up the lid that resembled a piece of flooring. He pulled out a small glass container with a deerskin lid, turning it in the light carefully.

"Per your instructions, Chae has made sure I've only been drinking water and broth. She has made sure no one else has had access to any of it."

"Who makes your juice?"

"I do. But honestly, anyone could have snuck in and tainted it. I'm either in the kith, the fields, or my work hut. I usually don't come back in here until bedtime."

He opened it carefully and sniffed, his eyebrows furrowing. "I can't smell anything odd, but if you'll let me, I'll take it back with me and test it."

She nodded, even as a sadness darkened her eyes.

"Hey, Zee. This is a good thing," he reassured. "We can find out what it was."

"That's not it."

"Then what is it?"

"What if someone else had gotten a hold of it?" she demanded, voice strangled with emotion.

"You said you were the only one…"

"But a curious child could have asked me for a taste. I drink it at dinner. What if I had decided to share it with you?"

Gwen set it down on the table and returned to her side, grasping her hand. "That didn't happen."

"I know, but it doesn't make it less atrocious."

"I agree, the act itself is monstrous. They were so blinded by their anger with you, they never considered others. They didn't care if there would be any innocent victims. Thankfully, you have weird taste."

Startled by his flippant comment, she scoffed then snatched her hand free as if offended. He chuckled at her reaction, moving back to the table to pack up the possibly poisoned apple juice.

"I'll take a look at this first thing when I get back to the castle."

"Can you stay tonight?" she asked, hesitantly.

"Yes, until daybreak at the latest. I told Taylor that I'd watch over you again, to give them a break. I don't know if I can come back tomorrow, but seeing that you're doing better, it's probably best for me to lay low as well. We don't know the true motive or who was involved so we should be careful. I will leave enough medicine and herbs for at least three days."

"Then come to bed," she responded. "I'm tired and would prefer to fall asleep with you next to me."

Gwen shook his head. "Anyone could walk in."

"My kithlin all believe I am dealing with a border concern. The only ones that will come in here is Tay and Chae." She frowned suddenly. "Unless, you don't…"

"It's not that, Zee. I know what your people would do if they saw me here. And I know what they would do to us if they found you in my arms. You're not strong enough to take on any kind of challenge because of me. And I'm useless in a fight."

Zawn didn't respond, but he could see her disappointment. She started adjusting the pillows around her and he returned to her side to help her until she could lay down comfortably. She rolled onto her side, with her back to him. He fixed the blankets, covering her up to her shoulder. He stared at her back, her silence tearing him to pieces, then he sat down by the fireplace. He glanced between her and the fire. He sighed, long and hard, before standing and undressing. He again kept his undershorts on, out of respect for her friends that might check in on them, then crawled into bed behind her. She didn't react at first, not until he wrapped his arms around her and pulled her against his chest. She laid her arms over his, then turned her head enough to nuzzle his cheek.

"If I had my way, I would be here every minute and hold you every breath," he whispered. "But I don't get my way. I can only find moments like this to hold on to."

"These are the moments we fought for, aren't they?" she asked, softly.

"They are. Sleep, my love. I'll be here until daybreak."

"I love you, Gwen."

"I love you too, Zee."

Reassured he wouldn't leave without her knowing, she closed her eyes and drifted off to sleep.

~   ~   ~

When he woke up, the sun was nowhere near the horizon. The fire weakly splashed light along the walls since the fuel had started to run low. He laid on his side, one arm over her shoulders while she laid on her stomach, her arms tucked under her chest. With her head turned toward him, the peacefulness on her face was surreal. He couldn't remember a night he ever got to watch her sleep. But without her having to rush back to her kith, she slept soundly beside him.

Seeing this side of her, knowing how rare it was to enjoy, he took in every detail. She was right. These were the moments they fought for....

He found himself falling further in love with her.

She took a deep breath then opened her eyes to find him watching her. She smiled dreamily, blinking the sleep from her eyes.

"Have I changed colors?" she asked, drolly.

"I've never seen you sleep," he admitted, brushing a lock of hair from her neck. "Almost didn't recognize you."

She chuckled, carefully rolling onto her side. "Usually, I have to keep an ear open for anything that would eat us."

"You were always on guard, weren't you?" He secured his arms around her and pulled her against him before kissing her, a gentle caress with no demands. "Did you sleep well this time at least?"

"It's the first time I slept well in a long while," she replied, then furrowed her eyebrows. "But now you have to leave, don't you?"

"I do. But I will be back in a few days. Will you behave yourself until then?"

She rolled her eyes. "Between Tay and Chae, it's not like I can get away with much."

"I knew I left you in good hands."

That made her laugh, which drew out his, too. He kissed her again before letting her go and slipping out of her bed. She sat up on her own, even though she struggled a little at first, to watch him dress. Her frown deepened with each piece of clothing, which caused him some distress. He moved back to the bed and kissed her lovingly. He traced her ear gently, making her do the same to his.

"I will see you soon, Zee."

"Don't stay away too long."

"Count the days. I know I will. I love you."

"I love you, too, Gwen."

~   ~   ~

Taylor retrieved Gwendin soon after he dressed, while Chae settled in to sit with Zawn. The children were having their lesson with Jheferin that day which meant Chaelene could hide away with her friend. Chae had snuck in breakfast after their kithlin disbursed, settling Zawn against her pillows so she could eat comfortably. She sat at the table nearby while the ill leader glared at her omelet.

"You're thinking too hard," Chae chided.

Zawn finished chewing then swallowed her mouthful. "Gwen is worried about us getting caught. What our people will do to him, to me, if they found us out."

"We know what would have happened when Medruano was leader. You are not him."

"No, I am not," Zawn responded, stabbing her food. "But how many of us still think the same way?"

"The question you should ask is, are our reactions to him out of hate or fear? He loves you, there's no doubt about that. But with our history, I think it's safe to say, we will always fear or hate men for one reason or another. Even those who we work with in the neighboring townships. I won't lie to you, Zawnie, but even Tay and I are cautious of him. Not because of who he is or what species he is, but because of who he works for."

"He's not like the Royal Family."

"That I know. But what if that lot find out about you? What will they visit upon us?"

Zawn didn't respond, afraid to admit to her friend that she already knew. Well, at least for Gwen and herself. But she wasn't sure if the kith would suffer the same consequences. She would need to speak with Taylor, in private. That had to be discussed.

Soon.

~   ~   ~

"What do you mean, deniability?" Taylor demanded harshly, glowering at her.

He had come in to relieve Chae during the lunch hour, which gave him the opportunity to update her on the kith's business. She let him rattle through all of the priorities before mentioning the plan if the Mehdehran King ever found out about Zawn and Gwendin.

"If it ever got out that I am involved with Gwen…"

"You dealt with that already, with Marassa."

"Yes, but Marassa isn't his only spy. What if Gwen gets caught here? What will stop an angry traitor or a lucky spy from sharing that? The kith must be able to deny any knowledge. Gwen and I are the only ones that should suffer for our…" and she blinked away her tears, "our love."

"If it ever comes to that," Taylor replied, carefully, as he took in her honesty about how she felt about Gwendin, "we will discuss it as a kith. Yes, I know you are our leader and all that. However, you are more than a leader. You are a friend, ally, champion. Our kithlin know that. It is only right that they have a say in what they will fight for and what they will not. Now, eat your lunch before my mate comes and thrashes me for not making you behave."

Zawn begrudgingly began eating, realizing that she would not win this argument. At least not at the moment.

"Love, huh?" he inquired. "Never thought I'd hear that come from you, Zawnie."

"There's no other word for it, Tay," she responded, before taking a sip of water.

"And have you said those words to him?"

She flashed a dark glare at her friend. "Why ask that?"

"Zawnie, I've seen the ring. I've seen the bracelet. You even celebrated your anniversary."

"We agreed to court before I challenged Medruano," she responded, shrugging nonchalantly.

"Should we expect something more in an announcement?"

She scoffed. "Why would we announce something private?"

"I just want to know if I have a brother."

She stabbed her food again with her fork.

"So, you haven't agreed to be mates?"

"We're devoted to each other, Tay. That's enough."

"For now," he retorted.

CHAPTER 34

Gwendin returned after three days, following Taylor closely as they snuck into the kith. He automatically set down his bags and removed his cloak, before kneeling in front of her as she sat in one of her chairs by the fireplace. He checked her over, muttering things under his breath. Then he glanced over his shoulder at Chaelene who sat in the other chair nearby.

"You've done a wonderful job," Gwen told Chae. "I can see a substantial difference in her already."

Chae looked proud of herself. "I've made all of her food. Everything is stored away from all others. She has even started eating more solid foods, like bread and potatoes along with vegetables and meats."

"Good. Keeping any opportunity slim for another dose has made all the difference."

"Do you know what the poison was?" Zawn asked.

"When I tested your drink, the only thing that got a reaction was centipede venom. Not an easy poison to manipulate. It had to be milked, purified, specialized, and added within hours of creation."

"We're susceptible to their venom," Zawn replied. "But we have an antivenom in place if someone is stung."

"You wouldn't've thought to use it if you were never stung," Chae pointed out, then asked Gwendin, "But your concoction took that into consideration?"

"Yes, centipede venom is one it targets."

"Someone had to know what it did to elves."

"That's a long list, Chae," Zawn responded. "Especially when compared to my nice long catalogue of enemies."

"With you out of sight," Chae said, frowning, "they may think they've succeeded."

"Let them assume. Taylor is still visible. They know better than to step up to him in my absence. This might give me time to recuperate properly and be ready to meet any challenges."

Chaelene didn't look swayed, but she nodded and stood. "I need to check on the kids. Who knows what they've done to their father. They miss you, by the way, but they believe you are doing noble things to protect the kith."

"I wish we didn't have to lie, but it's the safest choice. For now."

"Good night, Zawnie, Gwendin."

"Good night, my friend."

After Chae left, Gwen caressed her ear and kissed her lovingly. He cherished the embrace, trying not to think of these moments being stolen from them had the poisoner been successful. He didn't want to admit to her that after the first night he had returned to the castle and wept. Worry and fear had gripped him tightly and he laid in his bed, the bracelet pressed against his lips, as the tears ran down his face. The next morning, he dreaded returning to the kith, because he wasn't sure if she would start recovering quickly. She only proved resilient, settling his heart and mind immediately.

"You're doing a lot better. I don't think we'll have to keep up with the nausea preventing herbs if you've been eating that well."

"Chae shovels food in my mouth every time I open it," she responded, with a chuckle. "I feel like one of her kids."

"How's your energy level?"

"Decent. I'm not winded when I get up and walk. I'm lifting some things to regain muscle. And Chae has been feeding me a lot more meats and nuts."

"Good. You'll be back to fighting shape before you know it. Let's get you into bed. You still need all the rest you can get."

He helped her into her sleeping gown, but didn't move to undress himself.

"You're not staying?"

"I don't think I need to watch over you all night anymore. I'll get you settled and have Taylor walk me back."

Her frown deepened.

"And we've pushed our luck far enough, don't you think?"

She blinked at him, then shuffled past him into the bathing room. He heard a basket open, then close. She returned into the main room with something in her hands. She gestured for him to take it, and after he accepted the material, she walked past him and crawled into bed.

He stared at the neatly folded material, his heart warming. "A sleeping gown? For me?"

"Come to bed."

CHAPTER 35

It had been two weeks since Zawn was poisoned, and even though she was almost back to normal, she still had a hard time regaining weight. They kept the kith busy with spring cleaning and other tasks while telling them she was dealing with continuing border issues through diplomacy and it seemed to keep their kithlin satisfied.

However, some amongst the kithlin were not convinced.

One night, Zawn sat in her hut waiting for Gwen. It wasn't a particularly good day for her and Taylor had hovered over her most of the day. He only left her side when it was time to retrieve Gwendin. Taylor snuck the theurgist in while the kith sang in celebration of the new growing season. They spoke softly in her hut, but when the voices outside fell quiet, Taylor exited to keep an eye on the crowd but popped back in quickly.

Taylor looked dour. "Zawnie, you need to come outside."

"Why?"

"Our kithlin are demanding answers."

"Gwen, stay here, out of sight."

Zawn carefully exited her hut, using her walking stick to steady herself. She saw the square filled with her kithlin, but instead of sitting around, facing the fire, they had all turned toward her hut. They all looked worried and muttered to each other as they realized her condition. Their leader appeared weak, frail, tired. She saw their concern and forced herself to stand straight.

"I see that you have had some suspicions?" she inquired, her voice carrying stronger than expected. "Now that you see me, I guess you now all wonder what ails me?"

Murmuring answered her.

"Someone tried to kill me. They didn't challenge me, they didn't argue with me. They were cowards, poisoning me. But as you can see, no matter the tactics, I fought back and I survived."

"You hid this from us. Why?" Meagan demanded, the hurt evident in her voice.

"Because I didn't want to frighten you," Zawn answered, frowning. "You have all looked to me for guidance and strength, when things were scary and uncertain. If you saw me like this a week ago, what would have run through your minds?"

Her kithlin frowned, sniffled, and murmured fearful comments.

"It was not your burden to carry. Taylor stepped in when needed, Chaelene kept her eye on me. We got through this privately to make sure you all were protected. If I had believed any of you were in harm's way, by whatever hate brought this on, I would have told you. But I was the sole target."

Vergun approached her. "Who snuck in to see you?" he demanded, his deep voice booming throughout the kith. "They," and he pointed to Taylor and Chaelene, "are not the only ones who have been checking in on you."

She felt what little color she had regained drain from her face. Zawn debated on how much more she wanted to tell her kith. However, the sound of a door opening answered for her. Gwen exited her hut, glancing cautiously around at the crowd. Murmuring got a little louder, this time with worry and shock over a man being amongst them.

"He came to help you?" Nealon asked.

"I owed her my life," Gwendin responded, as he made his way to Zawn's side. "It was the least I could do."

Vergun slowly walked over and towered over the theurgist, eyes narrowed. Zawn tensed, unsure of the other elf's intentions. Taylor rested his hand on his hilt, but there was no need. Vergun held out his arm in friendship. Gwendin reached out as well and they grasped forearms.

"Thank you for helping our leader," Vergun said.

"It was my honor to help and to pay back my debt to her."

Then Vergun gestured that they all join the kithlin around the firepit.

"In a moment," Zawn responded, with a smile. "Please, eat. We'll be right there."

Gwendin helped Zawn back into her hut as the kith started to settle down for dinner. He closed the door behind them, his mouth becoming unhinged.

"That went better than I…" and his voice trailed off.

"And we're not dead," Zawn retorted.

He wrapped his arms around her, sighing hard. She didn't want to admit that her fears still were not completely relieved, but nuzzled his neck and inhaled his scent to calm her nerves. They stood together, filled with surprise.

"We need to go back out there," she said, with a chuckle. "Don't want to offend anyone after that."

"Can you handle it? Sitting up? Eating what's fixed?"

"I'll have to. Don't worry, I will use you to lean on if I need to. But I have to show them I'm healing, that I'm strong. It's just as important as resting now."

They exited the hut, making their way to the firepit. Taylor and Chaelene had left a space next to them, where Gwendin and Zawn sat down and stayed close to each other. Chaelene offered them a plate of food she said she filled herself. They ate off the shared plate and listened to the conversations around them, smiling as the children played and responding to any inquiries. Then a few of the kithlin began singing. They serenaded everyone with tales of victories and love.

Zawn looked over at Gwen, her heart warming. The smile on his face told her that he was not only enjoying himself but he felt incredibly welcomed. She was suddenly hit with a joy that she had never felt before. Her love and her kith, all together, and celebrating the day.

~ ~ ~

"What's wrong?" he asked, later that night as they cuddled in her bed.

"I am still amazed by their acceptance of you being here."

"I think it's because I was helping you and repaying a debt. Those are two very honorable actions that your people respect."

"You did respond properly to Vergun and the others."

"You sound surprised. You think I've learned nothing from you?"

She scoffed with a wry smile. "It's not that. I guess I'm still trying to wrap my brain around the fact that my two worlds have finally collided and it wasn't a catastrophe."

"I think you have too little faith in your kith and in your leadership. You have shown your people that life can be what they want it to be, not what their leader demands it to be."

"I don't know if I really had anything to do with…"

"Zee, you are their leader. You took a kith that was financially and spiritually in ruin and turned it into something thriving and happy. Your people sing at dinner, the children run and play. You told me you couldn't remember the days that were like this but you knew they existed at one time. You brought all of that back. You brought the pride back to your kithlin. No one else did that. Others helped, yes, but it was all you. I think if you wanted to make more changes, they'd accept them. Maybe not everyone, but I'd like to see someone try to argue with the majority."

She stared at him, eyes wide at the conviction in his voice.

He chuckled, pulling her in close. "Get some sleep, my love. This has been a very exciting day. And I think we'll have quite a few more in the future."

~ ~ ~

She woke the next morning, but he wasn't next to her. Confused, she raised up and glanced around. Gwen sat on the edge of the bed, looking out the window. He had moved the curtain aside, letting in some of the predawn light. She scooted along the covers, until she was behind him, and wrapped her arms and legs around him.

He chuckled, in surprise, then laid his arms over hers.

"Good morning," she whispered.

"Good morning."

"What's wrong?"

"Nothing. I was just listening to the kith. There are so many sounds I never thought about. People, animals, the forest around us, the firepits..."

"What does it sound like?" she asked.

"Sounds like home," he answered, looking over his shoulder at her.

Zawn smiled, kissing his cheek. "Good. That's what it's supposed to sound like."

"I should get going," he said, after a few moments of content silence between them. "Taylor should be here soon to lead me back."

"Maybe next time, I can be the one to walk you back?" she inquired, loosening her hold so he could stand up.

"Think you'll be up to it?" he asked, turning around and helping her to her feet.

"A walk will do me good," she answered, leaning into him. "I'm getting better, stronger, every day. I will continue to do so, thanks to you. The least I can do is walk with you."

"Then I will look forward to next time." He kissed her, lovingly, reveling in the tender embrace.

A knock at the door interrupted them, making him sigh. Zawn called out, permitting Taylor to enter.

"I'm sorry, but time to go," Taylor announced.

"I'll be back in a few days," Gwen reassured, hugging her gently.

~   ~   ~

A few days later, he returned, welcomed as a guest this time. Zawn had been pulled away from the firepit to help with the goats, a task that had been chaotic during the time of her illness. The rest of the kith sat in the glow of the fire, weaving and sewing. Chae stayed by Gwen's side, handing him a basket that had been half finished, while she started a new one. He observed her working the pieces together and once he felt he could handle the pattern, he started working on his. Even though he tried to concentrate on each tuck and pull, his thoughts dwelled on a subject that had been on his mind for weeks. However, with Zawn's poisoning, he had to put it aside. Surrounded by the sounds of laughter, chatter, and children, it rushed back up to the front of his mind.

"I do not like that look on your face," Chaelene chided.

Gwendin chuckled. "My face is always a problem."

"Because it gives you away."

"It does. My mentor at the College always said I thought too loudly." Gwen worked on his basket for a little bit before asking, "How did you know that Taylor was the one?"

157

Her eyebrows jumped up. "Oh, well… we grew up together, obviously. He would pull my hair and I would kick his shins. I didn't really even think about him that way until I found out he was talking about courting another. I had some devious plans for that girl, until Zawnie landed me on my back." She started to laugh. "I laid there in shock. She had never handled me like that before. Apparently, she had done the same thing to Tay. She yelled at both of us to get our shit together and realize how much we actually loved each other. And then… we did. We agreed to be mates and that was that."

Gwendin smiled as Chaelene glowed at the memory.

"Did… did you have to do anything special to agree to be mates?"

"Well, no. We don't have a big ceremony or celebration. That's expected for babies and promotions. When we agreed to be mates, well, it was an intimate moment that I will not detail but we just knew. We knew we loved each other and would covet no other." She fell silent, still beaming, then looked the theurgist up and down, suspiciously. "Has Zawnie said something to you about being mates?"

"No, of course not." He fell silent as he worked one stubborn piece through. "But I have had a lot of time to think lately."

"Do you love her?"

"Not allowed to."

"That wasn't the question."

He stopped working on the basket, meeting Chae's eyes without fear. "I love her more than I thought I could ever love someone."

"You've got a bit of a conundrum, don't you? She is not the easiest to love and not the easiest to persuade."

He laughed. "Loving her has never been hard. Persuading her on the other hand, well, that's definitely the issue."

"Can I ask you a personal question?"

"Of course."

"Have you… touched her ears?"

Gwendin stammered and blushed. "I never knew about that until she…" and he gently touched his own ear as he reveled in the memory. "And here I thought undressing for her was special."

She stared at him in awe, knowing what it took for Zawn to make that gesture, let alone accept him in an elven way. "It won't take much, Gwendin," she responded, after recovering from the shock of his admission. She laid a hand on his arm and squeezed it reassuringly. "If she shared with you that kind of intimacy… She loves you and I know she would be thrilled to be your mate. But you didn't hear that from me. I don't need to be landed on my back again."

"I can understand that."

"Do you?"

"I snuck up on her one time."

Chaelene winced. "Lesson learned?"

"Painfully, yes."

They stared at each other for a moment then started to laugh at their shared experience. Amused silence settled between them and they restarted their work.

~ ~ ~

Walking back to the storage hut, Satria frowned, deeply. She had approached Chae and the theurgist from behind to gather the completed baskets so they could be stored with the others for sale. She hadn't meant to eavesdrop, but the conversation was hard to ignore.

Ehdzia and Naji glanced up when Satria walked in, then asked her what was wrong. Apparently, her face gave away her mix of emotions.

"I heard something I don't think I should have," Satria responded, sitting down in the chair next to the table.

The two women joined her, one grabbing her hand and the other rubbing her shoulder.

"Was it that awful?" Naji asked.

"No, it wasn't something awful. I…" and Satria's shoulders dropped. "I think it was a secret. And I don't know if I should share it."

"But not a bad secret?" Ehdzia inquired.

Satria sighed. "No, I don't think so." She looked at her friends, her shoulders lowering. "I heard the theurgist talking to Chae."

"About?" Naji prompted.

"How he felt about our leader."

Ehdzia and Naji stared at her.

Then Naji responded, "I saw them embrace. It was… loving…"

The three women glanced at each other, unsure what to do.

CHAPTER 36

Mountainous in size, the width of his torso and hips taking up most of the hallway, Nicholaus strode down the corridor, making everyone else press against the walls to stay out of his way. His size did not stop him from walking softly, thanks to the porous skin that allowed for flight. Gargoyles were born from volcanic igneous, their bodies roughly riddled pumice, and his skin color matched the walls of the castle, dark and rocky. When a gargoyle claimed territory, they were able to blend into the rock around them. With no hair and a stony facade, he blended in well with the turrets when he was on shift. The only thing that would catch an onlooker's eye was his uniform which was a few shades lighter than his skin, but it had to be a concentrated effort.

Lately, he hadn't needed to take any shifts since their numbers had finally started to fill out. Those who were young when they had been trapped by Elixin were now old enough to learn the job. Thoughtlessly, he rubbed his arm a little harder than he meant to, causing the magical brand to burn deep into his muscle. He still cursed the King's former theurgist for teaching the maniac that enslavement spell. Years resigned to following his orders wore on Nicholaus, even though he tried to hide it from his clan. There was no release from it, unless Elixin died, which wasn't likely since he was unfortunately in good health. However, his people were all showing signs of exhaustion from the weight of that curse.

Nicholaus climbed the steps up to the northeast turret, having to angle himself a little sideways so as not to scrape against the narrow, rounded walls. He also had to wrap his wings around his shoulders like a cape, using the claws at the tips to hold them in place. He exited through a doorless arch, to find Marassa at her station. He watched her for a moment as she leaned against the wall and stared out over the forest canopy. Then he unfurled his wings and cleared his throat, causing her to turn around and acknowledge him. When she saw his irritated expression, she straightened to attention.

"There are reports of a man visiting the Whispering Hornbeam Kith. A man who looks very much like the theurgist."

Her eyes widened. "Nic..."

"You saw him with someone, didn't you?" he demanded, his gravelly voice low and menacing. "How dare you lie to the King?"

She stammered, which only stoked his ire.

"Who was he with?"

She finally found her voice, lifting her chin almost in defiance. "When I tracked him, he wasn't with anyone."

He regarded her, knowing that she was lying. "Zawn will have to answer for this, as leader of the kith." Then he began to leave.

"Nicholaus."

He stopped in the archway, doubting that she could say anything that would change his mind.

"Haven't we taken enough from her?"

The tone of her voice made him turn back around. Marassa still stood where she was, but her tears startled him. He hadn't seen tears from her since their enslavement. She hadn't even cried when she banished Zawn from her life, at least not in public. Shaken, he returned to her, grasping her shoulders.

"What are you talking about?" he asked.

"You're right. I did lie to the King. I did see him with someone. He was with Zawnie." She took a trembling breath. "I broke them up. I couldn't let her die over someone like him. I tried to keep them apart, I did. But it destroyed them, Nicholaus. He loves her. More than I ever could."

He felt the rest of his anger drain away. "She's in love? Marassa..."

"Please don't take it away from her again." She clasped his hands. "We took so much from her before our fall. I took away my love, you took away our friendship. And Medruano demoted her, stripped her of everything. Made her a sentry when she has always been a hero. Always a leader. Why can't we let her keep this?"

~   ~   ~

Deep in the night, when the overnight castle guard dozed off during his shift, they met high up on the roof of the stables. They settled along the ridge, blending in with the slate shingles. They varied in size and shape, but all had the same coloring. Male and female perched next to each other and watched him intently. Their night vision was enough to see each other, but it never rivaled a Goluean's. The gargoyles' specialty was long distance, pristine like a predator's.

Nicholaus glanced around at his clan, gargoyles who he had known all of his life or all of theirs. He spoke softly, even though his deep gravelly voice was reminiscent of stone on stone. "I'm sorry to have called you together at such a strange time of night, but it is the only way I know we will not be overheard."

"What has happened?" Aries asked, keeping his voice hushed, but his concern reflected in the faces of the others as well.

"As you know, the King has tasked us to keep an eye on his enemies, especially the Whispering Hornbeam Kith."

The gathered gargoyles frowned, their guilt evident about spying on their former allies. In the beginning, they happily reported on Medruano and his people. But since Zawn had taken over... They would never admit to Nicholaus' face that they had regretted their animosity toward Zawn over the decades. Hindsight gave them the opportunity to see the wrongs but never the ability to make things right.

"I ask that any details of a man among them be omitted from your reports."

They all glanced around at each other in surprise.

"We're to lie?" Mareah demanded.

"Omit," Nicholaus corrected. "He doesn't need to know who is visiting the kith. It would only cause more harm than good. I will take any responsibility if anything arises."

They all started to nod agreement, then swore to their leader that they would keep the information about Zawn's kith very limited and consistent when they had to report to the King.

CHAPTER 37

The whispering was expected. Not everyone knew what to make of the theurgist who came to their leader's rescue. Especially considering the years of animosity between kingdom and kith. However, the elves also knew humans who were kind, honest, and friendly. They worked for them, worked with them, and now they sold their goods to them.

He said he was repaying a debt. However, the more time he spent with the kith, it was obvious something else tied him to their leader. And Meagan felt the most recent whispering had taken a different tone. She knew just the elf to interrogate.

The younger elf walked past the baking hut, oblivious to her surroundings, when she was grabbed. Pulled into the empty kitchen, she was spun into a corner. Meagan blocked her exit, placing her hands firmly on her own hips to make herself bigger.

"What is going on?" Meagan demanded.

Naji blinked at her, innocently. "What do you mean?"

"Don't play coy. What's going on?"

~   ~   ~

"I need to talk to you." Meagan pulled Chae aside, her face serious. "I am afraid our kithlin are conspiring against our leader."

"What do you mean, conspiring?"

~   ~   ~

She knew her kith tolerated Gwendin's visits because he attended to Zawn's health. After a few weeks of Gwen visiting and sharing evening meals with her kithlin, it started to feel natural. He even got initiated by Talor and Chaen, who were very protective of their Auntie Zawnie and questioned him thoroughly about how he took care of her. They seemed satisfied with Gwendin's answers – even if they didn't quite understand everything.

They tried to keep their affection hidden, never touching or sitting too close. They would only kiss and embrace once they were behind closed doors. She thought they hid it well, because she didn't know how far the kith's acceptance would go. She found out one morning, at the firepit, when the men of the most prominent families cornered her. They had asked for a private chat in her work hut, but with their kithlin staring up at them in concern, she instead gestured for them to sit with her. They begrudgingly agreed.

"What's on your minds?" she inquired, as she nonchalantly ate her porridge.

Merded glared at her, as did some of the other men, but it was Vaghide who piped up. "We have concerns about this... man... visiting our kith. We understood that he did so out of repaying your life debt, but now he seems to, well, he seems too comfortable amongst us."

"Is that a bad thing?" she asked, setting down her bowl and looking each man in the eyes. "We deal with humans all the time. We work for and with them, as well as barter and visit with those in the nearby villages. And no harm has befallen us, has it?"

"You were poisoned," Duard responded, tone harsh.

"Yes, but that happened before he ever entered the kith."

"Maybe you were poisoned because of your visits outside of the kith?" Cadao retorted.

Her eyebrow rose up while her eyes narrowed. "I had believed I was poisoned because I took leadership. Unless there is something you know that I do not?"

Zawn stared him down until he couldn't stand it anymore and Cadao lowered his eyes. She could sense all of her other kithlin listening intently and she glanced around at the group. Then she cleared her throat, gaining all of their attention.

"You're right, Cadao. I have spent a lot of time with him, in secret. He has taught me that not all men are the same."

"Does he love our leader?" inquired Saronin, who sat a few seats away.

Zawn swallowed hard, unsure if she should be honest, but she knew she couldn't lie either. "We are in love, yes."

"About time," Naji stated, causing everyone to turn toward her.

"That is a crime," Vergun murmured.

"Is it?" Satria demanded, her tone causing all eyes to focus on her. "Have you watched them? I mean really seen them?"

"And why shouldn't our leader be happy?" Ehdzia asked. "If he makes her happy, then we should be happy for her."

Zawn tried to keep her face stoic, but the backing surprised her. Her heart warmed as more kithlin chimed in, in support of the couple. Her eyes landed on Meagan, who stood near the firepit that cooked their food, the smile on her face glowing with pride. Tay and Chae were nearby, wisely saying nothing, but the joy and relief apparent.

Zawn finally returned her attention to the men who confronted her. "It appears I have the majority on my side. Any other concerns?"

~   ~   ~

She had waited for him to arrive at their meeting place and she led him through the trees back to the kith. As they walked, she told him about the conversation she had with her kithlin. Because of the reaction by some over their relationship, they agreed to keep their physical affection private.

However, her kithlin had other ideas.

Dinner had been lovely, the kithlin sharing their songs and stories throughout the evening. As Gwen and Zawn sat side by side at the fire, they were approached by Meren, the child who liked to draw. He stood in front of them, grinning, before grabbing their hands and pushing them together. Confused, they laughed and tried to pull away. Undeterred, he kept putting their hands together. Gwen finally got the hint, grabbing Zawn's hand and holding it.

Meren's face lit up with joy, exclaiming, "Yes!" before darting off back to play with the other children, who had also been watching intently.

They stared at each other, speechless, but entwined their fingers tightly. Whatever campaign her kithlin had waged behind their backs, they made it very clear that the few naysayers were definitely outnumbered. Any challenge would be met with retaliation.

Later that evening, as the two lovers stood side by side in her hut, she watched as reality finally sunk in for Gwendin.

"I don't know how I feel about this," he admitted.

Zawn looked over at Gwen. "About what?"

"Actually spending the night with you, in a bed, with everyone in your kith knowing that I am here, with you, in your bed."

Zawn chuckled. "We could go back to the tent if you'd like."

"Even though I did appreciate the privacy it gave us, I have to admit that I don't miss the rocks and roots that stabbed me during the night."

"You were right though, back when we reunited. We want a world where we can be together, but we have to find a way to change minds. We will never change your people's, but maybe we've changed mine."

He hugged her tightly around her waist, then loosened his hold when he felt how slight she still was. "And it's just as scary as I thought it would be."

"Things have changed. We need to embrace new ways to survive. And new ways to keep us happy." She kissed him, running her hand up under his tunic. "Now, come to bed."

"I feel like I should undress for you again. It's been a while," Gwen joked.

"Never fear, my love," she responded, nuzzling his cheek while her hand caressed his chest. "You will always be strong enough for me. No matter how long we are apart. Now, come to bed."

"Are you… up to it?"

She smiled, slyly. "I may not have the stamina for our usual marathon and you may have to do most of the work."

His eyebrow rose up. "Putting me to work, my lovely leader?"

She giggled, then her amusement faded. "I do wish to lay with you. I want to be with you in my bed as I have dreamt of so many times."

She pulled him after her, and with each step, they helped each other out of a piece of clothing until they were naked and climbing into bed. He positioned himself above her and, as their bodies intimately connected, happy sighs escaped them. He moved gently at first, then hesitated for a moment, staring into her eyes. She could see his concern, which warmed her heart, but also made her smirk.

"I'm not fragile, Gwen," she whispered, running one hand through his hair.

"I don't want to run you down before we get to the best part."

She chuckled, a sultry sound that thrilled him. "Hm, then you better be quicker than usual. I don't know how long I can lay around like this. I might fall asleep before you get done."

"Oh, is that how it's going to be? Then tell me if this works for you?"

He started a fervent rhythm, making them both moan and giggle in excitement.

~   ~   ~

Afterwards, they kissed tenderly, wrapped up in her blankets to keep the warmth on their bare skin. The fire flickered shadows along the walls, as if the darkness and the light knew nothing but to dance with each other. He ran gentle fingers up and down her spine, making her snuggle up closer to him. They reveled not just in their pleasure, but the intimacy they had longed for since she had been poisoned. He had been careful with her prior, sharing undemanding kisses and gentle caresses, but hadn't made any other requests of her out of concern for her health. However, tonight, as they moved together, they delved into the depths of their love unlike they had before, connecting in body as well as heart and soul.

"Was it everything you dreamed?" he asked, teasingly.

"Hmm better."

"Yeah?"

"It's been a while," she lamented. "I almost forgot how good you felt."

He touched her nose with his. "I would have waited forever."

"Gwen…"

"I'm supposed to be a sexless monk, remember?" he inquired, his tone teasing, but the smile faded. "It wouldn't've mattered either way," he admitted, sincerely. "I would have stayed by your side."

"I would have been by yours, no matter what."

"I love you," he whispered, gently caressing her ear.

She copied the touch along his ear, responding, "I love you too."

He smiled again, this time slyly. "So, does that mean that you're my mate?"

She rolled her eyes and sighed, thinking he was joking. But his smile was chased away by the seriousness in his eyes, which took her back for a moment.

"We love each other," he continued. "You've determined I am strong enough for you, as you are for me. The kith has accepted me, even if some don't like it. There's nothing left holding us back."

Her heart pounded hard against her chest. The idea that they could be together, as mates, had been a fantasy of hers for a long time. She had feared taking that step though, because she hadn't wanted to jinx their relationship. They had weathered so much though and they were still together. Gwen promised her his heart every night they were together. She did the same. He was right. There was nothing left to do.

"I will be your mate," she replied, this time caressing both of his ears, "if you are mine. I will covet no others."

"I will be your mate until the day I die." Then he smiled again, returning the soft touch, making her eyes shut and tears to quiver underneath her lids. "And even after that. I will covet no others."

CHAPTER 38

"Crenast of Garadni, to see the King of Mehdehra!"

The King's brother arrived, again with his obnoxious flourish. Elixin greeted him cheerfully and they quickly made their way to the King's personal chambers to talk and drink. Kemberly and Valena curtsied as the two men passed by but, just like the last time, were not even recognized. They followed quietly behind, heading to their section of the castle and away from the two boisterous men.

~   ~   ~

It was late into the evening. Kemberly readied for bed, patiently letting her servants dress her in her sleeping gown and braid her hair away from her face. She dismissed them once the bed had been turned down and the fire stoked to last the night. Alone, she stood by the window, enjoying some peace and quiet for once. Elixin would leave her alone for the length of his brother's visit.

Tonight, he would drink himself dumb with Crenast.

With him distracted and Valena sent off that afternoon to the finishing school to keep her manners pristine, Kemberly could sleep in, skip breakfast, and take her time tomorrow. She would take full advantage of the rare convergence.

She took a sip of her water before setting the glass down on her nightstand. She started to climb into bed when she heard a scrape. Startled, she turned toward the fireplace only to see Crenast sneaking into her room from the hidden passage. She gasped, surprised he remembered how to get to her room.

"What are you doing here?" she demanded, keeping her voice hushed.

Crenast smiled, full of charm as usual. His puffy tunic and jacket were missing, as well as his boots. All he wore was his undershirt and riding pants. And a hopeful expression.

"I hope you're not mad I remembered your secret."

"No, not mad. But what…?"

"Your husband has drunk himself unconscious and will not miss me."

He approached her cautiously, but she didn't step away when they were face to face. His hands gently caressed her nightgown, before grasping the sides and pulling it up slightly.

"I wonder if I am still welcome in your bed?" he asked, his fingertips brushing her skin so slightly that her breath caught, his audacity exciting. "I have missed you terribly."

She lifted her arms over her head, inviting him to remove her sleeping gown which he accepted immediately. As it fluttered to the ground, he sighed happily as his eyes raked over her nude body. She hated what he saw. Her uneven breasts, stretch marks that scarred her abdomen and thighs, and the loosened skin around her belly. Elixin had always frowned until he no longer bothered with undressing her. She even believed that he fantasized about another while he submitted himself to his husbandly duties. She knew about the laundress and the stableman, after all, the household couldn't help gossiping loudly about her husband's dalliances.

Yet Crenast's response was the same as the first time he bedded her. "You are so beautiful. You are absolutely wasted on Elixin."

In the privacy of her bedchambers, she embraced him without hesitation.

~   ~   ~

The bed gently moved under her, signaling his exit. She opened her eyes, his body blocking the fading firelight. Then she raised up on her arm, watching as he moved around the room. The differences between Elixin and Crenast were not just personality but also physically. Crenast was shorter than Elixin, which made it easier for them to see eye to eye, especially when he was above her. His hair was longer, without the need to manage a crown, and he could pull it back in a small ponytail. She loved running her fingers through his locks when he focused on particular areas of her body. His skin was smooth, undamaged by war and conquest, reminding her that not all lives followed the same path. She wondered if that was the reason for Crenast's more carefree personality. He hadn't been hardened by death and power.

He noticed that she was awake, a smile on his face as he dressed.

"Elixin will wake soon," he explained. "I should be there when he does. Hm, I really do like being able to move through the castle without anyone seeing." Then he laughed. "I must remember to feign a hangover to ensure he has no suspicions."

"How long are you staying?"

"A week," he answered, pulling his pants up and fastening them. "I will spend most of my time with my brother of course. But in the evening, when he sleeps solid thanks to a little something I picked up on the way here, I will make my way to you, every night, to satisfy you in ways your husband refuses to." He sauntered back over to the bed and kissed her passionately. "Only with your consent of course."

"You always have my consent."

His smile widened as he stepped away to retrieve his undershirt from the chair nearby. She slipped out of the bed, not bothering to cover herself, making him sigh contentedly.

"Beautiful," he whispered, pulling her against him. Hands wandered and he finally laughed against her lips. "You drive me crazy." Then he turned them around and pressed her against the bookcase next to the fireplace, unhooking his pants. "I may have a moment to spare." He again kissed her with an urgency she still was unaccustomed to, but happily drowned in.

~ ~ ~

He kept his promise. Each night, Crenast would sneak into Kemberly's bedchambers and pleasure her in ways that Elixin could never fathom. She again felt like a woman worthy of a man's attention. She dreaded their last night, knowing that when he left, her life would return to dull shades of gray after he had painted it with colors of ecstasy and fantasy. His secret letters were never enough when they were apart to keep the vibrancy he brought in person.

They laid together in her bed, listening to the changing of the guard as their orders were called out and their stomping signaled the switch. He laid on his back while she cuddled up to his side, his strong arm laying along her shoulders. The night had been cool enough to leave a few windows propped open, which also meant they had to temper their volume even in their most ardent moments. She didn't mind though, it gave her an excuse to press her mouth against his wonderfully delicious skin and breathe in his sweet leather-like scent.

"I hate to leave you," he whispered, kissing her forehead. "But alas, I have no choice."

"I wish we could be like this forever."

He didn't respond immediately, his fingers dancing along her arm. "What if we could?"

"Elixin would never..."

"We wouldn't need his permission."

Surprised, she raised up on her arm to look at him. "What do you mean?"

"I have a plan. But I will need your help."

She caressed his face, reassuringly. "If it means we can be together, finally, I'll do anything."

~ ~ ~

Life at the castle settled back into its dour routine once the King's brother left. The servants were back to their gossiping and backstabbing, while the Castle Guard changed shifts precisely on time throughout the grounds. The gargoyles flew in and out of the turrets, spying on the enemies of Mehdehra.

But Gwendin felt that something wasn't right. He couldn't pinpoint exactly what was out of place, but he spent his free time magically feeling his way around the castle. He roamed the hallways, slipped in and out of hidden passageways, and strolled outside along the walls in hope of finding out what made the energy change suddenly. He knew he had to keep his suspicions to himself and tried to make his wanderings appear spontaneous.

However, they were anything but impulsive. He checked off each area on a map in his chambers until he was sure he covered the entire complex.

~   ~   ~

One morning, Gwendin made his way to the dining room to check on his sister. He made it a habit, just to annoy Elixin. But Kemberly wasn't at breakfast. Elixin ate alone, undisturbed by his wife's absence. Stomach twisting, Gwen rushed to her private chambers. He found her sitting on the edge of her bed, still in her sleeping gown, holding her head.

"Kem?"

She looked up, her face pale with a tinge of green. "Oh, I'm so sorry. I am not feeling very well this morning."

He checked her for a fever while rattling off questions about symptoms and reactions.

"Just very tired, nauseous, a little dizzy," she answered.

Gwen sighed, hard, moving his hand to her stomach.

She stared at it for a moment. "Oh. I hadn't thought of that. I didn't think... after the miscarriage..."

He stood, walking to her cabinet where she kept her teas and herbs that he had provided during the previous pregnancy. He started taking stock of what she had and what she needed until he heard her sob. Spinning quickly on his heel, he rushed back to her side to console his sister.

"I can't lose this one, Gwen, I can't."

"We will do everything we can, Kem, I promise."

He wrapped his arms around her tightly, as she cried against his shoulder.

CHAPTER 39

The two lovers met at their spot every time Gwen came to visit. Hand in hand, she would walk him to the kith, where he was greeted by most of the kithlin. The more he visited, the more natural it felt, and soon, even their critics begrudged him some interaction.

Months flew by and Gwen kept his masquerade up with the King. He helped Zawn cultivate part of her garden plot to support the herbs he used as an excuse to leave the castle grounds and soon his need to forage became just a quick stop by Zawn's garden.

One night, they met at their usual place, but Gwen's expression puzzled her. "What's wrong?" she inquired, reaching for his hand.

He entwined their fingers, grimacing. "Come, I want to show you something."

They walked back toward the castle, but before they reached the fork in the road, he led her down a path hidden by overgrowth and erosion. Their path was filled with loose rocks and twisted roots, so they stepped carefully until they reached a break in the foliage. There, a large rock face greeted them, with moss and slime covering it due to lack of sunlight. Gwen whispered a spell, causing a light to flicker from his hand. It cast light along the darkened wall, revealing an opening low in the rock. They ducked their heads as they entered.

With one hand lighting the way, he grabbed Zawn's with the other and guided her down into a tunnel. The uneven ground made them move slowly. Then the darkness began to creep away ahead of them. The tunnel opened up into a large cavern and his light flickered out as the glow surrounding them illuminated the entire cave.

The rock walls matched the dark color of the castle and cracked without a pattern. Blue and white in hue, the pulsing light reached out then pulled away almost in unison but without rhythm. Each slow ebb brought warmth, while each withdrawal cooled the cave. The static singing from the walls also made her neck hair stand on end, while her bark felt like it was drying up. She shuddered, wrapping her arms around her torso.

"What is this?" she asked, bewildered.

"Where our magic comes from. Why so many creatures exist, including us."

Zawn stared quietly at the glowing, surging veins. She remembered stories told to her as a child about the force that ran underneath their feet and not only empowered them but united them as magical creatures. "Life force?"

"Something like that. We call them energy lines. They run around the whole world. Sometimes they touch, they cross, but most of the time they run parallel to each other. They're everywhere. Even here under the castle."

It took a moment for what he said to register. "We're under the castle?"

"Yes," he answered. He saw the concern cross her face at the same time the energy brightened. "Don't worry, no one knows they're here except me."

"How did you find them?"

"I kept sensing something wasn't right after the King's brother left. Energy lines run everywhere, that's a fact, and I've always felt them when I've walked over them. But this feeling, it wasn't normal. Weird is the best way I can describe it." He sighed, hard. "So, during the day, when no one cares where I'm at, I've been investigating the grounds. You'd be surprised how many hidden passages this castle has. I guess Elixin's father was a bit paranoid and needed places to disappear into to avoid whatever plot he imagined."

She scoffed. "But he never imagined dying at his son's hand."

"I've been told that's never been proven."

"And it never will be. But those of us who know the truth speak it very quietly."

He nodded, thoughtfully, then shrugged. "One day, I got behind the wall of the throne room and followed a little secret hallway. That's when I felt the zap, the power surge. I knew there was something powerful behind that wall. I decided to walk around the outside of the main building and found this cave entrance. It was covered with different types of rubble, but I could move it easily. It was just time consuming so it took me a few days. They've been hidden neath for decades based on the debris I moved. But when I saw them... I just knew I needed to show you."

He watched as she walked along the cave walls, careful not to touch or step on the glowing veins. Her face was a mix of fascination and fear, the same look he had on his face the moment he first saw the cavern walls.

"I think it's best that it stays between us," Gwen admitted, glancing around the cave with concern. "To have access to this kind of power? Honestly, I don't think there's anyone who could harness them but..."

He watched her consider his suggestion before she shook her head. "No, I think your mentor at the College should know," Zawn responded, frowning. "If anything were to happen to us or something happened after we are long gone, something should be documented somewhere. The College would be a wise choice."

"What about your kith? Do you keep any kind of records?"

"We do." She glanced around the cave again, then nodded. "You're right, I should leave a note in one of our tomes too. Both human and elf should have a warning of this place."

"I'll send my letter out as soon as I can." He reached for her hand. "Come, let's block the entryway, document what we found in private, and then never speak of it again."

She grasped his hand, their fingers automatically intertwining. "Agreed."

~ ~ ~

She woke up before he did and hustled to the bathing room as quickly and quietly as possible. Then she vomited into the sink. She had never experienced nausea like that before. She tried to muffle her sounds, to hide it from Gwen. He was still sleeping in her bed, but he roused to the noises coming from the other room. She exited once her stomach calmed enough and had rinsed her mouth clean. Sitting on the bed, with his legs hanging off the side, he looked at her in confusion.

"I'm sorry," she said, grimacing, "I didn't mean to wake you."

"Are you sick?"

She made her way to the bed, standing in front of him and wrapping her arms around his neck. "Some nausea."

"Have you been poisoned again?" he asked, his face losing all color.

"No, I don't think so."

He appeared relieved then a thought crossed his mind. Gwendin's eyes widened, his hand reaching out to her belly. He laid his palm against the cloth of her sleeping gown, splaying his fingers out. His expression took her aback for a moment, not sure if he had hope or fear.

"You know that isn't possible," she responded, patting his hand. "No. I think it was the proximity to the energy lines. That's a lot of magic for someone like me to be around. And this appears to be a consequence."

"I'm sorry, Zee."

"If I didn't expect it to be this bad, how could you?"

He hadn't moved his hand, staring at her stomach pensively.

"What?" she inquired.

"Can you blame me?"

She furrowed her eyebrows, confused. "Have you hoped for an accident?"

"Hoped for a blessing, maybe. I know, it's foolish to think we'd... I've been thinking a lot lately, about a lot of things." Grabbing her into his arms, he sat her on the bed next to him. He took a deep breath, then continued, "I can leave my post. It would mean giving up most of my magic, but I'd give everything if it meant that we could truly be together. Maybe, if I leave the College, they would undo the spell..." Lowering his eyes, as if afraid to see her refusal, he grasped her hands tightly. "And-and we could see what the fates have to offer us, as mates."

"Gwen…" she stammered, breathlessly.

"I know your kith won't accept me as a permanent resident. I'm not so foolish to believe they would let me live here. But I'd gladly live in the tent for the rest of my life if it meant we could be together."

She freed her hands and cupped his face, making him meet her eyes. In his, there was hope, but she also saw fear there that she would deny him. She stared at him, dark thoughts running through her mind.

"You would risk everything?" she asked, "Your job? Your home? Your family?"

"You're my home, Zee," he replied, frowning slightly. "You're my family."

Zawn kissed him, ardently, loving him for his words. "You are my home, too," she whispered against his lips. "I would give up my kith if it meant we'd be together as a real family." Then she hesitated, glancing away.

"But what? What is it?"

"We should ask the kith first, if they'd accept you," she responded, watching as his eyes widened. "The worst they can say is no."

He grabbed into his arms, laughing against her hair. She clung to him too, not realizing how much it meant to her to offer him a place amongst her kithlin.

"What if they say no?" he asked, softly, his fears almost stealing his voice.

She leaned back, smiling slightly. "If they say no, well, then you can decide what to do about your post. You can stay there or live in your tent."

"I can agree to that," he replied, kissing her deeply before sighing. "The only thing I'd ask is if we can wait until the Queen gives birth. She's due in two months. I would hate to abandon her at such a crucial time. Especially after everything she's been through."

"Then we'll wait for the birth to make our appeal to the kith."

They embraced again, their future looking brighter than they could ever have imagined.

CHAPTER 40

Kemberly waddled down the hallway, her back hurting. This had been the furthest along in pregnancy since her son Vaeden. She stopped walking, her heart stinging with the memory of her precious son. She tried her hardest to remember him happy, healthy, and mischievous. But his sunken cheeks, hollow eyes, and sickly face haunted her still. She drew in a shaky deep breath, but her exhalation came out steady. Regaining her composure, she made her way to Valena's room. The door was cracked open and she stopped in the doorway.

Back from boarding school only recently, Valena sat in front of her vanity, a servant brushing her long brown hair before starting the braid. Both girls were oblivious to their audience. Once the servant was done, she turned and left without a word, but made sure to give a quick curtsey to Valena then Kemberly.

Valena turned around on her stool and stared at her mother.

"You're growing so fast," Kemberly lamented, crossing the room. "Before we know it, you will be engaged."

"What if I don't want to be engaged?"

Kemberly laughed, lightly. "That is not for you to decide, child. That is for your father to determine." The queen caught sight of two books sitting on the nightstand next to Valena's bed. "What are you reading now?"

Valena glanced over and shrugged. "Something with pretty pictures."

"Why aren't you reading about fashion and manners? That would do you better than pictures of," and Kemberly read the spine of one book, "mythical creatures?"

"I've ran out," the child responded, nonchalantly.

"Hm, I'll make a request from the College for newer reading material then. They had an agreement with the fashion guild to share texts as requested."

"I would appreciate that."

Kemberly walked over and stroked her daughter's face. "Always, my girl."

"You look tired," Valena pointed out as she cupped her mother's hand. "You should rest. I will keep myself entertained until lunch."

The queen smiled. "I have a nice nap in my future, I promise. See you at lunch, Valena."

"See you at lunch."

Kemberly exited and when Valena realized she was alone finally, she pulled another book out of her vanity's bottom drawer.

~   ~   ~

Valena sat in her bedchambers, curled up in her chair by the fireplace. In her lap lay a wide, thick book. It was so heavy that it took all of her strength to carry it from the library. She had snuck in after her parents settled down for the night, ensuring they didn't catch her. The only one who did was a young recruit.

Her eyes wandered off the pages and toward the fire. They had almost run into each other when they both turned the same corner from the opposite direction. He caught himself before careening directly into her, but she dropped her book in surprise at his sheer presence.

When he realized who he had almost run into, he had snapped to attention. The recruit, a teenaged boy conscripted into the castle guard as a child, had light blonde hair and pale blue eyes. Clean shaven, hair short and spikey in the required military haircut, his fair skin had a red tinge from a slight sunburn. His uniform has no creases or wrinkles and the buttons were immaculately shiny. Taller than most of the other recruits, she had noticed him out in the courtyard working through the required exercises. But this was the first time they had been face to face.

She glowered at him, but he continued to stand at attention. "You will not tell anyone that you saw me, do you understand?"

"Of course, my princess."

Silence held them as she debated if she could trust him or not.

"May I retrieve your book for you?" he inquired, his voice not unpleasant.

"You may."

He bowed his head, then bent over and picked up the heavy tome. He was close enough for her to catch the smell of laundry soap and sweat, but kept enough distance not to brush up against her. Straightening with his arms full of book, he finally met her eyes. "May I carry it for you, my princess?"

"You may."

She strode with determination down the hallway, the recruit following closely, thanks to his long legs. He held the door to her bedchambers while balancing the large book then set it down where she told him to before standing at attention again.

"What's your name?" she asked, curious.

"Marqut."

"Do I have your fealty, Marqut?"

"Forever, my princess."

"You will not speak of this to anyone?"

"Not without your permission."

"Good, or I will flay you alive for all to see."

Marqut couldn't stop the smirk that cracked his stoic visage. "Only if it would please you, my princess."

"Dismissed."

He had bowed at the waist, then left and closed the door behind him.

Letting the memory fade, she returned her eyes to the book in her lap. She would keep an eye on that boy. After all, he might be useful someday. She continued to read, relieved the book was written in Old Tongue. No one else knew that language, except for her tutor, who had been removed the year before after angering her father. Well, he said dismissed, but there had been another grave dug out in the outer bailey again.

She glanced over a sentence that seemed simple in its instructions.

Curious, she lifted her hand and pinched her thumb and index finger together...

CHAPTER 41

The night had finally become peaceful after such an eventful day. The Queen now rested in her bedchambers and the King had drunk himself unconscious in the throne room during a marathon celebration.

Gwendin stood over the sleeping infant, his heart full of hope. After the miscarriage, the Queen had a hard time conceiving, but when she did, she almost stressed herself to death. The entire castle household worked hard to keep her healthy, cared for, and most importantly calm. And there in the bassinet was the prize for all of their hard work, just two weeks earlier than expected.

The theurgist wasn't a religious man, not in the least, but he was raised believing in a higher power. He whispered one prayer of thanks and another for protection over the child. Then he left to rest for the night.

~   ~   ~

The next morning, he checked on Kemberly. Even though she was still worn out from the rough birth, her smile reassured him. She needed to rest and he knew immediately getting pregnant again would be the death of her. He couldn't trust Elixin, even if it meant the life of his wife. Gwendin added something to her morning tea without her knowledge, before helping her drink every drop.

When the time was right, he would counteract the contraceptive herb. She could at least relax for now and rebuild her strength so she could enjoy the curious, energetic baby boy that laid in the bassinet next to her bed.

~   ~   ~

That evening, he couldn't move fast enough. It felt like the trip from the castle to their meeting place lasted a lifetime. All he wanted to do was tell her. Tell her that their dreams could finally come true. Ask her to make the request

179

to the kith. For them to finally be together as a couple, as mates, and as a symbol of what life could be without hate or bias.

She waited for him near the old grandfather tree, lighting up with that beautiful smile as he arrived. He strode across the area and grabbed her up into his arms. He kissed her longer and harder than he usually did in greeting, making her laugh against his lips.

"What has gotten into you?" she demanded after freeing herself.

"She had the baby," he responded, his eyes bright with joy. "He's healthy. He's got all toes and fingers, screams like a banshee."

Her eyes widened. "Does that mean we...?"

"If you still want to."

"Or course I want to!"

He kissed her again, both giggling in excitement.

"We can ask the kith tonight at dinner," she announced, hugging him tightly. Suddenly, his excitement faded and he tensed in her embrace. She leaned back and saw his expression, making her frown. "What's wrong?"

"What if they say no?"

"We already talked about that, remember? We figured it out." Then she realized something. "You're really worried about your sister, aren't you?"

Guilt darkened his eyes. "I don't know if I should leave her so soon. It was a rough birth. Abandoning her now..."

"Then we can wait. Wait until you think it is a good time."

"Really? You're willing to wait?"

"Gwen, we've waited this long. What's a few weeks? Months? You know I'd wait forever."

He kissed her soundly. "I love you."

"I love you, too."

Then a sly smile crept across his face. He let go of her, but slid his hands down her arms until he grasped her hands. He pulled her toward the other side of the grandfather tree, making her laugh.

"We're going to be late to dinner," she chided.

"We'll blame it on... something..."

Once they were behind the tree, their giggles and moans filled the air.

CHAPTER 42

"Zee! Help me!"

Zawn bolted straight up in bed, sweating. She glanced around, looking for Gwendin, thinking he was in the hut. Then her stomach dropped when she realized he wasn't there.

However, the urge to run overwhelmed her.

She had to go.

Now.

She only bothered to dress in her tunic and pants, forgetting her boots. She grabbed her weapons and ran, sprinting out of the kith and down the road without recognizing anything or anyone. She ran as fast as she could, which felt as slow as morning dew dripping from a blade of grass.

She burst out of the woods onto the manicured surrounds of the castle… only to find the west side of the castle burning.

She unsheathed her haladie, then bolted through the battered gates into the outer courtyard. She dashed across the distance, then made short work of the inner courtyard. Battles were happening everywhere, bodies strewn throughout and screaming filled the air. She avoided each nightmare to make her way up the entry steps, past the throne room, and up the stairwell to the private bedchambers. She knew she had to go there. She didn't know how she knew where to go, or understood why, but she ran unerringly without question.

Whatever was guiding her took her into a vast hallway that led to different bedchambers. She caught sight of a familiar shape sprawled on the floor, in his theurgist slacks and tunic. However, the clothing wasn't only white. Blotches of red dyed the side of the cloth…

"Gwen!" she cried, rushing to his side.

She collapsed onto her knees, hands searching, trying to discern the extent of his wounds. She pulled up his tunic to find a ghastly gash running along his stomach. Blood gushed freely and she tried to staunch it with her hands and his shirt. His life drenched her hands, warming and staining them simultaneously.

The feel of her pressing down made him groan, in both agony and surprise. His eyelids flashed open and Gwendin grabbed onto her arm, gasping. "You came."

"You called."

"I got a f-f-few…" and he waved a limp hand toward the bodies nearby.

"You didn't need to be brave, my love," she responded, choking back her tears.

Gurgling escaped from his throat, a vain attempt to clear it. "Save… the baby."

"Gwen, no, I have to save you!"

"Too late f-f-f-or me," he wheezed, fumbling to place the dagger she gifted him back into her hand. "Save the baby." Then his eyelids grew heavy.

She cupped his face, trying to bring his attention back to her. "No Gwen, please, no, don't leave me."

His eyelids fluttered open again, those beautiful hickory brown eyes dark with pain as they searched her hazel ones. Somehow, there was a strength in his voice as he promised, "I will never be gone from your side." Reaching up with a bloody hand, he touched her ear. "I love you, Zee."

Shaking, she caressed one of his ears in return. "I love you, Gwen."

His eyes lost focus. She moved her hands back to his wound, trying again to save him. His blood stained her hands with its warm, thick stickiness. She could feel him trembling in pain, the spasms causing his breathing to shudder with each exhalation. The labored breathing punctuated the faint cacophony around them, like repetitive fatal blows in her chest. Tears ran down the side of his face and his eyes darkened, his pupils dilating to the point where his irises disappeared.

"Please, no, Gwen!" she sobbed.

Molten hot tears ran down her face as she felt his warm blood turning cold underneath her hands. She whispered pleas, prayers to whoever listened to stop him from leaving her. Her chest felt like it was sinking in, tightening and hardening to the point she struggled for her own breath. Pain burst through her as the vice squeezing her heart tightened. The thought of him leaving her, alone, helpless, abandoned. Her eyesight tunneled and she felt like passing out.

His last breath escaped him.

"No, no, no, no…"

That final exhalation was the only thing she could hear through all of the bedlam.

Her ears rang with that last rattle.

Then it faded and the sounds of the destruction around her blasted her senses again. Metal clashing, screams ricocheting, fire devouring.

Suddenly, through the chaos, she heard a familiar sound. A man stomping up behind her, lifting his axe for a death blow. All emotion fled and Zawn spun, swinging out her haladie and gutting him as his armor lifted up and exposed his belly. He staggered and fell backwards, the only thing catching her eye was the insignia on his shoulders. A tower surrounded in flames.

Zawn stood, turning her attention to the royal bedchambers.

~   ~   ~

A curved blade pierced the invader who stood over the fatally wounded king. The attacker gagged on his own blood as his executioner withdrew her sword. The man was shoved to the side, away from the furniture and the man bleeding on the floor. The King laid there, eyes wide in surprise, while his blood continued to stain the massive rug in a torrent. His breath rasped, not quite the death rattle she was familiar with, but it was close.

"Protect… my child…" he begged, softly.

"Why should I?" Zawn demanded, covered in blood as if it were ritual paint.

"Do not… let suffer… for the sins of… ignor…ant father…"

She scoffed, staring down at the man who led such brutal attacks on her people in the early days of his reign. Who had trapped the gargoyles into slavery. The man who had hated all that wasn't human.

"Only…" Elixin gurgled, "baby!"

"Maybe it is best to let your bloodline end."

The King rolled his head toward the bassinet, tears streaming down his cheeks. Zawn walked over, finding the baby unconscious. She could tell the infant had been crying based on the red cheeks and wet face, but he must have cried himself to sleep. Her heart shook for a moment, as his innocence hit her. She told herself that he was a prince, the son of the man that had put her people through so much hell.

Elixin reached helplessly for the crib, knocking his hand against the leg. The jolt startled the baby, making him cry loudly. As tears burst from his eyes and his terrified screams filled the room, he looked so vulnerable. Suddenly, she heard Gwen's voice in her head. Asking her to save the baby, a reminder that she was better than the man who laid dying on the floor. That the child was not guilty of his father's atrocities.

Her heart would never forgive her if she gave into the anger that tried to blind her. She sheathed her weapon, glancing over at the King. Then the man took his last breath, the rattling of his exhalation all too familiar.

Voices grew louder as more invaders moved closer…

~   ~   ~

Glass from the bedroom and nursery exploded out into the inner courtyard. Flames flashed and licked the window panes and curtains. The entire floor of private chambers became engulfed, causing shouts and panic from the household staff and the invaders.

The Queen and Princess, both held captive in the outer courtyard, screamed. They screamed for the King, who they knew had rushed in to rescue his son.

They screamed for the Prince, who they knew laid in a crib in the very nursery that now burned.

Their anguished sounds filled the area but it was all futile.

~   ~   ~

But out of everyone's sight flashed a corner of a white cloak as someone escaped the inferno and the castle grounds.

CHAPTER 43

Leaning against the door, so no one could come inside without permission, Taylor sighed hard. He had seen her rush back into the kith, wearing Gwen's cloak. He saw how the panic contorted her face and he followed her immediately. She almost slammed the door in his face but he caught it before it could impact. The panic turned into anguish then everything drained from her.

After she deposited her package on the bed and collapsed on the floor, she told him what had happened in a monotoned voice that left him speechless. Even the details of how she watched Gwen die and how she set the chemicals off in Gwen's apothecary to cause the explosion. It was as if she repeated some lesson from childhood, not describing the scene where she found her mate dying on the floor.

She either ran out of story or voice, he wasn't sure, but she fell silent. Zawn just sat on the floor, soot and blood still covering her. Gwendin's white theurgist cloak, singed and stained with the same debris, laid sadly next to her.

On her bed laid her prize.

The baby fussed, stretching against the ash-stained blankets wrapped around his small body. Zawn stared at the writhing human, pale with worry. Did she make a mistake? Should she have left the child behind? Her mind raced with questions and with ideas but wouldn't form a coherent thought. What was she going to do?

"How are you going to explain this?" Tay asked, trying to bring her back around. "No one has seen you pregnant, you can't pretend that you just gave birth overnight."

"I can if I lie," she responded, finally snapping out of her trance. "Tell everyone that Gwen hid my pregnancy with a glamour. We hid the birth because we didn't know what else to do. And because of his death, I have no recourse but to raise our child in the kith."

"Might be able to get away with that."

"Seeing that we're not allowed to breed, us hiding it with magic would be the sensible thing to do. And the timing fits with my illness a few months ago. The symptoms appeared to be some sort of morning sickness, remember?"

"What will you do as he grows up?"

"It's safer to lie to him just like I will lie to everyone else. I don't really have a choice."

"The Queen and the princess are alive, based on our spies' intel anyway."

"Yes, but when I got there, they were ransacking the entire castle as if they were making sure that no male in that family survived." Zawn shook her head in disgust. "Crenast marries Queen Kemberly, he secures the throne. That's why he killed his own brother. And he can marry off his niece Valena to secure any treaties he wishes."

"So the prince has to stay dead. That's why you burned the nursery."

"No one will be the wiser. I hope." She rubbed her face, smearing ash and blood. "It really didn't take much, the place was already burning and there were plenty of flammable items in Gwendin's…" and her voice faltered for a moment, "apothecary."

"And no one will think to look here because no one saw you?"

"Why would an elf be at the castle to begin with? We have deniability even if I was seen, but I doubt my presence registered with anyone. The only ones who recognized me are dead and burned. Hopefully this brother of the King will be too busy dealing with the fallout of his coup to notice us and our own drama."

Taylor watched his friend and leader carefully, realizing that even as the baby fussed, she didn't move to comfort him. She stared at him like it was a plague instead of a baby.

"You'll need stuff for the baby."

"I don't even know where to start."

"We'll start with the basics: a crib, clothes, food. We still have Minee's crib. I know Chae will happily give that to you. But we have no clothes left, we gave those to the new mothers weeks ago. As for food… I will have Chae bring milk and help you."

"Thank you, Taylor. I wish I didn't have to bring you into this. I am sorry to burden you with my… sin."

"At least this way, you have a partner in crime. I will admit to knowing your deceit and plans and have your back." He watched as the indecision and guilt clawed at her. "You did the right thing, Zawn. And in doing so, you showed that elf-kind are better than mankind."

"But at what cost?"

"Sleepless nights, dirty diapers, and a lifetime of worry." He stared at her, realizing that even with her reciting the events of the day, she hadn't absorbed everything. "Have you even mourned yet? For Gwendin?"

"Everything happened so fast…" her voice faded away into a whisper, "I can't feel anything right now."

Feeling helpless, Taylor turned toward the door. "I will go retrieve Chae."

"Thank you, my friend."

~   ~   ~

Chaelene entered the cabin as secretly as possible, with a large duffel hanging off of her shoulder. She found the baby fussing and wiggling on the bed while Zawn absent-mindedly had remained sitting on the floor. Taylor had warned her that Zawn was out of it and to handle her with care but also with surety. Zawn needed their strength if she was going to make it through the night.

"Taylor will bring the crib in a little bit," Chaelene informed her, but Zawn didn't move. "Zawnie, you must clean up before touching that baby again. Go, bathe. I will look after this darling wiggly worm."

Zawn blinked and nodded, then stood up slowly. She made her way into the bathing room, starting the water and stripping off her stained clothing. She climbed into the tub, the water not very deep, but enough so she turned off the faucet. She started cleaning off the charcoal and red. She felt like the wheel that was pushed by water to make the grinder move. Everything felt forced, mechanical.

But she cleaned up, noticing that she had a wound along her forearm and her feet were damaged from running on the gravel. After she got out of the tub, she caught herself watching the bloody water swirl, hypnotically, down the drain. She shook her head, snapping herself out of the darkness that tried to devour her. She dried and treated her wounds properly, just like Gwen taught her, then wrapped her arm to stop any more bleeding and put on socks to protect her tender feet. Then she slipped on a sleeping dress and dried her hair halfheartedly before pulling it up and back.

She returned to the main room of the cabin. She watched as Chae finished wiping the baby down and changing his diaper. Her friend made silly sounds, causing the baby boy to giggle. The infant looked over when he caught movement in his periphery, seeing Zawn and cooing at her. Zawn didn't move, making Chae grab her arm and drag her toward the bed. She pushed down on Zawn's shoulders, until she was sitting next to the baby. When Zawn didn't reach for him, Chae scoffed, picked up the baby and forced him into Zawn's arms.

"You cannot say he is yours if you won't hold him. If you won't look at him. If you won't love him. Now, look at that. He is completely taken by you."

The baby stared up at her, his wide dark brown eyes taking in her features as if memorizing her. Zawn trembled as she held the infant, unsure if she could ever love a human. Then she again heard Gwen's voice, reminding her that she loved him, a human, more than words could ever describe. And if she were to pretend that this child was theirs, she would have to love the baby.

Theirs. Their child.

After all of their hopes of starting a new life together, to have a family of their own, every dream they shared had burnt to ash in a single night. She had no mate, no partner to help her. Gwen wouldn't be there at her side, helping her with her new responsibility. Gwen was dead, gone from her forever. The realizations ripped a larger hole in her heart.

Tears blurred her vision and she started sobbing.

Chae sat down on the bed, arms wrapping tightly around Zawn. The sounds that came from her were unlike anything ever heard before. Chae whispered something as she hugged her grieving friend, helpless to relieve her of the pain that now tore through every muscle, vein and bone.

Taylor entered a little louder than he meant to with the crib, banging it against the door frame, to find his mate comforting Zawn. He set down the crib on one side of the bed, then stared down at his sobbing friend. He lowered himself onto the bed on her other side and wrapped one arm around both women and the other around the baby.

~   ~   ~

Zawn had collapsed after her tears ran out. She was asleep on her side, facing the crib, while the baby rested in Chae's arms. Taylor adjusted the height of the crib quietly, making sure not to disturb Zawn or the baby. It was just high enough for Zawn to see into it as she laid on the bed and she could reach in easily. He kneeled and stared at his friend for a few moments, then stood and approached his mate as she rocked the baby in her arms. He watched the baby sleep, his frown communicating the depth of his concerns.

"I'll stay with them for the rest of the night," Chaelene whispered. "He'll probably get hungry soon and she will need help."

"Are you sure?"

"Yes, go home. Help Momma with the kids."

He kissed her gently. "Good night, my love."

"Good night, my heart."

He glanced over at his sleeping friend again, then headed out. Once the door closed, Zawn inhaled deeply and opened her eyes, obviously hearing the exchange.

"You don't have to stay," Zawn said, her voice soft and gravelly.

"Oh yes I do," Chalene responded. "He can fight the battle for bedtime tonight. I've done it enough this month."

The baby stirred and started to cry. Chae immediately started bouncing him slightly. But that didn't appease him. "Now he's hungry. Come, sit up. Do you know if he was breastfed?"

"No, but I think I saw bottles like yours in the room."

"Then I'd assume she didn't nurse him. Either couldn't or wouldn't. He probably was used to nannies and the like. That should make this easy for us. As for milk, well, Naji produces more than she needs and shares with another who cannot produce any milk. I'm sure she can continue to help the both of you. She had some saved back, so I brought enough to get us through the night.

I stacked them into your chill box when you got quiet."

Chae transferred the baby back to Zawn's arms, who cradled him as carefully as she could. Her friend warmed a bottle over the fire, then wrapped the top with a fake nipple. She tested the liquid on her wrist first, smiled, then handed the bottle to Zawn.

"Do you remember feeding Minee? Same thing, be gentle and let him figure it out first."

The baby took to the bottle quickly, his little fingers moving as he nursed. His eyelids grew heavy after a while, making Zawn chuckle.

"Did I hear a laugh?" Chae inquired, teasing.

"He's cute for a human," Zawn admitted, with a shrug.

"He's a baby, he's cute no matter his species. We'll get him full and he should sleep for a while. Then we can get some sleep as well."

The baby started slowing his suckle, then he stopped. Zawn moved the almost empty bottle and he didn't react so she handed it over to Chae. The infant gave a big sigh, fingers no longer fidgeting. He pulled his arms in, making himself comfortable in her embrace, and he passed out with a full belly.

"Maybe I should give you to someone else," she whispered, mostly to herself.

Even with her back turned, her friend heard her. "Why?" Chae demanded, spinning around quickly.

"I'm not a mother. I have no instinct. I don't know how to do any of this. The only thing I've raised are goats. I'm a warrior, that's all I am good at."

"You are also incapable of giving up control. Who could you trust with this precious thing?"

"You?"

"I already have three and Taylor has been told in no uncertain terms, no more."

"Maybe he'd be better off with a human family."

Chae stared at her friend. "Do you really think you cannot care for this child?"

"I can barely take care of myself, Chae. Let alone the kith. How can I take care of baby, too?"

"Maybe this baby will change that. Or is that what you are afraid of?"

"No. I'm afraid I won't be able to," Zawn admitted, running a gentle finger over one of his tiny hands. "Not even for this baby."

Her friend watched her for a moment. "You changed for Gwendin."

Hearing his name choked her up. "Did I?"

"I watched you make adjustments to incorporate him into your life, as well as his lifestyle. He was an influence, I think, for you to step up to Medruano. You changed from someone who did what they were told, and broke as many rules as you could when those who gave orders weren't looking, to someone who fashions fair and just rules for all of us." Chae crossed the room and placed warm hands on Zawn's shoulders, making her look up. "You have changed before. You can change again. I see the look in your eyes, Zawnie, you see this child for what he is." The baby chirped in his sleep. "An innocent for you to protect. Not a human, not a prince, but your ward. Why else would you snatch him away from that place? Once you accept that, I know you will protect him with your very life. And you will make the necessary changes to do so. Because there is no one else who can do it for you. Now, lay him down in the crib. Let's get some rest."

~   ~   ~

She listened as Chae snored. Her friend was in a deep sleep, which made Zawn jealous. She had woken up after a short nap and now struggled with falling back to sleep. Then she heard something from the crib, making her raise up onto her arm. The baby was awake, cooing to himself and staring up toward the ceiling. She followed his eyes and realized he could see the night sky through her skylight. She looked back down at him and realized he had the same habit as Gwendin, who loved staring at the stars when they ate dinner and tell her tales of their creations.

She knew that she would share those tales with this baby. It would be a bedtime tradition, she decided, finally sitting up. The baby glanced up at her and giggled, then his eyes returned to the sky above. She knew she would never call him his human name. Watching him, she knew he would have an elven name, with a proper full name that would honor him, his family, and his kith. And his fascination with the sky even helped her formulate that name.

Suddenly, he made a weird facial expression just before the smell hit her.

She grimaced at the stench as the baby started to cry. Zawn nudged Chaelene awake, who in turn sighed and laughed.

"What goes in, must come out. Time for the diaper lesson."

They both got out of bed and Zawn picked up the crying baby. Chae waved her into the bathing room while she pulled a towel, folded it, and laid it on the counter. Zawn laid the baby on top of it, then started to unwrap him after Chaelene showed her how to unfasten the diaper. Before Zawn could move the diaper, Chaelene told her to wait. Then Chaelene grabbed a rag and laid it over the front of the diaper.

"Boys like to pee on you," she warned, with a chuckle. "Chaen got me once, the brat."

They maneuvered the diaper off without getting hit in the face with urine, even though the baby tried. Once it was safe to remove the rag, Chaelene gave instructions on how to clean the baby to avoid skin issues and lingering smells.

"We'll bathe him tomorrow, but for now just a wipe down will do."

"Do I need anything special for that?"

Chae smiled, proudly. "Good question. Yes, we will need to find a soap that won't bother his sensitive skin. He won't tolerate ours because it is a coarse soap. I will inquire in the human village when I go trade tomorrow, er, today. I know someone who will not ask too many questions. Once we figure it out, we'll make our own. Now that he's cleaned and changed, we'll give him another bottle."

"How often will he eat?"

"Probably every two to three hours. When they were babies, Chaen and Talor ate every two. Right now, Minee is every three, but she is eating more smashed food than milk. But, well, each baby is different."

Zawn watched as the infant rolled his head, trying to keep track of who was speaking. There was no fear, mostly curiosity. "He's awfully accepting of us. He has to know we don't look or sound like the people before."

"Maybe he can tell that we actually care for him. He is quite aware for his age."

"Gwen said he came into this world ready to take it on."

Her friend glanced between her and the baby. "He acts like he recognizes you. He has the same look Minee had when she heard your voice but couldn't see you."

"And yet I've never met him." As Zawn started to wrap the clean diaper around the baby's lower half, she noticed something on his thigh. "They branded him," Zawn whispered, her face crumbling. "What cruelty."

"Guess they have to make sure it's the right baby?" Her friend shook her head sadly. "Can't tell which baby is yours without marking them. Humans continue to disgust me." She watched Zawn's face as she finished adjusting the new diaper. "If this is how they treat their babies, he will have a better life with you. With us."

"Can you fix the bottle while I finish up here?"

"Of course."

As her friend busied herself with the bottle, Zawn finished securing the diaper and wrapping up the baby in the warm blanket. He smiled up at her, wiggling as if he could escape. Then she lifted him up into her arms, bringing him closer. He relaxed immediately and gazed up at her with those big brown eyes, as if she were the only person in the world.

"You poor darling. She's right, I'm afraid. You are stuck with me. And I am so sorry for that. You deserve better."

He fussed, struggling to get one arm free. She helped him get it out of her masterful wrap and he reached up and touched her lips with his uncoordinated fingers. She furrowed her eyebrows in confusion, then grasped his fingers gently and kissed them. That gentle touch, lips to fingers, made his smile widen.

"I promise to care for you, raise you, protect you, until my very last breath."

He sighed, settling in her arms more comfortably.

"Zawnie, it's ready," Chae called from the other room.

The baby's eyes got wider and he excitedly wiggled.

"Oh, you know that means dinner, eh? Come then, let's get you fed so I can get some sleep."

CHAPTER 44

Throughout the night, Zawn grew comfortable feeding the baby and changing his diaper, as well as holding him. After the last round, she had propped herself up on the bed and dozed off with the infant laying on her chest. His little head seemed cozy between her breasts, a delicate ear listening to her strong heartbeat. She secured her arms in a way to stop him sliding off and, in true Zawn fashion, she didn't move after her eyes closed.

That morning, as the two slept, Chaelene left to wake her own children and ready them for their day. When she succeeded in getting them and Taylor off in the right direction, she returned to check in on Zawn. The leader appeared quite harried, which was not since she had decided to announce the baby's arrival to the kith.

"I've fed him. I changed him. But he keeps crying every time I put him down. I can't get anything done if I'm holding him all the time."

"I told you not to hold him all night." Chae dug into her overnight bag then pulled out a mass of material. "Here, try this. Saved me with Minee until she got bigger."

They laid the fussing baby on the bed, Zawn cooing and making noises in an attempt to reassure him. Chae wrapped the loops of material around Zawn's shoulder and torso, then tucked the baby boy inside. He curled up in the sling, the only thing visible was the top of his hairy head. His complaints stopped, apparently the sound and feel of her heartbeat against his cheek reassuring him immediately.

"Now you can have him with you but not have your hands tied up."

"I can't wear my armor with this thing on."

"Do you think you'll need your armor every day?"

Zawn groused then demanded, exasperated, "How did you do this with three children?"

"I am ill in the head, apparently," Chaelene replied, her curt tone making her friend blush. "I had the help of Taylor and my mother. That was the only way I could do it. I was not alone." She finished fixing the sling, running a kind hand along the baby's back which made him sigh. "You are not alone, either, Zawnie. We are here to help you." She folded her arms over her chest. "But we need to know what to call him. You are about to introduce him to our kithlin, but does he even have a name?"

"Rynan," she answered. "Rynan, heir to the Haley family, our stargazer."

Chae looked at her curiously.

"Gwendin's father was named Rynauron. It is a nod to his family while Haley is a nod to mine."

"That is a beautiful name."

"Are you ready?" Taylor asked as he entered. "They are waiting."

She felt her nerves fray suddenly, then responded, "Wish me the guidance of my ancestors."

"I wish you the guidance of the entire kith's ancestors," Taylor retorted, straightening his shoulders. "But know you have our support. Whatever you need."

~   ~   ~

Zawn stood in the center of the gathered kithlin, trying to keep herself from breaking apart completely. She knew she would have to say the words, the words that made everything that had happened true. Once she said them, there was no going back. It took every last ounce of strength in her to speak without her voice quivering.

"As some of you may already know, Elixin has been deposed by his own brother, Crenast of Garadni. We don't know the new King's intentions towards us. We must be wary and must be aware."

Members of her kith nodded understanding.

"During the attack, our beloved Gwendin was killed."

Everyone in the crowd gasped, murmured, and some sobbed. The sorrowful sounds tested her resolve, making her swallow hard against the grief that tried to overtake her.

"He was my mate. And the fact that you accepted him as a friend of our kith meant more to him than you could ever understand. He had hoped to leave the College of Theurgy and be our theurgist and kithlin till the end of his days. He never got the chance to ask that of us, but I hope that posthumously, we would grant him that. And grant our child a place among us as well."

Confused exclamations rose from the crowd.

Zawn inhaled hard, then opened the sling enough to show the sleeping baby. "We had hoped to present him together, asking that you accept our family. We feared many things, from possibly miscarrying to another attempt on my life, so we hid the pregnancy with a glamour. But now, with him gone, I am alone with a child that will never know his father."

"That is an abomination," someone responded, his voice strangled with anger.

Instinctively, Zawn unsheathed her haladie, blocking the blade screaming toward her. Vergun looked startled, apparently not expecting her to react that fast. She pushed him back, wrapping her free arm around her infant, and securing her stance. She smirked, then parried straight on. Vergun stumbled backward and hit the ground, his sword clattering away. Zawn stood over him, placing one tip of her blade under his chin.

"Do you revoke your challenge, Vergun?"

"I revoke my challenge," he responded, voice quivering.

"Good, I would hate to kill you over this. You are too good a friend and metal worker. Get up." She stepped back, keeping her blade at her side while her other hand continued to hold Rynan against her in his sling. She glanced around the kith square, feeling her anger flushing her cheeks. "Anyone else want to challenge me? I'm quite in the mood to thrash a few more ignorant fools, even with a baby strapped to my chest."

"I challenge you," another voice boomed from behind.

Zawn turned to find Merded, the grandson of the man who she had bested to take the mantel of leader. His challenge was unsurprising. She measured him with a quick look over. He was taller than her and more muscular than any other man in their kith. His broadsword eclipsed her meager blade and his hatred for her in his eyes outmatched even his grandfather's.

"Fine." She turned to Taylor, dipping open the sling. "Hold my baby."

Taylor reached in and cradled the fussing infant as Zawn turned her attention back to Merded.

"I thought you could fight with a baby strapped to you?" reproached her challenger.

"I don't want him to be a distraction," then she raised her eyebrow, "for you."

Her challenger growled, offended.

"Do you have any affairs to put in order first?" she inquired, her snide tone making his eyes narrow.

"You're the only thing that must be put in order."

Her laughter in response held a darkness that worried her friends but it served only as fuel for Merded.

Without a second thought, he swung his broadsword. She hopped back, the tip barely missing her chin. She raised an eyebrow, then twirled her haladie. He slashed at her again, causing her to dance around the blade. Another close encounter from his broadsword and she spun away with ease. Her steps brought her to his left side and she kicked, landing a blow on his ass. Startled, he jumped away and growled at her in anger.

She wouldn't admit that she was toying with him mostly out of exhaustion and anger. But after losing her love, this pissant meant nothing to her. Embarrassing him seemed to be the only way she could get her point across to him and all the others that questioned her authority.

She waited for his next move. She had watched him spar long enough to know his favorite move: a crisscross swing then an undercut. Inwardly, she hoped he would be that predictable... but she'd had opponents change habits at the last minute.

Frustration got the best of him and he attacked. He swung his sword in a crisscross pattern then brought it up in an undercut to behead her. Instead of reacting in defense, which would have fatally driven her into his move, she played offense and slammed her haladie onto the edge of his blade before it got any higher than her hip. With the curve of her blade holding one side of his blade, she secured the other side with her gauntlet covered arm. A quick twist and the blade lurched from his grasp and she tossed it aside. Startled, Merded stood frozen and Zawn kicked him in the stomach then face, sending him flying backwards.

The former leader's grandson laid on the ground, groaning in pain. Zawn kept her distance, spinning her haladie, trying to decide if she wanted to finish him off. After all, he would continue to come after her as long as he lived. Then she heard Rynan cry, breaking through her deliberation. The thought of killing another's child brought her back to herself. She had to choose mercy, especially when it came to her own people. It was not an option that Medruano ever considered. And in that regard, she knew she was better than him.

"Do you revoke your challenge, Merded?"

"I revoke my challenge," Merded stuttered, the pain keeping him down on the ground.

"Good. Anyone else?"

Silence was the response.

She sheathed her blade and retrieved Rynan, who quieted down once she held him in her arms. She lifted him high enough so all could see the infant. "You all loved Gwendin, I know you did. I saw it on your faces every time he visited. You may disagree with my choices, and they may come back to haunt me later, but I am left to raise this baby on my own while leading you the same way I have for the last two years." She tried to meet every kithlin's eyes as she glanced among the group. "Look at us. Right now. We are flourishing as a kith and we have made ourselves an example to all other kiths that we can thrive without the help of men. We can fight amongst ourselves and fall into a spiral of destruction, or we can prove that we are better than that. Do not let your opinions of my personal life choices diminish the good we have done and the good that we will continue to do if we keep our heads."

"What are we to call this child?" Jheferin inquired, from his seat near the firepit.

The crowd looked over at him then back to Zawn.

"Rynan, heir of the Haley family, stargazer of the Whispering Hornbeam Kith."

"Then Zawn, *matriarch*," and the elder stressed that change in her status, "of the Haley family, daydreamer and leader of the Whispering Hornbeam Kith, we accept this child as our kithlin. And we will honor our fallen friend with his wish to be accepted into our kith. How shall we remember him?"

Zawn's lip quivered, having not thought that far. "Gwendin, patriarch of the Haley family... cherished one of the Whispering Hornbeam Kith."

"He will be entered into our texts as such." Jheferin blindly glanced around at the crowd that was torn by their grief, confusion, and adoration. "Unless there are other complaints?"

He was met with silence.

"We will recognize a day of grief for our fallen friend as well. Let us remember him fondly for his joy, his sense of humor, his willingness to help, and for his love for our leader."

Zawn tucked Rynan back into his sling, trying to hide her tears. "Yes, let us grieve for our friend."

CHAPTER 45

They wrapped flowers, limbs, and several types of leaves for the funerary before adorning it with the theurgist's stained cloak. They laid the effigy of Gwendin on the fire and let the flames devour each piece. Zawn stood at the head, baby strapped to her chest, with Taylor and Chaelene on either side. Saronin stepped forward to the foot of the effigy and began singing.

"Do not linger with us here/Time here is fleeting/When the time is right/We'll see each other again/On the other side of the canopy"

The song, known to all elves as the "Song of Farewell," took the last of Zawn's strength. She felt arms around her as she sobbed. Their support kept her on her feet while the warmth and gentle movements of Rynan kept her from completely collapsing emotionally.

"Lay down your weapons/And open up your heart/Finish your journey/We'll see each other again/On the other side of the canopy"

More voices joined Saronin's, the kith filling with sorrowful words but loving sounds.

"You may have left our side/But your memory will never fade/Embrace your time of rest/We'll see each other again/On the other side of the canopy"

A fitting farewell to the man who lived, loved, and walked among elves.

CHAPTER 46

Before he approached Zawn a few days later, he waited until she walked from her home to her work hut. Hesitantly, he knocked on the door, entering only when she gave him verbal permission. He noticed that her eyes widened when he entered. Merded sat down when she gestured to the chair on the other side of her desk, while her other hand cradled the baby in the sling against her chest.

Merded took a deep breath after swallowing hard. "I cannot follow you any longer. It was hard to do before because you killed my grandfather. Fairly yes, but that does not make it easier. And now…" His words began to fail him.

"What do you wish to do then?"

"I have a cousin who matched into the Whistling Cedar Kith. I would like to take my mother and appeal to their leader, to ask if they would allow us to join their kith."

"Taikin will accept you and your mother."

Merded stammered in surprise. "You already asked?"

"The moment I became leader, I knew not everyone would follow me," she admitted with an honesty that made him finally meet her eyes. "But I didn't want anyone left to the wilds. So, I reached out to Taikin and he is amenable. He is like me, wants elves to be with elves and to feel comfortable with their fellows. Even if it means leaving one kith for another."

"And you will let us go freely?" he asked, carefully.

"Why wouldn't I?"

"I challenged you."

"And lost," she retorted. Then she watched him for a moment, wondering if there was regret in his voice. "It's a right we all have, even if we sometimes challenge each other out of anger or revenge. I was surprised it had taken you so long."

"The good outweighed the bad," he replied, hands holding onto the other wrist's gauntlets. "You helped the kith get back onto its feet. You… changed not just lives but perspectives. I don't think I could have ever done that. I didn't know how to lead, let alone problem solve."

"Until now."

"No, I-I didn't challenge you for the job, just out of … I know I can never lead this kith and I can never make up for the dishonor my family has brought to this kith."

"Dishonor? How? By challenging me? Or putting up with me?"

"By betraying it. My grandfather. He… I found something when we were packing up."

He handed over a ripped sheet of paper, something that had been torn out of a book. It had amounts on it with dates. And a name.

"He paid Elixin to stay in power. Bribed him to leave us be so he could keep his leadership. And on the back… I think it's a list of kithlin he planned to sell to the castle, instead of paying coin."

Zawn stared at the piece of paper, the ink fading like a ghost in the shadows. She noticed that not only was it torn from a book, it also appeared to have singe marks on one of the edges. It had gotten near a fire but survived the attempt to destroy it.

"Do you agree with this tactic?" she asked, keeping her voice even.

Merded's face paled. "Absolutely not, Leader Haley. This is… disgraceful."

"Then the sin is not yours," she responded, laying the piece of paper on the desk. "Your grandfather paid the price for his greed. As long as you do not repeat his crimes, you will regain your family's honor."

"I will take steps every day to earn it back."

"I have faith that you will succeed in that endeavor."

Merded sat there, thinking hard before adding, "I do not know who poisoned you. No one approached me or my mother about the plan. But I believe it was agents from the Mehdehran castle, because you cut off their funding the moment you became leader."

"That I do not doubt. I gained more enemies than allies after my… promotion. Now, I will send a letter to Taikin and let him know of your request. And I wish you the best, Merded, in your endeavors and in your future. I hope you find peace and a place with Taikin's kith that is both satisfying and honorable."

"Thank you, Leader Haley."

~   ~   ~

The day had been a long one. After her conversation with Merded, Zawn had sent a letter to Taikin regarding his wish and the other kith leader's approval was quick. They agreed on a date and Zawn traveled with Merded and his mother to the Whistling Cedar Kith. When they arrived, Taikin graciously welcomed them and the kith helped their new kithlin settle in.

With Merded and his mother left in the good hands of their new kithlin, Taikin and Zawn spent some time together privately, discussing what had happened at the Mehdehran castle and Gwendin's death.

"I am sorry for your loss, Zawnie. I know you loved him greatly."

"It is a heavy loss, my friend. I'm struggling with it and… we… That's um not the only thing. I um… we have a child."

Taikin stared at her, face gone slack and drained of color. She worried over his expression until he grabbed her into a tight hug. She felt his surprised laughter rumble in his chest before it burst from his lips. She appreciated his affection and joy at the addition to her family even though he grieved for her loss of Gwen.

"What are we to call him?"

"Rynan, our stargazer."

"Who does he look… I mean…"

"He looks like his father," she answered, with a chuckle. "Nothing much we can do about that."

"Oh Zawnie… anything you need. Anything. Tell me and I will provide it."

"Thank you, Taikin. I mean that."

The call for lunch interrupted them. They released each other, sad smiles shared between them, then they rejoined his kithlin. After lunch, as she readied to leave, Taikin again pulled her aside. The smirk on his face warned her immediately that he had decided on his price for all of his previous help and rehoming Merded and his mother.

"What do you want?" she demanded, raising a suspicious eyebrow.

Taikin chuckled. "Who me? Asking for something in return? Ah, you know me well."

"Spit it out, I've a long walk home."

"You could stay the night. Start the negotiation fresh in the morning."

"I've a baby now, got to get home."

He groused, having already forgotten about her new responsibility. "Fine. I have a young elf by the name of Averell, who I'd like to spend time with you, in your kith. I want him to learn under your tutelage because of everything you have achieved. I have high hopes to train him to become leader one day, but…"

"What is his caste?"

"Warrior."

She rolled her eyes. "And so was mine."

"I did think that something in common would make the process easier. But I want him to experience different leadership styles. We know how I work but I am old and set in my ways. He needs to be able to adapt to different things, not just do the same things I've done. He should learn from someone who is younger, newer to the job…"

"And who's kith has been through different struggles than yours?" Even though she was frowning at him, she had to admit that his request was fair. She almost wished she had a similar option. "I can agree to having him stay with us for a while. I'll write to you when things have settled down, so I can make sure I have time to spend with him."

"Thank you, Leader Haley."

She grimaced. "It's still odd to hear that come from you."

"Ah, but it feels right to say it," Taikin responded, clasping her arm in friendship. "Safe journey back, my friend."

With that, Zawn headed back to her kith, thinking of everything she would need to accomplish in preparation for Averell's arrival. By the time she arrived home, she retrieved an excited Rynan and readied for bedtime.

Exhausted, Zawn finally fell asleep when Rynan passed out after his bottle. When she opened her eyes again, she saw Gwendin laying there beside her, on his side too and facing her. She gasped at the sight of him. He looked just like all the other nights they shared together, not like the last time she saw him. She searched his eyes in disbelief then reached out and touched his cheek, which made him smile.

"Gwen? No, you can't be here. You're dead."

"Doesn't mean you can't dream of me."

She sniffled. "I miss you."

"I'm always here." And he reached out and laid his hand against her heart. "I will always be here."

"It's not the same and you know it."

"Death isn't a cruel deity, Zee. She let me stay just long enough to see you again. She protected us as long as she could from the fight so we could say goodbye."

"I'm not angry with her. She's not the one who took your life."

"You're right, she didn't. But the man you killed afterwards, the one with the King? He did. You avenged me, my love." He caressed her ear tenderly. "I wish I had one more night with you."

"I wish we had a lifetime."

"We will see each other in the next life, I promise you, Zawn, matriarch of the Haley family, daydreamer and leader of the Whispering Hornbeam Kith. My love, my mate, my heart, my wife. Mother of Rynan, our stargazer." Then he leaned forward, gently kissing her before leaning his forehead against hers. "Remember, he may not be ours but he is our legacy."

She woke up with a start and once she realized he wasn't there, that it was really all a dream, she began to sob.

CHAPTER 47

She didn't know what made her more miserable, the baby waking up every other hour to be fed and have his diaper changed or the lack of sleep that came with it. Chae helped where she could, but she had three of her own, her mother, and Taylor to take care of. She didn't need to keep running to Zawn's aid every time there was an issue. Chae had been right that Zawn needed to change in order to raise the baby. The first thing she had to do was figure out a schedule where she could get some rest and still function during the day.

She wasn't succeeding as quickly as she had hoped.

~   ~   ~

One morning, with Rynan in Meagan's care, Zawn along with Chaelene and Taylor were clearing out some of the empty huts and determining which one would fit Averell's needs when Taylor stopped what he was doing.

He turned toward the road, "Zawnie, incoming," Taylor warned.

Zawn exited the hut to see massive creatures, limping or slowly walking into the center of the kith. Two of her sentries were leading them, trying to help them but the dark beings were too big for them to manage. Taylor and the other larger men joined in helping them.

"Nicholaus? Marassa?" Zawn rushed to the gargoyles, who were obviously injured. "What happened?"

"Crenast banished us after we surrendered," Nicholaus answered, softly, as if to protect the others from hearing their dilemma. "He said he had his army, he didn't need freaks like us. We didn't know what to do. We've spent days just…" His voice trailed off as he shook his head. "One of your sentries saw us, brought us here. We have nowhere to go."

"You are welcome here," she responded, in a low voice, then added, loud enough for the others to hear, "Come, everyone. Let's take a look at your wounds."

As they helped settle the gargoyles into their seats around the fire, Zawn called out for medical kits, water, and blankets. She noticed fresh blood streaking down from Nicholaus's heavy breastplate and called Taylor over to help her remove it. Taylor heaved it up and over the gargoyle's head then laid it against the bench. The wound was long and deep, worrying Zawn.

"We won't be able to stay for long," Nicholaus continued in his quiet voice. "We belong to the stone, we cannot survive without it."

"I know. But for now, you have shelter here. I trust my sentries not to be followed but castle spies are always on the move. We'll need to keep you hidden, just in case. We'll get you into this hut here once we're done. You need to sleep and eat."

Mareah, who overheard them as she sat next to Nicholaus, sobbed. "But where will we go?" she demanded, as Chae treated her torn wing. Nicholaus grabbed his mate's hand, trying to comfort her.

"I don't know, but we'll figure it out," Zawn replied, as she worked on cleaning the wound along Nicholaus's left side. "Maybe you can take to the cliffs around us, at least at night, and connect to the stone that way until we can resettle you." Then Zawn remembered a conversation from a few days ago. She looked over her shoulder, searching for Vergun. She saw him tending to the gash on Marassa's arm. "Vergun, how big was that cave?"

Vergun blinked, glancing around at the number of refugees in their care. "Big enough for a clan of gargoyles."

"We'll start there, then we'll find you a proper hold."

"Thank you," Nicholaus said softly.

"Now, stay still," Zawn ordered, "and let me get a better look at this gash."

As she moved to see his side better, she noticed a massive wound scarring up on his arm. She wisely said nothing, but made a note to keep an eye on it. She knew what had been there before. It was the mark of the curse Elixin had wielded. Now gone, they were finally free of it.

~   ~   ~

The next morning, Zawn strapped on her sling and cuddled Rynan inside. He had been fed well and his diaper changed before she even considering leaving her cabin. The air had a bit of chill to it, so she grabbed her cloak, tying it in the front and letting it fall over her shoulders to surround both her and the baby. She strode across the square and knocked on Merded's old hut. Marassa exited, looking exhausted. She closed the door behind her softly as if the others inside still slept.

"Did you get any rest?" Zawn asked, her voice soft.

"A little. It was hard not to be on high alert, even though we knew you all were guarding us. But the others have finally settled down enough to sleep."

"If you're still restless, we can check out those caves Vergun found last week."

"Maybe a walk will do me some good. But I think my bandage needs to be changed out."

"I can do that. Go sit by the fire, I'll get a kit."

Marassa waited patiently for Zawn to return with the medical kit. Zawn sat next to her, unwrapping the old bandage and assessing her wound. It didn't look like it had any infection, which relieved Zawn, but she still cleaned it carefully before slathering on the antibacterial salve and rewrapping it. As she moved, she noticed that Marassa had caught sight of something.

Marassa stared at her chest, her black eyes darker than Zawn thought possible. "A baby?"

"A son. Rynan."

"I didn't know," she responded, sadly. "He never let on."

"We had good reason to hide it."

"You did." Marassa couldn't take her eyes off of the hair that peeked out of the sling. "You never told me that you wanted children."

The elf shrugged, making the baby sigh. "You and I were quite young. I didn't really know what I wanted."

"We never told Elixin."

Zawn looked up, confused.

"When Nicholaus found out that the theurgist was coming here, I told him about what had happened. How I tried to pull you two apart. I asked that we keep his visits a secret. All of us agreed to not tell Elixin."

Zawn blinked her eyes a little fast, fighting back tears and unable to find words. She secured the clean bandage, then returned the remaining gauze and cream back into the kit. She caught a young man walking past and asked him to kindly return the kit to the healer's hut. He obliged with a smile and nods to both the elf and the gargoyle.

"Come," Zawn said, standing, "the caves are just down this trail."

~   ~   ~

The walk was refreshing for Zawn, who had been feeling cooped up with the baby, while Marassa seemed to relax as they moved farther into the thickening canopies. There was safety in the forest, for both of them, as they knew the humans were far enough away not to be a threat.

Zawn had to stop at a dead oak tree that had been struck by lightning, muttering the directions to herself, then she nodded and gestured for Marassa to follow her down the hidden path that laid behind the burnt wooden corpse. A few more strides and they found a small crack in the mountain that erupted from the forest. It looked like just another outcropping head on, but if one stepped enough to the side, the opening became apparent.

The two women walked inside, with Marassa glancing around and up toward the ceiling. The gargoyles would have to duck to enter, but the ceiling raised up high once they got past the opening. It widened in the middle, giving room for several people to mill around. It was also deep, narrowing slowly further in. In the darkness of the far back, stalactites hung from the ceiling, above the stalagmites that devoured their drippings to grow tall.

"Yes, this will do," the gargoyle murmured, mostly to herself. "We can stay hidden but also touch stone."

"You don't think it'll be too cold? We were thinking about turning this into a cold storage for large cuts of meat," Zawn explained, "until we could portion them out appropriately through the kith. But we're in no rush to do so since it is small game season."

Marassa chuckled. "We actually thrive in the cold. This will not bother us."

The gargoyle walked as far as she could before having to bend over, nodding and mumbling to herself. Zawn leaned against the wall near the opening, caressing Rynan's back which made him sigh contently.

"If you don't mind the cold, I might have a permanent solution for your people. There's a fortress that's been abandoned for a while now. It's high up, used as a strategic lookout before Mehdehra devoured Solata after the Purge. It's cold and it's difficult to get to if you have to walk. Think that might be a place you'd consider?"

"We don't need much, other than shelter and hunting grounds. It's how we survived before…" then Marassa fell silent.

Zawn tried to pretend that she didn't hear that part before Marassa quieted. "The surrounding forests are uninhabited and should provide enough prey. It's a midpoint between my kith and Taikin's. You'll have allies close by. We'll give it a look once you all have healed a bit more."

"Thank you, for everything, Zawnie."

"It's no bother."

"No, I mean it. After what I put you through when we broke up and then with the theurgist, after everything Nicholaus said to you after our enslavement, you could have turned us all away. To be honest, we would have understood completely."

"Yet you approached my sentries with hope that I wouldn't."

Marassa seemed to pale at the realization that Zawn had been told the truth. "Irai said we had to try, what other options were left to us?"

Zawn glanced around the cave, listening as the wind whipped along the opening but not finding its chilly way inside. "We have all lost something in this coup. If we are to survive, we must count on each other. Who else can we turn to? We cannot count on the humans, since they are the culprits every time we suffer misery."

"You've changed so much." The disbelief in the gargoyle's voice startled Zawn.

"I still hold some impressive grudges, Marassa, it's what I'm good at. But as a kith leader, I have learned that is not always a wise thing. I've also learned that it's not who we are as a people. We have so much to give to this world and to each other."

"I am sorry about Gwendin."

"The fool couldn't help but be brave in the end," Zawn responded, her anger and pain coloring her voice. Her tone disturbed Rynan, who moved against her. She rubbed his back and he settled back down.

Marassa got a curious look on her face. "Were you there?"

"I made it in time to say goodbye, yes."

"I didn't see you on the grounds. Your fighting style is quite unique compared to those of men. You're hard to miss."

"Maybe because I didn't go there to fight," Zawn replied, voice cracking. "My mate called for my help. But I was too late to save him. That is something I have to live with, something I will have to admit to our son someday." Rynan snored loudly against her chest then exhaled contently. She cleared her throat, struggling to stay stoic. "We should head back. This one can be timed between feedings. We'll get back just in time for him to tell us all about it."

CHAPTER 48

After hearing about what had happened to the gargoyles, Taikin agreed to hold off on sending his kithlin to Zawn while she cared for them. He also confirmed that the army Crenast arrived with had left the Kingdom to take on a fight with Sedora. She filed that information away, knowing she would have to deal with the new King head on soon.

They moved the gargoyles to the cave in the dead of night, keeping their location hidden from prying eyes. Zawn instructed her kithlin to hunt close to the caves first to ensure they could carry their prizes to the gargoyles before hunting for the kith. When some of the gargoyles felt strong enough to hunt on their own, they helped repay Zawn's kith by hunting for both groups.

Once the gargoyles' wounds healed to the point they didn't need constant intensive care, Zawn agreed to take Nicholaus and Marassa to the abandoned castle. They met in the kith square, Zawn wearing a heavier coat and pants than usual. She grumbled something about the rough terrain, which made the two gargoyles laugh, something they hadn't done in weeks.

"You forget so quickly," Marassa chided, a teasing tone Zawn hadn't heard since their affair. "We don't have to walk. We can fly."

Zawn rolled her eyes. "Yes, you fly, but not us elves. We're used to hoofing it."

Suddenly, Nicholaus scooped Zawn up into his arms. "Which way?" he asked after she squealed and admonished him.

"See that peak through the trees? That way."

And with a heave of their monolithic legs, both Marassa and Nicholaus took the sky. Zawn flailed then grabbed onto his shoulder straps that secured his breastplate, making him laugh. She growled at him, securing her grasp like they had taught her all those years ago.

Zawn had forgotten how amazing the act of flight felt. The exhilaration that filled her took her breath and caused her heart to race. The wind whipped her hair about her face and stung her eyes due to its strength and the drop in temperature. She turned her head to look over the gargoyle's shoulder, catching sight of Marassa nearby. Marassa's wings were spread wide, arching slightly after each large sweep. Zawn watched as Nicholaus adjusted his wings to glide on the draft that could take them higher. There was a dip then a rush upwards, until he had to beat his wings to gain more height. Clouds reached down and accepted them, soft dashes of moisture dotting her face and the gargoyle's skin.

"There?" he asked, his breath against her ear.

Zawn looked down toward the ground and saw the old turrets, jutting awkwardly out of overgrowth and fading snow. "Yes!"

He turned his body as he lowered one wing and swung them around into a quick circling motion. She forgot how dizzying landing was and had to close her eyes to settle her mind and stomach. She felt the thump and lurch of his landing, carefully opening her eyes and glancing around. Marassa landed next to them, folding her wings against her back as he did. The rustling of their wings sounded like dozens of birds fluttering around them.

Zawn slid out of his arms, exhaling and seeing her breath form in front of her. She looked at the two gargoyles, who didn't seem fazed by the cold, and groused as she fastened her jacket closed. They were too busy taking in their surroundings to notice her discomfort, then they gestured to Zawn to lead the way.

Zawn carefully made her way to the main entrance, picking her way through overgrowth and fallen stones. She heard the crunching steps of the gargoyles as they cautiously followed her. They made it inside and walked hesitantly through the halls, unsure if any critters had moved in since it had been abandoned a few decades before. But as they inspected the massive building, they found the fortress truly empty.

The wind whistled through broken shutters while weakened walls let the sun shine through where their mortar should have been. The ceiling had collapsed in one room, while in another it had a missing wall. Some rooms were not supporting structures, obvious additions with torn thatched roofs that had been used for storage. As they ventured deeper into the stronghold, Marassa and Nicholaus spoke softly to each other, agreeing that the building and the surrounding woods would work for them.

They found the staircase to the lower levels, where the kitchen and additional storage had been located. The plumbing and powerhouse were also housed underneath, near the other end of the property. They left Marassa foraging around the kitchen area to see what equipment worked and what didn't, while Nicholaus followed Zawn to the upper levels.

They walked around the private chambers up on the top floor of the west wing, being watchful of the additional structural issues. There were several bedchambers, bathing rooms, as well as open areas for dens throughout the level. The remnants of wooden shutters and furniture were brittle from time and weather, with some of the metal finishings suffering the same fate.

"We'll bring up some of my masons and metal workers to fix the structural issues," Zawn said, thoughtfully. "We'll have to work in phases, since it's such a large building. But we'll get the most important sections up and running first. It shouldn't take much to get you settled, but we'll make sure it's done right so it lasts you a while. Especially with the snow and wind that whips around up here during the winter."

He stopped walking, watching as she sauntered past him. "Zawnie…"

She tapped one of the shutters that laid on the ground with her boot. "We'll ask Taikin's woodworkers to make proper shutters, doors and furniture too." She rolled her eyes as the other elf's rascally face flashed before her eyes. "I'm sure he'll get some expensive favors out of me in return."

"Zawnie," he called again.

She kept walking, recognizing his tone and waving him off. "Nicholaus, please don't. Words are unnecessary and they'd probably come out wrong anyway. Besides, I already had a conversation with Marassa."

"Leader Haley," his voice boomed, making her stop in her tracks.

She heard rustling behind her. Hesitantly, she turned as Nicholaus lowered himself to his knees, making her step back in surprise. He wouldn't look at her, keeping his eyes on the ground as he abased himself.

"I was never proud of the words I said to you that day."

"Emotions ran ugly during that time," Zawn responded, blinking fast. Her own emotions were still raw and she folded her arms against her chest in hopes of controlling them.

"Blaming you for our enslavement was a terrible mistake," he admitted. "You warned us."

"Yeah, I did."

"We ignored you."

"Yes, you did," she replied, trying to keep her tone even. "I not only loved Marassa, but all of you. I thought of you all as members of my family, no matter what Medruano or the others said after your falling out. I warned you at a huge personal risk because I feared for you all and hated the thought of you falling to a bastard like Elixin. You knew I went to you against Medruano's orders, but you told him what I did anyway. I was in trouble from all sides."

"I was too angry at Medruano to think straight. I never thought about the consequences for you."

"I did. But I told you anyway." Silence. "You know he threatened to disinherit and banish me?" she finally snapped, unable to hold back any longer. "Leave me kithless? He thought it would be a better punishment than killing me. Thankfully, he only chose to strip me of all my responsibilities and left me to be a border sentry for the rest of my days. Can you imagine? A hero of the Purge demoted to sentry. It wasn't as bad as when you told me that I had failed you… I think that's the part that actually broke me. I learned at that moment the lesson about the price one pays for caring too much about others and the consequences of trying to help those who did not ask for it." A flash of Gwen dying shook her. She squeezed her eyes closed, trying to remember him smiling instead. "My other experiences in this life leave me picking my battles instead of fighting all of them."

"I don't know how I could ever earn your forgiveness. Or how I could ever thank you for helping my clan."

She rolled her eyes, rubbing her face to break free of her threatening tears. "Get off your knees, Nicholaus. Your acquiescence and apologies change nothing. As time has moved on, so have I. My kith will help your people." She started to walk away, pulling out a notebook from her jacket. "We need to make a list."

~ ~ ~

When Zawn asked her gifted masons and metal workers to assist with fixing up the old Solatan stronghold, they happily agreed. The gargoyles who had healed enough to fly helped transfer supplies and elves to the mountain fortress. Taikin responded to Zawn's request by sending his best woodworkers and a few others to help clean and find what still needed to be provided. Not to mention a list of demands in return.

It took some time. As each piece fell into place, and their healing continued, the gargoyles could finally call the fortress, renamed Brazen Fort, home. After helping them settle in, the elves returned to their homes and waited for the next challenge.

CHAPTER 49

Taylor was right. Sleepless nights. Diapers. Feedings. Babies were more work than Zawn could ever imagine. And the fact that she lied to everyone that he was hers, she couldn't just pawn him off on someone else and not face some sort of ramifications.

There were moments, however, where the baby did steal her heart.

One morning, she woke after a long night of dealing with the fussy tyrant. She opened her eyes, exhausted, to find Rynan on the bed with her still. She forgot for a moment that she hadn't bothered with the crib, because he started crying every time, so she had barricaded him with pillows and had curled up against one side. He had grabbed her hand, refusing to let her go, and had finally fallen asleep. Now, he looked at her and flashed a big toothless smile. She bopped him on the nose and he started gurgling at her.

"Now I know why mothers do not rid themselves of brats like you," she whispered, after grousing at him. "Those smiles are tricks that trap a woman's heart every time."

His only response was a giggle, while waving his arms up in the air as if he could grab the stars and play with them. She had named him aptly, he truly was a stargazer. Just like Gwendin.

She found solace in one exercise with Rynan. She would tell him stories about Gwen. How they met – minus the explicit thank you marathon – and how they learned to love each other even through their differences. It helped with her grief, remembering him lovingly instead of in the last moments of his life. Some nights his death would wake her from her sleep, but she would find Rynan awake as if knowing her nightmares, and she made herself talk to him about better times.

While she raised a child, Zawn found herself dealing with the passive-aggressive fallout from her kithlin over her falsified secret as well as a familiar aggression from the new King. It was too much sometimes, but she stood her ground, daring anyone who would challenge or insult her to her face with a glare that could set hair on fire. No one risked her direct wrath.

Then reports started coming from her sentries and the gargoyles about men cutting down trees, fleecing fruit, among other thefts. The elves chased off the trespassers but they always came back without concern. Angry by their audacity and disrespect, Zawn's next challenge was contending with the new King of Mehdehra. Crenast thought himself a greater King than his slaughtered brother, who could command anyone he deemed his subject. Little did he understand the damage his brother caused while he ruled and how his own naiveté would be his undoing.

With Taylor at her side and Rynan in Chae's care, Zawn traveled on foot to the castle. When they arrived at the gates, the guards reached out as if to take their weapons. Zawn laughed in their faces, holding her ground. Confused and frustrated, the guards waited for their new King's orders. The King gave permission for the elves to enter with their weapons. Even though the guards knew the dangers of letting in armed elves, they feared angering their new King more.

It had only been a few months and the castle hadn't been completely renovated yet. The private chambers that burned the night of the coup were still blackened shells. Her gut flopped at the sight, and tears threatened with the memories, but she told herself to focus. The dead King's brother needed to be set straight. She couldn't do that if she dwelled on the past. Or let her grief weaken her. Instead, she grasped onto the anger that simmered underneath. It was the new King who killed her mate and therefore, hatred for him would guide her. She focused her eyes on the back of the castle guard's head, inhaling deeply as they were led up the staircase.

The large doors to the throne room were left wide open, letting them walk straight up the stairs and onto the main receiving floor. There were still scars from the invasion along the walls, either from fire or weapon. The only items that appeared unscathed were the actual thrones.

The kith leader was led to the base of the dais, where she had to look up at the new King. Zawn kept a few feet away from the first step, while Taylor stayed by the doorway. Her fingers tingled, confusing her. Something was different, but she couldn't suss it out at the moment. Surrounded by enemy combatants, she took in every corner of the room, counting guards and courtiers, while keeping her eyes on the tableau laid out on top of the platform. Taikin's information was correct, there were no soldiers with that insignia that was burned in her mind anywhere in the building.

The Queen sat, as if just a puppet of her was left on the throne, her face drawn, eyes down, skin pale. Knowing what she had lost over the years made her the most tragic character in the whole lot. Also keeping her eyes lowered, the Princess, still a young girl, sat off to the side of the dais as if she was added as a last-minute thought.

And at the center of it all, stood Crenast of Garadni, the new King of Mehdehra. A middle-aged man with a girth of a well-fed sow. She had heard he let himself go the moment he came to the throne. He was shorter than his brother, but the hair, eyes, and ego were the same. His outfit was pristine in colors, shapes, and fit. His stance was straight and indignant as he received his guests.

"Welcome, Leader Haley," he greeted with an impressive but stern voice when he realized she wouldn't bow to him. "I must admit that I was surprised by your request for an audience. What brings you to the magnificent heart of Mehdehra?"

Zawn crossed her arms. "Your men trespass onto our lands without care," she responded, her voice as strict and loud as his. "They trample, chop down, and take whatever they wish. That is in conflict with the treaty set in place by our predecessors."

Crenast sat down and glowered down at her from his perch on the throne. "I hear you have an infant."

She lifted her chin, not surprised that his spies had learned about Rynan but she was annoyed by the fact he was using it as a deflection.

"Yes," she answered, with an even tone. "I have a child."

He sniffed, as if disgusted. "Then do the right thing and return to your hovel, care for your bastard child, and stay out of the business of men."

"Is that what mankind demands of their women?" she asked, her eyes moving to the Queen, who only continued to stare down at her hands.

"It is required of them," Crenast replied, his eyes so focused on the elf as if he could set her on fire.

"Then you misjudge our race completely."

"Oh, do I?"

She met his gaze, unfazed by the hate that burned there. "We are nothing like you men. We do not see the feminine as weak. In fact, we see it as it is."

"And what does that mean?"

"Come at an elven mother, you will regret ever having the notion."

The King scoffed at her. "We will do what we wish on whatever land we walk," he responded, indignant. "Now get out of here before that is not all we do."

"Then we will do what we must to protect our sovereignty."

Crenast appeared unmoved by her warning. With that, she spun on her heel and exited with Taylor right behind her. When they were safely away from the castle grounds, Zawn gave a subtle gesture and her hidden archers melted further into the forest. They all made their way to a hiding place and they waited long enough to confirm no one followed.

Taylor sighed. "Now what?"

All eyes landed on Zawn.

"We prepare for the worst," Zawn responded.

"You don't think he would attempt to invade?" Naji asked.

"He's now the King of Mehdehra," Zawn answered drolly. "Of course he is going to try."

With that, they started back to their kith.

~　　　~　　　~

Zawn pulled on her experiences during the Purge and other battles to secure her kith. She doubled the number of sentries along their border with Mehdehra. Instead of just having blade fighters, she added archers as well. She staggered the line so if the invaders made it past one sentry, there would be another a few lengths away and so forth.

She knew when Crenast's men moved en masse, she would change the line. While she waited, she worked on maps and plans.

~　　　~　　　~

She didn't have to wait long.

Within three days of her visit, Taylor entered her work hut as she thumbed through one of the elves' oldest tomes. She had pulled the massive text out of Jheferin's library when she realized why her fingers had tingled in the throne room. Something had been disturbed and she needed to learn more about what ran under the floors of the castle.

"We have confirmation that they are mounting an attack," Taylor announced. "Both our sentries and the gargoyles' have seen a buildup of weapons and men. They will probably be marching our way within the next day or two."

Zawn glanced up from her book, sighing. "Let's get our people prepared and march our visitors right into a welcoming party, shall we?"

~　　　~　　　~

As Zawn readied her plans, she absent-mindedly picked up Rynan as he fussed in his crib. She rocked and bounced with him in her arms before reality hit. She was going into battle, to fight for her kith and their way of life. But unlike all the other times, she was responsible for someone else. She stared at the baby, his big brown eyes taking in her features with a small smile of awe.

Taylor entered, frowning when he saw her expression. "What's wrong?"

"I don't know what to do."

"What are you talking about?"

"Rynan. I know the kith will move forward with you as leader but… What will happen to him if I do not come home? If I die in battle, who will take care of him? I never had to think about something like this. I've never had anyone…" She felt her throat constrict suddenly.

"Zawnie, if anything happened to you, Chae and I will take Rynan in."

"Chae said three was enough."

Taylor chuckled. "Despite her bluster, she adores him and would care for him if you couldn't."

"I've never had to leave someone behind before," she whispered, kissing the small hand that reached up. "I'm leaving my son behind."

Taylor wrapped his arm around her shoulders. "And you will come home to him, Zawnie. Knowing my mate and my children wait for me every time I step outside this kith, well, it drives me to come home every time. Now, for you, Rynan will be your reason to do the same."

~   ~   ~

Archers filled their quivers while the warriors honed their blades. Zawn laid out maps along a table set outside her work hut, with markings for her fighters. Chaelene and the other archers gathered around her first. The archers were marked in violet, lined up along the border between their territory and the Kingdom of Mehdehra.

"A staggered formation is required. Novices up front, high up in the trees. Masters back them up, but also stay lower on the limbs. Use the training arrows in the first few volleys," Zawn instructed. "We know they'll protect themselves immediately with shields, so don't waste the good ammunition. But do not fire any arrows until they step over the border. We cannot be the aggressors. Our stance is protection and response."

The archers, who were all women, nodded.

"Avoid fatalities if you can."

"You want captives?" Chaelene asked, surprised.

"I want leverage."

Halyn responded, "We will adjust our aim."

"Good. Do not forget, we are battling men. They will try to victimize us. If you must kill to protect yourself, someone else, or just to survive, do it." Then Zawn met the eyes of each archer. "Use your camouflage. They have been warned we would protect ourselves. They get nothing else."

All of the women nodded, then headed off in different directions to take their places. Next, Taylor and the other warriors approached her and she pointed to the jade marks on the map.

"Stay behind the archers. Those who avoid our volleys will run directly into you. Use your longer blades so they can't get a closeup kill. Disarm and bind as many as you can."

"A statement? You? Never," Taylor chided.

Zawn slapped his arm. "Just do it."

"We will follow your orders."

"Good. And I need at least four to help lead the others to safety before you join the ranks."

Four men raised their hands quickly.

"Thank you. Please follow me."

As they approached the square, Zawn frowned. The elderly, pregnant, and ill sat around the firepit, eyes lowered in shame because they couldn't join their kithlin in their battle. When they heard footsteps, each looked up.

Zawn regarded them for a moment. "You will all move to the cave system that housed the gargoyles for a while, at least until we straighten out these foolish men. Take only necessary supplies. I don't think you'll have to stay long, but you should be prepared for longer than a brief stay." Zawn met each set of eyes as they listened intently. "But there are very important tasks I require completed by the time we retrieve you. I need you to prepare medical kits for treating wounds, make meals to feed our hungry warriors, and also replenish our quivers. I do not have to tell you how important these tasks are, I think you already know, but I cannot give these tasks to any better kithlin. I know you will make us all proud."

Being entrusted with such tasks brought light to their faces and they answered that they would make her proud. She nodded, then gestured for them to start packing.

A very pregnant Satria approached Zawn before heading out, holding Rynan. Zawn reached for him, kissed and nuzzled his cheek, which made him squeal, before handing him back.

"I will take very good care of him, Zawnie," Satria reassured, seeing the emotions that rose up in her leader's eyes.

"I know you will," Zawn responded, patting her son's back. "That's why I asked you."

Satria nodded, with a sad smile, then waddled toward the pathway that led to the caves.

As the group thinned out, only one person remained. His blind eyes tried to make sense of the commotion around him, but inevitably, it was chaos to him and he groused. Sileas had told him he would take care of everything, but that didn't make sitting around anymore comfortable for the old elf. Zawn sauntered over, closing the gap between them to have a more private conversation.

"Jheferin, I have a rather large task for you. Something to work on while in the cave."

"Oh dear, what is that?"

"I want to make more than just a statement. I want to enforce my agenda for our kith."

The old man's eyebrow raised up. "And how do you plan to do that?"

Zawn smirked, then sat down next to her old friend.

CHAPTER 50

Early that next morning, they came. Two squads of Crenast's military stomped into the forest, their polished armor squeaking and steel swords sparkling. They marched proudly along the path that led into the forest. Their general shouted orders, which way to go and how fast to move, and as they got closer to the border, when to pull which weapons. They moved swiftly without any resistance until the first boots crossed the border into the elves' territory.

A shower of arrows landed, striking solid into the ground at the army's feet. The men stumbled to a stop in shock. They looked around, wide-eyed.

"Shields up!" shouted the general.

The sound of metal shields moving into position was met with silence from the forest around them.

"Forward march!"

Two more steps, another rain of arrows. The pings against their shields rattled their resolve, making them stop. They peeked over their shields, unsure exactly where the arrows were coming from.

Then a voice reverberated through the trees. "You have trespassed into the territory of the Whispering Hornbeam Kith!" Zawn announced. "Turn back now or face the full consequences of your transgression!"

The general scoffed. "Try your best, you fucking treelimb!"

Angered, she felt her toothpick irises widen into saucers. "He's definitely mine," Zawn whispered, before raising her arm and dropping it, sending forth her warriors.

The men in their heavy metal armor were no match for the lithe elves clad in cloth and leather. Every elf in the forest challenged more than one human, taking them down and restraining them before moving onto the next. When some of the men tried to escape the area, archers drove them back with well-placed arrows in the ground or nearby trees.

Zawn herself was on a mission. She darted around trees, jumped over roots and ducked under limbs until she came face to face with the insolent general.

As they met away from the main commotion, he sneered when he recognized the chunky necklace she wore as leader. She only smirked as she confirmed his rank by the markings on his upper arms. He raised his broadsword, swiping it in between them to intimidate her. Zawn scoffed, twirled her haladie with confidence and waited. Then the general attacked.

His sword, with its wide and long fuller, smashed against ground, tree, and her haladie with a vengeance. She blocked all the blows that made it to her blade, while dancing and avoiding several other swings in her direction. She made notes with every swing, with every move, with every step. When she could anticipate each of his moves, she stopped backing away and started her own attack. She swished and slashed with her haladie, catching his blade then his sleeve and last his arm. The vicious blow opened a gash in his arm, causing him to drop his blade and stumble back. The shock and pain made him cry out, giving her an opening to kick his stomach, making him trip and land on his ass. He grasped his arm, trying to staunch the blood that gushed from it.

"You bitch!" he hissed. "How dare you?"

Zawn kept her distance, but picked up his sword. "Do you yield?"

"Never. Not to the likes of you."

Zawn swung his sword from left to right, then buried it into the ground right between his legs, just barely nicking the exposed material next to his crotch. Then she lifted his chin with her curved blade.

"Do you yield?" she demanded, through clenched teeth.

"I yield," he snarled. "I yield!"

"Sound the surrender knell. Now!"

He fumbled for his horn then blew into it clumsily while trying to stave off the bleeding. But it was enough sound to halt the metal bashing in the distance. She heard her warriors whistle confirmation of their safety and their attackers' surrender. She dislodged his sword then leaned it against a tree behind her, so the general could not grab it, then sheathed her haladie. She ripped the piece of shirt that hung out under his breastplate, using it to make a tourniquet. As he watched her tend to the wound she caused, the general stammered.

Zawn scoffed. "If we wanted you dead, you would be."

The man stared at her, confused.

"Get up and march back to your men," she ordered, rising back up and fetching his weapon.

The general used a tree nearby to climb back onto his feet, then in defeat, shambled back toward his men. When they arrived back to where the main fight had taken place, the general found all of his men bound, some wounded, most just startled.

Taylor met Zawn at the edge, grinning in disbelief. "This is his best?"

"Maybe taking the castle should be our next step?" Eddard asked, staring down at the hog-tied human in front of him. "Then we would have no further worries about aggression from these pointless bastards."

Zawn glanced around, seeing the anger seething through her people. She would stamp out their aggression later, without human witnesses. "Come, let's secure our leverage. I have a meeting at the castle."

~ ~ ~

The gate guards gawked, useless. Zawn led one squad of men by one large rope. The rope itself was tied to a yoke, which was held up by the two men in front of the lines, one of which was the King's general. Attached to the yoke and the men were two longer ropes, which secured nine more men behind each of the leads. All were bound by their hands in a handcuff knot, with their hands in front of them. They trudged behind her like good puppies, even though they were exhausted and embarrassed and some limped due to injuries.

"Hello, boys," Zawn announced, as she directed her prisoners into the throne room. "I believe you left some trash in my forest."

She stopped at the dais, her prisoners halting their march behind her. She felt the eyes of the courtiers, the King, and the guards rest on her after taking in her parade. She glanced over at one uniformed guard, who had the mark of captain on his chest plate, then raised her eyebrow as if daring him to call his men to arms. He met her eyes, then lowered them, submitting to her control of the situation. She returned her toothpick thin pupils to Crenast and they slowly expanded into saucers as they adjusted from the sunlight to the dimmer light of the throne room and to her anger.

Crenast stood in front of his throne and the shock written all over his face filled her with perverse satisfaction. Footsteps from one hallway took her attention to the left and she watched as the Queen and Princess entered. They stumbled to a stop, their mouths gaping open at the scene in front of them.

Her eyes moved back up to the speechless King. "You have reneged on the treaty agreed by our predecessors. Your aggression against the Whispering Hornbeam Kith will not stand as just a misunderstanding. There has been a new treaty drawn."

Zawn dropped the rope then stepped onto the dais to stare down at Crenast from a very close proximity. He flinched when she reached for her belt, but she only pulled out a scroll, perfectly dictated by Jheferin to the eloquent hand of Sileas, and handed it to Crenast.

"There will be no negotiations. You will abide by the new rules of the treaty or you will have war. And you will lose. Do you understand?"

Crenast swallowed, hard.

"Do you understand?" she repeated, sternly.

"I understand."

"Good. I expect your signed copy delivered to me by the end of the week."

With that, she turned on her heel and strode past the prisoners, who bowed their heads to her. Out the door and into the courtyard, the remaining soldiers who were bound by the hands and left kneeling in the grass, lowered their heads as well.

Once free of the castle gates, a slight move of Zawn's hand released her archers from their ready stance and they peeled back layer by layer until most were walking in stride with her.

~ ~ ~

She received the signed copy of the treaty within a day.

~ ~ ~

Her kithlin returned from the cave once they knew it was safe. They had done as she asked, so they stored the arrows and medical kits away while sharing the food that had been prepared.

Zawn approached Satria from behind, but Rynan could see her over her shoulder and ruined the surprise with a squeal. But Satria didn't turn around. When Zawn walked around her, she could see that Satria was in distress.

Zawn took Rynan from her. "Chae! Meagan!"

"I'm sorry, I just," then suddenly a grunt escaped Satria.

Zawn held out her free hand and the younger elf grabbed it, squeezing it hard. "I think we've a baby wanting to join us," Zawn replied.

Chae and Meagan rushed up and each took hold of one of the pregnant woman's arms. Then they carefully started to guide her toward her personal hut. Taylor showed up at Zawn's side, a small smile on his face. Then they heard Satria call out to Zawn. She handed Rynan over to Tay before catching up with the three other women.

Before they knew it, a screaming baby girl arrived into the world, taking her place among the kithlin.

CHAPTER 51

"Leader Haley, we have visitors."

She rolled her eyes. "Not more ass kissers from the castle?" she demanded as she turned around.

She froze, startled to find three cloaked figures standing in front of her. Her stomach twisted as she remembered a similarly clothed figure that had walked along the road before being attacked by muggers. The only difference was the alternate color to the white, which was a light gray.

She swallowed against her tightening throat, then attempted to clear it in hopes to loosen the reacting muscles. "Visitors from the College of Theurgy? What are you doing here?"

One opened his cloak, removed something from his satchel, and held it out for her inspection. He had retrieved an opalescent gem, the length of his hand but thin as a dagger hilt. The name escaped her, but she remembered Gwen showing one similar to her ages ago.

"We have come to test your children for possible magical talents."

Zawn scoffed at their ignorance. "We are magic. You point that thing at any of us, it'll glow. See your way out of our territory."

The pair of theurgists in front stepped aside and allowed the cloaked man in the back to move forward. His hood and cloak were burgundy, showing him as a man of importance unlike his guides. He was even taller than Taylor and to watch him bow from the waist looked as if a tree had been chopped in half. He straightened, towering over his fellow theurgists, but didn't move any closer.

She could only see his mouth as he requested, "May we speak in private, Leader Haley?"

Zawn eyed him suspiciously, but gracefully bowed her head and gestured to her work hut. He glided past everyone and entered without another word.

Before she followed, she asked Taylor, "Care for our guests while I speak with their master? Water, food, whatever they require?"

Taylor nodded, then walked over to the two men and gestured that they take a seat at the firepit in the center of the kith.

Seeing that everyone was far enough out of hearing range, she entered the hut. The man had removed his hood, showing white hair and pale gray eyes. He was an older man, probably respected for the wisdom that came with his age, but she didn't know him. Gwen only spoke of close acquaintances and not the leaders of the college.

"Please, sit."

"Thank you." He lowered himself into the chair, sighing. "My name is Yunji, I am one of the councilors at the College of Theurgy. I appreciate you giving me time for a conversation."

She sat down across from him, cradling the baby against her chest as he slept in the sling. "My mind is made up, so there is no room for you to convince me to test our children. But I do understand saving face."

"Gwendin spoke highly of you in his letters to the college," he explained, a kind smile on his face. "He wanted us to understand that your agreement to let him gather on your lands helped tether the world of man to that of elf."

"It was a thin tether," she responded, carefully, "but a beneficial one."

"We received his letter of resignation the day he died."

Zawn glanced away, trying to hide her reaction. Tears stung her eyes and she blinked fast. She never knew he had given it to the messenger before the coup.

"We always knew he'd leave the ranks eventually," Yunji admitted, "but most felt that sending him here, meeting you and your kind, well, it made him run feral. However, I knew him better than most and knew his heart would always lead him to the right path. He had a meager savings back at the college." He produced a small belt purse that jingled with coin. "He has no other family to claim it, other than his sister but she refused it, so I thought it'd be used well by the elf kith he loved so much."

"We can't take that."

The man leaned forward, took her free hand and laid the purse in her palm. "Yes, you can. He would have wanted it that way. We would also like to continue the tithe, but in a different manner. If we were to give you a list of items needed by the college, would you have the people to do the gathering? We would of course raise the amount paid, to include time and effort, along with supply."

"Why not just take what you want?"

"You'd think that would be easier?" he asked, leaning back in his chair. "My dear, we know what lesson you taught Crenast. We may have gained some amusement out of it but we also took the message you sent him as being meant for all of us. Don't mess with the elves, especially those of the Whispering Hornbeam Kith."

Zawn smirked, finally. "Well, I hope that I don't have to teach that lesson again."

"One can only hope."

"So, the ruse to test our children? This was just to get my permission to meet with you? You could have sent a letter."

"Letters are easily ignored. And I wanted to meet the woman behind the notoriety. Curiosity got the best of me, if you will. I thought it also important to notify you that the College has cut ties completely with the Kingdom of Mehdehra. We will no longer provide them a theurgist or any assistance no matter how dire the situation. The death of Gwendin at the hands of an insurrectionist is unforgivable."

He looked at the lump against her chest, as a hand reached out toward her chin. She gently grasped it and automatically kissed the fingers, then tucked it back into the sling as Rynan sighed contently.

"Is that your child, Leader?"

"Yes. My son."

"If he shows signs of any talents, please, consider the College. We'd bring him in on a scholarship, no cost to you."

Her droll response, "I'm flattered, thank you."

"You should be, we don't take in mixed breeds."

She flashed a dirty look his way.

"I can see that he does not have elven features," he stated, matter of fact, "as I would have expected."

"Yes, well, he is still a child, not a bauble, and he has a name."

Yunji's eyes lowered, embarrassment coloring his face. "I guess I need to work on my tact? I spend so much time with facts and statistics, I forget the souls and lives behind the data." He returned his eyes to the baby. "What is his name?"

"Rynan, our stargazer."

"A strong name," he complimented. Then he met her gaze again. "Are you sure you don't want me to test Rynan before I leave? To see if he inherited any of your talents?"

Zawn frowned, peeking down at the sleeping infant.

"Or are you afraid he will take after his father?" he inquired.

"If I let you test him, what guarantees do I have for privacy?"

"It is only the two of us, and well, him, but there are no other witnesses. Who will believe who?"

She hated to admit that curiosity had gotten the best of her. Before the theurgists' visit, it hadn't even crossed her mind that Rynan could have magical abilities, but his relation to Gwen made it a possibility. Knowing now would prepare her for the future, especially if there were even a glimmer of magic. However, at the same time, she would find relief if he tested negative. It would make keeping him hidden easier.

"Fine," she replied, after a contemplative silence, "but if I hear that you spoke of this, your supply of herbs will dry up immediately."

"Understood, milady. Please, lay him in the bassinet and step back. I don't want a false positive because of your proximity."

Zawn reached in and pulled Rynan out of his safe cocoon against her chest. He made an upset sound, making her shush him, and she laid him carefully in the bassinet next to her desk.

The theurgist retrieved the crystal that he had in his satchel, then laid it on Rynan's chest. At first, the gem didn't glow. Not even a little.

Zawn felt relief relax her tightened chest.

Suddenly, there was a flicker. The light quickly grew so bright that the theurgist removed the crystal and dropped it on her table as if it were scalding. The glow throbbed a few times then started to fade.

The theurgist stammered, shocked by the reaction. "I've only seen it do that just a few times."

"What does that mean?" she asked, fearful.

"Is he Gwendin's?"

She dreaded answering that question, considering the situation. Zawn picked up the baby before he could fuss. She tucked him back in, and after he squirmed a little, he settled back into his nap.

"Leader Haley, please, I need to know if he is Gwendin's son."

"How could he be?" she demanded, indignant. "You made it impossible for him to have children."

"Nothing, my dear, is foolproof."

Zawn didn't respond and she knew he took her silence as confirmation.

"When he is old enough," he continued, his voice going from accusatory to kind. "I would think it beneficial for him to study with us. I know it is against your elven ways to trust a human. But, if he is as talented as this indicates, he will need proper training."

"I don't want him ripped from us as a toddler," she snapped back. "Not like you did Gwendin and all the others."

"You name the age and we will honor it. As well as the length of his education. Gwendin stayed beyond his graduation in hopes to teach, but ended up leaving to answer a call for help."

"I also wouldn't want him neutered," she added, thinking of all the possibilities that were lost to her and Gwen. "He deserves to have the life he chooses."

"We will also honor that."

Zawn looked away, her eyes settling on the baby in his sling. "I will consider your offer and I will write to you once I've made a decision."

Yunji bowed. "That is all I ask, milady."

"Can I…"

"Yes, milady?"

"Gwen told me that when he first arrived at the College, that he was scared and had nightmares. He said that one of the councilors helped him settle in, reassured him that they were only nightmares, and tucked him in every night. Was that you?"

Yunji grimaced. "He swore he would never tell anyone."

"He didn't say it was you."

"No, which I appreciate. We are not supposed to have, well, favorites. But I tested him, I brought him to the College, I felt… obligated."

"Thank you, for your honesty." She moved toward the door. "I will walk you out of our territory. And again, one word of this…"

"Milady, I will not even speak of this to my fellow councilors. This is an agreement between us only."

She continued to stare at him suspiciously, making him smile softly back in reassurance.

"Please, follow me."

~   ~   ~

Later that night, Zawn sat on her bed, baby sound asleep in her arms. He had his fill of milk and smiled as he enjoyed whatever images danced through an infant's brain. While she watched him dream, her conversation with the theurgist Yunji replayed in her own mind.

A knock on her door drew her out of her thoughts and she glanced over as Taylor peeked in. Seeing that she was awake, lounging on the bed, he entered. He chuckled at the expression on Rynan's face, slowly sinking down onto the edge of the bed.

"If they could only tell us their dreams at that age," he said, his voice soft in volume and tone. "All three of ours would smile and giggle in their sleep."

"I'm sure he dreams of milk and stars. What's on your mind, Tay?"

"I wanted to ask how your conversation went with the theurgist. You spent a considerable amount of time with him alone."

Her eyebrows jumped up and she sighed. "It was complicated. Gwen had money left at the College that they decided to bequeath to the kith."

"That was kind of them."

"He also asked if Rynan was Gwen's son."

"Why would he ask that?" he demanded.

"Rynan has magical talents."

"What? How?"

"I… I can guess." She questioned how much she should tell her friend, but realized that he needed to know everything. "The castle sits on multiple energy lines that cross."

He glared at her, suspiciously. "How do you know that?"

"Gwen showed me."

She saw how he disliked that answer. "Why Rynan?"

"None of the other Mehdehran royals were born in that castle," she pointed out. "The princess was born in the other manor. Elixin and Crenast were born in the old manor, because that castle wasn't built until their father started his reign. And the Queen was born in her land of origin. None of the family had been born on site before. Until the first son."

"You said that the Queen has had supposedly three boys while residing at the castle."

"Yes, the one that died as a toddler after some sort of illness, then the miscarriage, and..." she paused, then whispered, "Bryant." She let the name hang in the air for a moment before continuing, "Because that strong of magic had infiltrated the castle, it ultimately absorbed into their bodies and souls and I think the other two sons were not strong enough to survive. Bryant, well, he survived as long as he did. I think partly because he received the same talent as Gwen."

"Wait. How?"

"Gwen and Kemberly were siblings."

Taylor frowned. "So now, Rynan has abilities because of those familial ties and the energy lines."

"That's what I think influenced who lived," she replied, hating the thought about such power being so destructive. "The other sons were not strong enough."

"Rynan is?" he inquired, staring down at the sleeping baby.

"He has to be. What other choice does he have?"

"He's not there anymore, those lines no longer have influence on him."

"Not directly. They might not converge here, but they still run under our feet. They've already changed something in him. And now I have to consider his training. I can't teach him. I have shit control over the few talents in my own blood. Not to mention mine are nothing like his. And if that crystal gave any indication of his strength, no one else here has abilities that could ever match his."

"You think him that powerful?"

"You didn't see how the crystal reacted to him. Or how Yunji reacted to the crystal."

Taylor stayed silent for a moment, then sighed. "Well, if you decide to send him to the college, I will support it."

"Gwen told me what growing up at the college was like," she responded, her voice soft and sad. "Rynan will not have that same life. I don't want him snatched away too young. I want him rooted in our kith, so he never forgets where he comes from when he is surrounded by other humans."

"I know you will negotiate what's best for him." Then he chuckled. "But does the College of Theurgy know who they're negotiating with?"

She smirked, drolly. "Considering he also renegotiated the tithe?"

"Oh?"

"They will pay us more to do the foraging for them."

"They won't... take?"

"I believe the theurgists know to stay on my good side. Probably thanks to Gwen's letters to them, but Yunji admitted they took away the valuable lesson I taught Crenast. If they want to teach Rynan and to keep their steady stream of herbs and roots, they will follow my rules."

"Leverage helps."

"Leverage does indeed help." Zawn frowned, her mind tossing thoughts left and right. "I have a lot to think about, but for now, I think I need to get some sleep."

"Good night, Zawnie."

"Good night, Tay."

CHAPTER 52

After a month of consideration, Zawn sent her demands to the College of Theurgy, who responded quickly that they agreed with her terms. With that settled, Zawn readied herself for her next project: Taikin's apprentice. Even though she had expected him anytime, it still felt sudden, but Taylor had already helped her prepare everything long before the elf's arrival.

Late one morning, a tall, youthful elf strode into the kith on the heels of their scout, glancing around at the huts and people with his dark copper eyes. His pupils were mere slits due to the bright sunshine, giving the allusion that his irises glowed. Even though his hair was mostly black, and secured in a ponytail, it also had shades of bright greens like olivine and chrysolite. His overall skin color was a light jasper but his bark ran darker.

His clothing and armor easily identified him as a member of the Whistling Cedar Kith. His leather armor had facets like tiger eye, darker pieces accenting the lighter sections beautifully. The shoulder piece had metal spikes that protruded at a curved angle. They were intimidating as they glinted in the sunlight and used to injure an enemy with a good thrust. His tunic, pants, and boots were dark like the bark of a grandfather oak tree. A broadsword was sheathed to his belt, while a dagger was tucked in his breast plate.

Zawn stood in the center of the kith square, in front of the benches that circled the firepit. She wasn't wearing her own breastplate since she had to wrangle Rynan that morning, but she had slipped on her archer gauntlets and weapons along with her pants and tunic. Her hair was also pulled back into a pony tail, exposing the leader's chunky necklace and matching arm strap.

"Averell, welcome to the Whispering Hornbeam Kith," she greeted him, giving a subtle nod to him.

He approached her then bowed out of respect. "Thank you, Leader Haley. I hope to learn what I can and not be an inconvenience."

"Nonsense. This is a debt I gladly pay. Come, I will show you to the guest hut. You can settle in then join us for lunch. We can talk over a good meal about your requirements and my expectations."

"Thank you, milady."

~   ~   ~

He woke early, like he usually did, but had to take a moment to remember where he was. The bed in the guest hut was big enough to accommodate his large frame, which he was thankful for, but he still was unsure of the bathing room. He would have to figure something out if he couldn't fit in the bathtub.

With a sigh and grunt, he sat up and rubbed his face. He didn't hear anyone stirring outside, but it was still dark. Since it appeared he had time, he decided to rise and freshen up before heading out the door. Some cold water splashed on his face and a few stretching exercises helped shake off the remaining sleep from his body and mind, then he dressed in everything but his shoulder armor. He didn't see himself having to go into battle today, but he slipped on his breastplate and weapons just in case.

He stepped out on the porch, hearing a voice across the way in the stables. Against the rising sun's light, he saw the shape of a woman exit, followed by a crowd of rambunctious goats. There were quite a few, from older, arthritic bucks to just-born, bouncing babies and tolerant, steady nannies. The woman had something strapped to her chest as she corralled the group with vocalizations and clicks of her tongue. Once she had their undivided attention, she led them out to pasture. With each one out in the green acreage, she disappeared behind the larger homes that the families occupied.

Movement out of the corner of his eye brought his attention to the kith square, where another woman waved him over. He crossed the distance, noticing a large pot hung over the firepit. The woman who waved him over was tending to it, stirring and adding ingredients.

"Averell, right?" she asked once he got close enough.

"Yes, milady."

"Please, call me Meagan. Hope you like porridge."

"Smells delicious."

"Have a seat, I'll get you served. Zawn should be back in a few."

He looked at Meagan confused, which made the woman laugh.

"That was her with the goats."

"Your leader herds the goats?" he demanded, shocked.

"She's the only one they listen to."

"Who listens to who?" a voice inquired from behind them.

Zawn walked up to them, minus whatever had been wrapped around her. She was dressed modestly, in a tunic, slacks, and boots. She took a bowl from Meagan after she had served Averell, then sat down nearby.

"The goats," Meagan responded, settling down with her own bowl. "They only listen to you."

Zawn chuckled. "Oh, is that what you call it?"

"What do you call it?" Averell asked.

"Wrangling chaos," Zawn replied, with a shrug.

Averell felt confusion over her nonchalant acceptance of the chore. "But shouldn't a leader delegate such unimportant tasks?"

Meagan almost choked on her spoonful of porridge, wide eyes landing on Zawn's face. The kith leader didn't react, she only blinked as she stared at the young warrior elf.

"Is there such a thing?" she inquired, her voice dripping with sarcasm, before it changed into a serious tone. "Everything that happens from sunrise to bedtime is important to the kith. Even things that happen while we sleep." Then a droll smile crept across her face. "Now I see where we need to start. Eat up, Averell, it's gonna be a busy morning."

~   ~   ~

She had wanted to give him some time settling in, but after his comment at breakfast, Zawn took little pity on Averell. Her ego wouldn't let her. After everything they had gone through during Medruano's leadership, and the aftermath of his fall, she couldn't stomach the term unimportant. And that would be the most imperative lesson for her to teach him. Nothing in a kith was unimportant.

With him right on her heels, she started with checking on the animals, making sure the goats she let loose in the pasture were behaving themselves, along with the cows, sheep, and donkeys. Then she led him to the fields, to check in with Gaylon and the status of the crops he sowed, before walking over to the empty lots that were ready for manure and crops like lucerne. After that, they ate lunch with the rest of the kith. While her kithlin kept him entertained with the daily news and plans for the evening, she snuck off to check on Rynan who clapped and bounced at the sight of her. She stole a snuggle and kiss before returning to her day. And lastly, she headed off to the border, checking in on the sentries and discussing any concerns with them.

Averell tried to hide his boredom with the farming aspects but lit up when it came to the border concerns. That was something he understood, being from the warrior caste, and he enjoyed speaking with others from that world. Zawn begrudgingly let him converse with the different sentries, from Ehdzia to Darend, since it appeared to be a source of comfort.

By dinnertime, Averell looked exhausted. Having been to every corner of her kith on foot was normal for Zawn but for a warrior it had taken a little bit of toll. She told him to clean up before dinner, doing the same herself after retrieving Rynan. Apparently, he had a very busy day, falling asleep the moment she laid him in his crib. Sighing at the baby as he sprawled out, she washed up and secured him in his wrap against her chest. He was growing more every day, she realized, as one foot stuck out. She adjusted the sling to support his long legs then headed back to the square.

Even with her arriving a little late, her kithlin made room for her next to Chae and the kids. Averell sat on the other side of the fire, between some of the older kithlin. Food was served and everyone ate as they laughed, talked, and joked. Averell seemed uncomfortable surrounded by the joyous banter and giggles. Zawn admonished herself. She had forgotten that he was away from his kith. Away from the home and kithlin he had known all of his life. Granted, that was why Taikin sent him to her, because Averell could only think in terms of the world he knew. Taikin had kept the caste system in his kith because it worked for them. However, if Averell would ever be considered for the role of second or even leader, he had to know that there were other things that made up their daily lives.

She grimaced, then glanced at Taylor who sat nearby. She lifted her chin, subtly, and he looked over at the younger elf. Taking her hint, he moved closer and engaged Averell in conversation. She watched as the younger elf's shoulders relaxed and she finished her meal.

Then the basket weaving began. Another expression passed over Averell's face, something almost like terror, but a few of the women nudged Taylor out of the way to sit by the young warrior. They spent a little more time than she thought necessary showing Averell how to weave, but she wasn't naïve. The warrior was attractive and new to them.

Zawn scoffed, as Taylor crossed the square. He sat next to her, shaking his head. They drank from their mugs in silence, listening to the chatter around them.

"Did you really drag him all over our territory?" he demanded, keeping an eye on their guest and his admirers.

"He assumed certain things were unimportant," she responded, sipping her mead and rubbing Rynan's back. "I had to prove that everything is important."

"Well, he'll sleep good tonight."

They watched the women paying close attention to their handsome visitor. Charming smiles, gentle touches, and loud giggles were evidence of their infatuation with him.

"And not alone," he added.

"I'll need to discuss decorum, among other things, with our young women."

Taylor laughed. "I can have that discussion with him as well, if you wish?"

"Probably better coming from you."

They continued to watch the small group of women and Averell. Until the young male said something that made all of the women frown and he stood. Averell walked over to Zawn and Taylor, wished them a good night, then headed to the guest hut after Zawn nodded.

"Maybe I should drag him around the kith every day," she said, softly.

"Be nice, Zawnie."

"I have been in a mood all day," she admitted. "Why change it now?"

"Maybe focus that energy on the trespassers?"

"I've eyes on them. I will get a report in the morning and go from there.

However, for now, I am off to bed. I am jealous of this child's ability to sleep through everything."

Taylor chuckled. "He's getting as good at it as Minee. Good night, Zawnie."

~ ~ ~

The next morning, Zawn sent Averell to exercise with the other kithlin while she waited for her sentries to return. When Darend and the others strode into the square, she waved Averell over to join her, Taylor, and the others at the firepit. Zawn made sure her sentries had settled down with food and water before discussing the issue at hand.

Zawn leaned forward, keeping her voice low so as not to concern those walking past them. "What have you gathered from the settlement?"

"A family, with older boys," Darend reported, after swallowing his food. "They've started building protection for the animals, even though they are still living in the two tents. They have started to divert some of the river toward their settlement."

"You should disable their water ways," Averell suggested, "draw them out, then move in and destroy their structures. Then remove them by force."

"The King tends to redraw maps without telling us," Zawn responded, trying to keep her tone even. "They could easily have no idea that they've moved onto our territory."

"From everything we saw," Darend added, "they appear to be farming, not invading."

"They are trespassing," Averell retorted. "Why take pity on them?"

Zawn stared straight into Averell's eyes, the look on her face causing the others around them to hold their breaths. "This is why Taikin sent you to me."

"And why is that?"

"All you want to do is fight. Tackle the problem physically and not think through your actions or consider the consequences."

"Were you not raised in the warrior caste, Leader Haley?"

"I was. Why?"

"You are well known for your ability to fight," Averell stated, looking her up and down in a way that offended her. "But not much else."

Her kithlin sat in stunned silence and they glanced between their leader and their visitor as each spoke.

"Oh? Has my reputation as a nitwit finally run its course?" she snapped. "Apparently our teachers had different philosophies."

"Who taught you?"

"Brennan, our defender."

"I learned from Teneel, our champion."

"Champion?" She raised an eyebrow, while leaning back onto one arm. "Hm, only because he never had to challenge Brennan."

That made Averell bristle.

232

"I see I hit a nerve. Your enemies will use that to their advantage and the next thing you know, your ass is on the ground and you've lost your kith. To lead, you cannot be a hothead."

"I guarantee you that I could best anyone who insults or attacks my kith."

"Including me?"

His eyebrows furrowed in confusion.

"Well, I did just insult your tutor. Will you let that go?"

"No."

"Then let's have a go."

They moved over to the flattened area where her kith would exercise and learn how to fight. A crowd started to gather as word spread that the handsome visitor had irritated their leader enough to insult and challenge the youngster.

Averell glowered down at her. "No blades or other weapons."

"Agreed."

Zawn handed off her weapons to Chaelene while Taylor took Averell's. She rolled up her sleeves and tightened her boots while he worked his gauntlets and belt into a more comfortable position. Then he advanced.

Zawn played along with his grabbing maneuvers, ducking away, rolling around, and jumping back. But he concentrated on his size and brute strength, unable to catch the nimbler Zawn. Seeing that he wasn't changing his tactics, she decided to let him get a hold of her. Triumphantly, he clasped her arms, pulling her to him. He lifted and flipped her over, her head hanging down by his waist while her feet dangled over his shoulder.

As Averell held her like a bag of grain, Taylor and Chaelene glanced at each other knowingly.

"He fell for it," Taylor murmured.

"He sure did."

"He's going to throw her."

"He'll drop her."

"Want to make a bet?"

"A full month of baths and bedtimes."

They tapped fingers.

After letting Averell gloat for a moment, Zawn reared back then bit the exposed flesh that his armor didn't cover. He yelped, let her go, but she grabbed his arm, swung her body behind him, then struck the backs of his knees. They buckled and he fell forward, while she rolled away from him.

"Technically, he dropped her," Chaelene determined. "Even if she did hang on."

Taylor grumbled, annoyed.

Zawn stood over the groaning Averell, tapping his shoulder with her boot. He rolled over onto his back, staring back up at her in shock. She blew a puff of air out of the corner of her mouth, flipping the hair that escaped out of her face.

"You done?"

He nodded slowly.

"Good. Lesson for today: You can't always fight with fists. You have to use your brains too. And sometimes, teeth."

Zawn straightened her shirt, then sauntered over to her friends while the younger elf just laid there, probably mostly from shock.

"We corrected that weakness in our armor, right?" Zawn asked, quietly.

"Started the day you bested Medruano," Taylor responded.

"Good."

"Tay thought he'd throw you."

Zawn chuckled. "Yeah, I thought so too. That mean you lost the bet?"

Taylor grunted, affirmatively.

"Can you help him up? He might change his mind and throw me if I go and offer him a hand."

~   ~   ~

Averell spent the evening in the guest hut, even through dinner, and didn't come out until the next morning. When he did, he made his way directly to Zawn's work hut and knocked. She called for him to come in, while she shoved a blanket and an empty bottle back into a bag.

She could tell he had spent the night dealing with his wounded pride as he admitted, "I haven't been bested in years."

"And that did you a disservice. Our best lessons come from our mistakes. Trust me, I am the demigod of mistakes. It's taken me quite a while to realize that Brennan impressed upon me the most important lesson - stop and think. The best thing he ever did to drive that point home was to land me on my back every time I forgot. In the heat of battle, it is easy to thrash around like a bull. But when it comes to diplomatic matters, you can't just hit things. Words, thoughts, actions, they all must be weighed carefully. As do emotions. We are emotional creatures. Can we turn them off? No. Hide our feelings? Yes. But they are still there underneath our bluster."

"What will you do about the settlement?"

"I have sent three fighters, two masters and one novice, to speak with the trespassers. I'm waiting to hear back."

"You sent fighters even though you are approaching them diplomatically?"

"I'm strategic, not stupid," she replied, raising her eyebrow. "If the humans are hostile, I wanted our people to be able to protect themselves. Hope for the best, be prepared for the worst."

A knock at her work hut's door interrupted them. She called out permission and a young female novice warrior entered. She bowed her head to Zawn then waited patiently.

"Avari, how did the conversation go with the humans?"

"They apologized for their error. They thought the river they settled near was Myrianin, the one on their map. Iloran showed them the direction of the

Myrianin River compared to where they were and they again apologized. Cadao offered to walk them up to that area, which they accepted, and we were actually able to find them a nice plot to resettle. They turned down our offer for assistance moving, since they hadn't started to build much and only had a few head of cattle. We are keeping an eye on them to ensure they keep their promise, but by all indications, they are packing up to move to the plot on the other side of the river."

"I'm glad there was a peaceful and productive resolution." Zawn turned to Averell. "My suggestion this afternoon is to speak with Cadao and Iloran. Find out how they approached the situation and what their suggestions are for diplomatic agreements. For now, please join our kithlin for breakfast."

"I will do so, thank you, Leader Haley." With a dip of his head, Averell left.

Avari didn't move.

"Thank you for the update, Avari."

Avari bowed her head, then turned to leave the hut. She hesitated, then over her shoulder, inquired, "Leader Haley?"

"Yes?"

"They thanked us for approaching them kindly and for having a conversation with them. They had been told by the villages on the outskirts of the Kingdom that we are nothing more than savages and they had feared we would hurt them without cause. But they were relieved when we talked to them and stated that they were glad the gossip was wrong about us."

"Now you understand why I asked you to approach them first with words and not weapons?"

She could see Avari thinking hard. "The lesson you taught Averell yesterday, it was for all of us, wasn't it?"

"Do you think it was a necessary lesson for you and the others?"

"I agreed with his words," the younger elf responded, her voice soft.

"Then, yes, the lesson was for all of us. We are fighters, but we only fight to protect what is precious to us. We do not instigate, we defend. It is what has kept us formidable and honorable."

CHAPTER 53

The change in Averell was immediate. He listened. He watched. And he didn't spout off, even though there were times she could see him struggle. It was against his nature not to fight, not respond, which she understood more than anyone, but that didn't mean she didn't get some perverse enjoyment out of it. She kept her smirking to a minimum, not wanting him to become embarrassed or frustrated. That would undo all of his progress.

She also made sure he spent time with other kithlin, including Taylor, Gaylon, and Meagan. Taylor discussed with him what Zawn expected of him as her second, when he stepped in to assist and when she let him lead. There seemed to be a comradery between the two huge men, which Zawn saw as a plus. Gaylon took Averell through each step of sowing and growing, how the irrigation system worked – and sometimes didn't work.

Averell was referred to Meagan to learn about their business making the treats that they sold. However, Zawn didn't expect to find him baking alongside the cooks. When she walked in, she found their assembly line set up and Averell in the middle of it all. His hair had been pulled back, armor removed, and an apron covering his front. And even though the flour on his cheek diminished his fierceness, she could have sworn he was enjoying himself.

"What's on the menu this week, Meagan?" Zawn asked after she had taken in the scene.

Averell glanced up and smiled, then returned to whatever his duty assigned him.

Meagan sighed, an exasperated sound. "Well, the Crinstons' son is getting married, so they asked for pastries with the cream filling. They are expecting most of their township to attend, which means a large order."

"Guess you're glad that you have an extra pair of hands?" Zawn asked.

"Thankful for the hands and that he's a quick learner."

Averell chuckled. "I had to help my mother with dinner and breakfast. Between lessons and training, I was cooking."

"Hidden talents?" Zawn teased.

"Out of necessity," Averell replied.

"Anything I can do to help?" the leader inquired.

"More milk to make the cream would be helpful," Meagan answered.

Zawn nodded. "I will see what the goats are willing to give us."

And with that, Zawn headed back out and worked on wrangling the goats. As she led her trip of goats back to the stables so they could be milked, she caught sight of Averell standing in the doorway. His small smile conveyed amusement at the parade behind her, but there was something else. She clicked her tongue, while calling out entreaties, then turned her back to him as the goats hopped and bolted past her.

Averell's attention at first was flattering but then Zawn wondered if she was imagining things. Her grief still rattled her every day, which caused her to worry that she wasn't thinking straight. With a sigh, she entered the stables and helped milk the goats.

When she disappeared, Averell didn't move. He felt someone walk up to his elbow.

"Something wrong?" Meagan asked.

Trying to hide his real reason for watching the kith leader, Averell responded, "I still don't understand why she handles the goats. Shouldn't she delegate that?"

"Before she had to challenge our previous leader, he ordered her to clean the goat stalls. He despised her, and the feeling was mutual, so one day he gave her what he thought was the most demeaning task in the kith, tending to the beasts. I don't think he realized that her spending time in the stables would endear her to them. After she became leader, her affection for the goats paid off because they listened to her and made it possible to milk them without issue. She joked it was because she won a headbutting contest with them. She did try to hand them off to another kithlin but that went ugly fast."

Meagan laughed as she remembered the chaos and the kith leader's traumatized facial expression.

"The goats actually searched her out, found her in the work hut and rushed right in. Goats were on the tables, in the sink, on the chairs. So, she goes every morning to lead them to pasture and every evening to lead them to the stables. If we need to milk them, she wrangles them for us. They will follow her anywhere." Meagan smiled, a deeply affectionate expression. "Just like her kith. We would follow her anywhere." She shook herself and took a deep breath. "Now, come, those treats won't make themselves."

~   ~   ~

"You look confused," Taylor commented, snapping Averell out of his thoughts.

They lunched around the fire, Averell's shoulders a little achy from baking.

His height made it difficult to stand straight, because the tables were made for average height elves. He enjoyed it though, the bakers were funny and authentic in their joy. But his thoughts kept going back to their kith leader and the conversation he had with Meagan.

"Your leader confounds me."

Taylor chuckled. "Is that all?"

"She is a very confusing force of nature."

"That is one good way to describe her."

Averell furrowed his eyebrows as he stared at the older elf.

"She's been called many things," Taylor continued. "But none fully describes her. She's not like the rest of us. That is a good thing, to be honest."

"Taikin makes decisions based on facts and needs of the kith. Leader Haley makes decisions…" and the younger elf stammered.

"She makes hers based on emotion, feelings, instinct. Her heart. But she'd never admit that."

"How can she be like that after being raised in the warrior caste?"

"Why don't you ask her?"

"I do not know how to approach the subject without offending her."

"Oh but she's so much fun to offend."

Averell looked appalled by Taylor's amusement.

"You see her as a leader, as you should, but you must understand, I see her as my friend, as my sister. We may have fought in the Purge together but we have had each other's backs since we were infants. We grew up together, we were both trained in the warrior caste. But we also had my mother and a master who understood that we needed to see the world beyond swords and battles."

"I never thought of her life before being leader."

"You have had a life before your rank, before Taikin started training you. How do you think your kithlin will view you if you became leader?"

Averell thought about that.

"Ask her, talk to her. That's why you're here, isn't it?"

~   ~   ~

There was a knock at her door. She called out permission to enter, while she finished up her notes in the crop ledger. When she glanced up, she saw Averell enter cautiously. She closed her ledger after gesturing for him to have a seat, then moved it to the side. She waited for him to speak.

Averell sat in front of her, staring at his folded hands. His dark oak tunic hung off of his shoulders, but fit better along the arms and torso. His matching slacks crinkled in the thighs while tucked into his boots below the knee. He looked odd without his armor and weapons, but his meekness was even stranger.

"I don't understand you," he finally admitted.

Zawn couldn't help but smile. "You're not the first and I doubt you'll be the last to say that to me."

"You were raised warrior caste."

"Yes, I was."

"But you do not act like it."

"And how am I supposed to act?"

Averell didn't respond.

"Aggressive? Defensive? Offended?" Then her smirk faded. "Suicidal?"

"We were born to die."

"No, we were born to live, Averell. To live, to love, to have families and friends. I was never taught that by our leader, but from what I saw around me and who I interacted with, I learned that those things mattered as much as fighting did."

"What could teach you such a lesson?"

She hesitated, debating what and how much to tell him. "When I was born, I was parentless the moment I left the womb. Taylor's mother Inari agreed to raise me alongside him because when he saw me, he was taken by me immediately. She always called us her twins, even though we are several months apart. When we were old enough, Medruano decided that we were warrior caste because that was our fathers' caste."

"That is quite an honor, to follow in your fathers' footsteps."

"Inari never admitted that she had tried to intervene but I had overheard the conversation. She begged Medruano not to let her babies die the same way as their fathers but he disregarded her pain as hysterical blathering."

"A mother's love is absolute," Averell responded, the small smile on his face telling her that he was thinking of his own mother. "And there is nothing greater."

Zawn nodded, knowing that the same love was growing in her. For Rynan. "I remember the night Brennan came to our hut. Brennan and Inari thought we were fast asleep, but Tay and I listened intently by the door when the two spoke outside on the porch. Brennan promised to take care of her babies. That was his job. Inari finally agreed but threatened Brennan's life if so much as a bruise appeared on either of us, even in training."

Averell couldn't help his smile widening. "Inari sounds like someone I would've liked."

"I think you would have," she replied, then shrugged. "We both trained under Brennan diligently to make Inari proud. We also adopted him as a father figure since Taylor's father died during the same skirmish mine died in. Brennan took that role seriously, keeping us close at all times, which kept him close to Inari as well. They ended up being involved intimately several years before his death during the Purge."

"Did he die honorably?"

She glanced away, frowning. "He fell in battle. I wasn't at his side, but Taylor was. I heard Tay yell and left Taikin's side. We pulled Brennan to a fallback position, but the wound was fatal. It was almost too much for Tay. Thankfully, we were able to console each other once the fighting ended. We… loved him. We needed to and were able to grieve, the three of us, together. But Inari was never the same and soon followed Brennan to the other side of the canopy."

"I am sorry to hear that. They must have loved each other very much."

"They showed me what love was. I knew from a family perspective of course, Inari and Taylor never looked at me in any other way than family. But Inari and Brennan, even though they tried to be secret about it, showed me that there was more to our lives than dying. How even the smallest gestures could be a smile to someone that meant the world to you. No matter how much Medruano pushed for us to believe we were only good enough to fight and die, I always remembered Inari and Brennan."

Zawn blinked away the tears that threatened as she not only thought about Inari and Brennan holding hands but also how Gwendin's fingers entwined with hers. Over the dwindling fire's crackling, she heard Rynan murmur in his sleep in the bassinet behind her. She took a deep breath before continuing.

"It's taken me some time, but I have realized more and more that Brennan's lessons have molded my leadership style. And with Taylor having learned the same teachings, we work well together and understand what needs to happen to make the kith successful and our kithlin happy. I know I am not infallible, that I will make mistakes here and there, but because of our success, I know that I am capable. Decisions I have made turned profitable and lifted the spirits of my kithlin. I'm making a difference. Finally. And it's because I know what love is and I know how to love."

She looked up at the silent Averell, seeing his copper eyes darken with emotion.

"You have to lead the way that will work best for your kith, Averell," she continued, "But you have to also understand how all of your kithlin see the world. After all, not all of your kithlin were raised in the warrior caste. They will not understand your expectations and you will either end up with fear or disgust from them. You have to have all of your kithlin behind you. The only way to be a successful leader is to have the support of those you lead."

"Thank you, Leader Haley, for your honesty. I hadn't even thought about these things. I fear I have walked around with blinders on. I have a lot to think about. I wish you a good evening."

"Good night, Averell."

~   ~   ~

Tending crops, like weeding and feeding them vitamins, included all capable kithlin. They ate breakfast and headed out at first light. Laughter and chit chat filled the air, as well as a few well-meant wagers. After all, where was the fun in work unless you could beat someone and win a prize?

The day started out cool, but once the sun reached midday, the heat began to set in. Several individuals started removing their excess clothing to relieve their discomfort, or manipulated their clothing to allow better airflow. Even Zawn twisted her patched tunic up in the front and knotted it, baring her belly and lower back, and rolled up the legs of her pants. After getting comfortable, she returned to her work until she heard a nearby gasp.

Zawn glanced up, searching for the reason for the noise. The younger females nearby stared, mouths gaping open, and obviously the sources of the sounds. Most of the men had removed their tunics, tossing them into a pile off to the side of the rows. Including Averell.

She had to admit, begrudgingly, that he was a sight to be seen.

His multi-colored hair had been pulled up into a messy bun, giving his perspiration freedom to run down his back and torso. His chest was wide, the muscles underneath moving like ripples of water after a pebble toss. Each muscle in his arms clenched as he lifted heavier objects, like rocks and machinery, then relaxed when he set the objects down. Moisture trickled along his muscular arms, getting lost in the dark shades of his skin that accented his athleticism acutely. His sweat adhered his beltless trousers to his hips, which slimmed down magnificently from his abdomen. The legs of his pants were also rolled up, exposing the fit calves that led to quite a few assumptions.

There was little left to the imagination, but Zawn knew the women around her were using theirs to undress him completely.

Apparently feeling eyes on him, Averell looked over at Zawn. A sly smile spread across his face when he saw her staring at him. She raised an eyebrow before rolling her eyes and returning to her work.

~   ~   ~

The weeks flew by and Averell felt more like a member of the kith than she had expected. He helped wherever he could when requested, but tried to spend as much time with Zawn too. She appreciated his curiosity and found his happy-to-help attitude refreshing, considering their first few days together. She had gotten used to him being around, meeting her for breakfast, spending time with her, and wishing her a good night.

It had been a rather long day in the fields, leaving Zawn exhausted and sore. However, the work had been shared amongst the kithlin and the crops were hearty this season. She couldn't help but beam with pride. She made her way to her work hut, Averell on her heels, and she dug into her cold box for ice to cool their glasses of water. She handed him one while she sipped from hers, a content silence between them.

Then she noticed that he glanced over her shoulder. She looked over, finding Rynan's supplies laid out along the counter.

"You talk about a child," Averell pointed out. "But you never mention a mate."

"Some things are personal. And some things are not easy to talk about."

"I heard stories that you didn't take an elf as a mate. I never thought I'd hear of such a thing in my lifetime."

"Obviously, you've never followed your heart even if you knew it'd get you killed. I may have been named the daydreamer of our kith but most called me a nitwit." She chuckled. "Tried everything in my power to earn that moniker. Loving someone even though it was a crime seemed to be the best way to do so."

"Was he your only one?"

She raised an eyebrow. "That is a very personal question, Averell."

"That didn't come out the way I meant."

"Ah, but it did. Just like everyone else, you wanted to know if laying with a man has ruined me."

"That is not what I asked."

"Then what did you really want to know?"

"If you would ever take another chance. With someone new? With an elf?" Then he hesitated before adding, "With me?"

Zawn's eyes widened and she felt her breath catch in her throat. He reached out cautiously, cupping her face with his large hands. His touch was gentle, reverent. One thumb caressed her cheek in a manner she never expected out of him. The look in his copper-colored eyes reflected an honest attraction to her.

"I have found it surprising at how easy it is to talk to you. I am comfortable with you. You have been welcoming and patient and kind. Even when you tease me over a foolish question, you still answer it with detail that makes me think you wouldn't do that just for anyone."

"I am to teach you how to be a leader, Averell."

"You're teaching me more than that," he whispered, leaning in as if to kiss her.

She stepped back and out of his hands, blinking fast and trying to calm herself. She wasn't angry or offended, she was flabbergasted. Surprised by him, startled by how she felt. Her heart was in her throat, threatening to burst free and run out of the hut. She cleared her throat, then tried to talk her way out of his honesty and her own attraction to him.

"I'm sorry, if I made you believe there could be more. I am a mateless mother and a kith leader. There is nothing more for me in this life. Including lovers."

His face crumbled. It wasn't disappointment, like a man who had hoped to bed her. It was something more like heartbreak.

"I am grateful for your honesty," he responded, speaking carefully in an attempt to hide the pain in his voice. "And I am sorry for overstepping. I bid you a good night, milady."

~   ~   ~

Taylor was walking from the armory to his home when he saw Averell leave Zawn's work hut. He saw her face before the door closed then watched the other elf as he strode, head down, back to the guest hut. He sighed, torn over who to go to first. He chose Averell, because he'd get more information out of him than Zawn. But first he grabbed two mugs and filled them with mead, before heading over. He knocked hard, to make sure the other knew it wasn't Zawn, and the young elf opened the door slowly. He saw the two mugs, grimaced, but opened the door further to let Taylor in.

Taylor handed over one mug to Averell before sitting down in one of the chairs. Averell followed, lowering himself into the other chair. He stared down into the mug, then downed a substantial amount in one swig.

"What happened?" Taylor asked, his tone flat.

"I… tried to…" and Averell covered his face with one hand.

"You made an overture."

"I did."

Taylor tried to quell a smirk, not surprised. He had watched them interact ever since she landed him on his back and could tell Averell was falling for his best friend. "Well, you're not a bleeding lump of pulp, so she didn't get too angry."

"Her words were blunt enough."

Taylor exhaled, hard, staring at the rather morose younger elf. "How much has she told you?"

"What do you mean?"

"I assume she's told you some personal stuff? Her experiences color her leadership style quite a bit. As they do her personal decisions."

"I know that she fought in the Purge, so she is much older than I thought at first. I know she has a child, but no mate. Not anymore, anyway. From rumor and now her own admission, I know he wasn't an elf. She told me about your mother and your mentor, how they taught her about living life and loving others. That's about it."

Taylor shook his head, disappointed. "She always holds back. I'm going to tell you some things that if you tell her I was the one who spoke of them, I will deny it and they will never find your body."

Averell's eyes widened, but he nodded slowly, accepting the other man's terms.

"Before becoming leader, Zawn never met a rule she liked. The first time it bit her was when her first love turned their back on her when she tried to help them, against our leader's orders, and lost almost everything in return. She spent a long time alone, as if paying a penance, until she met someone new." Taylor paused, his heart warming but hurting at the memory of Zawn and Gwendin together. "They loved each other beyond any love I have ever seen in all my years, but their relationship broke rules, laws, and a few stigmas. He died when Crenast came to power, leaving her with a newborn. She has tried to figure out how to be a mother along with the many other hardships that come with leading a kith. It has taken her a long time to figure out what rules work for the greater good. She has come a long way and I am very proud of her, seeing that she is the closest thing I have to a sister. However, she grieves her lost love daily, as she is reminded of him every time she looks into their son's eyes."

"I can see why she wouldn't want to talk about those things. That is a lot of pain for one soul."

"And yet she gets up every morning. I don't know how she does." Taylor took a final swig from his mug. "You are attracted to her, and that's not something to be ashamed of; she is an amazing woman."

"She is a light," Averell admitted, softly.

"But she is a force of nature with unseen scars. You can ogle her from a distance, but keep that distance at all times. If she were to ever see you as more than some student from a friendly kith, she will let you know without innuendo. However, do not expect it."

Averell nodded, slowly, then grimaced. "I do not wish to be sent away because of my error. I have to figure out a way to apologize to her."

"If being sent home was your punishment, you would already be walking. No, she must have recognized that you meant no ill will. Let her come to you. She will tell you your penance."

"Thank you, Taylor."

~ ~ ~

Zawn reclined in her cushioned chair, in front of the fireplace, Rynan laying on her chest sound asleep. A light knock on her door brought her out of her thoughts and she glanced up to see Taylor slipping in through the door. He closed the door softly, then made his way to the end of the bed. He stared at the sleeping child for a moment before speaking.

"He told me what happened."

Zawn remained silent.

"He regrets stepping over the line."

"He already apologized," she responded, in a whisper. "And I didn't thrash him for it."

"No, you were kind enough not to beat him for his attempt." Taylor sighed, sitting down. "I know it's still fresh but…"

"I cannot be a leader to a lover. I'm to teach him not lay with him."

"He finds you attractive. Out of all the women here. We both have seen how the females in our kith watch him. Any one of them would take him up on an offer of companionship." He scoffed. "I think even my Chae would."

Zawn chuckled at that, then the humor faded away. "He should make an offer to another," she replied. "He deserves the energy of someone his age and the freedom of a childless woman."

"Zawnie…"

"He's half my age, Tay."

"Gwendin was younger," he countered, his reward a dark glare from Zawn.

"I can't expect someone to be responsible for a child that is not his."

"Yet you expect that out of yourself."

She didn't respond.

"I don't want you to be miserable for the rest of your life. That's a long time, Zawnie."

She scoffed. "Have I not always been miserable? It's the constant state of my being." She rubbed Rynan's back when he moved, reassuring him back to sleep. "I know what Gwendin would want, what he would say to me. But I am still grieving, my friend." Her voice shook as she continued, "I close my eyes and see him dying in front of me. I still hear his last words ringing in my ears late at night. I break down when no one is looking or when I am alone too long. I even regret not letting that soldier strike me down too."

Taylor straightened at that admission.

"I still get so angry thinking about him being brave enough to protect this baby. The only thing that gets me to put my feet on the floor every morning is our kithlin and Rynan." She stared down at her baby, frowning. "It is hard enough that I am having to change my ways for a baby that looks at me like I am the only thing in his world that matters. I need to figure me out before I can drag anyone else into this messy life of mine. And I refuse to use Averell because he deserves as much respect as I do."

"Then you need to tell him that. And I think you should tell him more about what you've been through, so he can make up his own mind about what he wants from you. Right now, he sees you as an impressive woman, unlike anyone he's ever met before. You can't expect him to understand your resistance by kicking him out of your hut or sending him home. I think you two could have a better connection if you told him more about who you are and what it has taken for you to get here."

"I told him some stuff."

"But was it the right information?"

"I'll talk to him in the morning."

"Nicely?"

She rolled her eyes, before taking a deep breath and shushing Rynan when the movement disturbed him. "I'll be diplomatic. Happy?"

"Yes. Because thrashing him once was enough for the one lesson."

"That's why I didn't do it again. It didn't fit the situation. Go home, Tay. Leave me to my sleeping baby and my thoughts."

"Good night, Zawnie."

"Good night, my friend."

~   ~   ~

The next morning, Zawn summoned Averell to her work hut. He sat after she gestured to the chair, then she lowered herself in the one that faced him. She stared at her hands as they twisted together in her lap, then made herself take a deep breath.

"I know I told you about how I learned to be different, that I learned about love from those around me. But I have also been through many heartbreaks, Averell. Most of my own doing, but there is one choice I made that I will never apologize for, even though we didn't get our happily ever after. Gwendin was my mate. More than a mate, he was my true love. I didn't know I could be in love like that until I met him. I would have given everything up for him. Not many can understand that, beyond the romantic notion. And I would never expect someone your age and status to ever understand that. I am very protective of his legacy and how he is remembered, because he was a man among elves. I loved him and now I am left to grieve him, while raising our son and making sure he never forgets his Dadda."

She let her words hang in the air, unsure how he would react. She sighed when he didn't respond.

"If you think that our misunderstanding has destroyed any chance of you continuing your lessons with me, I will not be offended if you wish to learn under Taylor or if you'd rather just return to your kith. To save face, we'll come up with an explanation that makes our separation reasonable and my fault."

"Leader Haley, I appreciate you trying to soothe my ego with diplomacy, but I know that I have a lot more to learn from you. And I want to get to know you better, since you have lived a life that, even though we come from the same caste, does not run parallel to mine. I can handle my wounded pride if you can pretend that I didn't make an overture."

Zawn smirked. "As long as we agree to hide our awkwardness from the others?"

"Gladly."

"Good."

He paused. "I am sorry for the loss of your love."

"Thank you. Please, come, we've discussion about our next crops that you should observe."

"Lead the way, milady."

"Call me Zawn."

CHAPTER 54

Zawn handed off Rynan to Chaelene before Averell met her at the work hut. When he arrived, she led him out to the fields where they worked side by side. They helped with picking some of the vegetables that were ready while pulling weeds that popped up. They talked quietly to each other as they made their way through the rows, while laughing with the other kithlin who told stories and jokes.

When their shift was done, she sent him to clean up while she bathed away the dirt and grime. She changed into more comfortable clothes and walked back to her work hut to wait for Averell. She caught herself trying to fix her hair in the looking glass that hung in the work hut's privy room. She looked bedraggled and exhausted. She rolled her eyes, knowing it was hopeless. There was nothing she could do to make herself look less worn out.

She heard the knock for permission, which she yelled out, then walked into the main room at the same time as Averell entered. She gestured for him to sit down, then offered to answer any questions he had.

"Your kithlin answered all of my questions. I am honored by their willingness to share their knowledge with me. You were right, there is more to the kith than fighting and winning. Nothing is unimportant. Before, I never thought about where my food comes from, or my clothes. I finally understand that everything is important in the kith. I don't think I would have seen any of these things if Taikin tried to show me." He frowned. "I'm sure he tried."

"Again, that's why he sent you to me. I am not afraid of pushing you out of your comfort zone."

"And straight into the mud."

They laughed.

"I can only hope that I raise my son to understand the same things. That there's more to the food on our tables, the clothes on our backs. And to respect each trade as if it were the most important one in the entire kith, because each is equal in its importance."

Averell blinked, his mouth falling open in shock. "I just realized something. I haven't met your son."

Zawn shrugged. "He spends his day with Chaelene when I'm so busy. He is in good hands. You don't need to worry about it."

"I would like to meet him. He is one of the most important people in your life."

She stared at him for a moment, her stomach turning. The honesty in his eyes showed that he wanted to know more about her life, her son included. "Um, stay here. I'll be back."

Zawn retrieved her son, who had squealed in excitement when he saw his mother, then returned to her work cabin. She entered nervously, carrying her baby on her hip, something he enjoyed because he could look around. Once he learned how to hold his head up, he demanded to be carried that way. She would laugh when he got excited at something he saw, because he would bang his hands against her chest or shoulder.

Averell turned and watched her walk in, eyes looking the boy up and down. "Taikin said your child was, well, special. He didn't say he was so damned cute. May I?"

As he held out his hands, Rynan reached out, too. Cautiously, she handed Rynan over. He held the baby high up on his chest, then started making baby noises and cooing, making Rynan laugh at him.

"I am the oldest of six children," he responded, reading the confusion on her face. "Babies are not strange to me. What is his name?"

"Rynan, our stargazer."

"How old is he?" he asked.

"Um, almost six months."

"This is when it gets fun. Babies want to be a part of everything."

Then Rynan reached out and grabbed a hold of Averell's lower lip.

"And gwabbing ederting," Averell added.

"Rynan, stop, silly," she chided, stepping closer and freeing Averell's lip.

Rynan squealed with disappointment. Zawn chuckled, kissing the hand that had held the lip. Rynan babbled in response. Then he fussed again.

"Chae said you hadn't had your bottle yet," she said, reaching for him.

"I can hold him while you make it," Averell offered. "I can tell he is a handful. I don't mind."

She smiled her thanks, then headed into the small kitchen area. She always kept supplies in a bag that she carried from her personal hut to her work hut daily. Milk was placed safely in the chill box, while diapers, toys, and blankets remained inside the satchel. As she worked on warming his bottle, she kept them in view. Babbling and babytalk escaped the massive mountain of an elf, all the while Rynan cooed and giggled and wiggled in his arms. Zawn started to slowly relax, watching Rynan win over Averell. But she apparently still had a baffled expression on her face, because Averell laughed at her.

"Why the look?" he inquired.

"I have been met with many strong opinions."

Averell sighed, then nodded. "Because we are not supposed to do certain things, doesn't make them impossible. You said he was your true love. If this lovely little wiggly worm is the product of that love? It must have been an epic one."

She felt a blush warm her face. Clearing her throat, Zawn crossed the hut, then reached for her son again. This time Averell readily handed him over because Rynan recognized the bottle and wriggled in excitement. She held him at an angle and gave him his bottle. As usual, his suckle started loud and impatient then began to slow as he got near the end of it. As he dozed off, she set the bottle down and laid him down in the bassinet behind her desk. The moment he touched the mattress, he started to cry, making her sigh.

"Chae says you go straight to sleep for her on the bed," she admonished him, but gave in. She grabbed the wrap, secured it, and put him inside. He had grown so much that his legs now hung down and his arms stuck out. But with his head against her chest, he heard her heartbeat and fell happily back to sleep.

"He knows his mother and has his own preferences when it comes to her," Averell responded, his tone kind.

"He's spoiled," she retorted with a smile.

He chuckled, covering his mouth to muffle the sound so he wouldn't disturb the baby. "That too."

She sat back down finally, one arm wrapped protectively around Rynan. She stared at the baby for a few moments, then glanced back up at Averell. He had been watching her, quietly, apparently surprised by this other side of her.

"Now you've seen what my days are really like," she admitted, with some chagrin. "When it's not as busy with the growing season and all that, I have him usually all day. He's been to every corner of the kith. And Chae steps in when I can't have him with me. Sometimes Meagan helps out too if Chae has a big lesson with the children. I am fortunate that I am not alone in my parenthood. Even though it has been a hefty change for me to get accustomed to."

"It only makes you a better leader, don't you think?"

"When I announced that I had given birth to Rynan, I was challenged by the former leader's grandson."

"Merded?"

She nodded. "I was surprised it took him so long, but I think I hadn't given him a good enough reason before then. But a hybrid child? An abomination? That was enough. He was formidable, but it didn't take much for me to beat him. I had the choice of making him rescind his challenge or kill him like I had his grandfather." She paused, rubbing the baby's back when he moved in his sleep. "Rynan started crying. It was then the warrior in me was reminded by the mother in me that taking a life can never be done in whimsy. Because the person on the end of your blade is someone's family."

"Teneel never taught us that perspective. It was always attack because it was either you or them."

"Brennan had a similar warning. But he always knew I had my own point of view and I tried to break the fight instead of flight lever in my brain." She chuckled. "It was a lot of work. But after the Purge, after everything I saw, and now with how much my life has changed, I have had to see the bigger picture."

"Is that why you approach things as diplomatically as you can?"

"That and I have seen wars start over slight misunderstandings that a mere clarifying question could have cleared up without one life lost. Been around a long time. It's the curse of the elf-kind."

"I am glad I haven't had to live as long to learn those lessons."

She raised her eyebrow.

"I've had a good teacher."

CHAPTER 55

That night, dinner had been served and Averell ate with everyone as usual, then excused himself before the storytelling. Confused, Zawn watched him walk to his hut and when he didn't return immediately, she stood and made her way over. She knocked on the door, entering after hearing his permission. She slipped inside to find his duffel on the bed. He was gathering his clothing from the drawers, folding them neatly and placing them inside the bag.

She frowned. "Packing already?"

"I do leave tomorrow," he responded, with a chuckle. "Probably should have started sooner."

"I probably kept you too busy to think about it," she said, shrugging.

"You have, indeed."

As he continued to adjust items in the bag while adding more to it, she suddenly realized that she hated seeing him go. Quietly, she admitted, "It will be odd not to see you every day."

"Knowing Taikin, he will send me back a few more times so you can land me on my back."

"I look forward to that."

They both laughed, then their smiles faded away. Averell stopped packing and turned toward her. He took her hands in his, his expression serious.

"When I made the overture a couple of weeks ago, it was because I found you physically and intellectually attractive. You are unlike anyone else I have ever met. And yes, you bested me, which made me quite smitten. But spending so much time with you, learning more about you and how you see the world, and then meeting your son, it makes me have a greater respect for you. Not just as a leader, but as a woman. I hope that we can continue our friendship even after I leave tomorrow."

"No matter where you go or how long your absence," she responded, trying to fight away her disappointment over his departure. "You will always be a friend and ally, Averell. And you will always be welcome here."

"I am glad to hear that. May I hug you farewell?"

"You're not leaving until tomorrow."

"Yes, but I don't know if I'll be strong enough tomorrow not to give myself away in front of your kithlin."

She pulled her hands free, which he respected but looked a little worried by her actions. She raised up on her tiptoes and wrapped her arms around his neck. She felt him sigh in relief before bringing his arms around her and pulling her close. They stood together in silence, pressed closely, taking in the other's smell and warmth.

"We will see each other again soon," she whispered.

~   ~   ~

Over the next few months, Averell did get sent back, but more for keeping a strong bond between the two kiths and not necessarily for punishment. He would only spend a few days before heading back, but those days were spent at Zawn's side. He helped her with whatever tasks were on her agenda and there were times that he even toted Rynan around, entertaining the boy when Zawn needed her hands free.

CHAPTER 56

She wasn't in the work hut like he had expected. Assuming she had stepped out briefly, Averell set down his bags and unbuckled his armor. He piled his shoulder armor and breastplate in the corner, out of the way, but she still didn't show up. Concerned, he walked around toward the center of the kith and he heard it. A crying baby and a hopeless voice trying to quiet him. He strode over to the hut at the very edge of the kith and knocked on the door. He heard her curse then she opened the door.

Zawn still wore her sleeping gown, with her hair pulled back into a messy bun. She stood there, crying baby in her arms, and she looked as if she were about to cry herself.

"Oh, Averell, I am so sorry. I forgot you were coming."

"Everything all right?"

"No. Rynan is teething and sensitive and just a handful right now. I haven't gotten any sleep or gotten anything done these last few days. But it wasn't fair to stick Chae with him today, since it's an adventure day for the older kids."

He gestured to be let in and she backed away toward the fireplace and chairs. He shut the door behind him and closed the distance between them.

"What have you tried for the teething?"

"Everything known to an elf. I'm afraid there's a human element I don't know what to do with."

"My momma always gave us a mix of chamomile and vanilla extract. And gave us chilled fruit in a cloth."

"None of that worked on this tyrant." Then she paused. "But we didn't use fruit. We just used a cube of ice in cloth."

"Maybe it was too cold? Here, sit. If he keeps fussing, try gently rubbing his gums."

"I've done that, he just bites me."

Averell chuckled. "Keep doing it a little longer."

With that, Averell was out the door and she could hear him speaking with

Meagan. Exhausted, she sat with the wailing Rynan in her arms, maneuvering him to free one hand, which allowed her to softly massage his gums. She could feel the hard nubs on the bottom jaw, but she made sure to massage both sets just in case. She rocked him gently in hopes of soothing his anxiety, but she felt helpless with her son being in pain and her inability to fix it.

Averell returned, with a clean cheesecloth that held something inside. He knelt by her chair and swapped it for her fingers. She could feel the chill of whatever fruit he chose, realizing that it was cool but it wasn't ice cold. Rynan began to chew and rub his gums on the cheesecloth. The tears and screams stopped for the first time in hours.

Zawn sighed in relief then burst into tears herself. Averell murmured something sympathetic, pulling her into a hug. She sobbed into his neck as he rubbed her arm understandingly, giving her the time to get her exhaustion out of her system. When she finally caught her breath, she groused at herself.

"I am so sorry," she said, sniffling and sitting back up straight. "This isn't how a kith leader should treat a visitor."

"Are we still leader and visitor?"

She frowned, using her sleeve to wipe her nose.

"You're my friend, Zawnie," he replied, rubbing her back. "And you have had one of the worst nights a mother can ever have. I think you're allowed a breakdown every once in a while."

"What do you mean, one of the worst?" she demanded.

He laughed, sitting back on his legs. "He hasn't been sick?"

"No, he's been fine. A little fussy, that's all. Well, there was the snot incident. But nothing serious. Until this."

"Then you're lucky. Here, let me take him. Go clean up."

"Thank you, Averell. Really. But this isn't fair to you."

"I vaguely remember a certain leader telling me that sometimes you have to count on others for help and that you cannot be expected to do everything on your own."

She didn't respond.

"Hand over the tyrant and go clean up."

She rolled her eyes, but followed his orders. She handed Rynan over, who was still gnawing on the cheesecloth, then stood and walked into the bathing room. She heard Averell cooing at Rynan, who grunted as he gnashed, and she splashed water on her face. She grabbed a washcloth and wetted it, laying the cool cloth against her tear-streaked face. She closed her eyes and took several deep breaths before reopening them and removing the cloth. She stared at herself in the looking glass, seeing the pain and exhaustion on her face. She hadn't realized it was so obvious. She needed to work harder to hide it. There was no reason to worry the others.

She had to get better control of herself.

Once she felt she had a better handle on her emotions, she stepped back out. The scene left her speechless, making her lean against the doorframe.

Averell had taken her seat, still babbling to the baby until he started to doze off. The man fell silent as Rynan gave a big sigh and started to lose his grip on the cheesecloth. Averell caught it before it fell, smiling down at the child in his arms. He limited his movements to make sure he didn't disturb Rynan, keeping the cheesecloth in hand and slowing his rocking motion.

She walked back over after taking in the scene. She laid a kind hand on Averell's shoulder, making him carefully look up.

"Thank you," she whispered.

"You're welcome. Please, lay down and try to get some rest. You can only sleep when he does at this juncture. I'll keep an eye on him."

"Are you sure?"

"Zawnie, of course I'm sure. Get some rest."

~   ~   ~

She didn't know how long she slept. She only knew that Rynan's giggling roused her. She slowly opened her eyes, to see Averell and Rynan sitting on the floor by the fireplace. Averell had his legs splayed out in a way that kept the boy from crawling away while Rynan sat in between them. Apparently, the cold fruit had taken the sting out of his gums, because Rynan laughed at Averell who played peek-a-boo with him.

She laid there, watching them, her heart warming. Then she felt it crack when she imagined Gwen doing the same thing. Breathing became difficult. She had been missing him severely lately, but as she laid there, she heard his voice telling her to enjoy the tableau in front of her. The younger elf seemed as carefree as Rynan in their play. She knew Averell's care for Rynan stemmed from his misguided affection for her, but at that moment, the two of them entertaining each other was, for her, the simplest moment of pure joy.

Averell glanced over at the bed, as if checking to make sure they weren't disturbing her. He smiled widely when he noticed that her eyes were open.

"Look, it's Momma," Averell whispered, pointing toward the bed.

Rynan looked over and squealed joyfully. Zawn chuckled, sitting up and slipping off the bed. Rynan reached for her to pick him up, which she obliged, kissing his cheek.

"Feeling better, my darling?"

"Every time he woke up, I gave him the chilled fruit. Meagan looked quite baffled when I came out with him in my arms, but she gave me what I needed each time. The swelling's down and he seems to be feeling better."

"I honestly can't thank you enough, Averell."

"Nonsense. You've given me so much of your time and patience and knowledge. If I can return some of it by babysitting and helping you get some sleep, I will always oblige."

He noticed that she still looked sad, even though she seemed entertained by her son. He patted the floor in front of him. She lowered herself to sit down, all the while Rynan jabbered. She laughed and asked him questions, which only extended his incoherent story.

"Apparently, you did a good job babysitting," Zawn said with a chuckle. "At least, according to Rynan."

"I'll take the compliment."

He wrapped his arms around her and pulled her closer. She didn't relax immediately, leaning slightly away from him but she did not push him away. He refused to be offended, because he understood her hesitation. But she needed some reassurance and as he held her, he hoped that she would eventually seek it from him.

"Chaelene, Meagan, and Taylor all checked in on you two while you slept," he informed her. "They tried to take over but I knew they all had things they had to take care of. I only left to grab lunch and came right back."

Their tightknit proximity let Rynan reach over her shoulder and grab Averell's nose, making the big man laugh. The sound and feel of his laughter eased her tension and she leaned back against his chest. Incrementally, she started to settle in his embrace.

"You didn't have to," she replied.

"No, but I wanted to."

Rynan grabbed onto her shoulders and pulled himself up onto his feet, teetering on her thigh. He lost his balance and she held tight as he landed back onto her lap. Frustrated, he cried out, making her kiss his forehead. He sighed, then started to plot his next move.

"I slept through lunch?" she asked.

"Not too long. Hungry?"

She groused as her stomach growled. "Apparently. I don't even remember when I ate last."

"Well, lunch was just cold meat sandwiches and vegetables." He paused, while Rynan tried to stand on her legs again. "I made you a plate and put it in your chill box."

"You didn't have to."

"You do realize that's not the point?"

She didn't respond.

"I know it's hard for you to accept help when it comes to your son. Especially mine, knowing how I feel about you. But take it, Zawnie. I would be nowhere else, doing nothing else."

"I don't want to mislead you. I also don't want you to think I expect you to help raise my son. You're young, with the world laid at your feet. You should be with those your age and mindset."

"Do you think me carefree?" He shook his head, smiling mirthlessly. "Taikin wants me to be his second, and quickly, because Darion isn't getting any younger or healthier. Taikin wants him to retire and enjoy the rest of his final days on this side of the canopy. So, if you think I'm sowing wild oats and adventuring, I'm flattered, but those days are over for me. And to be honest,

I've had my fill." He bopped Rynan on his nose, making the infant laugh. "I care about you and your son probably more than I should. I know we will never be more than this and I have accepted that. But let me keep this at least."

Guilt darkened her eyes as she stared at him. "It's not that I don't think you're strong enough…"

"You didn't give me the chance to prove it to you," he chided, with a smirk. She rolled her eyes, shifting in discomfort.

"But no, I don't think you have ever questioned my strength. Only the possibility of you wasting my time or hurting me. I will never stop caring about you, no matter what, because you are my friend, Zawnie."

"I would be," and she paused, thinking, "honored if you were a part of Rynan's life. Even if only here and there."

"Good. Because I would be honored to be a part of his life. And yours." Silence. "Hand over the tyrant and go eat."

"Next you'll be telling me to put pants on?"

He laughed. "I wouldn't dare."

Reluctantly, she handed her child back to Averell, then opened the chill box. She tried to sit at the table to eat, but Rynan kept crawling over Averell's leg to reach his mother. Sighing, she returned to her seat on the floor. Her son settled down, at least in trying to escape Averell's barriers, but he crawled over them and grabbed onto clothes and hair. The two adults sat closely, with the infant trying to stand on his own and Averell trying to keep a hold of him so he wouldn't fall over and hurt himself. Then she tried to divert his attention with food, which worked and he happily sat down, gumming some squash.

"Can I ask you something personal?" he inquired.

"You can."

"Were your tears just from lack of sleep?"

She glanced up at him, surprised, then focused back on her carrot. "Rynan is almost a year old."

He furrowed his eyebrows together in confusion, then they unkinked as he realized what that meant to her.

"How much time did he get to spend with his son?"

"Only a couple of weeks."

"Such a short time," he whispered, sadness in his voice. "It must have hit you quite hard that he has missed so much."

"They want to hold a great celebration for his first birthday, but it's hard to think of planning something joyful when there was tragedy so close."

"I never knew Gwendin," Averell responded, carefully. "However, I think he would want you to celebrate not just birthdays and other milestones, but also, every day. You can grieve him, miss him, but you have so much to rejoice for him, about him. Rynan included."

She looked up into his eyes, seeing his honesty. He wasn't placating her or faking the heartfelt words. He reached up and brushed away the hair that escaped her bun, making her realize how close he was to her. He gave into temptation, letting his fingertips trace her cheek gently. She swallowed hard, deep feelings stirring in her that she had hoped were dead.

A knock on the door made Zawn stiffen. She stood up and set her plate on the end of the bed, then answered the door.

Chaelene stood there, relief on her face. Suddenly, Rynan shrieked and laughed, waving his hands at Chaelene as he sat in front of Averell.

"You are definitely in a better mood," Chae responded, smiling at the child, then returned her attention to Zawn.

"Did the children have fun today?" Zawn inquired.

"They did. Many new critters for them to talk about. And how are you?"

"Rested. Thank you for helping."

"Averell did all the work. I only made sure he ate. Will you be able to join us for dinner?"

"I think so. I got a pretty good nap. And now that we know how to manage his teething…"

"Good. We'll see you three then."

~ ~ ~

As the sun set, the fire flared up and everyone gathered in the square. Taylor, Chaelene and their three children took over one bench, saving a spot for them. The two older children ran around the bench, giggling and insulting each other. The youngest, Minee, laid in Chae's arms, face down in the nook of her elbow. Zawn was always amazed at how that girl could sleep anywhere and in any position.

Averell sat next to Zawn as she held Rynan, giving him his bottle after he got tired of stealing off of her plate. Chatting and laughing filled the air, lulling Zawn. She let go of her anxious thoughts and enjoyed every voice, every story, and every smile.

Zawn felt Rynan squirm then glanced down at him. "I will be right back."

"Everything all right?" Averell asked.

"Yes, he is just making, well, that face. Diaper change imminent."

Her friends laughed at that.

She stood up, then carried her baby back to their hut. She laid out the changing blanket and put Rynan down. However, as she unwrapped the diaper, she stumbled back at the smell. "Oh, Rynan Haley, what on this side of the canopy!?"

She took a deep breath before wrapping him back up and carrying him into the bathing room. Chae had warned her that diarrhea was a side effect of the teething phase, but his diaper was… epically disgusting. She started filling the sink, but she decided to spray him off with the tub nozzle first. She tested the water before running him under the stronger stream, making him whine in annoyance.

"I know, my darling, but you have gotten it in every nook and cranny. This is the easiest way I know of to get it all."

Once she got what was visible off, she moved him to the sink and turned off the faucets. Then she bubbled up the small bath with soap and scrubbed her baby. As she cleaned him up, she sang to him softly, a practice that kept him calm. He always enjoyed listening to her, either talking or singing, and he watched her face intently when she did. He stopped fussing at her for the scrubbing and smiled up at her with his discolored gums. When she looked closer, she saw the tips of teeth peeking out from his bottom jaw. The shapes looked similar to hers, only smaller. Elves had more canines than humans, but the molars and front teeth were very similar.

"Ah there are the troublemakers!" she whispered in a teasing tone. "Now you will learn how to chew food that you have never eaten before and you will get fat."

He laughed then slapped his hands on the water. He splashed her just right and water rolled down her neck and into her shirt. She shook her head at him, then scrubbed his ears, which he hated, and he screamed his displeasure. It was her turn to laugh at him. She lifted him and checked every crack and crevice, confirming she had gotten all the diarrhea, then rinsed him off and wrapped him in a towel. She drained the sink and carried him to the bed.

A knock on the door and then, "Zawnie?"

"Come in, Tay."

Taylor peeked in, seeing her wrangling her child in the towel. "That bad?"

"I think I will be burning that diaper just to put it out of its misery."

Taylor chuckled. "I was glad when Minee finally got through the teething phase."

"Chae says it seems to last forever," she responded while she dried her baby. "But not to lose hope, because eventually it does end."

"It will, eventually."

Rynan rolled over and tried to crawl away, enjoying his nakedness. She grabbed him and laid him back down, making him squeal in anger. He fought her while she tried to put a clean diaper on him. She tweaked his ears and feet, making him shriek and giggle, which was enough distraction for her to finish wrapping the diaper and securing it.

"Let me finish getting him dressed and I'll be right out."

"Good, because Averell was about to send in the cavalry."

She shook her head, slipping her baby into a sleeping gown. "Never seen a man so high strung over a child that wasn't his."

"You know he is fully aware that you are a packaged deal? One comes with the other, no matter what."

"I know."

Taylor chuckled. "What did they used to say about us?"

"Where there's one, there's the other."

"That's you and Rynan now." He regarded her quietly. "Chae said the two of you looked quite cozy earlier today."

"Spying was she?"

"Making sure you were awake before knocking." He watched as she finished dressing her son. "You know that he still has feelings for you, don't you?"

"I do. He has been very honest about that. Fear not, he and I have come to a mutual understanding. However, he will soon be too busy to worry over me and my son."

Taylor frowned, confused.

"Taikin wants Darion to retire soon and for Averell to take his place."

Taylor's eyebrows jumped up in surprise. "He's that bad?"

"Sounds like it. I expect that Taikin will be distracted as Darion gets worse. We'll need to prepare to support them as needed."

"Of course."

Zawn put on her wrap and slipped Rynan inside. He squirmed at first in rebellion, but ended up getting comfortable, then his eyes grew heavy as he listened to her heart beat. "There. All set. Let's go back. As of right now, the only planning we must start is for this little one's birthday."

~   ~   ~

After the birthday celebration, where joy and community made the kith glow, reality set in. She could count the days from Rynan's birth to Gwen's death with little effort. She couldn't stand hiding away in her hut, so she packed up her son, some necessities, and headed out for a night away from her kith. She left Taylor in charge and she only informed him where she was headed. Her kithlin watched with understanding and their own sadness as she headed out to grieve in private with her child. After all, the man they called friend was someone she called her love. As much as they had secretly hoped Averell would be a loving substitute, they knew their leader's heart was still healing.

Zawn walked for a while, disappointed that it had taken her this long to show her son such a special place. However, she knew the right time was now. As she approached, she heard the roar, smelled the blooms, and felt the humidity. She pushed back the brush and stepped into a welcoming opening. Morai Meadow sprawled out in front of her. She glanced down to find Rynan sound asleep in his wrap, making her chuckle. She stood at the edge and took a deep breath, feeling the mist of Irem Waterfall caress her face and arms, as if greeting her like an old friend.

Memories flooded her like the waterfall filled the lake below. Gwen and her swimming, laughing... loving each other. The thoughtfulness each had for their anniversary; her bringing him here, his special brew to mark the occasion. And of course, their debauchery.

That term made her laugh again, even though tears rimmed her eyes. It was bittersweet. They loved each other so much, fought so hard for their happiness, and to lose him in such a way was unbearable. Yet her heart reminded her that he died protecting the one other thing he felt was just as important in this world as their relationship. The baby that slept against her chest, who kept her up at all hours, and flashed that gum-filled smile. He gave his life so this child could have his. She had to honor that, even if she wished he hadn't.

Apparently, he was braver than she could even imagine.

With a sigh, she walked around the lake and found the spot where they had set up camp. New grass had grown tall, but the smooth ground hid underneath and made it easy to set up her small tent. She started a fire, tweaked the tent, and her movements finally jostled Rynan enough to wake. He fussed at her, making her coo soothingly, before removing him from the wrap. She sat down by the water's edge, letting the wide-eyed boy take in his surroundings. His awestruck smile reminded her of Gwen's reaction.

Then she whispered, "Watch this," and reached into the water. She tapped her fingers gently, causing ripples to cascade along the glass of the lake. A diffused glow grew from deep down in the water then the single light burst into dozens, as small luminescent tadpoles swam to the surface.

Rynan squealed in delight, trying to reach down into the water but Zawn held him back so he wouldn't fall in. When the creatures flickered and faded, he cried out in disappointment and leaned back against her chest.

"They can't stay forever, my darling," she responded, hugging him gently. "I'm sad to say they will not react to you, but I will always ask them to visit when we come here."

He sighed, squeezing her arm with his fidgeting hands. Then he gurgled and wiggled in excitement. Confused, she followed his eyes back into the water and there, just under that glass top, was a smiling face.

A nymph. Not just any nymph, an eahzal. Black eyes and sea green skin, black kelp for hair, and deep green lips. They were beautiful, mysterious, and based on legends, treacherous. However, under the wise leadership of the Sedoran Queen, they never came off as dangerous. Just cautious, and around Zawn, curious. Maybe because Zawn's heritage wasn't just elven.

With a kind expression, the eahzal broke the water's surface to meet Zawn and her son face to face. She cocked her head to the side, inquiring about something.

Zawn blinked, unsure what she was thinking, then came to a realization. "The Whispering Hornbeam Kith has a new kithlin. My son, Rynan, our stargazer."

The eahzal's smile widened, her joy obvious at the news. But for a moment her eyebrows furrowed, apparently noticing the difference between the mother and son.

"He takes after his father," Zawn answered. "Were you the one that saw us here almost two years ago?"

The nymph nodded and seemed to blush. Another curious expression as she glanced around.

Zawn felt tears threatened. "He is on the other side of the canopy. For a year now."

The other woman frowned, reaching out and gently touching Zawn's knee in a comforting gesture. Rynan reached over and laid his hand on the eahzal's, who smiled affectionately at the boy. Reluctantly, she bowed her head in respect, then splashed backwards into the water. She disappeared into the deep, dark water, leaving Zawn and Rynan alone.

Rynan stared in awe then startled babbling, as if trying to explain what he saw. Zawn listened intently, trying to hide her amusement at his excitement. When he finally exhausted his limited vocabulary of noises, she kissed his cheek and stood, returning to the fire and settling in for the night.

They watched the stars peeking down through the canopy, the trees around them shifting in the wind. Rynan cooed and babbled, reaching up like he could catch them. She started to tell him the tale of the twins, brother and sister, torn apart by a cruel fate but reunited forever in the celestial plane. Suddenly, a flicker and flash of a falling star lit up the sky just above them. Zawn smiled at Rynan's enthusiasm, while memories of watching celestial showers with Gwen flooded her mind. It made her miss him more.

Then Rynan turned those bright brown eyes to her. "Dadda."

CHAPTER 57

A few months later, the days finally longer and warmer, another group of visitors walked into the kith, led by a sentry. Their white cloaks and hoods made them glow against the earthy colors of the forest. Flanked by his entourage of hooded theurgists, Councilor Yunji's eyes searched each face that passed by in hopes of quickly finding their leader.

"Running low on apprentices to send out?" Zawn inquired, leaning against the porch post of her work hut.

Yunji turned toward her, chuckling. "Thought a walk would be nice."

"Are you well?"

"I am."

When he didn't elaborate, she looked him up and down. "Are we revisiting our agreement?"

"I'm always up for a good negotiation."

"Then come inside, let's talk."

Zawn waved to one of her kithlin to tend to the other theurgists while Yunji and Zawn moved inside.

Rynan was barricaded in a playpen, standing and bouncing as he held onto the sides. He looked up at the theurgist and almost fell backwards because the man was so tall.

"He has grown so much since the last time," the older man observed, sounding shocked.

"The way he eats, you'd think he'd be as tall as you by now." She sat down, gesturing for him to join her. "But no signs yet."

"I have a feeling that he will be a late bloomer," he admitted.

"Meaning… puberty?"

"That would be my guess. Gwendin was a late bloomer, even though he learned the mechanics starting at a young age."

"Is that why you didn't counter my terms?"

The theurgist smiled. "I told you I'd respect them."

She scoffed, then glanced over at Rynan who fussed about being left out of the conversation. She stood and picked him up, then grabbed a cup of water for Yunji while Rynan watched from her hip. She handed over the drink to Yunji then sat down and settled Rynan on her lap. Her son stared at the theurgist with wide eyes and his usual joyous smile.

"He uses that smile as a weapon, doesn't he?" Yunji asked, with a chuckle.

"You have no idea."

"But you are well?"

"I am," she responded, then raised her eyebrow. "Even though I am suspicious of your visit."

"I came to speak with you because of your request for certain books."

"You could have just responded to my letter."

He regarded her carefully, trying to gauge her mood. "I felt as though a face-to-face conversation would be more beneficial. Especially considering the books you are inquiring about. Am I correct in assuming that you feel it, too?"

"Depends on what you are referring to?" she countered, her tone casual.

"There's a darkness coming," he responded, face shifting into a grim expression. "I don't know what it is or where it is coming from. But it's in the air."

"I feel it, too," she admitted, her voice soft, as if to keep her words from carrying too far. "The wind whispers of tragedy and anguish. It is unsettling."

He watched her for a few moments before asking, "You know where the ill wind comes from?"

"I can only guess."

They watched as Rynan grabbed Zawn's left hand, playing with her fingers by separating them and then pushing them together or crossing one over the other.

"And?" Yunji prompted.

"The King of Mehdehra's castle smells as foul as the harbingers."

He nodded, solemnly. "What led you to that connection?"

"There is a convergence of energy lines underneath the structure."

"You've seen it?"

"Yes, Gwendin showed me. I've been around long enough to know that anytime that much magic is in one place, nothing good comes of it. We both agreed that he should tell you."

Yunji humphed. "Is that why Elixin's father built there?"

"I doubt he was unaware. His theurgist had to know."

"Another man dead at the hand of Crenast."

Zawn looked at him, confused. "There was another theurgist with Gwen?"

"No, the theurgist before him moved onto another post after Elixin came to the throne. Elixin disliked our kind and had basically banished his father's theurgist." Then he added, carefully, "The only reason Gwendin was appointed here was because of his sister."

"Kemberly."

"He told you that as well?"

"We tried to keep no secrets from each other."

"I'm glad. He struggled with the fact that his sister married that monster. But cruelty seems to run in the family. Crenast, on his way to overthrow his brother, searched out certain allies and associates. And killed them."

Zawn sat there, fingers drumming against the arm of the chair. "He left a larger swath of destruction that I realized."

"Yes, he was notoriously flippant regarding the sanctity of life. But you stopped it when you negotiated your new treaty. He backed down and halted all murders."

"That we know of," she replied, her tone dark. "I stopped him from killing us and our allies. But things can happen behind walls and transgressors will hide or skew the truth."

"Agreed. But the view from the outside is that Crenast is weak compared to," and he stared pointedly at her, "the Queen of the Elves."

Zawn's eyes widened, exasperated. "I am the leader of one kith."

"Most only know of the one kith, thanks to your legendary show of force." She rolled her eyes.

"There are other rumors as well. That he disappears from time to time, leaving his audiences alone in the throne room. Sometimes he is found wandering the hallways, sometimes studying in the small library." Yunji set down the cup and pulled a small book from his cloak's pocket. "He must know the same things we do and who knows what he plans to do with that information. Seeing that you are feeling the same things as I, I will grant you the use of the books you have asked for. Here is the first one. When you are done, hand it off to our messenger and we will send the next one the following week."

As Zawn reached for the book, Rynan tried to help, grabbing her arm and the book. Even though the conversation was dark, the two adults could not help but laugh at his fearlessness.

"You have quite the study mate," he pointed out.

"He is into everything, that's for sure. I will have to be careful though, he hasn't gotten his drooling under control yet." She held the book in one hand and kept her other arm wrapped around Rynan. "Thank you, Yunji."

"You are welcome, milady. And please, anything you find that you think may be of any use, send it on to me."

"I will."

Rynan squealed, banging his hands onto her arm.

"Will you stay for lunch? The least we could do is show some of our elven hospitality."

"That would be lovely, milady, thank you."

"Come, let's join my kithlin. I hear them gathering now."

~   ~   ~

They sat around the firepit, eating lunch and listening to the conservations around them. Zawn had Rynan in her lap, sharing her meat rolls with the impatient child. Once he got his fill, he started looking for something else to do. He slipped out of his mother's lap, holding onto the bench to steady himself. He took a couple steps to the left, smiling with pride, until he bumped into another's leg and looked up.

Rynan reached for Yunji. The theurgist set his plate down on the bench, then grabbed hold of the child. He let the boy sit on his knee, where he stared up into the gray eyes of the older man. As Yunji watched Rynan smile up at him, Zawn witnessed a kindness in the man she hadn't seen before. It was more than kindness. It was a level of affection that an uncle would have for a nephew. Gwen had told her that Yunji was his mentor, and that they were close, but seeing how he interacted with their son, she wondered if Yunji considered Gwen more of a son than a student. She knew the older man probably wouldn't admit to that, but she could see it in his eyes.

"Now, I may have a story about your Dadda that your Momma might not even know."

Zawn chuckled. "Oh, I can't wait to hear this."

CHAPTER 58

Zawn was half-dressed when the moment came. She heard sobbing before the person banged on her door. Zawn opened it, only to find Amna, tears pouring down her face, her mouth quivering. She stammered some syllables which didn't make much sense, but Zawn knew that if Amna was upset it could only mean one thing. She grabbed her pants and jumped into them before rushing across the kith to a hut she knew well. She strode in to find him in bed, looking as if he was still sleeping, but she knew better. She sank down onto the edge of the mattress, feeling her heart shatter.

"Oh, Jheferin," Zawn whispered, laying her hand over his, then she slid her fingers to his wrist where no movement could be felt. The hand itself was cold and stiff, indicating he had died earlier in the night. "Safe journey to the forests on the other side of the canopy, my friend."

She looked toward the doorway and saw Sileas, whose tears streamed down his face like rain. She stood up slowly, then reached for him. "My dear Sileas," she whispered, hugging him tight. Jheferin's great-great grandson began to sob, his body shaking against hers. "You took such good care of him. He could not have asked for a more honorable and loving child to be at his side."

"What am I to do now?" he wailed, clinging to her.

"Grieve. Everything else can wait," she responded, not letting him go. "We will help you every step of the way. Anything you need. Now, come, let us ready him for his journey. He would want no other to lead the way."

Sileas nodded against her shoulder before she released him to the care of Amna. She closed her eyes briefly and sighed, then exited the hut. Their kithlin hovered, everyone knowing him their whole lives, tears drenching their cheeks.

"Today, we mourn the loss of our precious historian and archivist. We will bid him a hero's farewell, thanking him for his service to the kith."

Sobs and sniffles were the only responses. They embraced each other and whispered their prayers for his safe journey. Then they moved away, preparing for the funeral for their kithlin.

CHAPTER 59

Years flew by and before Zawn knew it, Rynan was ready to start his lessons with the other children. He chanted his numbers with pride, told her the stories he learned in his lessons that day, and entertained her with reenactments of the great battles of days past. She didn't bother telling him that she was there for most of those battles, especially when he interpreted the ghastly but epic deaths of heroes and villains with such gusto. She found herself wondering if Gwen had the same energy and imagination as a child, even in the halls of the College of Theurgy.

When he got old enough to choose, he took on the haladie and short sword like his mother. Even though he was adept at bow and arrow, he wanted to be just like his mother. She even sparred with him, teaching him tricks she learned from Brennan and those she fought beside during the Purge like Taikin.

The thoughts of who he used to be and who he was kin to had vanished over time and Zawn only saw him as her son. Hers and Gwen's. They were his lineage, his family, along with Taylor and Chae and the rest of the kithlin.

The only thing that made him stand out was his physical appearance. She could pick him out easily in the crowd. It was known that she had a child, that he was mixed. It concerned her only when it came to enemy spies, if a kidnapping ever crossed their minds. Being different never seemed to bother him, maybe because he never really focused on his reflection, but she knew one day his differences may dawn on him and she would have to figure out how to reassure him.

As for Gwen, he visited her in her dreams intermittently throughout the years. It was always them in bed together, facing each other. When she asked why one night, he answered that it was because they had fought so hard for those moments that he never wanted to let them go. He would always remind her of how much he loved her and how proud he was of all the things she accomplished. Including Rynan.

Each dream ended with him caressing her ear and telling her how much he loved her. It took a long time before she no longer woke up sobbing. When the tears stopped, she feared so would the dreams. However, Gwen didn't fade away and she could remember him during waking hours in the moments that they had fought so hard for without falling apart. She could even make it through telling Rynan stories, who was getting old enough to understand and react to her emotions. She found herself smiling more during those private moments with her son, which helped her recognize that grieving Gwen took many forms. But most importantly, loving him also took many other forms she never considered before. Learning from that helped her grow as a leader and as a mother.

~   ~   ~

It was late at night, the chilly air whipping through the bones and canopy. The rainy season had started to move in. Faint tapping of precipitation echoed through their home. They had a hard time falling asleep, both laying on their back and staring out into the darkness that hovered over the skylight. The stars hid from them behind the clouds but the moons peeked out here and there, sharing their shy greetings.

Rynan rolled over, sighing. "I miss the stars."

"They'll come back," Zawn replied, mirroring her son. "Every year they play hide and seek in the clouds. Then they get bored with that and they come back and entertain you for the rest of the year."

Rynan reached up and touched her earlobe. "Mine aren't like yours."

"That's because we are not exactly the same."

"My eyes aren't either."

"Because I am an elf and you are a human."

"But you're my Momma."

Zawn frowned, suddenly realizing how complicated things were now that he could start putting things together.

"Yes, I am, but your Dadda wasn't an elf," she responded, carefully.

"I look like my Dadda?"

Zawn stared into those big brown eyes. His freckles splashed along his nose and that one little wrinkle along his forehead reminded her of Gwen. His laugh was an echo and his voice a mimic as well.

"You do," she confirmed. "You have his eyes, his smile."

"Can I look like you someday?"

She chuckled, caressing his forehead gently. "No, my darling. You will always take after your father. On the outside, anyway. And you have Gwen's heart, this I know. But your spirit will always be elven. I will teach you everything you need to know about your elf side and how we live, how we fight, and how we love. Because that is just as important as your father's side."

~   ~   ~

Time ticked by as the boy became a young man. The child of the leader started to learn his place in the kith while he grew up and looked more like Gwen every day.

CHAPTER 60

There was a crash and yelp, then a flash of a long-legged, wiry pre-teen, with wild hair running. Zawn caught the speeding shape entering her personal hut. She glanced over at the source of the smashing sound to see Taylor walking toward the square. The startled but expectant look on his face told her everything she needed to know. She nodded, setting down her bowl and striding straight to her hut. She opened the door quietly, so as not to alarm the occupant, and entered without a word.

Rynan sat at the table, his expression contorted with frustration. Slowly, starting with one item then several, books and knickknacks lined along her bookshelf started to rattle. She sighed, sitting across from him and reaching for his hands that were gripping his book tightly. Once her hands grasped his, the clattering stopped.

"Looks like it's time," she admitted, rubbing thumbs along his skin.

Her son sniffled. "But I don't want to leave."

Her shoulders slumped, then she smiled kindly. "Oh my darling." She stood up and moved around the table, pulling on his hands to make him stand. He rose to his feet and she wrapped loving arms around him. "If we could teach you all that you needed to know, and help you handle your magic, you wouldn't have to. But you need to be taught in a way we cannot teach, by those who understand better than us. That is why your enrollment to the College was set in place when you were still a baby."

He hugged her back, a sob escaping.

"Do not forget, your mother is a brutal negotiator. You are not being dismissed from your kith, my darling. You will be home during breaks and holidays. You will graduate and you will come home. You will return to us as our theurgist like your Dadda had hoped."

He stood wordlessly in her embrace and she could feel his ear snuggly pressed up against her chest, earnestly listening to the sound of her heartbeat.

"It will be a good thing. You are going to learn all the things you must to be

271

a better person. You will meet people from different places and different backgrounds. And you will share with them your home and your life. You will meet people who look like you but will not have the same spirit. Remember, you may look and be part human but your spirit is elven. You will be an ambassador for our people in ways I could never imagine." She kissed the top of his head, his wild hair tickling her nose. "I can't tell you how proud I am that you can follow in the footsteps of your Dadda."

She could still tell he wasn't completely convinced. She hugged him tighter for a moment then released him. She cupped his face, making him look up at her. He blinked away his tears and sniffled again.

"You already know Yunji, so there will be a friendly face there awaiting you. You will write me every week. You will tell me all the things you've learned and ask me any questions you might have. And who knows? Maybe I will take time away from the kith to frustrate Yunji and the other councilors by visiting... unannounced."

Rynan finally giggled, imagining the look on Yunji's face if she showed up without telling him. She leaned back further, making him look up at her. The tear streaks along his cheeks and his reddened eyes broke her heart, but she smiled kindly down at her son.

"There's my favorite sound in the whole world. Now, go, wash up. I'll send word to Yunji and tidy up the preparations. Then we will have the entire kith see you off in the best way possible." She kissed his cheek. "But you won't be leaving today. So, clean up and complete your chores. Taylor is waiting."

"Yes, Momma."

~   ~   ~

With Rynan calmed and back at his chores, Taylor made his way to the work hut. The door was cracked open, allowing him to peek in first before entering. His friend sat at her table, pen and paper laying in front of her, her expression solemn.

"So it's time?" Taylor asked, hesitantly.

"He's the right age for a late bloomer," she responded, rubbing her face roughly. "Yunji had warned me when it would manifest."

"Even with the warning, it wasn't predictable."

"Did he hurt anyone?"

"No, just scared himself. And me, to be honest. No one else saw what happened."

She sighed, fiddling with the paper in front of her. "Feels surreal to write this letter."

"Do you think they'll demand him to go immediately?"

"No, I made sure I would have a say as to when. It's mid-semester anyway. I'd think they'd take him in after solstice break. That will give us the holiday before the farewell."

"Will you be all right?"

She scoffed. "I have to be."

"Do you want him straight back when he's done with his chores?"

"No, let him play. Minee will help keep his mind off things for now."

CHAPTER 61

Zawn was correct. The College of Theurgy agreed that Rynan would start his education during the new semester, which started after the winter break. Rynan had stared up with wide eyes at his mother, worried about leaving but relieved he would have time to absorb his new reality. He had to promise, however, to watch his emotions and keep calm so he didn't have any other incidents. That was easier said than done, considering he was becoming a young man and puberty meant an emotional battle for the boy.

It also gave her time to prepare. The thought of her son not waking up every morning by her side, not seeing him at every meal... she didn't know how she was going to handle his absence. Not to mention the fact that she had protected him every breath of every day. Yunji guaranteed his safety, especially with the fear of an ally of Crenast's or another enemy finding out who he really was, and even allowed her to interview the leader of the guard at the College within the last year. The tall man, who appeared a little too thin for Zawn's comfort, proved himself a creative and imposing fighter. She, begrudgingly of course, approved.

But Zawn was not prepared for the day Taylor marched Rynan straight into her work hut and made him stand in front of his mother.

"Tell your momma what I caught you doing," Taylor ordered, trying to keep his tone strict.

Zawn's stomach dropped. She already had every talk she could with the boy, especially about his changing body and his possible thoughts, but what could have been so awful that Taylor dragged the boy home?

"I was talking to a girl," Rynan admitted.

"What kind of girl?" Taylor prompted.

"A human girl, one who lives in the castle."

Zawn stammered, her stomach now flipping. "And what does this girl do at the castle?" she asked, her pitch a few notches higher than normal, which made Rynan's eyes grow wide.

274

"She's a servant. I found her one day on our land. I saw her washing her clothes in the river so I asked her why and she said because the King doesn't want people like her using his facilities. Her name is Eriselda. She is very nice, Momma, I promise. She even started using the soap I taught her about so she doesn't pollute our water. She isn't mean. We just talk."

She stood, speechless, and Taylor's facial expression radiating his amusement didn't help.

"Are your chores done?" she managed to stammer out.

"I need to help with lunch," her son responded.

"Go help then. I need to think on this."

"Yes, Momma."

And Rynan darted out of the hut before she could change her mind.

Once he believed the boy was out of hearing range, Taylor started to laugh. "He has your spirit."

"Shut up."

"What? It's true."

"I need to change my pants. I think I shit myself."

"What would you have done if he said it was the princess?" he asked, keeping his voice low. "Deny him his friendship? Order him away from her?"

Zawn sighed, rubbing her face. "I don't know what I would have done. Thankfully, I don't have to make that decision."

"But you knew this was going to happen eventually. Him finding a girl interesting."

"Yes, but I had hoped for a nice elven girl from our kith... not a human."

"This is natural though. She looks like him." Taylor shrugged. "What I saw was very sweet. They were sitting shoulder to shoulder on a fallen tree trunk, just talking and smiling. I have never seen him so comfortable, let alone content."

She barely heard a word her friend said as she ruminated on the idea of her son with a girl. "I want to meet this... girl," and she said that last word with gritting teeth, "I do not believe she is some innocent."

"Then ask your son, nicely, to set up a meeting. As leader and as his mother, you have the right. But also, as leader and mother, you need to respect the situation for what it is."

"And what is it?" she demanded.

"A friendship."

~　　~　　~

They walked along his little path, one that Rynan had worn down with his weekly trips. Once they made it to the river, someone sat on a fallen log with their back to them. A small bag of snacks was held in one hand while the other retrieved whatever was inside.

"Seldy?" Rynan called, making the girl turn around.

When the human girl saw Rynan, a joyful smile lit up her face. Then she saw the well-armed elf that followed close behind him. The smile faded and all color in the girl's face disappeared. She jumped to her feet and took a step back before he reached her, but she tried to steady herself as he grabbed a hold of her arms.

"It's all right, this is my Momma."

Zawn stood a few lengths away from them, glaring suspiciously at the young girl.

"Momma, this is my friend Eriselda."

Eriselda shook herself, then stepped away from Rynan and curtseyed to Zawn. "Milady."

Zawn looked her up and down. She was definitely of meager means based on her clothing, which had patches and darns similar to those Zawn had growing up. Her low status was also reflected in how she braided her blonde hair out of necessity not for fashion. Her skin had patches of dryness, so she didn't have some fancy skincare routine that would make her princess material. She was thin, most likely from the paltry diet allowed her. Her gray eyes had a playful glint in them when she looked at Rynan, but darkened with fear when she looked at Zawn. Her features looked nothing like the Mehdehran royals. She had bruises along her right arm, as if knocked against something hard, and she also had what looked like burn scars from hot surfaces like a clothes' iron. Simple things that would have been ignored by someone trying to infiltrate her kith as a spy. Zawn knew immediately that she really was a maid.

"Have a seat, you two," Zawn ordered, folding her arms over chest as they settled down side by side on a fallen log. She watched as they adjusted themselves to sit closely, shoulders touching. She felt her stomach quiver when it reminded her of… "You travel quite the distance just to wash your clothes. This river runs close to the castle itself."

The girl glanced at Rynan, who nodded reassurance, before answering, "I only get one free day, milady, and I try to stay away from the castle as long as I can on that day. A few weeks ago, I just threw my laundry in a bag and started walking. I followed the river. That's how I can come so far without getting lost."

"And she follows it back and makes it home before dark," Rynan added.

"I take it you've walked her back a few times?" Zawn inquired.

Both Rynan and Eriselda looked away, guilt draining the remaining color from their faces.

"Have you stepped foot in the castle, Rynan?" his mother demanded.

"No, milady!" the girl responded. "We would both get into trouble. I make him stop a few lengths from the tree line so no one sees him."

"And I hide up in a tree to watch and make sure she gets back safely. No one sees me."

Zawn glared down at them. "How long have you been meeting here?"

They began to stammer, annoying her even more.

"Have you told her your schooling will start soon?"

Eriselda raised her fawn-like gray eyes to meet Rynan's. "You're leaving?"

"I was going to tell you but I got caught and Momma wanted to meet you. I'm sorry, Seldy. I was going to tell you, I swear."

Gwen's voice chastised her for being so cruel. And as the children sat there staring at each other, oblivious of the elf's presence, she knew there was more to these two than just friends. After all, this seemed to be a legitimate, shared relationship that meant these two children cared greatly about each other. Just like Zawn and Gwen had, even though some thought it was illegal or a flight of fancy.

"He leaves in a few weeks," Zawn said, managing a kinder tone than even she thought possible. "It has been set since he was a baby. But we will be able to maintain contact via letters. If you wish to write him while he is gone…"

"I can't write, milady, let alone read."

Rynan appeared devastated. "I didn't know that."

"Why do you think I made you read things to me?"

"I thought you liked listening to me."

"Well, I do but…"

Zawn rolled her eyes, then cleared her throat, silencing the children. "We'll… work something out, if that is amenable?"

"I would like that very much, milady."

"Yes, thank you, Momma."

"I will leave you to your visit," Zawn said, resigned. "I will think about some options for when Rynan leaves."

Turning on her heel, Zawn started to depart until the girl's voice stopped her.

"Milady?"

The elf turned back.

"Are we in trouble?" Eriselda asked. There was worry in her voice and it caused Rynan to reach and grasp her arm to comfort her.

"Why do you ask?"

"Rynan is my friend," the child stated, a strength in her tone that impressed Zawn. "And he is my secret."

Zawn suddenly felt deeply for the girl. She understood where the child was coming from, considering her relationship with Gwen. She wondered if Eriselda felt like Zawn did when Marassa threatened her secret. When that thought hit her like a punch in the stomach, Zawn knew her grilling of the pair was unfair, even for an overprotective mother. Sighing, she took responsibility for her cruelty and knew it had to be rectified. Zawn refused to let them suffer like she did.

"Do you think I will report you to your masters?" she asked.

Tears welled up in the girl's eyes and Rynan's hand slipped into hers.

"I have no intention," Zawn reassured. "Neither of you are in trouble, at least not at the moment. Spend your time together. Do not dally too long, Rynan, you still have a few chores to finish."

"Yes, Momma."

~   ~   ~

"When were you going to tell me?" Zawn asked her son that night, as they laid in bed staring up at the stars that winked and glittered down at them through the skylight.

"I don't know," he replied, softly.

"You will miss her the most, won't you?"

"Momma…" and he sat up, fearing he had offended her.

Zawn chuckled. "No, it's understandable. She is your friend. That is a special person, a friend. That is how your Dadda and I started. Friends…" and a sly smile cracked her face, "allies."

"I don't want to leave."

She stared at him for a moment, seeing the absolute heartbreak on his face. She wondered if Gwendin felt the same way when his parents sent him away to live at the College. Then she remembered that, even though life there for him was tough, he wouldn't have been happy with his parents either.

Zawn had ensured that Rynan's childhood was different from Gwen's, she made that promise the moment she decided to keep him. It was hard for her to see him feel so distressed about leaving and she knew it was her fault.

"I know," she responded, sitting up as well. "But you understand why, right?"

"I do, I guess."

"What do you mean, you guess?"

"I guess you don't want me blowing things up all the time."

"Well, that is one reason," she agreed, then wrapped her arm around his shoulders. "But I also want you to learn all you can about the world. You've been living in a very small part of it. We can only teach you so much. The College will teach you so much more."

"But why? Why can't I just be a warrior like Minee or a mechanic like Chaen? Why do I have to learn more than them?"

"Because you are your father's son."

"I am also your son."

Her eyebrows raised up. "You are. You are the son of a kith leader and the son of a great theurgist. You have opportunities others do not. And you are unique, special, and that should be nurtured." She could still see he remained unconvinced. She sighed hard, trying to figure out another way to persuade him. "It is no different than when we foster others from Taikin's kith and he our kithlin. You will learn and you will bring back that knowledge to us, just like our kithlin do when they return from working with Taikin and his kithlin."

"I'm a bridge, aren't I?"

"Who used that word?"

"Minee. She used the same comparison."

"Minee is a very smart girl, you should listen to her."

278

He rolled his eyes, but she knew in his heart he agreed.

"Before you go." Zawn pulled out a hand-woven bracelet of juniper, pear, and amethyst, with beads of fluorite and amethyst simply interwoven from under her pillow. "I gave your Dadda one, to remember my love for him when we were apart. I give you one now, to remember my love for you."

Rynan's eyes filled with tears and he grabbed her tightly into a loving embrace.

"Thank you, Momma."

"You're welcome. Now, let's get some sleep. It's been a busy day."

CHAPTER 62

The entire kith turned out to watch as Rynan left for school. Zawn made sure his departure fell on Eriselda's day off, so the two could say farewell before the College of Theurgy came to gather him. They hugged for a long time, not even saying a word for most of it. Once they separated, the girl stood next to Zawn's elbow. As he mounted his horse and started off, she caught tears in Eriselda's eyes. It was bad enough her son was leaving, but seeing the young servant girl cry as her friend left her behind, Zawn felt more of her own tears escaping down her cheeks. She tried to subtly wipe them away so the child wouldn't notice.

"Thank you, milady," Eriselda whispered. "For letting me say goodbye."

Zawn stared at her for a moment, eyebrows furrowing. "Goodbye is too final. This is only a temporary farewell."

The girl didn't respond, only stared down the road where Rynan had disappeared.

"Do you fear that he will forget you?" Zawn asked.

"Won't he? He will be around others who are smart and talented like him. I'm just a servant girl who can't read or write or do anything smart. I will just end up dismissed into memory once my name no longer crosses his lips."

Zawn watched as the younger girl's tears continued to stream down her cheeks. The elf tried to hide her own heartbreak as she remembered thinking the same thing about Gwen. When she had to end it to save his life, thinking all that time he had someone else. Someone else that would make him forget her.

Then Zawn started to walk away. "Come. I want you to meet someone."

The girl didn't move.

"Follow me."

Zawn led her over to Chaelene, who had settled next to the firepit. Eriselda stared up at the elf, eyes wide with unsurety, trying to wipe her face dry with her worn-out sleeves.

"Eriselda, this is Chaelene. She teaches the children of our kith how to read and write. She offered to teach you too so you can communicate with Rynan while he is gone."

"You'd really teach me?" Eriselda asked, her voice small.

"Of course," Chaelene responded. "It is what I do."

Eriselda lowered her eyes. "But I may be too dumb."

"Nonsense. Do you know how to count? Understand the weight of each potato so as not to overflow the stew? How to measure the detergent for the laundry?"

"Yes, milady."

"Then, child," and Chaelene reached over and touched the girl's chin, making her look up, "There's hope for you."

~   ~   ~

It took a few months, because she could only meet with Chaelene once a week on the day she did her laundry, but she was determined to learn. Chaelene would send her back to the castle with workbooks that she smuggled in her bag then would return with them completed for Chaelene's review. They added her laundry in with theirs, keeping her free to focus on her lessons. They also fed the girl during her visits, ensuring that she would get at least one decent meal a week.

They kept Eriselda's visits and her lessons secret from Rynan until she felt comfortable enough to write her own letter to him. She took her time, secretly writing it in her bunk at the castle. Once she was happy with the result, she asked Chaelene to read it and confirm that it was coherent. Chaelene was so proud, she bearhugged the girl without warning and nearly took all her breath. They folded it neatly and slipped it in the envelope with Zawn's letter, then handed it off to the messenger who picked up the herbs and dropped off the tithe.

The next week, along with the book Zawn had requested, two letters arrived from the College. One was addressed directly to Eriselda. The girl cried out with joy, her very first letter received. She rushed to a tree, sitting against it to read her letter privately.

"You have done a very good thing, Zawnie," Chaelene said, smiling at the servant girl's reaction to Rynan's words.

"Me? You're the one putting in the work."

"That girl would have never known how smart she was had you not asked me to teach her."

"Hm, as far as that girl's concerned, you offered."

"Must you hide your affection for this girl?" Chae demanded, exasperated. "I know she is not an elf, but still... There is more to this than just her being your son's friend."

Zawn groused at her friend, then responded, "You didn't see how they were together."

"I did, just before he left," Chae replied. "They reminded me a lot of you and Gwendin."

"Yeah, me too."

Zawn opened her own letter from Rynan and the first sentence made tears well up in her eyes.

Thank you for helping my friend.

CHAPTER 63

Zawn hated being so foolish, allowing another human to visit her kith, but Rynan's friend was a sweet girl who only wanted to find somewhere to fit in. Even Minee befriended her, especially since Eriselda spent so much time with Chaelene catching up on all the lessons the elf children her age had already learned. She kept a careful eye on the human girl but didn't spend much time with her. That wasn't the point of her visits anyway. If Rynan wanted this girl to have any kind of relationship with him, even just friendship, she needed to understand where he came from.

But his thanks still got to Zawn. That simple sentence made her proud to be his mother and confirmed for her that he didn't want to forget Eriselda. She wanted to honor that even if her nerves were rattled.

One day, she sat on the edge of her garden, with a basket in her lap. She hadn't much to pick, since everything was out of season, but she checked the soil while she had a free moment. Then she heard someone walk up on her and she glanced over her shoulder. Taylor leaned against the wall of her hut and watched as his friend picked what vegetables had volunteered a few late treats.

"You let that child come here and learn," he pointed out. "You let her write letters to your son. But you avoid talking to her for too long. What am I missing?"

"Nothing, Tay. I care about my son and, if he is happy, then so am I."

"Zawnie, that's a half truth."

She stopped plucking through the leaves and glared up at her friend. "What do you want me to say?"

"I don't expect you to say anything, to me anyway. I think it only fair that you interact with the girl you have brought under your wing… even if you only let one feather tip touch her."

And with that, Taylor left her alone in her garden.

~   ~   ~

Zawn caught herself staring at the girl as she studied next to the firepit. She devoured every lesson Chaelene gave to her and seemed to revel in the knowledge. She also seemed to enjoy the puzzles that Minee tried to solve. Both girls would sit for hours in contemplative silence, only saying something when they had an idea. But Taylor was right, Zawn had avoided spending too much time with her.

She noticed she did that often with anyone new. The last person she let get anywhere close to her for long periods of time was Averell, but that was because she was teaching him. Even that blew up in her face, when he admitted feelings for her. But his overture was too soon after Gwen's death and she still struggled over life without her love. Zawn chastised herself for thinking about that incident. She would never admit her regret over that, but she remained thankful that Averell was willing to remain friends afterwards. Averell's visits were always a welcome breath of jovial laments that she enjoyed.

Reluctantly, Zawn made her way over to the firepit. The girl was oblivious to her approach, engrossed in whatever lesson assigned to her. Zawn peeked over her shoulder out of curiosity and found that she was reading a text from one of the elders. She paused to read a few sentences and realized that it was The Accounting of the Purge.

"That's pretty heavy reading," Zawn commented, sitting down catty-corner to the girl.

Eriselda finished the paragraph she had been reading, then slipped a small torn piece of leather between the pages to mark where she left off. It was dyed lavender, probably a remnant from a larger hide. Naji must have given the scrap to her. Eriselda closed the book and stared at the embossed leather cover for a moment.

"They don't talk about history in this way. Banquets are always full of tales of triumph, but never of the treaties and comrades that helped them win these types of wars."

"Humans like to hear themselves speak. We prefer to write it down to ensure the accuracy of our history so that we learn from it and avoid repeating it."

"Is that why you hate humans?"

"Hm, hate is a strong word, Eriselda."

"It seems to fit."

Zawn stared into those fawn-like gray eyes, seeing the girl's disappointment that Zawn lumped her in with the others. Rynan's words describing the girl as not like the others rattled in her head, making her grimace.

"A long time ago, there was an incident we now call the Purge, which is the topic you are reading about. Old gods looked at those of us who walked these lands and decided the imperfect must be eradicated. Human, elf, gargoyle, among many others, were targeted. We fought side by side to survive. Those battles have been largely forgotten, only the victories that men claim was theirs alone, which are being retold at banquets. When Elixin came to the throne, he made it clear that his only intention as King was to conquer. He attacked the gargoyles first, enslaving them to his stone castle. He had his choice of who to conquer next. He decided, before he moved on to the Riders, Golueans, nymphs and Elementals, he would come for us elves."

"What happened?"

"Only half of his battalion survived to retreat. The other half died in the first two waves of fighting." Zawn scoffed, the memories of the fight ringing in her ears. "We suffered very few injuries, but had no casualties. I think he believed we had settled into our peace for so long that we had gone soft. He was quite surprised to have been so wrong. Our previous leader, Medruano, had a treaty drafted and he and the King went back and forth during negotiations. It took longer than we had hoped, but we stood our ground about our autonomy. They finally agreed to a tentative peace. That lesson, however, was never imparted to Crenast after he overthrew Elixin, so it was my turn to teach a King the lesson that elves never soften. We only strengthen our ranks with each generation."

"No wonder you find me repulsive."

Zawn sighed. "I do not find you repulsive. I am wary. But I trusted a man once and he turned out to be the love of my life. And the father of my child. I hope that my faith from that experience doesn't fail me with this one."

"I hope so too. I like coming here. I like learning too. Your kith is everything the castle isn't."

"And that, my child, is on purpose."

She watched the girl think hard before she spoke again. "Maybe, if we talk more, if we learn more about each other, you won't be so wary of me?"

"It's worth a try."

"I would like that very much, milady."

~   ~   ~

Zawn kept her word. Every visit, she spent time with Eriselda. Sometimes it was by the firepit, other times in her garden, and even in her work hut. She made sure not to interfere with the girl's lessons, because she didn't want Chae chastising her, but Eriselda started taking more of her lessons with Zawn instead, determined to learn more about the kith leader.

Eriselda was very attentive, noticing that when the messenger delivered items to the kith, there was a larger envelope meant for Zawn and bore the Haley name. The papers inside as Zawn removed them also had Rynan's information and his full name also included Haley.

"Why does Rynan carry your family name and not his father's?" Eriselda asked, eyebrows furrowed.

"Elven tradition is that the family name that one carries is the one that has greater standing in the kith." Zawn smirked, shrugging. "No greater standing than that of leader, is there? And if one of us were to take a mate, they would be of the Haley clan as well."

"Does he know his human family name?"

Zawn cocked her head to the side. "He's never told you?"

"I never thought to ask."

"Ah. Yes, he knows," the elf answered, as she removed the book and remaining letters from the larger envelope. "If he didn't offer it freely, then he has a reason to hold it close." She handed the girl the letter addressed to her. "I will leave that admission up to him. I hope that doesn't offend you?"

"Of course not, milady," she responded, holding the letter reverently in her hands. "I will ask him when the conversation is properly timed."

"I know he would appreciate that."

CHAPTER 64

Rynan wrote that he would be heading home for holiday the following week. Zawn couldn't wait to see the boy, but she knew Eriselda anticipated the visit more than anyone else. Zawn made sure that Chaelene didn't have any assignments for that day, only to give her something to read after she returned to the castle. Then Zawn asked the kith to set up a celebration meal while she readied her hut for his stay.

~   ~   ~

The arrival of a young man in a theurgist's cloak caused a cheer to explode among the crowd as they awaited him. He pushed back the hood, the light amber lining making him appear more mature than his age. But the smile was all boy.

"Rynan, our stargazer, welcome home!" Zawn shouted over the cheers.

She hugged her son tightly, realizing that his head rested against her shoulder instead of her chest. She felt emotional when she realized it was no optical illusion… he had grown tremendously during his absence from the kith. She finally released him and let the others greet him in a similar manner.

While he was preoccupied, she grabbed Eriselda and positioned the girl in front of her. When Rynan turned to say something to his mother, he found his friend standing there instead. He gasped then grabbed her into a tight hug. They clung to each other, oblivious to their surroundings.

Zawn backed away a few steps to stand beside Taylor. She folded her arms across her chest, sighing. "Well, now we know what their letters were about."

"You kept their friendship alive, Zawnie," Taylor replied, nudging her with his elbow.

"It's more than friendship," she responded. "I knew that the moment I saw them together."

"As did I. They are both better for it. As are we."

Zawn rolled her eyes, then stepped closer and admonished them softly, "Listen, you two, everyone wants to eat. Let go."

Rynan and Eriselda laughed, embarrassed, then released their hold on each other. Zawn waved everyone over to the tables, benches, and food, but just inside her periphery, she watched as the two held hands, their fingers entwined lovingly. Everyone plated food and shared laughter as the cooks argued who had the best dish. Zawn and the children sat with Taylor and his children, while Chaelene helped a new mother with her fussing infant.

Rynan and Eriselda sat close, sharing a plate between them. Rynan kept his shoulder against hers, while on his other side, his elbow kept in contact with his mother's. Before the two teenagers realized it, it was time for Eriselda to head back. Zawn led them to her work hut, where the girl's satchel had been tucked away. She walked them to the entrance of the kith, then, begrudgingly, suggested that Rynan walk his friend back, but to be careful about how close he got to the castle. Without argument, he grabbed the girl's satchel and tossed it over his shoulder, then clasped her hand and the two were off into the forest.

Taylor walked over and stood by Zawn, as she stared off into the trees. "You've got your hands full with those two."

"Don't I know it?"

"It's nice to see you spending time with her, you know," Taylor admitted. "I see her light up when you two talk, just like she does with Rynan."

"You were right, it was important that I have a relationship with her. She is the dear heart of my son, but she is also a friend to this kith. I see her settling with us when the time comes."

"And you will allow it?"

"If I deny her, what will stop my son from doing the same thing I did with Gwen?"

Taylor chuckled. "He does have your spirit."

"We'll continue to teach her and train her in all things a young kithlin would learn. And then she will have to make her decision when the time comes."

"Well for now, let us celebrate. Also, I wanted to ask, who gave that boy permission to grow that much!?"

Zawn started to laugh. "I almost didn't recognize him and he's my son!" She shook her head and sighed. "At least I know he is being fed well at the College. Come, let's rejoin our kithlin. He'll take his time getting back."

~   ~   ~

Later that night, Zawn and Rynan settled down in their hut. Both dressed in their sleeping gowns and climbed into bed. They laid on their backs, staring up through the skylight, and tried to name the stars that greeted them through the clouds.

"So, how are your lessons going?" she asked once they ran out of guesses.

"Good. Yunji has taken me as his apprentice. He gives me a lot of homework, but it's really interesting. I never really thought I'd be happy to study, but... I did learn something useful recently."

Zawn laughed, rolling her head so she could look at him. "Isn't it all supposed to be useful?"

"Supposed to be, but not really." He sat up and held his fingers together in front of his eyes. "Here, watch."

Rynan closed his eyes, whispering an incantation under his breath. She waited good-naturedly but she saw the frustration manifesting on his face. It was taking too long apparently but she didn't say anything. He had to be patient, especially with magic. Then a glimmer. A flash. He opened his eyes. At the tips of his fingers, a small flame. It was faint like the flame of a candle at the end of its wick. But it was there. He did it. Then he shook his fingers, dismissing the flame easily.

"Still a work in progress," he admitted, sheepishly.

"It was wonderful. I'm proud of you."

"Only because you're my Momma."

She smiled. "It's my right indeed."

"He also tells me stories about Dadda."

"He knows more about your Dadda than I do. You will have to share them with me. Have you made any friends?"

"No, I guess I'm a little scared. I never knew there were so many people in the world. And different people, with different skins and hair and beliefs. Oh and different languages. And so much noise. Not like the kith, very different. It's been hard to sleep because of it."

"You aren't in the dorms, are you? I made sure that was part of the agreement."

Rynan smiled. "I have Dadda's old room."

"What?"

"Yunji kept it for me. So I could connect with Dadda and feel at home."

She felt tears mist her eyes. "Oh, my darling, that's wonderful."

"I found his old notebooks, filled with spells and remedies. He really studied hard."

"His magic took work. It didn't readily come to him. But what he could do," and she smiled at the memories of him caring for her when she had been poisoned, "he was brilliant at it."

"Yunji told me he knew the moment Dadda visited, after spending time at the castle, that he had found someone." Rynan's fingers lingered along the woven bracelet on his left wrist. "Dadda didn't hide the bracelet on his wrist. Yunji knew what the colors and stones meant, based on his studies of the elven culture."

Zawn scoffed, surprised at how naïve she had been all those years ago. "I didn't even think about Gwen wearing it where it could be seen."

"He says mine is similar but not the same."

"Probably because I made both of them. The pattern is simple enough, but

I'm not very good at it. Never have been." Zawn frowned. "I wasn't able to save Gwen's when he died, because of the fighting..." and her voice faltered.

"Did Dadda give you something in return?"

"Actually, he gave me something first." She rolled over and grabbed something out of the small selenite bowl that sat on the table next to the bed. "He gave me this." And she handed the ring over to Rynan, before sitting up too. "He found the stone, made the setting. So, I made him his bracelet."

"You always wear it, but I didn't know Dadda gave this to you. You never told me."

"I probably did."

Rynan glowered, partly embarrassed, partly annoyed that she would accuse him of forgetting.

"You were probably too young to remember," she reassured, even though she laughed at his reaction. "I told you a lot of stories when you were a baby. Some I may never have repeated."

She watched as her son fiddled with the ring, letting the firelight glint off the stone and tarnished metal. The patina created by her skin's oil had darkened the silver over the years, but she couldn't bring herself to clean it because it would change the connection between her and the piece of jewelry.

She could see Rynan's thoughts as they ran around in his head. She tried to hide her concern, not knowing exactly what he was debating, but she knew it had to do with Eriselda. She sighed, caressing his face gently.

"Talk to Chae in the morning. If she can teach me, she can teach you. But for now? Sleep. The day has been eventful and your old momma is exhausted!"

~ ~ ~

Even though he stayed for a week, his return felt brief. The days moved by fast and before she knew it, she was helping him pack. Eriselda was able to see him again before he left, further cementing their connection.

CHAPTER 65

Seasons started to trade off and the weather began to warm up. Chaen, Talor, and even Meren were offered places in Averell's kith, giving them opportunities not afforded them in the Whispering Hornbeam Kith. Chae took it hard, because her babies were moving on, but the pride both parents felt could not be denied.

One day, Eriselda stood at the edge of the kith, pale and unmoving. Out of the corner of her eye, Chae caught sight of her and she startled at how the child looked. She approached the girl with some caution, then saw the girl holding her bag in one hand and the other wrapped in a stained cloth.

"Eriselda?" Chae inquired, making the girl look up. "Are you hurt?"

"They said I needed to learn my lesson." Then she raised her poorly wrapped hand. "I shouldn't've have grabbed the pan."

"Oh, child, what happened? Come, sit."

Chaelene guided her to the firepit, taking her bag and making her sit down. She carefully unwrapped the cloth to see a vicious burn on the girl's palm. She glanced over her shoulder in time to see Zawn walking toward her work hut.

"Zawnie!"

Zawn stopped, turned to look at who called her, and saw the concern on Chae's face. She strode over to them, eyebrows furrowed.

"She burned her hand. I don't think it's been treated."

"Oh, what on this side of the canopy? Stay here, let me get a kit." Zawn rushed off and returned with a medical kit in hand. "When did this happen?"

Eriselda stammered, her voice cracking. "I got up early to help in the kitchen before coming here… I was asked to. And the pan got knocked off. I just… I just grabbed it."

"Damn instinct," Chae muttered, as she dabbed pain relief on the blisters. "Thankfully it's not your writing hand. But why didn't the house manager do something to treat this?"

"Said I should have known better," the girl whispered.

"And you walked this whole way in pain?" Zawn demanded as she prepared a clean wrap.

"Pain?" Eriselda blinked, dazed. "Am I in pain?"

"I think she's still in shock, Zawnie."

"I think so, too. Let's get her hand wrapped and have her lay down." Zawn sighed. "The guest hut is a mess. We'll take her to mine."

"I don't mean to be trouble," Eriselda responded, bursting into tears.

"Not trouble, we promise," Chae assured.

Zawn pulled the girl into a hug, shushing her as Chae continued her work. Eriselda collapsed against Zawn, her gasping sobs tearing at both women's hearts. Zawn gently rocked her, making sure she didn't interfere with Chae's treatment. The reassurance finally broke through the young girl's distress and she started to calm down.

"We take care of each other, Eriselda," Chae added, once she knew the girl could hear her. "That's what we do. Now, can you walk? We want to get you comfortable."

Eriselda nodded, a jerking movement. With Chae on one side and Zawn on the other, they led the girl to Zawn's personal hut. They sat her down in front of the fireplace, removing her worn boots and darned clothing. Chae ran a damp cloth over the girl's face, cooling her tear-streaked cheeks. Zawn slipped one of her old sleeping gowns over the girl's head, then carefully pulled her arms through. Chae made a cup of tea that would help Eriselda relax and once she drank it down, Zawn helped her lay down in her bed. She tucked the blankets around the child as she started to drift off.

"That castle riles me up more and more," Chaelene responded, staring down at the child. "They let that child suffer. For what?"

"Cruelty is the point. When you own someone, they are only worth the distaste you feel for them. Gwen hated the castle. He always said it was busy but empty. No one cared about each other." The leader shook her head. "One day they will consider her unnecessary and decide her parents' debt paid. They will dismiss her, not caring if she has anywhere to go."

"One can only hope it will be someday soon. We'll have to help her find someplace."

Zawn patted Chae's shoulder, smiling. "Go, tend to the children. I'll work in here today and keep an eye on her."

~ ~ ~

Later in the morning, before lunch, a deep inhalation and confused moan signaled that Eriselda was waking up. Zawn stood and walked over to the bed, sitting on the edge. Eriselda opened her eyes, then scrunched her eyebrows in confusion.

"How did I get here?" the young girl asked, her words slightly slurred.

Zawn frowned. "You don't remember?"

"Everything's blurry."

"You walked all the way here on your own," Zawn responded, gently brushing some hair from the girl's forehead. "You were quite dazed with shock."

The girl looked at her wrapped hand. "I didn't know what else to do."

"I'm glad you came to us. We got you patched up pretty quickly. Are you in pain?"

"Throbs a little."

"That's normal for that kind of burn. We'll redress it in a little while. But first, you need to eat something."

"I am a little hungry," the girl replied, sheepishly.

"Can you sit up?"

Eriselda nodded, pushing herself up into a sitting position with her uninjured hand.

"Good. Stay there. I will be right back."

Zawn returned with some soup and bread, then paused in the doorway, realizing that the girl couldn't hold the bowl. She set the food down on the table and helped Eriselda into a chair. She rested her injured hand in her lap and slowly sipped the soup off the spoon, keeping her eyes focused on the bowl while Zawn pulled the bread apart in more manageable pieces for her.

"I'm sorry for being a nuisance, milady," she said, voice soft.

"What makes you think you're a nuisance?"

Eriselda stayed silent, not lifting her spoon from the bowl.

"If you were a nuisance, you would not be here and we would not be getting to know each other." Zawn watched as the girl started eating again. "We'll clean your hand and redress it before you leave. Also give you supplies to treat it on your own."

"Thank you."

"You are welcome. Now finish eating."

Eriselda hesitated, then set down her spoon and stood up. Zawn rose to her feet as well, prepared to support her, but Eriselda collided against her. She wrapped her uninjured arm around Zawn, flattened her ear against the elf's chest, and hugged her. Caught off guard, Zawn stood there for a moment, then sighed and held her. Eriselda immediately settled into the embrace. She noticed that the child didn't back away immediately and that her ear was pressed in the vicinity of Zawn's heart.

"You are not a nuisance, my child," Zawn whispered as the girl clung to her, "and you are welcome here anytime. You need not ever apologize for asking us for help. If you need anything, we are here for you." Then she ran her hand over the girl's head, fingers tangling in her hair. "Do you understand?"

Eriselda nodded, sniffling against Zawn's chest.

"Good. Now finish eating. If you get it all down, there may be a treat for you."

The child finally loosened her hold on the elf and looked up, a small smile adorning her face. "Can I pick the treat?"

Zawn chuckled. "Maybe. We'll see how clean the bowl is when you're done. Now, go, eat."

~   ~   ~

After she finished eating, the elves were able to check and rewrap her hand. Zawn let her choose a treat to eat while they worked on her hand. The salve they slathered on had taken out most of the inflammation, but the skin had stiffened. Chae added a skin softener to the salve she packed for Eriselda, something she admitted Gwen had taught her. Before she had to head back to the castle, Chae went over the directions with the girl, who nodded and hugged the elf in thanks.

"Minee?" Zawn called out, getting the girl's attention.

Minee trotted over to her auntie and momma, catching a glimpse at Eriselda's wrapped hand. She frowned, concerned, but didn't ask any questions.

"Can you walk Eriselda back?" Zawn asked. "Only to the tree line, of course."

"Happily," Minee answered, holding her hand out to Eriselda. "I'll carry your pack for a bit."

With another around of hugs, Eriselda headed back into the forest with Minee at her side. The two girls chatted as they walked, probably about Eriselda's hand.

The two women watched as the two girls disappeared. Zawn must have had a peculiar look on her face because Chae sighed, nudging her friend with her elbow.

"What is it?" Chae inquired.

Zawn waved her hand, dismissively. "Nothing."

"Zawnie."

"I sent one child to school and ended up with another in his place," the leader responded, exasperated.

"Is that a bad thing?"

"No, it's not a bad thing," Zawn admitted with a shrug. "Keeps me from missing him too much."

"Then what is it?"

Zawn didn't respond immediately, her eyes still trained on the path the girls had taken back into the forest.

"Zawnie?"

"Am I the right person?" Zawn asked.

Chae chuckled, crossing her arms over her chest. "By the look on Eriselda's face every time she sees you? Absolutely."

CHAPTER 66

Eriselda's hand healed quickly under the acute care of Chae and Zawn. She followed their instructions each week after they checked her, keeping her medications hidden in her bunk. When visiting the kith, she was relegated to reading for a few weeks, until the skin regained its color and elasticity. She had discoloration along the palm, where the hottest part of the pan had been grasped, but she was able to use her hand without permanent disability.

One thing that did change, however, took some getting used to for Zawn. When Eriselda saw the kith leader, she hugged her in greeting, and when it was time for her to leave, she hugged the elf in farewell. Zawn secretly appreciated the gesture, knowing that the girl hadn't seen any kindness from others, and she also used it as a substitute for Rynan's missed hugs.

Even after being cleared to return to her usual physical activities, the girl didn't rush and wanted to wait at least one more week. Neither Chae or Zawn argued, respecting the girl's hesitation. Eriselda had been sitting at the firepit, reading a smaller book that was easier for her to hold with one hand because her injured hand still tired easily. Zawn sat nearby, cleaning mechanical gadgets that she would use to replace the worn-out pieces in the irrigation system. Their comfortable silence ended with the closing of the book and Eriselda sighing.

"Milady?"

"Oh please call me Zawn already."

Eriselda's eyes widened. "I don't know if I can."

"You can try."

"Zawn," she said, with hesitation, then her face contorted like she ate something sour.

Zawn started laughing, setting the sprocket down into her basket. "It's a start. What's on your mind?"

"Um, I'm reading about the Nymphs of the East. I, um, what makes elves different from nymphs?"

"That's a good question," Zawn admitted, placing her brush and cloth inside her basket. "Legend says that the gods wanted us to be different, because they enjoyed variety and wanted a world full of it. We elves are nature based as much as we are magic, just like the Nymphs of the East, but we are not relegated to residing in a tree, water, or whatever element those nymphs are created from. We don't rely on the talented to communicate. We derive sustenance from food like you do, not from the soil or other elements. We also reproduce like you do, not by a seed or whatever it takes to make baby nymphs."

Zawn felt the girl's mind whirling.

"It's fine, ask."

"That's how you could have Rynan?"

"Yes, same mechanics." Then she smirked, seeing the girl's next question without her asking it. "And that's how Rynan will have his own children."

Eriselda's blush deepened.

Zawn regarded the girl for a few moments, before inquiring, "Has anyone talked to you about certain things?"

"Some things offhand," she answered, keeping her eyes on the book in her lap, "but no one thinks about educating the servants."

Zawn folded her hands on her knees, reading Eriselda easily. "Would you like to ask more questions?"

"Yes," she replied quickly, looking back up at Zawn. "Can I?"

"Of course. If you find someone who you're comfortable with, I'm sure they'd be happy to…" Zawn suddenly realized that the girl stared at her, anxiously. "Oh. Me? Um, let's go somewhere more private?"

~   ~   ~

Later that night, Zawn sipped her apple wine. She thought having the talk with her son was difficult, but Eriselda was different. Maybe because she had so much misinformation, thanks to cruel individuals at the castle, or because she was an awkward child to begin with. No, that wasn't really it. It was the fact that the girl loved Rynan. She knew where their friendship was headed and to be the person to explain sex and intimacy to the girl who would more than likely be her son's mate…

Zawn sighed, shaking her head.

She did a good thing, she knew that. Eriselda wanted someone to talk to, about anything, and someone to look up to. Zawn thought for sure it would have been Chaelene, but no, Zawn ended up being that person. She questioned again if she was the right person, but Chae's voice repeated that she was, because Eriselda chose her. Not only chose her, but trusted her, and Zawn mused privately, loved her too. The poor girl had been handed off to the castle at a young age as collateral and never knew affection from a parent.

It reminded her of Gwen's childhood.

She took another, slow drink. Reluctantly, she had to admit the truth. If Eriselda and Rynan grew out of their love for each other, Zawn knew that the girl would still be considered a friend of the kith and offered a home when the time came. Because either way, Zawn accepted Eriselda as her daughter, in her heart and her mind.

~   ~   ~

Zawn caught Eriselda on her next visit watching Minee and the other children in her age group working on physical exercises. She stood off to the side, clutching the book she probably got from Chaelene against her chest. Her eyes darted back and forth between each pair as they participated in either hand-to-hand combat or sparring with weaponry like staffs and khukuris. She seemed completely riveted by their movements and unaware as the elf walked up to her side.

"We all learn how to fight, starting at a young age, even those not of the warrior caste," Zawn informed her, making the girl jump. "We believe everyone must be taught how to protect themselves."

Eriselda stammered, wrapping her arms a little more tightly around her book. As Minee flipped her opponent over, making him land on his back on the ground, Eriselda gasped.

"Can I learn to fight too?" she finally asked, her voice a mere whisper.

"If you wish. But be prepared for bruises, both physical and ego."

~   ~   ~

Between her lessons with Chaelene, Eriselda trained with Zawn. The timid girl began to crack her shell, but it took something other than a book in her hand to do so. Zawn started her out with a staff, which she used to gently tap the dummy constructed of hay, twigs, and wood. However, as her confidence began to build, so did the strength of her strikes. She listened to Zawn intently as the elf explained tender spots in the anatomy of humans. One she didn't quite believe, until Zawn gave Eriselda a whack, and she didn't question the kith leader after that.

When she felt the dummy wasn't enough to hone the girl's skills, Zawn switched her to a live opponent. She didn't want to throw her into a group of children that were several steps ahead of her, so the elf took it upon herself to spar with her. She knew what the girl's level of mastery was and didn't try to push her too hard.

Until the day Eriselda landed Zawn on her back.

Laying on the ground as the girl stared down at her, mortified, Zawn chuckled. "I think you can join Minee and her group now."

CHAPTER 67

The rainy season rolled in loudly, with thunder and lightning, then settled into the light rains during the night and days darkened by clouds. Zawn laid in bed, listening to the pattering, remembering her nights with Gwendin. They would cuddle in his tent, letting the rain bounce off the material, while they talked and loved each other. Then she thought about Rynan's reaction to hearing thunder for the first time. He had stared up at the skylight with wide eyes, trying to catch the path of the lightning and laughing at the rumbling as it vibrated through the floor.

The weather quickly stole her ghosts away. As the rain quieted and the thunder faded away, she was left alone. Again. Gwen was gone and Rynan was away. And Zawn was by herself in an empty bed. She buried her face into her pillow for a moment, frustrated at how hard the emptiness of her hut hit her. She reached her arms around the pillow but her hand encountered something hard. She lifted her head, finding a book laying nearby and tracing gentle fingers along its binding.

She had brought it to bed with her like she had done before when her heart hurt. She lifted herself up on one arm and opened it gently to where three dried tulips had been pressed thoughtfully into the pages. Red, white, and yellow. She carefully touched the red one, remembering her fears and hopes during that fortnight when she didn't know what had happened to Gwen. Those tulips stayed fresh until they met again, when their vitality started to diminish but she was determined to save them. He never knew she had preserved his sweet love letter to her during their time apart. Now, she held onto them in memory of their time together and in hopes of seeing him again in the next life.

She realized with some heartache that Gwen had been in her life for such a short time. Only a few years. In comparison, to the dozens of decades an elf lived, it was so miniscule. However, his impact on her was enormous.

She sighed, making herself sit up and stretch. She closed the book again then picked it up and held it against her chest. She whispered against the binding before slipping out of bed and placing it back on the bookcase near her table.

As much as she wanted to hide away with her heartache and memories, she didn't have the luxury of lying in bed and feeling sorry for herself. She had her kith and her responsibilities.

She got dressed, slipping on some older clothes and soft deer hide shoes instead of her boots. She made her way to the firepit, where breakfast was being doled out, and she ate with a cluster of children around her. They talked and laughed, entertaining her while she finished her coffee. She left her wares with the breakfast crew, who smiled and thanked her for her compliments on the meal.

That was the last of her respite for the morning. She was glad to have eaten a hearty breakfast once she started learning about leaking roofs. With a deep sigh, she jumped in to help. She added her knowledge and hands in helping fix the thatching on the damaged roofs.

She had just finished the last hut when she heard greetings from behind her, making her turn toward the main entrance to the kith. His sheer size made him instantly recognizable as did his bright copper eyes.

"Averell! What are you doing here?"

"Oh you know Taikin, after he got your letter, he jumped at the chance to help. And of course, always happy to barter in return."

"What is that lunatic plotting now?"

They laughed and closed the distance to hug. With all of his armor, she carefully reached around his neck while he wrapped his arms tightly around her torso. They hadn't seen each other for several months and neither seemed to want to rush the hug. She let herself soak in his warmth, inhaling his distinct sandalwood smell. Then she broke their hug, being the first to step away.

"Our kith found those roots you were looking for," Averell responded, opening his satchel and letting her peek in.

"Fantastic timing, the College will be sending their courier in a few days. But we've funds in reserve to pay your kith. Come, let's get them in the storage hut and I'll gather the coin."

Zawn led Averell to one door that led to their cool storage underground. She had him pour the roots into one empty woven grass basket and covered it with a cloth lid. He obediently followed her to her work hut, where she opened the safe with her key and counted out the coin. After handing over the money, she locked the safe.

"That should cover the time and labor. If Taikin takes issue, let him know the door is open for negotiations but he'd better have some tantalizing proof for a raise."

Averell chuckled. "I will pass that along."

Zawn sat down in her chair with a sigh and a smile, then gestured for him to sit as well.

"So how are you?" he asked as he settled into the chair across from her.

"Hm, busy. As usual."

Averell shook his head before lamenting, "A curse of all kith leaders."

"Are you well?"

"I am," he answered, "even though that walk was a bit brutal through the pass because of the weather."

"Are you required to return today?"

"Well, you know how Taikin feels about dawdling."

Zawn rolled her eyes. "Do you want to stay?"

"Honestly? I would love to get some rest. It's a long, lonely walk and I'm not looking forward to doing that again today. I'd have to leave now to make it by bedtime."

"We've the guest hut you can use," she responded, with a wry smile. "We just need to tidy it up. And if Taikin complains, blame us for the celebration we dragged you into."

"What celebration?"

"The sun rose again?"

Averell laughed. "Your kith certainly celebrates just about anything."

"Come, get out of that leather. You can leave it here until the guest hut is set up for you."

She helped him out of his armor, frowning as she ran her hand underneath the shoulder guard.

"Why did you really take this horrible assignment?" she demanded, frowning.

He looked at her confused. "Horrible?"

"Your armor is still wet from walking through that storm."

He reached out and cupped her face, staring straight into her eyes. "I wanted to see how my friend was faring."

"You could have sent a letter," she retorted, then shrugged. "She fares well. Even if her hut is the cleanest it's ever been." She laid her hand over his. "I miss my son like any mother would. But I had to change my ways to accommodate a child. Now I must adapt again. Seems to be a theme in my life."

"Life is nothing but change, Zawnie. Don't tell me you wouldn't make any other changes if the opportunity arose?"

"Depends on the opportunity, I guess."

She felt awkward suddenly, with Averell so close and that honesty in his eyes giving him away. She stepped back, clearing her throat. He exhaled hard then continued to remove his armor. She took each piece from him and laid them out near the fire.

"Come, lunch should be ready. Let's get you fed."

~   ~   ~

Averell spent the rest of the day eating, drinking, and catching up with his friends in the kith. She stayed by his side briefly after lunch, enjoying his tales of misadventure, until her responsibilities pulled her away. When Zawn excused herself, she swore she saw disappointment in his eyes. Or maybe she was seeing things she wanted to see. She didn't want to admit to him that he had been on her mind lately.

She sighed as she walked away, feeling foolish. He was a friend and he was here because of orders by his leader. And she, as leader, had her job to do too.

Even if that meant climbing down into an irrigation ditch with no shoes or pants on.

~   ~   ~

With Zawn knee deep in sludge, Taylor and Averell sat at the firepit. They enjoyed the comfortable silence they shared, but they were both thinking of their mutual friend.

Taylor took a drink from his mug before admitting, "I'm glad you took the assignment."

"Thank you for reaching out," Averell responded. "She says she's fine. But how is she, really?"

"She's been quiet, withdrawn since Rynan went to the College. She's fought through the loneliness as best as she could. But it's been worse since Rynan's last visit."

"I would have been here to support her," Averell replied, gritting his teeth in frustration. "I would have seen him off had I known the date."

"I think she hoped that if she didn't announce it, it wouldn't happen. But she knew how busy you've been lately, taking on more responsibilities because of Taikin's health."

The two men sat and drank in silence.

"It is nice to see her as herself again," Taylor admitted. "She hasn't laughed this much in weeks."

"Oh, should I stay longer?"

"Taikin would have your hide."

"Eh, I don't really need all of it."

Taylor shook his head. "Her life has changed again, despite her best efforts."

"She admitted as much."

"I hope she finds herself soon. Or at least a version of herself she's comfortable accepting."

"She's talked me into staying the night, but I didn't tell her I had already planned to. I will entertain her as long as I'm here."

They tapped mugs in salute. "Glad to have you here, my friend."

CHAPTER 68

After the rather putrid job of unclogging the irrigation ditch, Zawn scrubbed herself clean for quite a while in her bathtub. She swore she removed at least a full layer of skin before the stench finally relented. Then she lathered a flowery lotion all over, hoping the perfume would hide any residual smell. She slipped into another tunic and cloth pants that were loose and warm. She braided her hair away from her face and stared at herself in the mirror. Maybe with everyone wrapped up in Averell's visit she could hide away in her hut. She could cuddle in her bed and try not to think.

Then someone knocked on the door. She groused, but opened it, to find Averell standing there.

"Are you coming to dinner?" he asked.

She chuckled, mirthlessly. "I could ruin it. I don't know if I got the stench off."

"We'll sit downwind," he replied, offering his hand.

She glanced between his eyes and his hand, then grasped it and let him lead her out into the kith square.

~   ~   ~

Every time he sensed her mind wandering inwardly, he would get her attention with a gentle touch or something whispered in her ear for only her to hear. Whatever comment he made would cause her to laugh or glare at him, which in turn made him chuckle. After the festivities of dinner and the nightly storytelling died down, Averell retrieved his items from her work hut and she led him over to the guest hut. She opened the door and headed toward the fireplace, while he sighed and dropped his armor and duffel next to the bed.

"Ah the guest hut, how I have missed you," he lamented with a wry smile.

"Come now, this was your home not too long ago. For a few months anyway."

"It's been over twelve years."

She blinked, surprised. "Time has flown by, hasn't it?"

She stoked the fire, causing the flames to erupt in yellows and reds. Then she checked the bathing room to make sure it had soap, towels, and other amenities. Pleased that Meren had stocked the hut up appropriately, she tweaked the bedding and started toward the door.

"Looks like you're all set. Have a good night, Averell."

He reached out an arm to stop her from leaving. He looked at her, his expression serious. "Zawnie, honestly, how are you?"

"Why do you keep asking that?"

"I had to drag you to dinner. You hardly spoke all evening."

"You dominated the conversation," she retorted.

He dropped his arm, exasperated. "You didn't even interrupt me."

"And you're complaining?"

"Zawnie, I know you well. And I know that you are not yourself. Your son is off to school. You can't hover over him anymore and you cannot be there to protect him against everything you deem a threat. You've spent years with that child by your side or under your feet. Now, he's not. That has to be stressful."

"Would have been worse if they took him at the age they usually do," she admitted, folding her arms across her chest. "I got more time with him than most parents who have talented children."

"That's because you are a brutal negotiator."

Zawn chuckled. "That I am." She shrugged, the humor leaving her. "I am fine. But thank you for worrying about me. I forget sometimes that some people do."

Averell stepped closer to her, those copper eyes of his intently watching her hazel ones. He caressed her cheek, making her close her eyes briefly.

"I have never stopped caring about you, Zawnie."

Her eyes narrowed even though she kept her tone joking. "Did you take this assignment to have another swing at the old widow now that her nest is empty? Even though I had rebuffed you quite soundly?"

"You know that's not why."

"Did Taylor ask you to visit?"

"Someone told me that you had mentioned that I hadn't visited in a while. Mentioned it more than once. I took that as an invitation because it was evident you might have actually missed me."

"I didn't miss you," she responded, indignant. "I just…"

"Just what?"

"Noticed it'd been a while, that's all."

"You missed me," he retorted, narrowing his eyes in annoyance. "Admit it."

"No. I just thought it odd."

"You can't say it, can you? Is it so hard for you to admit that you have feelings like everyone else?"

"I don't have feelings like everyone else."

"Is that so? Do you not love your son? Or Taylor for the brother he is to you?" He searched her eyes. "You have no affection for me?"

"I can never love again," she whispered, after swallowing hard, "not like that."

"I have always known that no one could ever replace him. I just held out hope that you would consider another companion someday, on your own terms." He smiled, almost sadly. "And I'm not asking you to love me."

"But you deserve love, Averell."

"Don't tell me what I deserve. I know what I want."

"What do you want?"

"Nothing more than to be your anchor."

"Why?" she demanded, her voice trembling slightly.

"I can't let you drift away into the darkness. You're the light that guides not only your kith but all kiths. Including mine. And especially me. You've been my guiding light every day since we met. That's why I humbly make this request. Stay with me tonight."

He leaned in, slowly enough to give her time to back out. She didn't step away. He kissed her, at first softly then ardently when she answered him. He pulled her into his arms, pressing her against him as they continued to kiss. As much as he wanted to drown in her, he finally came up for air, staring down into her beautiful hazel eyes.

"I don't want to be alone," he whispered. "Do you?"

~   ~   ~

She had feared that she would compare the two men and ruin the experience. However, with each touch, each kiss, she only saw and felt Averell. No other thoughts intruded. It may have been the way he undressed for her, displaying that body of his that she had only caught glimpses of. On hot days, he had been known to take off his armor and tunic, but to see him remove his shirt in the firelight, just for her, it felt like a treat. She had never seen anything beyond that, so as he removed his boots then his slacks, she was rendered speechless at his beauty.

Once he was naked, he waited to see what she would do. There was still that shadow of fear in his eyes, like he expected her to bolt out the door and leave him there. That darkness dissipated when she reached out a hand. He clasped it as he bridged the distance between them. Once he got closer, she fumbled for his other one. As he stood closely in front of her, she raised up on her tiptoes and kissed him. She took those hands, hands that had worked, fought, and reveled alongside hers, and placed them on the hem of her shirt. Taking her hint, he reverently undressed her as well. When she was completely nude, she heard his breath catch, as if every fantasy he had couldn't compare to the reality. Finally, he lifted her up and took her to bed.

Now, cuddled up to his side, after he had shifted onto his back sometime in the night, she watched him sleep. That affection she had for him, that she thought she hid from the world, remained even as she laid next to him. She was astounded, not just by his deftness and stamina but also by his tenderness. His dedication to her satisfaction surprised her. She felt a smile creep across her face when she thought about him making sure her satisfaction was plural. And when he reached his end, he avoided collapsing and crushing her under his weight. Instead, he kissed her passionately and rolled them onto their sides. He kept her close, leaning his forehead against her chin. She felt him inhale deeply, as if trying to stay awake, making her whisper, "Sleep." She heard his breath slow and she followed him into a peaceful slumber.

She watched him just a little longer then closed her eyes again.

~   ~   ~

When he opened his eyes, she wasn't next to him. Startled, he glanced around until he found her slipping out of the bed on the other side. He took a moment to enjoy how the shadows from the dying fire danced along her back and hair. But he couldn't see her face, making him anxious.

"Leaving?" he asked, his voice thick with sex and sleep.

Sitting on the edge of the bed for a moment, she glanced over her shoulder before standing. "I do not think it's wise for my kith to catch me in bed with you. Assumptions will be made."

"You could stay a little longer."

Zawn scoffed, putting her pants back on. "You have a long walk home. You need your sleep."

"But how can I sleep, all alone?" he asked, making his voice sound a little pitiful.

He caught her rolling her eyes. "You'll sleep just fine without me."

"I'll have to head out first thing," he warned her, as he sat up in bed. "Taikin will be expecting me to return as early as possible."

"At least stay for breakfast," she replied, searching around the bed until she found her shirt. "Can't walk all that way on an empty stomach."

"Will you have breakfast with me? See me off?"

"It's the least I can do."

She walked over to his side of the bed and kissed him gently. He reached up and ran his fingers along her cheek. Slipping his hand behind her head, he drew her back toward him and kissed her deeply. Their lips lingered, passionate caresses shared between them. Then she pulled away, taking a deep breath finally.

"Good night, Zawnie. I will see you at breakfast."

"Good night, Averell."

~   ~   ~

That morning, at breakfast, Zawn and Averell met at the firepit. They plated their food, then quietly sat shoulder to shoulder. Eating in comfortable silence as they had done many times before, they watched as the kith moved around them. Conversations, laughter, and sounds of different activities ebbed and flowed.

"I was thinking," he began, then paused, twisting his fork in the remaining scrambled eggs on his plate.

"About?"

"That I could continue to take these assignments. Would that be amenable?"

Zawn started to respond that it was up to Taikin, then realized the leader in her wasn't who he wanted to answer. He wanted to hear from the woman he had laid with the night before. And she knew she wanted to see him again, in that private way.

"It would be amenable," she replied. "You have been missed."

"I have missed you, too."

"Tell Taikin that you would be expected to stay the night because I will not allow you to catch your death unnecessarily."

He tried to keep his face stoic as he responded, in mock seriousness, "I will pass that on."

They heard greetings from behind and Zawn turned to see Eriselda entering the kith. The girl caught sight of Zawn and smiled, then it faded and her eyes widened when she realized she didn't recognize the elf sitting next to her.

"Excuse me for a moment." Zawn set down her plate, stood, then approached Eriselda. She hugged the girl, whispering, "He's a friend. Now, go, set down your laundry and see Chaelene in her hut."

Eriselda nodded, releasing her and following her instructions.

Zawn returned to Averell's side, feeling his curiosity. When she sat down, she picked up her plate and waited for his questions. He stared at her as he chewed. She knew he was enjoying the uncomfortable silence, dragging it on as long as he could, wanting to see her squirm. She refused.

"Did you forget to mention having another child?" he asked, drolly.

"She is Rynan's friend," she replied, nonchalantly. "She stays with us during her days off."

He regarded her for a few moments, then shook his head. "That big heart of yours."

"Shut up."

He continued to eat with a smirk while Zawn glared at him. However, once he finished, the reality set in. He would leave, they would carry on with their lives, and not know if and when they would see each other again. Averell was determined not to stay away for long, but he didn't have any control over that.

She took his plate and handed it off, along with hers, to one of the kithlin collecting the dirty ones. Then she stood and he followed, heading back to the guest hut to gather his stuff. She walked him to the entrance of the kith and blinked up at him for a moment, almost unsure what to say.

"Come back soon, Averell."

She wrapped her arms around his neck. As he hugged her back, he was aware that it was a longer embrace than usual. With her body pressed against his and her breath in his ear, he felt his heart warm. He would remember this embrace more than any other, holding it in his heart forever. He wanted to say something, but as always, he feared how it would come out. But he couldn't leave without saying how he felt. Telling her what it all meant.

"No regrets," he whispered in her ear, causing her spine to stiffen. "You were worth the wait."

Zawn felt her heart leap, surprised by his words.

"I hope we take the time," he added, "and continue to put in the work."

When he released her finally, she nodded clumsily. He smiled, squeezing her hand gently.

"I'll come back soon."

She stood, wordlessly, and watched him walk down the road until he disappeared into the morning's lingering mist. She shook herself, trying to gather her thoughts, but could only head to her work hut. She entered, then turned to shut the door, only to find Taylor hot on her heels. She rolled her eyes, gesturing for him to enter so she could close the door.

"What did he say to you?" Tay asked.

"Farewell, that's all."

"Farewell does not leave you speechless," he retorted. "And it doesn't take that long."

"He said I was worth the wait," she responded, but couldn't look at him. She stared at the paperwork on her desk, fingers barely tracing the lines of text.

Her friend's eyebrows rose up while a sly smile materialized. "What happened last night?"

"Averell and I, we, um," then she exhaled hard.

"Finally."

She looked up, surprised.

"What? You think I didn't notice that he still held out hope?" he demanded, exasperated. "I got to watch him pine for you every visit for the last twelve years. But he respected your wishes. Every visit."

"I still don't know if it was a good idea."

"What do you mean?"

"I… I don't want to hurt him."

"I doubt that you could."

"He deserves better, Tay."

Taylor sighed, hard, crossing the room and grasping her shoulders gently. "Have you ever considered that Averell was sent to you for a reason. You don't know what interactions happened to bring you two together."

Zawn rolled her eyes. "You know I don't believe in those kinds of things."

"No, but I do. You know what Gwendin would want, what he would say to you. That is why I can say for sure that you can still love Gwendin and find love with someone else."

She didn't respond immediately, but after a deep breath whispered, "I made a promise to him. I vowed not to covet another."

"You are not betraying him, Zawnie."

"My brain knows that, but my heart disagrees quite vehemently."

He shook his head. "I think it's the other way around."

"I know what Gwen would want. I know what he would say. But it still doesn't feel..." her voice trailed off. "What about Rynan?"

"Averell has accepted him." Then Taylor nodded knowingly. "You think your son would not approve? He's known Averell most of his life. He adores Averell."

"Yes, but that's before knowing this man has seen his mother naked."

Taylor chuckled. "I think he'll be fine with it. There is no one else in this world who wants you to be happy more than your son."

"Other than you and the rest of the kith?"

"Yeah, other than the rest of the world. Zawnie, I am happy for you. Now, I just have to remember to knock before entering when he is here."

CHAPTER 69

Zawn sat on her porch, darning a set of socks she refused to give up. It was another reason why she made sure no one else did her laundry. She knew someone like Meagan or Chaelene would burn them immediately when they saw them. But they were one of the first pair made by the older kithlin after she took over as leader. There was pride and love in each knitted row and she had a hard time giving up something so precious. They also kept her feet warm but not enough to make them sweat.

As she worked quietly, her thoughts kept lingering on Averell. He sent a letter not long after his visit, stating that this way he could take the time to say what he wanted and honestly without her interrupting him. She rolled her eyes again, imagining Averell saying that. But he was right, she would have resisted listening to him, still concerned over making a mistake and hurting him. With more time to think because of Rynan's absence, she had found herself wondering about her relationship with Averell.

She heard a small whistle in her right ear and a fluttering. She thought her ear was ringing, so she continued to work on her socks. She heard it again, but, again, ignored it. Until something bumped into her head. Startled, she looked up to find a hummingbird flitting back and forth, from her head to the corner of her hut. She furrowed her eyebrows in confusion. When the bird started darting from the corner to behind the building, she set down her socks, stood up, and followed it. As she made her way around the building, toward her garden, she found the hummingbird hovering over three colorful flowers. Zawn approached them and realized they were not just any flowers.

They were tulips.

Three tulips, one orange, one red, and one pink, swayed gently under the wind of the hummingbird's wings. The bird twittered again, whistled, then disappeared into the sky.

Zawn kneeled down and touched them gently. They magically fell into her palm, nothing connecting their stems to the ground. She heard herself sob before she felt her body shaking. She knew. She knew it was him. And he wanted to make sure, through such a beautiful sign, that he accepted her relationship with Averell.

"Oh, Gwen," she whispered, holding the flowers against her chest.

CHAPTER 70

About a month later, Averell walked back into her kith. His towering shape was unmistakable, as was his booming voice as he responded to greetings. He kept glancing around until he found who he was looking for, even if he held down his hopes.

She stood in the doorway of her work hut, leaning against the doorframe, her arms crossed. She wore just her tunic and slacks, feet bare and weapons missing. Her long hair was braided and twisted, laying over her shoulder and running the length of her torso. Her signature smirk brightened her face, but in a mischievous way, as did her raised eyebrow.

"What are you doing here?" Zawn inquired.

Averell smiled, as he would any time he visited, even though he didn't know what to expect. "Found more of those roots for the theurgists."

"Oh, that'll make them happy. I swear, I have never seen them so excited about plants in my life. Come, let's tend to business."

First, the storage unit where he deposited the roots. Then her work hut, where she handed over payment. He tucked the money into his belt purse, trying to hide his concern that she would dismiss him immediately. Everything seemed normal, like before. But she had kept her distance, as well as her voice even and professional.

"Is our business complete?" he asked, cautiously.

"Kith business, yes." She moved closer and unfastened his shoulder plate, causing the heavy piece of armor to thump to his left on the floor. "But personal business?" His breast plate was next, falling to his right. "We haven't quite got started, now, have we?"

He grabbed her into his arms. They kissed, groped, stumbling back toward the desk which he trapped her against. She started working on his pants when giggling startled them. They paused, until they realized the sound was from the firepit, and no one was close by. They laughed at themselves, then resumed their undressing until they were nude enough in all the right places to greet each

311

other properly.

~   ~   ~

Sitting on the floor could cause them to catch a chill, considering their lower halves were unclothed, but they were close enough to the hearth for the small fire to keep them warm. Averell reclined against the chair, while she straddled him. Only wearing his tunic, he held Zawn against him. He slipped his hand underneath her shirt, running fingertips lightly along her back. She twirled her fingers in his hair as it trailed down his shoulder and chest. The tenderness they shared was in stark contrast to the passion they exhibited during their fervent greeting.

"Can I have that kind of greeting every time?" he asked.

She started to laugh, which drew a chuckle from him. "As long as we remember to lock the door behind us."

"Ah, I knew I forgot something."

They laughed again, then they settled into a content silence.

"I'm glad," he added.

She looked up at him, eyebrows furrowed in confusion.

"That you are willing to continue this," he said, his eyes searching hers, "whatever it is."

She sighed, hard, resting her chin on his shoulder. "I've had time to think. You've given me the time."

"Hm that's one thing I learned when we first met. Everything is on your timeline, no one else's. It's just how you are."

"Now you know why I've had so few partners," she responded, voice soft. "I'm very difficult to live with."

"Most of the time its endearing. Good thing I've always liked a challenge."

She groused at him, sitting back. He grabbed her by the hips, stopping her from sliding off his lap.

"Not complaining," he reassured.

She leaned forward again, resting her head on his shoulder. "Your letter also helped."

"I meant every word."

When she glanced away, he squeezed her. "Even the part about, um…?"

"Every day. No matter how busy or tedious or dreadful my day, I always wish you good night. And every morning, no matter how early or late, I always wish you good morning."

Sounds of laughter and conversations ebbed and flowed past the hut's closed door.

"Lunch time already?" he inquired.

"Sounds like it. We should make an appearance before my kithlin get suspicious. Come, let's get decent and share a meal."

"Wait."

"What?"

He ran sure hands up her back and pulled her in close again, then kissed her, deeply. Every one of her muscles relaxed as they shared the passionate embrace. She finally pulled away, sighing languorously.

"Something to tide us over until bedtime," he said, his lusty tone making her blush.

"This will be the longest afternoon on record," she retorted.

He started to laugh again and her own giggles followed.

"Before we head out," she added, as she stretched, "help me fix the furniture."

~ ~ ~

Averell's visits were not always consistent, but when he found the time, he made the trek to see his lover. Even though it was always under the guise of kith business, gossip started its rounds. Not only in her kith, but his was well. Because after all this time, the pair didn't hide that they only had eyes for each other. But Zawn and Averell didn't confirm or deny anything. They let the others make their assumptions while they carried on behind closed doors.

~ ~ ~

Zawn sat down, opening her letter from Rynan. Eriselda had already snatched hers from the courier and was reading it as she sat against her favored tree. Zawn cuddled up in her chair, smiling as she read about his different lessons and how he has learned so much under the guidance of Yunji.

Then a new paragraph: *I hear Averell is visiting more often.*

She felt her chest tighten. She hadn't even figured out how exactly to tell him about their relationship.

I'm glad, Momma. He is a good friend to you and a good man. I know you have always enjoyed his company. And you two have always cared deeply for each other.

She felt tears threaten. Then her door opened and Averell entered. He saw the look on her face and frowned.

"What's wrong?" he asked, dropping his duffel and kneeling next to her chair.

She showed him the letter, folding it so he could see his name and Rynan's words.

"He approves?" he inquired, his voice soft. He reached up and hugged her, then kissed her forehead. "I'm glad he approves. I worried." He groused. "But what does he mean he has to have the talk with me?"

Zawn started to laugh. "Well, I am his Momma."

~ ~ ~

313

That night, Zawn led Averell to the guest hut. He had his duffel over one shoulder, breast plate in the other hand, while Zawn carried his shoulder plate. When they had walked far enough from her kithlin, their fingers reached out and entwined gently. She only pulled away when she had to push the door open. They both dropped his armor along the wall next to the hearth. After the door closed, he sighed heavily.

"Am I to remain relegated to the guest hut?" he asked, drolly.

She turned around and stared at him for a moment. Then he watched her expression change from contentment to grief. He dropped his duffel, then reached out for her. Blinking fast, she stepped back. He kept his distance, unsure if he hurt her with that question.

"I'm sorry, Zawnie."

She leaned against the back of a chair, taking a deep breath. "No, it's... you're right. If we're to be lovers..."

"Zawnie, it was a bad joke. I'm sorry."

She didn't move toward him, staring at the fire. He could see her thinking, maybe a little too hard, making him worry.

"It's still the bed I share with my son," she replied.

"And you shared it with Gwendin?"

She nodded, folding her arms over her chest. "After I was poisoned, the kith had accepted us because he helped me heal. He was able to stay here with me. For a little while."

He finally grabbed ahold of her arm and pulled her into a hug, making her melt against him immediately. "I know we've only been at this for a few months. I guess knowing you for so long and now knowing your son accepts us, my expectations became accelerated. I will only share your bed when you are ready."

"You have been too patient with me, Averell."

"You require it." He leaned back, his expression sly. "I will stay in the guest hut as long as you want me to. As long as you lay with me, naked, every night I'm here."

She looked up at him, a smile finally breaking through. "I would be nowhere else."

They kissed tenderly, until he realized something and his eyebrows furrowed. He pulled away, looking confused.

"Wait, when were you poisoned?"

CHAPTER 71

Rynan came home soon after that letter. He asked Averell to step away from the group so they could talk. Based on Averell's body language, Zawn knew it was torture for her lover. Her son, on the other hand, had to be enjoying himself greatly making the other feel incredibly uncomfortable. She tensed when they rejoined the group.

Averell walked past her, grumbling. "I need a strong drink."

Rynan sat down next to her, looking rather pleased with himself.

"Been waiting for weeks to get that out of your system?" she demanded, glaring at her son.

"He had to know what my expectations were," he responded, tartly. "Especially regarding siblings."

"Oh?"

"I'm too old to be a brother."

She chuckled. "Oh but you would always be my favorite."

"Not funny."

She watched him grouse, bumping his shoulder with hers.

"Are you upset about us?" she asked, softly.

"I meant what I said in my letter. I know you will always love Dadda. I will never doubt that one day in my life. But he wouldn't want you to stop living. You also put everything on hold for me, I know that. If Averell makes you happy, then I am happy." He wrapped his arm around her shoulders. "I need to know one very important thing. Has there been naked business in your bed? Because if so, I may need to burn down the entire hut."

She started to laugh. "We have defiled the guest hut only." Then she paused, smirking. "And my work hut."

He made a disgusted sound in response, making her laugh harder.

~   ~   ~

Months passed. Averell visited when he could. Rynan came home during breaks and holidays. There was a rhythm in her world, even if some of it was uneven. Her kith thrived, her allies too.

But she kept a secret from all of them.

Her studies of the texts from the College and the texts Jheferin kept, which were now Sileas's responsibility, brought her little hope. She read the dire warnings of places like the castle, where energy lines converged. But they provided little else. She shared her disappointing news with Yunji through letters and he agreed he found nothing more in the texts he had access to at the College. He had reached out to other libraries in hopes of information passed down in another kingdom but he wrote that he didn't have any hope.

Then Yunji made the trek to the kith, his usual bodyguards surrounding him in a blur of white. However, they all had been to the kith enough that they were greeted with cheers and joyful words. Zawn exited the barn to greet them as well, followed by the herd of goats. Yunji stopped and chuckled as the kith leader and her legion of goats stared back at him.

"I still haven't gotten used to that," Yunji said with a shake of his head.

"To what?" she demanded.

"Your four-legged army."

Zawn chuckled. "I never thought of them that way. Maybe I need to teach them how to attack? Might instill a whole new level of terror in our enemies."

"They would probably do so at your order. Please, just don't let them attack me."

That made her laugh harder. "Go ahead into the work hut, I'll be there in a moment." Then she turned to his four companions. "Theffy, Churron, there's stew, help yourselves. Melcum, Thenious, there's staff practice behind the old pine tree if you wish to join."

The four young men glanced at Yunji, awaiting his permission, even though they knew he would give it. However, Yunji hesitated, out of spite of course, knowing his theurgists grew impatient under his torture. He saw Zawn cross her arms and raise an eyebrow, making him chortle.

"Go. Enjoy yourselves."

And without another breath, all four young men disappeared into the kith. Shaking his head, Yunji made his way to her work hut and she returned the goats to their grazing grounds. When she entered, she found her guest sitting in one of the chairs, resting his feet against the hearth.

"That bad of a walk?" she asked, heading into the kitchen and pouring two glasses of apple wine. She handed him one glass, which he took without hesitation, while sipping from the other.

"Age is catching up with me."

She plopped down in her chair with a sigh. "We are definitely not getting any younger, are we?"

"I think myself spry enough to keep up with the youngsters, until I have to make this trek."

"Maybe it's time for a beast and wain?"

Yunji scoffed, offended. "And give those youngsters something to crow about? Absolutely not!"

Zawn started giggling, which coaxed out his own laughter.

"Speaking of youngsters, when will Rynan return to his kith?"

The older man's eyebrows raised up, annoyed with her change in topic. "You know, he really should be assigned elsewhere."

"That was not part of our agreement, Yunji."

"I know, but I must try to persuade you. I think he would benefit with experiencing the human world beyond the walls of the College."

Zawn grimaced. "If that world knew where he came from, they would not only cast him out, they may even kill him. That is not a world that would accept him and I will not take that chance."

"You should have him home by winter solstice. Is that satisfactory?"

"No, but do I have a choice?"

Yunji chuckled. "Not really."

They sat in contemplative silence until he sighed.

"Theurgists like your son are being trained to fight against an unknown enemy. We suggest that you and your kind do the same."

"Hard to prepare when you know nothing of the threat."

"Agreed. But we have to do what we can in hopes of saving lives." Yunji stared at her for a moment. "The ill wind has reached out farther and darker than before."

She frowned. "It gains strength every day."

"You know more than you let on, milady. What have you learned from all those books you have borrowed?"

"Nothing I didn't already know. What about you? You said you were going to expand your research to other libraries in neighboring kingdoms."

"Yes, my fellow theurgists dug through their respective libraries, sent me the books that referenced our topic of interest, but same thing. They haven't found anything new that would tell me what we need to know."

Yunji took a long drink, the lowered the cup back down on the arm of the chair. As it sat there, his fingers tapped on the glass, thoughtfully.

"Who do you think has disturbed the energy lines?" he inquired.

Zawn shrugged. "The only new variable is Crenast. I doubt it would be any of his soldiers or courtiers. They don't take a piss without his permission. And as a megalomaniac, he would be the one to do something stupid."

"On purpose or by accident?"

"That remains to be seen. All I know is that something has changed and it isn't good."

Yunji cleared his throat roughly. "There is something in one of the texts. Someone of mixed blood being able to control the lines." He paused, swirling his wine. "Rynan…"

"I will not sacrifice my son," she snapped.

"Good. Because I would not let you."

Silence froze them for a moment, then Yunji sighed.

"I'm glad we see eye to eye, milady."

"Me, too."

~   ~   ~

Zawn lied to Yunji. She knew of a creature with mixed blood lines having the ability to control the energy lines like no one else could.

As the child of Elven and Elemental blood lines, Zawn fit that description.

Under the pretense of errands, she made her way to the place she took both Gwendin and Rynan to - Morai Meadow. It held a secret she never spoke of and knew no one else was aware of it. Behind the waterfall, near the edge of their territory outlined by the mountain, was an exposed energy line.

One had to climb a specific tree to find it, but the sliver of light was there. When she got to the right height, she asked the old grandfather oak to move her closer. He obliged, shifting and stretching his limb to accommodate her. There, hiding amongst the moss, a glow.

Zawn inhaled deeply, then reached out toward the pulsing light. The heat emanating from it wasn't surprising, but when her fingers touched it, the burning made her snatch her hand back. She cursed under her breath, looking down at her fingertips. Blisters already started.

With her unharmed hand, she pulled out a folded sheet of parchment, where she had scribbled notes. The instructions said to touch the vein directly. None of the books mentioned injury.

That wouldn't do.

She folded the parchment and slipped it back into her purse, before shuffling down the tree. She needed to think this through.

CHAPTER 72

Rynan's homecoming was the most anticipated event of the year. He had finished his education, graduated with the honors he earned, and now he was returning to his kith permanently. Days filled with cleaning and cooking took up most of the kithlins' time, as did happy chatter about the arrival of their favorite son.

The day he was supposed to arrive, the kith waited impatiently. Morning turned into afternoon and worry set in. Then as the late afternoon sun ticked across the sky, someone in a white cloak with light amber lining strolled along the road up to the kith.

Zawn stood at the entrance, hands on her belt and smirk on her face. She watched as the hood flipped back and the face of her son, all grown up, glowed with joy. The boy who left returned a young man, and even though he had visited often throughout his education, it still surprised everyone how much he had grown up in his absence.

He was taller than his own mother, but not quite reaching Taylor's height. His shoulders were broad and his body sleek, but still muscular for a bookworm. After promising his mother, he kept up his exercises and training with the College's head guard during his time at the College. His shaggy, dirty blonde hair reminded the kithlin of his father Gwendin, as did his dark hickory eyes. His smile seemed to reflect his mother though, while a dimple flashed when those lips turned up in mischief.

Their kithlin waited for him to reach his mother, who embraced him heartily. They stood in each other's arms as if it had been forever. He buried his face into her neck, nuzzling her black and emerald hair. She ran fingers through his hair with one hand as the other held him close to her.

"Welcome home, my darling," Zawn whispered in his ear, then turned toward the rest of the kith. "Rynan, heir of the Haley family, stargazer and theurgist of the Whispering Hornbeam Kith, is home!"

The entire kith erupted in cheers and laughter. Zawn stepped back and watched as the kithlin rushed to welcome her son home. It started with Taylor and Chae, along with Minee as well as Chaen and Talor who were there for the special occasion. Next Meagan and Saronin... until it was a blur of elves.

Behind the mass of people, Eriselda fidgeted in her fine dress, one that Zawn had gotten custom-made for her, unsure of herself. But when Rynan's gaze found her in the crowd, she stopped worrying and felt her heart jump. He cut through the people, striding directly to her, and no one got in the way. They hugged, whispering and laughing, forgetting everyone else around them. Just the tone of their hushed voices gave away everything between them.

Then Zawn raised her voice to the crowd. "Come, to the firepit! Serve the food, pour the wine! We celebrate!"

With the bustle of the kith moving away, Eriselda and Rynan finally loosened their grip on each other, moving enough to lean their foreheads together.

"I'm glad you're here," he whispered.

"I can't stay long, I'm sorry."

"Seldy, you're here. That's all that matters. It made coming home even better."

"I'm glad you're home, Ryn," she replied, swallowing hard against the lump in her throat. "I liked it better when we could talk."

"Me too."

She exhaled hard, trying to fight back a sob. "I need to go. But I can come back on my next day off. If you want?"

"Of course I do." He pulled her back into a full hug, squeezing gently. "I'll walk you back."

"No, you should stay..."

"I have all night with my kith. I only have the walk from here to the castle with you." He released her then grabbed her hand. He led her back to the crowd and searched out his mother. "I am going to walk Eriselda back. I won't be gone long."

Zawn refrained from rolling her eyes at the two lovebirds. "Fine, be back before dark."

The two headed out, then Zawn felt a presence at her elbow. She glanced over to find Minee watching them walk away.

"Want me to follow and make sure that nitwit doesn't get lost?"

Zawn chuckled. "Probably wouldn't be a bad idea. But give them some privacy."

"I will stay far back enough that they won't know I'm there and I won't see anything gross."

"Thank you, Minee."

~   ~   ~

As the evening started to wind down, Zawn nudged her son's arm and motioned him to follow her. They walked toward the cabins, but they didn't approach hers. She led him to one that was just a few lengths away. She opened the door, entering and stoking the fire back to life. Rynan glanced around the smaller hut, confused.

"What's this?" he asked.

"Your personal hut."

Rynan's mouth dropped open. "M-mine?"

"Well, you are now the kith's theurgist, not to mention a young man. You need your own space." She watched him look around with a surprised smile. "What, you thought you'd live with your mother for the rest of your life?"

"I hadn't even thought that far."

"Hm, good thing I did, huh?" She moved into the kitchen area, gesturing to the counter space. "It has a bigger kitchen than most, so you can work your potions and herbs. Bigger kitchen however means smaller bathroom, so no bathtub but the shower will probably fit your needs better. Plenty of shelving and large windows for plants too. You didn't leave much this last visit, but I moved your things into the chest there, put your notebooks on the bookshelf over there. And it looks like Minee put your College satchel over here by the bed."

"Momma, this is…" he stammered, touching the kitchen counter, reverently. "Thank you."

"You're welcome. Now, get some rest. It's been a long day for you, I'm sure you'd like to get some sleep."

Rynan chuckled. "All the excitement has kept me going until now. But, my own place? After all of my time at the College, this is… this is the best thing ever."

"Well, don't get too loud with your potions. Just remember I am your neighbor on the west and Minee is your neighbor on the east."

He grabbed his mother and hugged her tightly. "I'm so glad to be home."

"We are glad you are home too." She paused, taking a deep breath, relieved. "I'm glad you're home, my darling. Now, bed."

~   ~   ~

She left her son to settle into his new hut, chuckling to herself over his excitement. In her own hut, Zawn sat near her fireplace, darning a shirt along its hem. She didn't know when or what had snagged the shirt, she assumed maybe one of the goats, but the original hem had gotten pulled and unraveled. She didn't notice until she washed it and now, she had the annoying task of fixing it.

She heard a knock on her door, making her glance up. Rynan peeked in, shyly, to find her still awake.

"Can I come in?" he inquired.

"Of course." She returned her attention to her darning, frowning. "Can't sleep?"

He stepped inside, closed the door, and sat on the edge of her bed. He wore his sleeping gown, his skin freshly scrubbed. He watched her work for a few breaths, then shrugged. "I don't know if the adrenaline is keeping me awake or what."

"It'll run out soon enough."

"It's also very quiet in the cabin," he added, furrowing his eyebrows. "I'm used to people milling around at all hours, either studying, partying, or panicking."

Zawn chuckled. "Sounds like you'll have to reacquaint yourself to the quiet, mild life of the kith."

"I've missed it terribly."

"You've been missed as well," she responded, tying off the thread and cutting it.

Silence answered her, making her look up. Rynan was laying on her bed, eyes closed. Then a soft snore escaped him. Sighing, she shook her head. She got up from her chair, folding the shirt into the seat, and walked over to her son. She nudged him, making him adjust himself on the bed, and she pulled the blanket up over him.

~   ~   ~

About a week after Rynan returned to the kith, Averell paid them a visit. The tall elf glanced around for his lover and found Rynan instead. The young man stood in the doorway of his mother's work hut, arms crossed. Averell stopped in front of him, waiting for the other to speak.

"Glad you could finally make it," Rynan quipped.

Averell dropped his duffel onto the porch before grabbing and hugging the boy. "I am sorry that I'm late. We had a big harvest."

Rynan snorted. "Momma said you've been busy."

"She inside?"

"No, she had to go deal with the irrigation system again. Gaylon asked her last night to check on it today. I swear, no matter what she does, it always clogs up because of the soil shifting. She thought you'd be stopping by so she asked me to keep an eye out for you."

Rynan gestured for him to join him inside, where Averell set down his duffel and started removing his armor.

"How does it feel to be home?" the elf asked.

"Surreal," Rynan answered, then scoffed. "I kept hearing the other students talking about assignments. A lot of them were anxious about where they were going to go. I uh… I wondered what it would be like to be sent to a place I didn't know. I worried that the College would renege on its agreement to return me to my kith."

"Your mother is someone I wouldn't want to betray and I know Yunji wouldn't dare either. She has too much leverage over the College. And she uses it wisely."

"Yunji is a good man, a great teacher," the young man responded. "He wasn't the one I worried about."

"Well, the College did what they promised. You're home."

"And that I am very glad about."

Then Averell smiled slyly. "How are things with Eriselda?"

Rynan blushed, stammering.

Averell chuckled. "Sounds like we are brothers in that feeling?"

"Can I ask something, well, personal?"

"Of course."

"How did you know Momma was the one?"

"Oh, well, when I first saw her, I thought her beautiful. But we didn't agree on several topics, so we butted heads immediately. Then she thrashed me and well, the rest was history. Is Eriselda the one for you?"

"I knew the moment I first saw her."

"Then I don't think your question is if she is the right one, but if she thinks you are the right one."

"I've loved her since we met."

"If she has stuck with you this long, my dear boy, she believes you are the right one for her. All you have to do is ask her what you want to ask her. I am sure she will say yes."

"Thanks, Averell."

Then they heard Zawn's voice as it approached the hut, both men smiling at her annoyed tone and braced for her entrance.

~   ~   ~

The kithlin surrounded the firepit, their joy palpable. They talked, laughed, and after the food was eaten, some sang tales of love and adventure. Averell sat on one side of her while Rynan sat on the other. Taylor, Chaelene, and Minee were nearby on another bench. Zawn reveled in the moment, surrounded by everyone she loved. Then as the night wore on, the group thinned out and soon Zawn and Averell were readying for bed. They watched Rynan retire to his own hut before leaving the square.

"He is finally home," Averell said. "How does it feel?"

"Good. The kith feels... almost complete."

"Almost?"

She held out her hand, which he happily grasped, then she led him to her personal hut.

CHAPTER 73

Eriselda waited for Rynan near the kith's edge, but per his instruction, she didn't enter. She stayed by the overgrowth next to the old pine tree. His kithlin hadn't gotten to that side of their living area, which they tried to keep tamed to avoid sneak attacks and forest fires. When he arrived, he grabbed her hand and led her into a hut from the back.

When they entered, she didn't recognize the hut. She only knew Zawn's personal and work huts, as well as the guest hut where she had to study inside during the rainy season. It was the same size as the guest hut, but the kitchen seemed larger than the one she had seen in Zawn's. She glanced around and saw items that reminded her of his theurgy, glass and ceramic containers that varied in size and color. Small plants kept in vases along the window to get sunlight. There was simple set of drawers next to the bed, which took up the right side of the room, and on top were usual night stand items: candle, glass of water, handkerchief. There was a table with two chairs near the hearth, leaving room for one person to walk between it and the end of the bed.

She suddenly realized that this was his hut.

He looked at her, sheepishly, which amused her but also flattered her. Knowing that he was sneaking her in and that, after all these years, together and apart, they were finally alone and... somewhere private.

Then he began to undress for her...

~   ~   ~

They laid together in his bed, together in a way they had only dreamt. Rynan held Eriselda close, listening to her soft breathing and enjoying the tickle of air against his chest. He never understood all those stories his Momma told him until now. What love was. How it felt. What it meant to find the one person you couldn't live without.

They had said the words for years... it slipped out one night before he headed back to the College and took them both by surprise. But neither of them could deny that they loved each other. They whispered it to each other as often as possible, even though they tried to keep it between them.

He would no longer hide those words from his kithlin. She was his love, his lover, his mate. Content with that private affirmation, for now, he closed his eyes and drifted off, not caring if they would get caught.

~   ~   ~

It was still dark outside. Eriselda had started to dress, her brain still reeling from their intimate night together. She shyly glanced over her shoulder, seeing the naked backside of Rynan. She felt her heart beat faster as her face warmed with a satisfied blush. She watched dreamily until he turned and caught her. His face reddened at her attention, but at the same time, his eyes wandered along his lover's half-dressed body.

Lover. She had yearned to call him that for so long. After their night together, she could call him that freely.

He turned away reluctantly, to pick up his shirt, and that's when she noticed something on the back of his thigh. She knew the color drained from her face and was thankful that he didn't notice. Because on his thigh, in the same vicinity as Princess Valena's, was a brand. A mark that proved his bloodline. His royalty. She swallowed hard against the lump in her throat and pushed the realization to the back of her mind. Especially as he walked around the bed to pull her into his arms.

He kissed her lovingly and she used that wonderful sensation to chase away her worries. "I hate that you have to leave so soon," he whispered, leaning his forehead against her temple.

"It may be our first time, but I doubt it will be our last," she assured, slyly smiling then kissing his chin.

Their lips caressed again, making time stand still. He tightened his arms around her, pressing her against his chest. Through the cloth and his skin, she felt his heart beat. Feeling it beat in time with hers, she knew they were truly united.

"I love you, Seldy."

"I love you too, Ryn."

As he walked her back to the castle, hand in hand, she told herself that what she saw, what she knew, didn't matter. It didn't seem to matter to him. Whatever story explained his mark wouldn't change how she felt about him. Nothing could change how they felt about each other. He was her love, her lover, and her heart. And if he didn't want to talk about it, she wouldn't bring it up.

~   ~   ~

Zawn worked thoughtfully on her machine parts on the porch of her work hut, before dinner was served. Out of the corner of her eye, she noticed Eriselda entering the kith, greeting those who called out. However, instead of heading to Rynan's hut, Eriselda approached Zawn first, her face drawn with worry.

"What's wrong?" Zawn asked, frowning.

"May we speak privately?"

"Of course."

Zawn led her inside, closing the door behind them and waving for the younger woman to sit. As Eriselda slowly sank down, Zawn took her seat in the chair across from her.

"You've got me worried, girl," Zawn admitted. "What's wrong?"

"I have been deemed too old to reside at the castle."

"You've been dismissed?"

"No, I still have debt to pay off. But recently, my duties have changed from drudge maid to the princess's morning maid. I help get her ready in the morning, then tidy up her chambers and then… that's it. I don't have to be there all day and night. I have been told by the house manager that I am at the age that they believe is unwise for me to live within the walls."

Zawn sighed. "You're at the age that riles men's temptations?"

"It is easier to banish me from the dorms than to manage the men."

"I guess that's for the best," the elf chided, disgusted. "But they don't pay you anything to subsidize rent or to build a place of your own."

"No, they don't. All my earnings go to the debt. I don't know what to do."

"Have you told Rynan?"

Eriselda shook her head. "He wouldn't understand, let alone know of a proper outcome."

Zawn stared at the girl, fingers drumming against the armrest. "There would be some strict rules, stricter than usual, if we were to take you in. If anyone at the castle knew we let you live amongst us, it could cause some issues. Mostly for you."

Eyes wide, the girl stared at her, speechless.

"There are spies who like to keep an eye on us, reporting anything new to the castle or other enemies. I'm sure they're aware of you visiting, but living here may be a bigger issue. You will need to wear elven clothing when you're here to blend in a little better. When you go to the castle, you'll only wear your work clothes. The sentries already keep an eye out for you so that won't change. But you'll have to rethink how you travel. It's not like you'll be off doing your laundry or sneaking out of the castle. You may have to deviate from the main road and take less well-known paths to cover your tracks since you'll be traveling here daily."

"Live… here?" the young woman whispered, in shock.

"Do you really think we'd abandon you, too?" Zawn asked, smiling wryly.

Eriselda sniffled, tears rolling down her cheeks. "I didn't think about living here."

"You are the closest thing I have to a daughter, Eriselda. Where else would you go?"

The girl didn't respond, wiping the tears from her cheeks.

Zawn chuckled, handing her a handkerchief. "I have a feeling that if you told Rynan your circumstances, he would have come up with the same outcome. But he wouldn't ask me for permission."

Eriselda stared at her, confused.

"He'd continue to sneak you into his hut and pretend you weren't spending the night."

The girl's face drained quickly of its color.

"Didn't think I noticed, did you?" Zawn inquired.

"You didn't say anything."

"As kith leader, I am annoyed that my son would blatantly ignore the chain of command. And annoyed with you too, seeing that you've been taught our ways."

Eriselda lowered her eyes, not quite in shame but more in embarrassment.

"But as his mother, I understand my son's behavior. I have very little to stand on considering my misbehavior in my younger years. After all, if I had followed the rules myself, I wouldn't have had him." Zawn leaned back in the chair, smirking. "Tell Rynan your situation. And when he tries to find a way around my rules, tell him I am not stupid and to come see me. I will ask his intentions toward you and then offer him a few options."

Eriselda sat silently, then exhaled. "I do love him, Zawn."

"And I know he loves you. You two have been in love for a very long time."

"We really have."

"Is this outcome amenable?"

The young woman nodded, clumsily.

"Good. Now go rile up my son into righteous indignity before you send him over."

~   ~   ~

It wasn't immediately after she left. Zawn waited patiently, honing her short sword. Then there was a knock. She called out permission and watched, amused, as a sheepish Rynan entered.

"Seldy told me to come see you," he admitted, closing the door carefully.

She raised her eyebrow, then sheathed her blade. "Did you come up with a master plan to skirt around the rules?"

"I did. Then she told me you knew."

"Rules are meant to be broken?" she inquired, drolly, gesturing for him to sit.

"It wasn't that," he replied, lowering himself into the chair across from her. He stared at his mother before shrugging. "I just... we wanted to be together but didn't know if it would have been acceptable."

"I see no issues," she responded, furrowing her eyebrows. "The kith loves you and adores her."

"We love each other."

"About time you two admitted it, too."

"We've told each other for a while now. We just wanted to keep it private for as long as we could. I guess it felt more special that way."

His mother laughed. "You may have kept the words secret but your body language gave you both away since day one."

"So, she can live here? Live with me?"

"Do you want her to?"

"More than anything."

"Then we will make it official," Zawn said with a smile. "She will be presented to the kith and I have no doubt that she will be permitted as kithlin."

"And as my mate?"

Zawn's eyebrow rose up. "Are we already there?"

"I knew the moment I saw her washing her clothes in the river," he answered, his voice soft with love and honesty.

"Yeah, I knew the moment I saw you two together for the first time. My rebellious son, the things you have put your mother through."

He stood up, closed the distance between them, and hugged her tightly. "And I am thankful that you are my Momma."

"Humph. Go back to your hut. We'll announce at dinner. You'll need to name her."

"I thought you would do that."

"I named you and I named your father," she replied, exasperated. "I don't know if I have another in me."

Rynan pulled away just enough to meet her gaze. "It would be our honor if you named her."

Zawn sighed. "Fine. I will… think on it. But if you two don't like it, too bad. She is stuck with it for life."

Rynan chuckled, kissed her on the cheek, then darted out the door.

~   ~   ~

That night at dinner, Zawn shouted for everyone's attention. They all settled into a nervous quiet, unsure why their leader would call silence to their revelry. It usually meant something big was about to happen. Zawn stood, glancing around at every face, holding her cup with both hands.

"My friends, today has turned into a more important day than even I could have foreseen. My son, Rynan, our stargazer, has asked that we consider his mate, Eriselda, as kithlin. You all know that I do not take a decision like this very lightly. But we have all gotten to know Eriselda over the years, as she visited and learned and helped. I believe it would be a great honor for her and for us to have her join our kith. Any disagreement to this decision?"

Not one soul said they disagreed. Exuberant expressions amongst the kith glowed in the firelight. The crowd murmured in excitement and affirmation that they approved of the new kithlin.

"If there are no challenges, then please, Eriselda, stand."

Eriselda rose up, glancing nervously at the smiling faces surrounding her.

"As mate of Rynan, our stargazer, Eriselda is now heir to the Haley family, starlight of the Whispering Hornbeam Kith. Welcome home!"

Cheers burst from all over the square, while clapping and stomping accompanied. Rynan stood and hugged her, whispering happy words. Suddenly, everyone was on their feet, surrounding the couple.

Zawn watched their faces and felt her heart thump hard. Their happiness meant more to her than she thought. As the revelry sparked singing and dancing, Zawn wiped away the tears that had escaped. Then she felt arms wrap around her. She chuckled as Rynan and Eriselda embraced her. Whispering her own congratulations, she held onto them as long as she could before they got dragged away to dance in celebration.

After everything, from her falling in love with Gwendin, to making him her mate and a member of the kith posthumously, she finally found a way for her kind to accept others as part of their family. Even with all the pain caused by man, they couldn't hold on to the idea that all men were alike. There was hope, there was love, there was more to them than assumptions. She smiled as she watched her son and his mate celebrate.

She only wished that same cold wind that haunted her long ago hadn't settled in her bones again. Things were changing, like Yunji had said, and all they could do was prepare.

~   ~   ~

After the revelry drove many to bed, Zawn walked Eriselda over to Rynan's hut. He had darted off a few moments before, probably to straighten it up after his morning of remedy making. They hooked arms and walked slowly, trying to give him enough time.

Once they made it to the porch, Zawn turned and hugged Eriselda again. She found it astounding at how tall the girl had become. She remembered the first time Eriselda hugged her, when she had burned her hand and wandered to the kith, knowing that they would be the only ones that could help her. The girl's had ear rested easily against Zawn's heart. Now, as they embraced, the young woman's chin hooked over the elf's shoulder and she was able to nuzzle the dark locks that had escaped Zawn's tight braids.

"Welcome home, Eriselda, our starlight."

"Thank you, Zawn."

"You're officially family now, my dear. Call me Momma."

She felt the young woman quiver. "Thank you, Momma," Eriselda whispered, sniffling.

"Go, be with your mate. But do me a favor? Don't make me a grandmother too quickly."

Eriselda giggled, then stepped back to look at Zawn. The tears that streamed down the younger woman's face made the elf's heart warm because she knew, for the first time, those were tears of joy. Zawn caressed her cheeks, wiping them dry while smiling, then nodded toward the hut. She watched as Eriselda, her son's mate and her new heir, entered the hut before turning away and heading to her own.

CHAPTER 74

The days and weeks flew by. The kith felt complete with the addition of Eriselda as kithlin and she could finally call it home. She could finally say she had family. Still under contract, she continued her work at the castle, but once completed, she headed home to her mate and her kith. She helped out with meals and laundry, all the while making time to spar with Minee and her other friends.

Late one night, after the moons had decided to return to their shelters, Averell and Zawn laid in her bed. She cuddled up against his side, resting her head on his shoulder. He was propped up by a couple of pillows, which gave them a good enough angle to watch the fire glow and crackle. She could tell something was on his mind that evening but he didn't want to discuss it in front of the kith. She raised up on her arm, making him look up at her.

"What's wrong?" she asked.

"Nothing."

She raised her eyebrow. "You know that doesn't work on me as much as it doesn't work on you."

He sighed, hard. "I don't want things to change…"

"But?"

"There are things that are out of my control."

She caressed his cheek gently. "Talk to me, Averell."

He grabbed hold of her hand, kissing it before resting their clasped hands on his chest. He stared at their fingers as they entwined, unable to look her in the eyes. Whatever was on his mind weighed heavily.

"Taikin wants to step down," he finally responded.

"Which would make you leader."

"He deserves to retire, Zawnie, I know that. Ever since Darion died, his own health has deteriorated and I know he longs for the day when he can see him again."

"And this is what he has trained you for, to take over," she replied, proud.

"You'll make an excellent leader, Averell. You've proven that with everything you've taken on already."

"Thank you, that's high marks coming from you."

"It is," she agreed with a smirk. Then it faded as she watched his eyes darken with worry. "What? Haven't you chosen a second?"

"No, I have. Darion's great-nephew, Aric, he's been a great help. Our kithlin listen to him and honestly, they love him. He'll make a great second."

"But?"

"I will have even less time for other things. Like traveling."

Her eyes lowered, realizing what he meant. Less time for them. After all the years of waiting for her, now he feared losing her to his responsibilities... similar to the fears she once had with Gwen. Ever since they had given into their feelings, she had wondered what it would be like when that time came. What changes would come when he became leader.

"My son is grown," she responded, slowly, "and doesn't need me hovering over him all the time. He has his mate and they are sharing a life together now. Taylor's children are grown too and he has stepped into more roles in the kith." She returned her eyes to meet his, a smile growing. "I think I could find time to travel outside the kith, if it were to keep our relationship."

"You would...?" he asked, then his voice faded away in surprise.

"Why wouldn't I? We've made adjustments for each other already, what's one more?"

He pulled her over on top of him, making her straddle him as he sat up. She laughed at the move, settling on his lap while he wrapped his arms tightly around her.

"Be my mate," he said.

She sighed, staring into his hopeful eyes. "Averell..."

"I know you are still devoted to Gwen, I know that he will be the one that you share your afterlife with when you move on to the other side of the canopy. But until then... Let me have the rest of this life. If you mean it, that we can stay together no matter what, then be my mate. Be my mate and I will covet no others." Then he smiled, wryly. "Which won't be difficult since I haven't desired another since we met."

Her heart leapt, recognizing that not only hope resided in those beautiful copper eyes, but also his love and devotion. She couldn't say she didn't feel the same. She knew how she felt, something she thought she would never feel again, but it was only for Averell. And she knew he was right, that they both had been devoted to each other longer than their physical relationship, neither looking at anyone else.

She reached up slowly, cupping his ears first before tracing them slowly. He shut his eyes at the sensation, tears escaping his eyelids as she made her way to his earlobes.

"I will be yours as long as you are mine," she whispered, wiping away his tears and leaning her forehead against his.

He reached up and touched her ears in the same manner and with a gentleness she had never felt before from him. A deep shuddering breath and tears running down her cheeks solidified their oath and bond to each other. They embraced each other tightly, sighing into hair and trembling with the love they had expressed.

~ ~ ~

That morning, as he readied to leave, she watched him. She had dressed already, but languorously laid across her bed, bare feet hanging off the edge. She kept finding herself giggling, her mind still whirling through their promises to each other last night.

He glanced over at her, furrowing his eyebrows in confusion. "What?" he asked.

"I think this might be the first time two kith leaders were mates."

He thought about it, then nodded. "I think you're right."

"That causes a predicament."

"Does it?"

She sat up, still grinning. "Yes, who's name do we share?"

"I didn't even think about that. Should we change our names?"

"If we did, I'd think you'd have to take mine."

"Is that so?" he demanded, teasingly. "And why is that?"

"Seniority."

Averell laughed, crossing the room. He pulled her to her feet and hugged her. He stared down at her, his smile wide, before kissing her soundly.

"I'll have to think about that," he replied.

Her eyebrow rose up, annoyed. "Oh?"

"Well, it could cause confusion. Someone asking for Leader Haley... we'd have to ask which one."

Zawn giggled. "I didn't think about that."

"We'll discuss it next time we see each other," Averell suggested, kissing her again, this time a little longer. "Maybe you can take a walk next week?"

"I think I can fit one in my very busy schedule."

"Good. See you soon, my love."

"Safe travels, my love."

CHAPTER 75

It was another dreadful day at the castle. Eriselda arrived early, waiting for the princess to wake. She patiently bathed the princess, then dressed her. She watched the princess leave for breakfast, before straightening up the bed, bathing room, and the sitting area in front of the fireplace. Once she had everything tidied, she started to leave. However, as she made her way down the hallway and servant staircase, she caught sight of Crenast walking swiftly down an unused passage. Eriselda brushed it off, knowing the rumors about the King's disappearances. When she turned on her heel, she found the princess following him. Valena gestured for her to join her. Eriselda grimaced, but she had to obey.

They followed him, jumping behind doorways and archways every time they thought he'd turn around to check for stalkers. But for the most part, Crenast seemed to care little if anyone was following him. He finally stopped at a plain, blank, very unassuming wall, making both young women hide in one of the archways in the concourse. Then he started murmuring something against the bricks.

Valena grabbed Eriselda and pulled her close. "What is he saying?"

"I don't know," Eriselda lied. She listened intently while the princess was distracted, memorizing syllables and cadence. She recognized the enchantment, but didn't want to let Valena in on how much knowledge the servant girl had gained from the elves or from her mate.

Suddenly, part of the wall popped open. It dragged along the floor, making an eerie sound, and gave way to a flight of stairs that had been hidden behind it. Crenast again appeared unconcerned, not checking around him before heading inside.

"Stay here," Valena ordered, darting across the large concourse to catch the door from closing. After a glance around, the princess followed Crenast down.

Eriselda remained where she was, impatiently waiting for Valena to return. She feared that the princess would be caught by her uncle and that the consequences would be dire. After what felt like forever, Valena reemerged from the hidden doorway and ran back to her servant. Then Valena grabbed her hand and dragged the girl back to her bedchamber.

"What did you see?" Eriselda asked.

Valena stammered then shook her head to get her senses back. "I don't know. What were those?" Valena seemed to ask herself, voice still hushed. "It was a weird cave. What is Crenast doing in there? Why?" Valena's mind was running faster than Eriselda could ever imagine. "Stay here, I want to check one other place."

"But milady, I am not supposed to stay later than lunch."

"I am the princess, I outrank that horrid house manager. Now stay. I will be back."

Eriselda stood in the princess's receiving room, wringing her hands.

~   ~   ~

Valena first checked the library, finding that Crenast had not returned there. The candles had been extinguished but the sunlight streaming through gave her enough light to glance around. However, all she found were spaces where books had stood but now were missing. She knew immediately which ones were gone, she had read all of them when she was younger. A memory suddenly surprised her, one where she lied to the theurgist Gwendin about why she had decided to read certain books. The theurgist never questioned her after that when he saw her reading. She had memorized them all since.

But what did Crenast know that she didn't?

She spun on her heel and made her way to his private chambers. She wanted to know what he had learned. As she hastened up the main stairs, she made up an excuse in her head to be there. She needed to confirm some trivial information with her mother. After all, her mother shared the chamber with Crenast and she would use that to her benefit.

When she arrived, the guards were not patrolling the hallway and the double doors were closed, which meant neither Crenast or her mother Kemberly were inside. She cracked one slightly open, slipped in, then starting looking around. She spent several moments checking bookcases, cabinets, and tables but she didn't find any books or notes. Then she heard voices from the direction of the staircase.

Crenast and Kemberly.

Cursing, Valena exited their chambers but had nowhere else to go. She glanced around for a hiding place and jumped into half-empty linen armoire in the hallway. She kept one door cracked and she watched Crenast and her mother stroll toward their rooms.

"Why must you stay in those dreaded caves at all times of the day?" Kemberly demanded, frustrating darkening her voice. "You've left me handling all of the important matters again and people are gossiping."

"I have told you from the very first day," Crenast responded, exasperated, as they walked in front of the armoire. "If we can harness the energy lines, we will rule not just Mehdehra but the entire world. From the Riders' land to the other continent. No one will be able to overthrow us."

Kemberly turned on him suddenly. "But it has been almost twenty years, Crenast. You are no closer to ruling the world than you were when you killed Elixin."

Crenast's jaw locked in anger. "Must I remind you that you were involved in that insurgency as much as I was?"

"Because you filled my head with lies. And then you killed my brother and my son... the one thing you promised not to do..."

"I did not kill your son," he snapped. "His protection was your responsibility. You were supposed to be in the nursery. You were to protect your children and feign hysteria. My men knew if they saw you, they were to leave. You weren't there. And your brother... trying to fight my men...?"

"It wasn't my fault Elixin changed his schedule, that he sent my daughter to another part of the castle. He wasn't supposed to be in the bedchambers."

The two conspirators glared at each other, anger flushing their faces.

"Nothing we had planned came to fruition, Crenast," Kemberly complained. "What do I have to show for my submission to you? No power, no wealth... no other children. I am left wanting."

"I will give you the world, my love," he placated, reaching out to grasp her arms. He showed her more tenderness in private, faking their animosity only for the public. "Just bear with me, just a little longer. I will keep my promises."

Kemberly stared into his eyes for a few moments before she sighed, then nodded. "My patience wanes by the day, Crenast. Please remember that."

"How could I forget, with you looking at me that way every day?"

Another stretch of stressful silence. "We should retire to our rooms until dinner. But you must tend to the business at hand before hiding away in the caves. The people must see the strong King taking control and fixing problems, not the Queen who is only permitted to take notes."

"Agreed. We will hold court appropriately, traditionally. And if there are any wagging tongues..."

"We shall cut them out," Kemberly replied.

The malevolent laugh that erupted from Crenast made Kemberly smile just as maliciously. They clasped hands and entered their bedchambers. Once the double doors closed and the guards started their march in the other direction, Valena slipped out from inside the armoire. Fuming at her mother's duality and her stepfather's plan, she snuck off of their floor and rushed back to her bedchamber.

~   ~   ~

"What happened?" her servant asked after she returned.

Valena must have had quite the look on her face for her servant to sound so concerned. "Nothing. I thought I'd find something in the library but Crenast must have his notes in his chambers. I still don't understand what he is doing."

"You may need to keep those thoughts to yourself until bedtime, Your Majesty," Eriselda suggested.

"Why?" the princess demanded.

"You can't hide it very well. And you've dinner with him tonight."

The princess growled a curse then sighed hard. "You're right. I will need to hide my suspicions. I forget myself sometimes. Now, I will require you to stay here tonight."

"But Your Majesty…"

"No buts. I have a feeling I will need your help keeping my mother distracted when I am investigating. Now, help me ready for dinner. That other servant isn't as good as you at braiding my hair."

~ ~ ~

With Valena tucked in bed and finally asleep, Eriselda took a deep breath and slipped out of the bedchambers. She snuck across the hallway into an empty bedchamber, locking the door behind her. First, she lit a candle and made her way to the window, an opening that faced the main road into the forest. If her kithlin were watching, they needed to see that she was alive. She ensured her face was lit properly and she waited several breaths before moving away. Then she walked over to one side of the dead fireplace and tapped part of the mantle that connected to the wall. The wall clicked open and she was able to access the secret passageway.

She traveled as far as she could in the secret hallway until it ran out. She exited into one of the hallways that lead to the main concourse. She knew that the guards were in another part of the building doing their sweep, so she made her way to the hall where they watched Crenast disappear. She forgot how eerie the castle could get at night, with no one moving around except the ghosts. She always called them ghosts, but she really didn't know what the random twinkles of light along the walls and floors were. She only knew that they felt like lightning when she got too close.

She had told Rynan about them, which surprised him and that was when he suggested that maybe she had magic of her own. She didn't believe him, until he tested her, but they kept the truth secret from everyone. She would never get to learn the way Rynan did, but he did teach her some tricks of the trade when he visited. Including languages.

Glancing over her shoulder to make sure no one was around, Eriselda walked up to the wall and repeated the incantation Crenast had chanted earlier. She heard the magical lock disengage and the wall popped open. She slipped through the thin opening and pulled it closed behind her. Then she descended the stairs.

She tiptoed down as quietly as she could, unsure if the chambers below were empty. A light below grew brighter and brighter with each step, making her shield her eyes. As she neared the last step, the illumination was almost too powerful and she had to blink fast and hard to clear her vision. Once her eyes adjusted, she could see the cave walls and the veins of light that pulsed.

She didn't know what she was looking at immediately, but as the warmth reddened her skin and the static electricity spurred her arm hairs to stand on end, she slowly realized that they were the energy lines she had read about when she was younger. They were mentioned in several books, but the one that gave the best detailed description was the tome that spoke about magic and the different creatures that lived in the world, including the elves. She also knew from that book that it was unwise to stay too long, especially for anyone without a strong magical lineage. She scanned the area quickly, trying to memorize everything in the cave. Her eyes stopped for a moment when she saw the trunk that was tucked away in a corner. It blended in so well with its surroundings that she almost missed it. She knew immediately that was where Crenast hid his notes. Then she spun around on her heel and darted back up the stairs.

~　　~　　~

Zawn led the goats back to their stalls to be milked after Meagan listed all of the treats they needed to make for the upcoming fair in the neighboring township. Many of the goats that she had befriended during her required chores had passed due to old age, but their descendants, and their newest offspring, learned from them that Zawn was the leader of the pack. She smiled when she remembered Averell's shocked reaction to the kith leader managing animals.

The thought of him made her cheeks blush. She had recently returned from an overnight stay with Averell. Spending time with him in his kith made Zawn realize how he had taken her lessons to heart. Seeing him working side by side with his kithlin, taking on tasks that his younger self would have considered below him, made her heart warm. He became the man Taikin had hoped for, thanks to the tutelage of Zawn and her kithlin.

The goats settled in, munching on oats while the younger women milked them. Zawn left them to it, but not before sharing a few scratches with the older nannies, and stepped out of the barn. On her way to her work hut, she was met by her son, who looked rather anxious. She reached out and grasped his hand, pulling him close.

"What's wrong?" she asked.

"Eriselda hasn't come home," Rynan replied, keeping his voice low. "I'm worried about her. She had said things at the castle were, well, weird."

"We'll send sentries out to the tree line, to see if they can get eyes on her."

Rynan tried to suggest something but his frown deepened.

"Theurgist or not, it is not safe for you to be on those grounds," Zawn responded, reading him correctly. "I know she is fine, we have taught her everything she needs to avoid trouble. But if things are worse than usual, she may have to make a decision about staying. Debt paid or not."

"We've talked about that. She wants to leave."

"Then we will work something out when she comes home. Come, let's talk to our sentries."

~   ~   ~

The sentries confirmed seeing Eriselda that night, in the window. They knew she was safe. But why she had been sequestered to the castle remained a mystery.

~   ~   ~

A few days later, Valena was called to the Queen's private chambers for lunch. Eriselda was left in her bedchambers, dreading the idea of being trapped in the castle one more night. She wanted to go home, to feel Rynan's arms around her and the kith's protection. She whispered to whatever gods were listening to free her from the castle and from Valena's constant orders.

For the past few days, Valena had been coming and going constantly, leaving Eriselda behind to make excuses if anyone came looking for her. She didn't know where the princess was going but she knew that the princess was looking for answers. But Eriselda knew that Crenast would make sure nothing helpful would be available. He had hid this secret for so long that he believed he had everyone tricked.

Eriselda just wanted to go home.

Most importantly, she needed to warn Zawn.

~   ~   ~

Valena waited until her servant left to fetch something frivolous that she had demanded. Once the door closed, the princess turned to her vanity.

"My queen?" the princess called. "Are you there?"

Her reflection stared back, making Valena frown. She straightened, running anxious hands down her skirt. Disappointed, she started to turn away… until she heard her name whispered. She spun on her heel to find a mesmerizing swirl darken the mirror.

"My goddess?" Valena responded.

No face manifested, but two hands pressed against the glass. Valena reached out, placing her hands against those reaching out to her. She could feel the cold steeliness of the surface, but she knew the iciness also emanated from the other side where her master resided.

"Talk to me," the disembodied voice answered.

"I found the entryway, but cannot get in. I cannot find his notes. I am lost at what to do."

A chaotic laugh shook the glass. "You know what to do. We have our plan, child. Fear nothing."

The mystical swarm faded and left Valena alone with her reflection. Then the door opened and the princess turned to her servant. She returned empty handed, but before Valena could pounce, the plain girl cleared her throat.

"The King and Queen have asked for your presence."

~   ~   ~

Valena crashed back into her bedroom, tears of anger burning down her cheeks. Eriselda had leapt to her feet in shock, unsure what had had transpired. Valena had a scroll in one hand, the seal broken, and clenched tightly in the other a crumpled invitation.

"I am to be married off!" Valena screamed, throwing the smaller piece of paper into the fire. "Married to something I have never met nor could ever love!"

Eriselda wisely kept her mouth shut. She knew the princess and the guard's captain were too close for their own good, but Valena would never admit to any impropriety.

Valena then spun on her heel, facing Eriselda. She held up the scroll in front of her, laughing slightly madly.

"But I have a plan."

~   ~   ~

The sentries were able to get eyes on Eriselda briefly a few times before the next reports back were of her and another young woman walking through the woods. Zawn and her archers headed out to meet them, the kith leader knowing exactly who traveled with her daughter. She wondered, rather annoyed, what the human wanted. After all, the moment she stepped into the kith's territory, it would be considered breaking the agreement Zawn forced Crenast to sign. And she would also be considered a political prisoner if Zawn so chose.

She stopped near the river, motioning for her archers to take positions around the area. Better safe than sorry, if their guests were a diversion for a bigger problem. With her kithlin hidden in the trees, she ensured she was the only one seen.

Zawn could hear someone fussing about the foliage in her hair and pulling on her clothing, while stomping loudly through the leaf covered terrain. Then two young women walked out of the bushes and stumbled to a halt when they saw who awaited them.

"Princess Valena," Zawn acknowledged, crossing her arms over her chest, mainly to hide her drawn dagger. "What do we owe for the visit?"

The princess' eyes narrowed with indignation, angry that the elf in front of her didn't fall to her knees in fidelity. "Your loyalty and your deference."

Zawn started laughing. The princess stared at the elf, offended, while her servant looked concerned.

"You are not in your castle, child. You are in our territory, trespassing to be exact. So you will want to adjust how you talk to the one who makes the decisions in these woods."

Valena's chin lifted a little, almost in defiance. Her servant, Eriselda, who the princess did not know was kin to Zawn, blinked and then lowered herself to her knee. Valena watched aghast, then flashed fuming eyes at Zawn.

"Your servant apparently knows her place," Zawn said, with a smirk. "Now explain your presence in my forest before I consider this an act of war by the Kingdom of Mehdehra."

Suddenly the flush of fury drained from the human's face. Valena swallowed hard, as if shoving down her pride, before answering, "I have been sent by my father."

"Don't you mean stepfather?"

"No, my father." Then the princess produced a rolled-up parchment, the seal of the King broken in half. "He requested my mother give this to me when I was a certain age." She glanced around the forest, apparently feeling the eyes on her. "The details I will only share in private with you, Leader Haley."

Zawn regarded her for several breaths, before making a gesture with her dagger. To Valena's surprise, several other elves exited the shadows and foliage, surrounding them with bows and arrows in hand.

"I will take you somewhere private then," Zawn responded, but the smile that graced her face changed into something malicious. "But we cannot let you know exactly where we go." She made another gesture and both the princess and her servant had bags suddenly secured over their heads. "Fear not, we will guide you."

~   ~   ~

Valena was unsure how long they had walked, but the moment her shoes contacted wood, the bag was removed and she found herself inside a hut. It was simple; two chairs, a table, and a bed, along with a washroom and fireplace. It reeked of the forest, not pleasantly perfumy like her bedchambers. She refrained from pinching her nose, trying to remain diplomatic. The elf queen waved everyone out, including Valena's servant, then gestured for the princess to sit down. They sat across from each other at the table, Valena keeping her back straight and proper while the elf leaned back leisurely.

"You asked for this audience," the elf said, her patience lacking. "Say your piece."

Valena handed over the letter, which Zawn took firmly and opened. As she read, the kith leader tried to avoid rolling her eyes.

"So, he's telling you to start a war?" Zawn asked, drolly. "Instructing you to gather others who hate Crenast to help you? He's rather earnest for a dead man."

"That's my father you're talking about," Valena snapped. "Show some respect."

"Child, I knew your father and I remember him well. Very well. He has earned zero respect from elf-kind."

The silence crackled with anger.

"I will not help you overthrow your uncle. He has kept his end of the deal I drew up after he killed your father. There have been no transgressions against my kind, therefore I cannot transgress against him."

"But it is only a matter of time before he changes his mind."

"Agreed. Eventually he will think himself mighty again. But until then, I will stay on my side of the border."

Valena scoffed. "I see my father was mistaken in his opinion of you."

"When he wrote this, he probably would have been right about me. But this was written, what? Almost twenty years ago? A lot has changed over that time. I have many more responsibilities than even you could imagine, princess." Zawn stared at her a little longer, then sighed. "I can send word to the Gargoyles that you wish to meet with them, but I will warn you now that you will not get a favorable response. Years under your father's cruel thumb have soured their views on humans in general."

"I would appreciate that, Leader Haley."

"And you can rest here until they respond. After that, you will have to decide where to go next. I cannot endanger this kith or my allies by hiding you here. Because, if I read your reaction earlier correctly, you left on unfavorable terms."

"A marriage arrangement against my wishes. Words were said. My absence will no doubt cause a search."

"And they cannot find you here," the elf responded, sternly.

"I understand."

"Good. Rest. I will send your servant in."

With a swift move, the elf was back on her feet, dropping the letter back into Valena's lap and disappearing out the door. It closed behind her with a sharp click, leaving Valena alone in a very different world than she was used to.

~   ~   ~

Not long after the elf queen left her alone, there was a knock at the door, making Valena stand up nervously. Her servant had already come in to check on her, then left to gather some food and drink, but she wouldn't bother knocking. The door didn't open, which meant they waited for consent. She called out permission, then the door creaked as the other pushed it open. It was a young man, a few years younger than her, with dark blonde hair and dark brown eyes and a small satchel in hand.

"You're not an elf," she said, startled.

"I am," he responded, with a wry grin. "I just look more like my dadda."

She furrowed her eyebrows. "That is a crime punishable by death."

"Is it?" he asked, drolly. "Well, I guess that is where we differ. It's acceptable here."

She stared at him in disbelief.

"Your friend said you got hurt," he added.

"She's not my friend," she retorted. "She is my servant."

Rynan quietly seethed at the disgust in her voice, but forced himself to keep cordial. "Apologies, Your Majesty."

She frowned, shoulders dropping. "No, I apologize. It's been an awful day."

"Will you permit me to look at your injury?"

She gestured for him to sit down as she moved to the other chair. As he lowered himself into his seat, she followed and pushed up her sleeve. The gash wasn't deep but ugly enough to warrant some concern. He excused himself and disappeared into the bathroom, soaping up a hand rag and returning with it. He carefully cleaned the scratch, making her hiss.

"I know, I'm sorry. But it's to get the dirt out and help avoid infection."

"You sound like a theurgist."

"That's because I am one," he responded, opening his bag that he set down by the chair and pulling out some salve.

As he slathered her arm, she raised an eyebrow. "Half human, half elf, and a theurgist? You are indeed different."

"I've been told I am unique. I consider it a compliment. There. That should take care of any pain and keep infection away."

"My thanks, theurgist."

"You're welcome, Your Majesty. Good night."

And with that, Rynan gathered his satchel and exited the hut. He passed Eriselda as she returned to her master's side with a plate of food and mug of mead, avoiding any recognition. They had enough time to hug and whisper their greetings while their mother and the princess spoke, but that was all. They would have to catch up later.

~   ~   ~

"Milady is asleep, finally," Eriselda announced as she stomped, tiredly, to the firepit and collapsed on the bench between Rynan and Zawn. Rynan wrapped his arm around her shoulders, making her lean in. She felt comforted by his love and by the protection Zawn exuded. Being trapped at the castle, unable to come home, had torn her apart.

"Good, now we can talk," Zawn responded. "Minee? Can you keep an eye for any movement from the guest hut?"

"Yes, Auntie," Minee responded, stepping away from the fire and guarding their group diligently while keeping her eyes trained on the guest hut.

"Eriselda, why is she really here?" Zawn asked. "It's more than some foolish letter left by Elixin."

"She was to be married off."

Zawn scoffed. "She made mention. Does she really want to start a war because she refused to be sent off to a fat man with several sexually transmitted diseases?"

"Fat is an understatement," Eriselda replied, her face contorting in disgust.

"Saw him for yourself?" the leader inquired, drolly.

"The Kingdom sent a portrait along with the offer to take Valena off her parents' hands."

Zawn glanced back at the hut, eyebrows furrowed. "What does she think will happen if she bests Crenast? Her own father's laws ban her from reigning over Mehdehra."

"I do not know what she hopes for, other than maybe having a choice in husband?" Eriselda shook her head. "All I know is we rushed off in the dark with no real plan. Let alone proper food or camping supplies."

Zawn handed her a piece of bread. "So you haven't eaten at all?"

Eriselda smiled her thanks as she accepted the bread. "What little I grabbed was devoured by the princess halfway here." She frowned and took a bite, her face giving away her concerns.

"What is it?" Rynan asked.

"I've noticed a lot of odd things happening at the castle. The King would disappear for hours on end and would never discuss where he was going and what he was doing. He's the King, why would he? But Valena decided to follow him. We watched him disappear into a hidden entrance. She followed him down but couldn't describe what she saw. So, after everyone went to bed the other night, I snuck in. I heard his incantation while we hid and it was pretty straightforward. The secret doorway led into this weird cave. There were these glowing veins all along the walls. I've never seen anything like it. But I remember the books Chae had me read when I was younger, talking about energy lines."

Taylor glanced over at Zawn. "The King has been trying to harness the power of the energy lines that run under the castle."

"So there are conjurers in the family," Zawn said, quietly.

Taylor grimaced. "You said he had visited the castle while Gwendin was alive. He must have realized what lay underneath and that's why he killed his brother. He could rule the land while gaining power from the natural source of magic. But didn't you do something about the entrance Gwen found?"

"Gwen found an entrance outside of the castle. We had collapsed that one, but neither of us realized you could get to it through a doorway in the castle. Never even thought of a secret passageway."

"So you knew about them?" Eriselda asked.

"I did. We also informed Yunji, so the College is aware too."

"Now what?" Rynan inquired.

"I need to send a message to Yunji. I told the princess she can only stay until the gargoyles turn down her invitation to join her. Then she must leave." Zawn looked over at Eriselda, who had lost color in her face. She reached over and brushed her loose hair out of her face, while tracing fingertips along her daughter's cheek. "Don't worry, we will find a way to keep you with us. If she left the castle on bad terms, then you have to remind her who you owe your debt to. It's not to her, it's to the royal family. And then we will make sure you never go back there again."

"Thank you, Momma," Eriselda whispered, closing her eyes.

"You need to get some sleep," Zawn murmured. "You look exhausted. I'm afraid she'll expect you at her side first thing. But go, sleep in your own bed. We will place guards at her door so she can't wander. Minee? Can you ask Avari to stand first watch?"

"Of course, Auntie."

"Thank you."

"I'll line up the rest of watch," Taylor suggested. "You need your rest as well, Zawnie."

"Agreed. Even though I doubt I will get much sleep knowing who stays a few strides away."

CHAPTER 76

The sun rose, the light creeping along Valena's face and waking her up. She rolled over and glanced around, realizing that her servant had left sometime in the night. When she sat up, the door opened briefly and the brown-haired girl entered.

"Where were you?" Valena demanded.

"Asking when breakfast would be ready," the servant responded.

"Soon I expect."

"Yes, I'm to queue up at the firepit in a few moments."

"Then go, now. I'd prefer it hot off the stove."

"Yes, milady."

Valena slipped out of the bed and entered the washroom. In the privacy of the privy, she used the time to conjure. She removed the stones and herbs from her belt purse. The spell she needed to use took time. She had started the incantation last night when Eriselda thought she had fallen asleep and left, but now she had to focus her intentions. Then a knock on the door. She quickly hid her paraphernalia and exited the washroom.

The door opened once she called out permission. It was the theurgist again, smiling kindly.

"I came to check on your injury."

"It's doing much better, thank you." She watched as he bowed politely before moving to leave. "I've never met a theurgist. My uncle doesn't believe in them. And I guess the College respects that."

"No, there is no respect," Rynan responded, a little strongly. "After his coup cost a theurgist's life, the College blacklisted the Kingdom of Mehdehra."

Valena scoffed. "Crenast omits so much. He acts as if it was his decision to disallow the College's participation."

"He may believe that, but the rest of the world knows the truth."

"Did I make a mistake coming here?" she asked suddenly, startling him. "I am a princess from a Kingdom you must hate. You must think me a monster.

I still call the one person who has been by my side a servant even though she's done so much for me. My uncle has committed acts of aggression against your people without consideration of the consequences until it's too late. And he had one of your colleagues killed."

"Do you support those actions?" Rynan asked.

"No, I don't."

"Then he is the only monster I see in this world."

Valena lowered her eyes.

"But my opinion means little. The only opinion you need to have in your corner is our kith's leader. Whatever you've held back, it will do you no good. You must be honest and upfront with her."

"How did you know I've omitted anything?"

Rynan smiled, wryly. "You're a princess. I think knowing what to say and when to say it is a job requirement."

"Can you ask for Leader Haley to speak with me?"

"I can." And with that, Rynan exited the hut.

Valena, left alone again, smiled. Now she knew what protections the theurgist had marked on him. The Old Tongue glyphs glowed faintly along his wrist. And she knew how to get past them.

~ ~ ~

Zawn looked at little annoyed with Rynan for getting involved, but he did have a point. The princess was holding something back. She needed to find out what it was, and if the princess was willing to divulge it thanks to Rynan's suggestion, Zawn should at least listen. A strong knock on the door and a regal voice answered.

Zawn entered, finding the princess standing in the middle of the room. She gestured for the elf to sit and lowered herself into the other chair. They stared at each other for a few moments before Valena sighed, looking a bit demure.

"Your theurgist is wise beyond his years," she admitted.

"Theurgists generally are," Zawn responded.

"It is more than just the letter from my father, or the forced marriage to the Carmanic prince. My uncle killed to get the throne, married my mother just to use her to keep the throne. He is cruel to her, he is hateful to all that he believes does not serve him. He often speaks of the elf queen who had the audacity to show him as weak, which he had tried to hide. His strength lies in fear and murder, curated by his elite guard."

Zawn didn't respond.

"Crenast will move on you. I know he plots every day and every night on how to take you down. And he knows if the great elf queen falls, everyone will follow like dominoes. So yes, I came here out of a selfish reason, but the enemy of my enemy. Who else could help me stand up against this murderous fiend?"

"Knowing that he plots daily on how to take me down changes nothing. I already know this. How could he not think of ways to destroy me? I know what it meant when I walked in with his men tied like cattle. I'm sorry, princess, but it's not enough to start a war and put my kith in directly in harm's way."

"I see. I am sorry to hear that. I had hoped to head him off at the pass, as it were, but if I am to do so, I guess I will go it alone."

"I hope whatever gods you pray to, princess, give you all the strength you need."

The elf stood up and moved to leave, but Valena gently clasped her wrist. She felt Zawn stiffen and knew she saw that as an act of aggression.

"But know this," Valena responded, keeping her tone even. "If I unseat my uncle and return my Kingdom to its rightful place in the world, it will not be on the backs of those around us. I will work toward peace throughout the region, somehow."

"That is good to hear, Your Majesty."

Valena released her, and without another word, the elf left the princess alone.

~   ~   ~

The theurgist checked on her again that night, after her servant left to gather her dinner. He sat in the chair across from her, but Valena knew she needed to touch the young man. She pushed up her sleeve and showed him her scratch.

"Does this look infected? It got red all of sudden."

"Oh, let me take a look."

"I haven't asked your name, theurgist," she said, as he gently touched her arm so he could turn it toward the firelight.

"Rynan."

"Rynan, what an interesting name."

"Yes, unique, just like me," he teased, glancing over at her with a wry smile. "I think it's red from rubbing. Probably your sleeve. You should consider letting it air by keeping the sleeve pushed up."

"I will do so, then," the princess conceded, reaching out and tracing his face, whispering something. She watched as the glittering manifestation of her spell swirled into his eyes, nostrils, and mouth. How simple it was, three little words and she had him in her sway. "Now, dear theurgist, I would like to know more about you. Without you editing anything out."

He nodded, dreamily.

"What is your name?"

"Rynan, heir of the Haley family, stargazer of the Whispering Hornbeam Kith."

She frowned, not expecting him to have responded with an elven name. Then she cocked her head, curious. "Haley? You are related to the kith leader?"

"Yes. She is my momma."

"And who is your father?"

"Gwendin Graywhim. Theurgist."

"Gwendin? That can't be. He was my mother's brother. She told me he hadn't married, nor ever confessed to any children."

"He died right after I was born."

Valena started calculating. "So did my brother. He died with your father, while you lived on with your mother and I with mine. My goddess was wrong. Here I came looking for leverage and found a cousin." She shook her head, that theory not feeling right. "But you don't look like your mother at all."

"I take after my dadda."

"Yes, well you do remind me so much of my mother. But your chin, your ears… they look like mine. And I take after my father in that regard. Tell me, Rynan, do you have any birthmarks or brands?"

Rynan took a deep breath, suddenly blinking fast. "I'm sorry, what were we talking about?"

"My wound," Valena responded without missing a beat. "You said it wasn't infected."

"I think it's red from rubbing. Probably your sleeve. You should consider letting it air by keeping the sleeve pushed up."

"I will do so, then, thank you, Rynan."

"Have a good night, Your Majesty."

And with that, he was gone. Valena fumed, unsure why her spell wore off so quickly. She had honed her abilities early on, practicing diligently on the castle guard. She hadn't lost control of anyone since the early days, when Captain Marqut had snapped out of it too early and confronted her. A cruel smile crossed her face as she reflected on his anger, slamming her against the wall, demanding her intentions. His fury tasted delicious, but underneath... Well, she didn't need to use a spell on him, he admitted. He loved her enough to do as she wished without any additional prodding. That was the night they sealed the details of their agreement and campaign against Crenast, after a rather lengthy negotiation in her bed of course.

She would have to lure the theurgist back, somehow. He wasn't just a long lost relative, but the son of the kith leader who she needed to manipulate. With him under her control, she could infiltrate the elf queen's resistance. She knew she couldn't keep using her self-inflicted scratch as an excuse, so she would have to conjure him back to her.

~   ~   ~

Left alone again, she wondered why they kept her and her servant separate at night, but she assumed it was for leverage. They must have believed that Valena wouldn't try anything if she found her servant with a dagger to her throat. She scoffed. Little did those elves know that she could care less, but if it gave them a false sense of security, then she let them believe what they wished.

It was for the best really. She spent most of the evening wishing him back.

The next morning, her spell worked. After eating her breakfast and given time to bathe, she paced away time until the knock on the door. They participated in small talk until her incantation worked. In her thrall, the young man sat in the chair trapped in a dream state.

"Tell me, Rynan," she said, not willing to waste time. "Do you have a birthmark or brand of any kind?"

"I do."

"Do you now? Show me."

He stood and dropped his pants. There, on his inner thigh, a mark just like hers.

Just like hers.

Valena blinked, her breath stolen for a moment. "Do you know what it means?" she finally choked out.

"I am a descendant of the Royal Family of Maroe."

"Oh my dear boy," she whispered. "That's a lie."

The theurgist started blinking rapidly and she knew her time was up. She ordered him to put his pants back on, then to sit down.

"Ask me about my brother, about your mark," she suggested, focusing her intention before she lost her hold on him.

When he came to, she started to laugh as if reacting to a joke. He smiled, a little confused, but she played it as if they had been discussing daily things.

"You are very charming, Rynan," she mentioned, folding her hands. "You remind me so much of my father, it's… it's scary."

"You are fortunate that you had time with your father," he admitted, his smile fading.

"Despite his reputation, he was a good father. I miss him dearly."

"Must be difficult to live with the man who caused his death."

Valena scoffed, eyes misting. "You have no idea. But when you are just a princess, and have no say, you deal with it as best as you can. It may have been more bearable had my brother survived the attack."

"What happened to your brother?"

"Which one?"

Rynan furrowed his eyebrows in confusion.

She smiled, sadly. "I had three. The first died of an unknown disease as a toddler. The second was a miscarriage. Mother almost didn't recover from that one. Then Bryant, he uh, he died in the fire that destroyed the private chambers. It was set by Crenast's men, to ensure both my father and brother were dead."

"I'm sorry. That is a lot of loss, not just for you but for your mother."

"It changed her. I haven't recognized her for a long time. I think the hardest part was not being able to mourn Bryant. We were able to bury Father, with Crenast's blessing of course, but we had nothing of my brother to lay to rest. The fire must have destroyed his little body. Sometimes… well, it's fanciful thinking that maybe he survived. That a maid or servant whisked him away to be raised in secret. I know, it sounds so foolish but…" Valena giggled, shaking her head. "I dreamt that he'd arrive at the castle, drop his pants, and show the world who he was, leaving Crenast weaker than your elf queen did."

"Drop his pants?" Rynan asked, incredulous. "That's a crude introduction for anyone."

"At birth, members of the Royal Family of Mehdehra are all marked. Inside the thigh. Easy to hide but difficult to remove. It is the crest of Mehdehra, which is rather distinct."

Rynan looked away, a confused expression on his face as he stared at the fire for a moment.

"What is it?" she asked.

"I uh… I didn't know other Royal Families did that."

"What do you mean?"

"I've a mark too. Inside the thigh. I was told it was because of my father's side of the family."

"Are you related to the Mehdehran family?"

"No, I was told my lineage can be tracked back to the Kingdom of Maroe."

"I do not know which families participate in that tradition, but may I see yours? I could probably tell you if it's related to my family."

He hesitated, then stood and unfastened his pants. Keeping his undershorts on, he let his trousers lower to show the small mark on his thigh.

Valena faked her surprise, letting her well-practiced tears burst out of her eyes. "No, no you can't be!" She jumped to her feet and hugged him tightly, sobbing just enough to be convincing. "Oh Bryant, oh it's really you!"

"No, I'm Rynan. Son of Gwendin and Zawn Haley," he stammered, shaking at her reaction.

"You are my brother. No one else would have that mark. No one."

"How?" he choked out, his brain unable to make any connections.

"I don't know, you'll have to ask your so-called mother." She leaned back, cupping his face. "But be careful. She's lied to you your entire life. Making you believe that you were someone you are not. She could spin any tale to save face. But, here and now, I promise you that I will never lie to you like that, ever, Bryant. Honesty will be the only thing that will allow us to rule fairly and justly."

"You're right, I need to talk to her. I need to find out the truth. I… excuse me."

"Of course, this is such a shock to you as it is to me." Then Valena whispered another spell, just a small one before adding, "It's time to confront your dear mother with all of your questions."

He blinked and shook his head, regaining his senses, before he nodded thanks, then exited the hut.

~   ~   ~

Zawn sat at the firepit, keeping watch for Rynan. He was spending too much time with the princess, making her hackles rise. As he exited the guest hut this time, she could tell something was wrong. She waited as he slowly approached her, asking for a private conversation. She agreed, walking him to her personal hut.

She stood by the foot of her bed, waiting for him to speak first.

"I've been spending a lot of time with Valena."

Zawn raised her eyebrow. "I've noticed."

"She keeps telling me that I remind her a lot of her father. Even my smile. I have to ask…" and he stumbled over the words.

"Ask what?"

"Gwendin wasn't my father, was he?"

Zawn felt her throat constrict and her knees buckled, causing her to sit hard on the bed. She tried to wrap her mind around the idea that she had to finally tell him the truth. Who he was and who he wasn't. She had practiced a speech when he was still young but as the years flew by, the speech faded as it became, as she had selfishly thought, unnecessary. It hit her harder than she expected, considering how she knew the truth this whole time. Maybe it was having to tell him…?

"Momma?"

"I uh, never thought this day would come," she admitted, voice soft.

He furrowed his eyebrows, anger manifesting in his usually kind brown eyes. "So Gwendin wasn't my father."

"No, he is not. Not your natural father anyway."

"Who is my father?"

She didn't know how to soften the blow of her words and they tumbled out. "King Elixin. Which means Valena is your sister."

"You had an affair with the King? How? The way you talked about him…"

"No, no, I did not have an affair with that… man," she retorted, feeling disgusted by his accusation. "Gwendin was the only human I was ever with, thank you. No, I'm not…" and she tried to say the words. An admission that she knew would haunt her forever.

"You're not…?" he began, then he started shaking his head. "No, you said I was your son."

"I rescued you when Crenast was ripping the castle apart, trying to kill off all the male heirs to Elixin. You were an infant, not long on this earth, when he killed your father. Gwendin begged me with his dying breath to protect you, to save you. I made up the story that you were ours to keep you alive."

"For what?"

"To live," she replied, jumping to her feet and cupping his face. "They were going to kill you in your crib, without a second thought. But your mother had a hard time having you and… and Gwendin knew you deserved to have a life without such terror. He died trying to give you that life. And I honored his wishes."

"Are you even related to me?" he demanded, face contorted in betrayal.

Zawn felt the tears threaten. "No. But Gwendin, my love and my mate, he, uh, I found out that his sister is your real mother. He was your uncle."

"So, I am not elven at all. Nothing in me?"

"Your spirit is."

He ripped himself from her hands, seething. "That's not enough."

"It's been enough your entire life," Zawn snapped back.

"Well it's not anymore."

Chilling silence smacked against the walls.

"I need…" Rynan stammered, "I need to be alone."

With that he left, slamming the door so hard it swung back open.

~   ~   ~

His head felt like it was on fire. The anger, the confusion, it all ate away at him. He found himself storming into the forest, pausing at the edge of the kith, then walking back to the guest hut. The princess ushered him in kindly and he could see that she restrained herself from hugging him again. He sat down, breathing hard, fury shaking his very bones.

Valena walked behind Rynan, placing a cool hand on his shoulder. She closed her eyes and whispered an incantation before strolling back in front of him. His unstable emotions opened him up perfectly. When she was sure it took, she leered and leaned in closely.

"You know who you are now, Bryant. And you know that you do not belong here. You know what you must do. Fear not, cutting ties with her will bring about your destiny. Remember, she has lied to you all of your life. She does not deserve any kindness or empathy. Now go."

Without responding to her, Rynan stood and exited the hut.

~   ~   ~

He didn't bother knocking. The door slammed open, banging against the wall and straining the old hinges. His entrance made Zawn jump to her feet, instinct pulling her khukuri, almost as if to ward off a physical attack.

"I am human, a man!" Rynan shouted. "I will walk side by side with my sister and take back our birthright. Then we will reevaluate our treaty with the elves."

Zawn's eyes narrowed. "Do what you think is right for you and your 'sister.' But remember, I will do what's right for my people. And like your father and your uncle before you, I will teach you any lessons necessary."

"Fear not, Leader Haley. I will never set foot in this kith again and neither will our soldiers."

"Hm, those are only words, dear Prince."

"We will not respect your kith either. We will turn our backs on you in your hour of need."

"It is man who always begs for help, not us elves. So be very careful who you ask for help in your time of need."

"Fuck you."

Just then, Averell walked up to the hut as Rynan's voice rang out.

"You don't talk to your mother like that," Averell chastised.

"She's not my mother." Rynan watched the confusion wash over Averell's face. "Oh, so, she lied to you too?"

Zawn clenched her fists. "Get. Out."

The young man scoffed then vacated.

Averell turned toward Zawn, baffled. "What did he mean?"

"You should go home, Averell."

"Not until you explain why Rynan would say that."

Anger overrode diplomacy and she snarled, unable to stop the words that came out next. "Because I'm not."

"What are you talking about?"

"When Crenast invaded to overthrow Elixin," she explained, unable to control herself. "I took the baby before they could kill him."

"You stole a baby?"

Those words burned Zawn. "Get out."

Without another word, Averell stormed out, leaving her door wide open. Taylor and Chaelene entered, confused and concerned. But Zawn lashed out at them as well.

"Get out, both of you. Now."

Shocked, they backed out and watched as the door slammed in their faces.

"You grab Averell," Chaelene ordered, her anger coloring her face. "I want to thrash Rynan myself."

Taylor nodded, sharply. "Agreed."

~   ~   ~

Chaelene shouted his name, causing him to stop on the porch of his hut. He turned on her, face twisted with anger. "I have nothing to say to you, Chae," snapped Rynan.

"I know you don't. It's your mother you should be apologizing to."

"Fuck that. She lied to me, my entire life."

Chae's eyes narrowed, her anger finally boiling to the surface. "She lied to you to save your life. She lied to the world too. She put her life on the line for yours."

"I didn't ask her to."

"No, the man she loved did. Your uncle. And so did your father."

"Two dead men who can't back her claims," he snapped back.

She looked at him with disgust. "You really think she took you from the castle out of spite?"

"We know how much she hated Elixin. How much she hates Crenast. Why wouldn't she?"

"Then you are not just a fool and nitwit, but a fitting example of the Royal Family of Mehdehra."

For the first time, Rynan wanted to hit someone. However, the knowledge that Chae would thrash him within an inch of his life cooled him. Shaking, he knew in that moment he had to leave. He didn't belong here, he needed to go where he would fit in. Without responding, he spun on his heel and stormed into his hut.

"Get your stuff, we're leaving," Rynan ordered, grabbing his satchel and packing.

Eriselda stood on the other side of the bed and watched, face blank but eyes glowing with rage. He knew she had heard everything, even his argument with the woman who wasn't his mother. She had to be angry, too. But Eriselda didn't move and she didn't speak.

"I said start packing. We're leaving."

"No."

Rynan looked up in surprise. "What do you mean no? We're leaving. We're going home. And we're going to take back my throne."

"That horrible place is not my home. This is my home, my family. I am not leaving this kith. Not for you and some misguided hope and sure as hell not that monster of a princess. If you want to be King then you do that on your own."

"I have every right to take back what was taken from me. Both by Crenast and mm-Zawn. And you are to join me, as my mate."

"If you are so blind that you cannot understand what Momma did, then I cannot support you. I will not help you. And I cannot see myself…" and she swallowed hard, "staying your mate."

"Seldy -"

"If this is what you want, then go. I don't want that. I know you can't see that Valena is manipulating you as a means to an end that will benefit her. But you should be able to see how I feel. Can you not consider my feelings as well as yours?" When he didn't respond, she shook her in disgust. "Then you can go fuck yourself." And she marched out of the hut.

~   ~   ~

She had hoped things would lead to blows. Violence always tasted sweet. She had enjoyed setting the castle guards against each other often. However, the division was sufficient. Valena grinned maliciously, until a knock on the door.

By the time she swung the door open, she morphed into a concerned sister. "Bryant? What's going on?" she asked, frowning.

"It's time to regain our birth right."

She curated her smile into a hopeful expression. "I'm ready when you are."

"Grab your stuff and let's go."

~   ~   ~

The kith watched him leave. Him, alone, with that princess. That human. Everyone, but Zawn. She was oddly absent.

Even Eriselda watched, but didn't make a move to join him. He glanced over his shoulder for one last look, seeing the faces of his kithlin frowning or glistening with tear streaks. The fury that rode him started to shake loose. His heart shattered at that moment, realizing that he would never see them again. He would be King or he would be dead. He turned his attention back to the road, trying to hold his head up while he felt his spirit die with each step.

~   ~   ~

Zawn stared into the fireplace, lost in her pain and her grief. She knew opinion would not take kindly to her actions but she also knew it didn't matter. Sacrifices were made for the greater good, even if those who made the sacrifices would be eventually deemed the villains.

Footfalls broke the spell of the flames and she glanced up at the door. Averell stood there, shoulders slumped and face distorted by his conflicting emotions.

"I wanted to apologize…" he began.

"Get out."

He held out his hands, helplessly. "I didn't mean..."

"Oh, but you did. I am a baby thief, never mind the motives." She looked at him, her eyes harsh but expression blank. "You should go home, Averell. There is nothing here for you now."

"Nothing here?" he whispered.

As they stared at each other, he could see her turning cold. He could see her light, the one he loved and let guide him, dimming with each breath.

Then she returned her eyes to the fire. "I'll reach out to you when I'm ready."

"No, you won't."

Zawn scoffed in annoyance. "You're right, I won't." Heartbreaking silence settled heavy in the hut. "Leave, Averell. Please, don't make my final act today be your banishment."

Averell stood there for a few moments, then resigned himself to her decision. He nodded, slowly, then gathered his stuff and left her hut.

Taylor stepped inside, having heard the exchange while waiting on the porch. He watched as Zawn turned away from the fire and moved to pull out her duffel, lifting it onto the bed and she started to fill it with her own items.

"Where are you going?"

"My dishonorable actions have come to light," she replied, not even bothering with folding any of the clothes. "It's best I leave before our kithlin decide to banish me. Let this be my decision. At least give me that."

His response sounded too matter of fact. "They will not banish you."

"Won't they? I brought a human child into our kith and lied that he was mine. They have dealt with me long enough anyway. They know you are to take my place. They will appreciate someone with an even head over my nitwit ways."

"You can't step down and you can't leave, Zawnie. Now, you are allowed to feel sorry for yourself. But your work isn't done."

Zawn stared at her friend, shocked.

"Whatever happens at that castle will have consequences for not just our kith but for all of our kind and our allies. Whoever sits on that throne will decide that it is again time to handle those dirty elves. And when they're done with us, they will move onto our friends, our allies. You're the only one that has knocked that lot on their backs more than once. You may think you're done as leader but you are mistaken. I cannot protect our people like you have for all of these years. Even the years before you were a leader, back when you saved so many lives during the Purge. Unpack your shit and start figuring out how you're going to protect us."

With that, Taylor stomped out and slammed the door behind him.

~   ~   ~

The next morning, Zawn sat at her small table, nibbling on some apple bread and bacon. She had gotten little sleep. After Taylor left her, she stared at her duffel and resigned herself to his orders. Throwing her clothing back into their baskets and tossing the duffel under her bed, she stood helplessly in her hut. Deflated, she rested her forehead against the binding of her book for several moments before pulling it out. She set it on the bed and she turned each page reverently. She touched the tulips, both sets, softly and lovingly, then the piece of cloak she had cut off before it was burned at Gwen's funeral. Her hands lingered a little while on the earliest letters Rynan had sent from the College and the letter Averell had sent her after their first night together. She had lost so much and she didn't know if it was worth trying to hang on to whatever was left.

The whole night she sat, alone, with the ghosts of her past consoling and haunting her simultaneously.

She sighed, sipping her coffee, as she let it sink in. Rynan was gone, so was Averell. All she had left was her kith. Taylor was right, a new storm was stirring as Elixin's children rushed to win their birthright back. If they won, they would soon turn their anger back on her. If Crenast succeeded in keeping his throne, he would turn his attention to the one who had taken away his original opportunity of killing Elixin's male heir.

Her work was far from done. But maybe, once she secured her kith's safety and sovereignty, she could step down. Say it was time to retire. Taylor would be in a secure position and have no worries from the humans. Her kith would continue to strengthen themselves against any enemies. She could leave with a lightened heart.

A careful knock on her door drew her out of her thoughts. She glanced up at the door and saw him peek in cautiously. She waved him in, trying to hide her annoyance that he didn't follow her orders. He entered but stayed near the door as if he expected the need to escape quickly. He stared at her, his face giving away his anger and heartbreak.

"I told you to leave," she pointed out, lowering her eyes back to her food.

"You did," Averell answered. "But you didn't say how far to go."

"I recall clearly that I said to go home."

"You forget, this is my home just as much as my kith."

She glared at him, irritated by his maneuvering around her orders.

"Where did you stay?" she inquired.

"Guest hut. Taylor told me to stay there and stay out of sight until morning."

She tried to hide the rolling of her eyes. "And he says he's not ready to be leader."

"I meant it, Zawnie. I wanted to apologize."

"Your immediate reaction has always been the most honest."

"And usually, the least thought through. Tell me what happened."

"What is there to say?" she demanded, face burning with disappointment and anger. "I stole a baby. No explanation can change that."

Her mate shook his head and leaned back against the doorframe. "You may call yourself a nitwit, but if there's anything I've learned about you over all of these years, you don't do anything without a reason. Even if it's an emotional response to a situation. There's always a reason. I know you well enough to know that about you."

She stared into her mug, watching the remaining liquid swirl due to her movements. She heard Gwen's voice, yelling out to her, waking her in the middle of the night, begging for help. "Gwen called to me. Woke me out of a dead sleep and all I knew was I had to help him. I ran as fast as I could to the castle, but by the time I found him…" Gwendin's bloody face flashed before her eyes, making her stomach twist. "He was mortally wounded. The fool had tried to protect the prince. He told me to find the baby. And I did, in his crib, with Elixin bleeding out nearby. The King even begged me to save Bryant. They both knew that Crenast was determined to kill any male children of Elixin's, because then there would be no challenges for the throne. But I didn't take the baby for that reason or for Elixin. I did it for Gwen. He had made that request with his dying breath."

"You saved the baby's life."

"Because Gwen asked me to."

"And you raised him as your own."

"What else could I do? I had my mate's nephew in my care. Not just his nephew, but the prince of an enemy kingdom. I couldn't hand him off to someone else, I couldn't guarantee his safety that way." She straightened her back, resting her folded hands on the table. "So I raised him as my own. Despite the anger and resentment of my kithlin, despite the dangers of raising a human among elves. Now you know the truth. I know it gives you little comfort. It gives me none."

"How many here knew?"

"Only Taylor and Chae. No one else was told, to ensure the safety of all." She sighed, rubbing her face with one hand. "Please, go home. I have to reckon with my kith and the consequences of my actions."

"I'd rather stay," he responded. "If you are driven from your kith, I will walk you to my own."

"No." She finally raised her eyes to meet his. "If I am banished, if I am challenged and I lose but live, I will leave these woods. I will walk away from all elf-kind. It is what is for the best anyway."

"And what of us?"

"I don't know."

Averell stood there, words failing him.

"You should go home, though," she continued. "Prepare your kith for the worst. And we need to warn our allies as well."

"I can send messengers north, if you can send them south."

"Agreed. Word will spread faster that way. Thank you, Leader Dylan."

She watched him stiffen. She had never called him by his family name. Never.

"I'll send word once my messengers have been dispatched, Leader Haley," he responded, stepping out of her hut and into the morning mist.

~   ~   ~

Minee approached the hut, peeking in the window first. She saw Eriselda sitting at the foot of her bed, staring at the quiet fireplace. She hadn't even changed her clothing and her face was red from crying. Taking a deep breath, she knocked on the door but didn't get an answer. She popped it open, just enough for Eriselda to see her. Eriselda wiped her face with one hand to hide her tears. Her friend entered, closing the door behind her before leaning against it. They had both watched as Rynan walked toward an unknown future. One without either of them. Now they were left without guidance.

"He is a nitwit," Minee stated, folding her arms.

"I told him I didn't want to be his mate anymore." Eriselda tried to choke back a sob, looking down at her hand. Laying in her palm was the bracelet Rynan had made her. "I couldn't go with him. I refused to go with him."

"But you know he's gonna get himself killed."

Silence, punctuated by Eriselda's sniffling, settled over them.

Then Minee scoffed. "I'll go get my weapons."

~   ~   ~

Later that morning, after breakfast, Zawn exited her hut and made her way to the kith square. She knew they would speak of her mistakes while they ate and she didn't want to complicate that by being present. However, as she walked to the firepit, the square was empty. That didn't make any sense to her. They should have stayed, to give her their decision. She knew they had made one.

But no one remained.

Taylor approached her, face stoic. "They refuse to congregate."

"What are you talking about? They were all told to meet here after breakfast so they can render my punishment."

"It is very simple, you nitwit. If they do not meet, then you cannot make them punish you."

"Then what am I supposed to do?" she demanded, exasperated.

"Like I said last night, protect them. Protect all of us. Do your job."

As if the thought just came to her, Zawn turned to face Taylor. The annoyance on her face didn't need any translation. "You know you're going against a leader's orders just as much as they are?"

His eyebrows raised up. "How? I'm here, meeting with you."

"I'm sure you spent the morning conveying your expectations from our kithlin." He didn't respond, even while fighting back a smirk. "I'll consider your punishment later." She spun on her heel and strode to her work hut, where she started to plan.

~   ~   ~

She tried anyway. She sat at her desk, with her maps, her paper and her pen, but she couldn't seem to grasp a decent train of thought. She couldn't focus. Her brain kept going over her fight with Averell, with Rynan, and with Taylor. Gwen's bloody face even haunted her, his last breath still rattling in her ears. She needed to stop overthinking the past, it was too late to fix. But she couldn't.

She retired that night without a plan. Without even a note for a foundation for a plan. She couldn't turn off her brain. She couldn't push out the painful expression on Averell's face when she told him there was nothing left for him. Tears threatened but didn't fall. Then she reflected on Rynan's face when he realized that she wasn't his natural mother. Nausea surged but nothing happened. She readied for bed and climbed in, but she tossed and turned all night.

With her sleep affected, it made it difficult to function the next morning. She tried again to work on her plan but nothing seemed to make sense.

"Where is she?" a voice echoed throughout the kith.

Startled, Zawn jumped to her feet and ran out of her hut.

In the center of their kith stood Yunji. When he saw Zawn, he looked worried, almost panicked.

"Who put chains on you?" Yunji demanded.

"Chains?" she asked. "What chains?"

He bridged the distance between them with so few strides and grabbed Zawn by the shoulders so quickly that she didn't have time to step back. He looked her over, muttering what sounded like incantations, then he released her and grabbed something from his satchel. Before she could react, he smashed a sugar ball over her head. The liquid ingredients burst over her head, hair, shoulders… drenching her completely. As the contents drooled down her body, she felt a violent jolt as if hit by lightning. Then a bright light emanated from her chest, arms, and legs, until it burst free and illuminated the entire kith. And as if freed from the restraints, her legs gave way and she collapsed, shivering violently.

But she didn't hit the ground. Strong arms had caught her and were wrapped around her like a blanket. A heartbeat against her cheek soothed away the shakes. When she could finally open her eyes, she found Yunji holding her and staring down at her in concern.

"I am sorry, milady," Yunji said, not letting her go. "I couldn't take the chance that the conjurer would stop me."

"Conjurer?" she mouthed, her voice gone.

"Did they stay for a while?"

Even through the fog in her mind, she finally understood and nodded numbly.

"Where did they stay?"

"Guest hut," she croaked, her voice shredded by whatever he released.

He looked up at someone who approached. "Hold her, Taylor. She mustn't be alone."

Next thing she knew, Taylor was holding her against his chest as Yunji disappeared into the guest hut. Another round of incantations and a flash of light blasted out of the windows and doors. The curtains furled as if swept up by a tornado and the doors slammed shut and swung open on their own accord. Then Yunji exited, suddenly looking exhausted, and he slowly made his way back to Zawn. He collapsed onto his knees next to her and Taylor, breathing heavily.

"What don't we know?" Taylor asked, keeping Zawn safe against him.

"I usually can sense your kith, and Rynan, through the energy lines. It's a gift I have. One day, I lost touch with all of you. I feared the worst. But when I saw Zawn, I knew there had been a conjurer in your company. They bound you, my dear. Binding you helped them cause chaos to reign over the kith. Tell me, have you all been arguing? Saying hateful things?"

Taylor sighed. "We have been just short of physical violence."

"Who was it?"

"Princess Valena," Zawn answered, her voice sounding stronger.

What color Yunji had in his face drained immediately. "So it's not just

Crenast?"

"Appears so."

"Can you stand?"

Zawn took a moment and a deep breath, before nodding. Taylor let her go but held onto one hand while Yunji took her other hand once he returned to his feet, and they helped her up. She wavered on her feet but adjusted her stance to save herself.

"What did you hit me with?" she asked, watching as the liquid turned into crystals then to dust. The fine grains dislodged and blew away in the soft breeze.

"A few choice herbs. Including a few you've harvested for us."

"Ah, that's why they were so important? They challenge the power of conjurers?"

"They challenge the power of evil."

"We should have you both sit," Taylor suggested. "Neither of you look steady yet."

"Come, let's sit by the firepit. We will fill you in."

"Good." Yunji glanced around. "Where's Rynan?"

CHAPTER 77

It took a few days for her allies to coordinate their return. They hid in the forest, protected by the tent provided by her allies. Valena regaled Rynan with tales of greater days under her father, all the while keeping him in her magical thrall.

Valena and Rynan used the dark of night to sneak into the castle. Valena's knowledge of every nook and cranny kept them out of sight. They had assumed more guards would have been placed on shift because of Valena's disappearing act, but there was a chance Crenast hadn't even noticed. Or maybe even Kemberly had soothed his concerns because she knew her daughter wouldn't survive in the forest around them.

They ran toward the lower level, where the ground sloped down drastically. They slid down the hill, landing near the entryway the kitchen drudge used to move trash out. They snuck through an old doorway, where the wooden door only half-hung on its hinges, which meant they didn't have to touch it and make noise. As they entered an abandoned back hallway, they were intercepted by the Captain of the Guard and several well-armed men.

Valena halted their advancement, staring down the men. "Good evening, Captain Marqut."

"Your Highness," he responded, tone even. Then a smile cracked his stoic visage. "They are in the throne room, lightly guarded by friends of ours. We will make sure you are not interrupted. Anyone who tries to rush to their sides will be killed without question."

"Thank you, Captain. We will make short work of them so you can cut down those in the ranks that will not bow to me."

The captain and the men around him all bowed to Valena, before turning away and jogging down the hall.

Valena turned to Rynan. "Come, this way. We'll enter from the back."

They tiptoed up the servant stairs which led to a hallway that ran behind the throne room. They could hear voices, a man and a woman.

Crenast and Kemberly.

Rynan couldn't make out what they were saying, but it sounded like a disagreement. Then he heard something about marriage and knew instantly that they were discussing Valena. He glanced over at her and in the dark, he could see her eyes narrow in anger. Her eyes landed on his after a few breaths.

"Are you ready, my brother?" she asked.

"Let's end this tyrant's reign," he responded, making her smile.

They burst through the doors with a grandeur that even impressed Rynan. They strode towards the dais, watching the jaws drop open on both Crenast and Kemberly. Rynan knew Valena reveled in the surprise, but he kept his eyes on the guards lining the walls. The Captain had said they were friendly, but his warrior training taught him to always be alert especially because someone could make a foolish decision at the last possible moment.

"Good evening, Uncle," Valena said, her voice echoing throughout the throne room.

"What are you doing here?" Crenast demanded. "You should be packing. And who is this ruffian?"

"My name is Prince Bryant, son of King Elixin and Queen Kemberly," Rynan responded, feeling the temperature drop at that announcement. "And I am the rightful heir to the Mehdehran throne."

Kemberly's knees buckled and she collapsed onto her throne. "Bryant?"

"That's right," Valena responded. "You failed to end the male line of Elixin. He has been hidden neath all of these years." She barked in laughter. "An infant outsmarted you, you bastard. And now, together, we take back our inheritance as the children of King Elixin."

Crenast scoffed. "You think you can overthrow me, you little bitch? I am more powerful than just some monarch on a throne." Crenast held his hands out to his sides, reciting an incantation that sounded familiar to Rynan. It was what Yunji called a "come hither" spell, one that called the forces of whatever power around them to the conjurer. His hands began to glow, first an ebb than a burst. Then he raised one toward each child.

In response, Rynan raised his hands, whispering words in another language, manifesting a silver and purple shield to block Crenast's bolt of energy. Valena ducked away from the blast aimed her way.

Rattled, Rynan dropped his hands and took a deep breath. He had done the shield spell before, several times at the college, but here it felt… different. Shuddering, he felt a power surge striking through his feet. He never knew what tapping into a convergence felt like, but as it occurred, it scared him.

However, by the look in Crenast's eyes, the murderous King and uncle reveled in it.

Crenast began another chant, drawing in the magic faster than Rynan anticipated, and Rynan couldn't create another shield fast enough. Crenast hit him twice as hard, throwing the young man several horse lengths away. He landed loudly on the ground, his head knocking against one of the cobblestones. He blinked. The firelight pulsed and glittered, then flickered. The blow seemed to crack the haze Rynan felt he had been looking through these last few days.

"You impudent vagrant," Crenast snarled, striding over. "Time to disintegrate you from this very existence!"

Suddenly, Crenast was surrounded by silver lightning bolts, electrocuting him repeatedly. Rynan looked over toward the source and saw Valena, encircled in a bright silver light, her hands sending the bolts directly at their uncle. The light drew through her feet, like Rynan had felt when he protected himself, and knew immediately that she had harnessed the energy lines.

"No, Crenast, it is you," Valena snapped back, "who will be removed from this existence!"

She cupped her hands as if they held something and kept them together. Then with a light filled flourish she ripped them from each other. The gesture split Crenast in two. His body thumped dully onto the dais, while his head bounced down the steps. All light disappeared from the air except for the candelabras. Valena was left panting, Rynan seeing her legs shaking from exhaustion. She stumbled to the nearest chair, leaning on it but not falling into the seat. She glanced over at him, laughing even as she tried to catch her breath.

"We won," she crowed. "The monster is dead!"

Rynan rolled onto his knees and climbed to his feet, his ears still ringing from the magic and the knock to the head. Once he straightened, he looked over at the other woman, sitting speechless on the throne. She had been glancing around, trying to figure out what had just happened, until her eyes landed on Rynan. Quivering, she rose to feet. Reaching out with her hands, she walked carefully to the young man in front of her.

After closing the distance between them, Kemberly cupped Rynan's face, tears rimming her eyes. "Bryant? Is it really you?"

Rynan stared into the eyes of his mother, at least who he knew as his natural mother, and saw the family resemblance. He had her eyes, her nose. Which meant that she and Gwendin shared those features because he had been told for so long how much he had looked like him. But he had noticed that his chin looked like Crenast's, as did his hair line, which only confirmed to him that Elixin had been his natural father.

Valena responded, almost dismissively. "It is." She straightened and stretched, reaching up as if she could reach the ceiling. She wiggled her fingers, smiling as she started taking stock of her next steps.

"How?" Kemberly demanded, in disbelief.

"My dda…" Rynan stuttered, then taking a deep breath so he could speak clearly. "Gwendin made sure I was saved before Crenast could kill me."

"He sent his elf whore to grab him away from you," Valena replied, walking up the steps to stand on the second dais that held up the King's lone throne.

The haze seemed to finally lift, with each throb in his skull. "Watch what you call her," Rynan snapped at Valena, feeling suddenly protective of Zawn. "She was his mate."

"Gwendin found love?" Kemberly whispered to herself, surprised.

"She saved my life," he continued, not hearing Kemberly. "She protected me so I could come back and change the course for Mehdehra. We owe her and her kith our thanks not insults."

Valena didn't react, but she glanced around the throne room proudly. "We are where we belong. Finally."

"The rightful rulers," Kemberly announced, coming out of her thoughts. "Your father would be so proud. Both his son and daughter taking back what is legally theirs."

Valena started ticking off things to do. "We must work through the ranks and make sure there are no Crenast loyalists, then we will use our might to quash those who think they can skirt our rule. The elves, the gargoyles, all of them will kneel or die."

Rynan frowned. "Sister, that is unnecessary."

"Is it?" she demanded, whipping around to glower down at him. "I heard you argue with your kidnapper. You know what she is, what she has done. What she is willing to do. She cannot be allowed to commit anymore crimes. We will subjugate the elves so they are law-abiding." Valena sniffed, disgusted. "It is obvious she will never kneel to our throne. I cannot have disloyal subjects in our borders."

"Our border ends where theirs begins," Rynan corrected her. "They are not our subjects."

That made his sister's eyes narrow. "Is that so? Then we will take their land and make them our subjects. We will have unified lands as far as the eye can see and we will do so by whatever means are necessary."

"You sound like Crenast," he warned.

"Do I? Hm, looks like my spell over you finally broke."

Rynan seethed. So he was right, there had been something over him that was dislodged the moment his head hit the ground.

"No matter," Valena continued, stepping down from the daises to stand in front of her brother. "I will do what is necessary to strengthen Mehdehra. I will succeed where Crenast had failed time and time again. This is a new day in Mehdehra and our Kingdom will continue to grow through victories."

"I also know what you said to the kith leader," Rynan retorted. "You promised peace on the land finally, but all you want is war and bloodshed? This is not why I returned to this place. This is not why I helped you take our throne back. I told her we would never step into their territory again."

"Promises that were not yours to make. And I knew you would always favor the kidnapper who warped your mind all these years. Guards, take our brother to a bedchamber and lock him in there. Maybe a good rest will bring him back to his senses."

Rynan knew he couldn't fight his way out, not with so many trained guards. He let himself be taken into custody and dragged out of the room.

Kemberly sighed. "We will set him right. It will take some doing but…" She turned to see her daughter staring at the thrones. "He will rule as you deem appropriate, Valena."

"Like Crenast?"

"What are you talking about?"

"Did you conspire to kill my father?" Valena demanded, the anger strangling her voice.

"What? Of course not. Crenast killed your father, forced me to marry and lay with him." Kemberly crossed the dais and grabbed her daughter by shoulders, making her turn around. Valena's anger vibrated off of her, shocking the Queen. "How could you think I'd willingly participate in such horror?"

"So you didn't help Crenast overthrow Father?"

"Of course not," Kemberly replied, pulling her daughter into a tight hug. "I loved your father. We were a love match in the truest of terms."

Valena didn't respond, even as the squish of her dagger penetrating flesh echoed throughout the empty chamber. Kemberly gasped, then gagged, stepping away from her daughter. The blade stuck out of her abdomen, blood seeping from the edges of the wound.

Valena scoffed. "Love match, you say? Was it love when he beat you every month you weren't pregnant? Or when he blamed you for the miscarriages and Vaeden's death? You did not love him and he did not love you. And I know you planned it all with Crenast, Mother, I heard you talking about it. I am not upset that you killed Father, really, but the fact that you faked everything with Crenast... I can't forgive that. Now you can join him and Father on the other side. I pray they are your judges, determining the punishment for your corrupt soul."

Without another word or sound, Kemberly crumpled into a lump of flesh and material. Just as she admired her work, she heard footfalls. The captain of the guard and his trusted lieutenants approached the dais.

"Who do you serve?" she demanded.

"Valena, Queen of Mehdehra," they responded, proudly and they all kneeled to their new queen.

After they returned to their feet, Valena waved for the guards to remove the bodies. As they scurried away, she turned and raised her eyes up to the crest flag of Garadni. She snapped her fingers and the flag caught fire, shedding embers and singed pieces down onto the room below. Silence followed and she turned to find herself standing on the top dais. Finally. Once she was left alone in the throne room of her ancestors, she slipped comfortably onto the King's seat and surveyed her Kingdom.

Not the King's seat. Not anymore.

Hers.

It was all hers.

~   ~   ~

The door slammed and the locks engaged loudly. The men didn't bother bringing light to the room. It was dark, cold, empty. The fireplace lay dead, the bed made with sheets only, pillows and comforter missing, and a window that appeared painted closed.

Rynan huffed, angry at his sister, at himself, and at the fact that he couldn't fathom a way out. The castle wasn't a place he was familiar with after all. He'd had to count on Valena to lead him around. How he wished Eriselda was there, but she had smartly refused to join him on this fool's errand. He regretted not listening to her.

He hated how he left things with his Momma… his… Leader Haley…? No, he knew she was still his Momma, she was the woman who raised him, taught him, loved him. How easily he betrayed her devotion by calling her sacrifices monstrous. The two men that he would never meet, his natural father and his uncle who he had believed was his father, both begged her to save Rynan. She fulfilled that request and then he had broken her heart by hating her for it. He frowned, knowing that whatever spell Valena cast probably made him act that way towards her. However, his words, no matter the instigation, damaged his relationships with not just his mother but his mate, cousins, and kithlin.

With one last idea, he ran his hand up the flue of the fireplace, hoping for an opening. It had been bricked up inside… but on the ledge of the lowest bricks he felt something. A pile of something crinkly. He grabbed the stack and pulled out several opened envelopes. And inside, letters. He sat carefully on the edge of the bed, laying them gently in his lap. They were old, weathered, but the writing still legible. As he read what turned out to be love letters, a realization ran his blood cold. The dates, they were less than a year before his birth, and they were written by Crenast.

To Kemberly.

Was Elixin even his father after all? Or was it the man that had tried to kill him?

He flopped onto the large bed, staring up into the stony ceiling. He found himself longing for the stars. If he could see the stars, he could find his way. Then he exhaled hard, realizing he was truly lost in the world of men.

Lost in his thoughts, he didn't hear the scraping. But he heard the rustling that followed, making him sit up and glance around. In the corner, next to the fireplace, the shadows of a few bricks moved. He realized suddenly that someone was pushing through the wall. He jumped to his feet, ready to fight hand-to-hand, if necessary, since all of his weapons had been confiscated. The secret door finally opened up wide enough to let someone in.

Eriselda peeked out from behind the secret door, looking around to make sure he was alone. He hesitated approaching her, unsure of her loyalties. After all, she had told him she wanted nothing to do with his campaign. Or him after their argument. And she wasn't just his mate but his sister's servant. She could be here because she was following orders, which would be easier than her heart. But as she stepped out further, he saw her carrying his haladie and khukuri.

"Seldy, what are you doing here?"

She waved him over with her free hand. "Come, this way. We can get outside the inner courtyard and follow the path to the forest."

"Why are you helping me?" he demanded, his hurt coloring his voice. "You told me to go fuck myself."

"Yes, I did, but I followed you anyways because I love you, you nitwit. I watched you fight. And I heard everything."

"But…"

"And I respect our Momma more than your sister, more than you even. Come. I don't know how much time we have."

~ ~ ~

They were able to get past the inner courtyard before their secret hallway ran out. They had to hide behind some hay for the horses when the guards made their rounds along the inner courtyard wall. They could see the gate from where they squatted down, but the guards were on heavy rotation. They counted between each pair, realizing they couldn't get across the yard without being seen by the approaching pair.

"What now?" she asked. "I didn't think this far."

"We could fight our way out."

"You'd be on your own, I am no warrior."

He laid his hand on her shoulder, making her look over at him. "You learned how to fight from the best warrior in all the kingdoms. We can take two guards."

"Yes, but how much noise would we make and how much attention would that bring?"

He grimaced. "You have a point." Then he noticed the carriage, still tied to the horses, as if waiting for someone. Had Crenast planned a journey? Or was it to carry Valena off to her new husband? "How about a distraction? Think you can land a rock on a hindquarter?"

"From here?" Eriselda glanced around the ground, then found a good-sized rock. "I can try."

"Do your best."

She took a few deep breaths, briefly closed her eyes, then flung the rock across the yard. It struck squarely on one horse's buttocks. The horse screeched and bucked, startling its partner, and both horses bolted. The carriage lurched and rattled behind the panicked animals. The guards yelled and tried to chase down the animals. With everyone looking one way, Eriselda and Rynan darted off in the opposite direction to slip out the back gate.

As they made their way into the tree line, he heard rustling nearby and raised his haladie. A shadow emerged, her granite gray eyes angry and focused solely on him.

Minee glowered at Rynan. "I will thrash you later. Right now, we have to get moving."

"We have to move fast," Eriselda responded. "Valena killed the Queen, she's in full control of the castle guard."

Minee nodded. The two girls started off into the dense darkness, but Rynan didn't move.

"I can't go back with you," he said, glancing between the two girls as they looked over their shoulders at him. "I have to leave this forest. I can't stay here, I can't go back to the kith. I'm on my own."

"Your mother didn't raise you to run away," Minee snapped.

"She's not my mother."

Eriselda whipped around, then stormed towards him. The next thing he knew, she had him slammed against a tree. "No? Did she not raise you? Teach you? Love you?"

"Seldy-"

"She may be angry at you for taking another's side, Ryn, but she's still your mother. And her people, her kith, they are yours as well. You can't leave your kith to your sister's revenge. They need to know she plans to invade."

"They already know. My momm-Leader Haley made it clear she knew Valena's intentions before we ever stepped foot back in the castle. Just as she was clear that I was never to return to her kith."

"So you will not fight for either side? You'll just run? You are not who I thought you were."

"Seldy, I've never been someone anyone thought I was. I don't even know who I really am."

She laid her hand on his heart, making him grasp it gently. "You are what's in your heart."

Rynan's eyes began to fill with tears as he thought of all the times he doubted himself. It was always Zawn who would bring him back to reality, who reminded him what lived inside his heart even if he couldn't see it himself.

"She always told me," he responded, voice quivering, "that my heart was instilled with Gwendin's goodness and his hope."

"Those are quite important qualities, Ryn."

He frowned, shaking his head. "My name is Bryant."

"No, it's not. It's Rynan, heir of the Haley family, stargazer of the Whispering Hornbeam Kith. My mate, my love, my family. No throne, no royal title will ever take your true name's place."

"We are kithlin. Now, you go back to our kith," Minee added, "and you fix things with your mother."

"She's not my..."

Eriselda smacked him on the arm. "No, that woman in the castle wasn't your mother. Zawn raised you, loved you, sacrificed for you. Kemberly would never. Zawn saved your life just like she saved mine."

"Who attacked you?" he demanded.

"No, not like that." She paused. "When you left for school, I wasn't in a good place. I thought how you would forget me quickly and I'd nothing to live for because life at the castle was…" She shrugged, sadly. "It would have been so easy just to jump off a turret."

"You never told me that," he responded, choking up.

"She didn't want you to feel guilty," Minee replied, trying to subtly wipe her cheek.

"Your mother," Eriselda continued, glancing over at Minee, "your kith, took me in. Gave me tools to thrive, gave me the chance to keep you in my life. Gave me something to look forward to, something to enjoy. The same thing that I'd only felt with you."

"Seldy…"

"So you can be angry at her for not being completely truthful. But you saw how Crenast reacted to you being alive. She saved you from that monster."

Rynan glanced between his mate and someone he considered more a sister than cousin, unsure what to do.

~   ~   ~

Valena entered Bryant's prison, expecting him to abase himself to her. However, the bedroom laid empty. Out of the corner of her eyes, she saw the wall next to the fireplace at an odd angle. Furious, she screamed, causing the windows to rattle.

She turned on her guards, who backed up in fear.

Then movement against the other wall beckoned her. She rushed over to the full-length mirror hanging from the wall. Hands splayed against the glass while a voice whispered what had transpired.

Valena fumed. "I will lay waste to that kith."

"Yes, you will, my dear child. With my help."

CHAPTER 78

Averell returned a few days later, with a cadre of his strongest warriors. They were suited up for war, armor and weapons Zawn hadn't seen since the Purge. Averell gestured for the fighters to mingle with the rest of her kith, before he approached Zawn. Then she heard gasps and joyful welcomes when Merded was recognized as one of the warriors. Merded glanced over at Zawn and they nodded to each other out of respect.

When Averell got closer, she realized that she had a hard time looking in his face, so she focused on his shoulder that had the large leather armor piece with spikes on it. After bowing his head out of respect, he stood at attention as he spoke.

"Our messages have been received in the north. Our allies are preparing."

"As are ours in the south," she responded, voice sounding more stern than she meant.

He caught her glancing back over at his comrades.

"Merded volunteered. They all did. It took everything I had to stop Taikin from coming," Averell admitted. "He is still a fierce warrior in his heart, even though his body has failed him. But he works with Aric, who is leading our kith in their preparations, so we came to help yours since you will be the first target."

"We appreciate the assistance, Leader Dylan."

They stared at each other in silence.

His lower lip quivered a moment. "May, may I have a word in private, Leader Haley?"

Zawn hesitated, then nodded, "Of course, please," and gestured to her work hut.

He led the way and she followed a few steps behind. Once they entered and she shut the door, Averell didn't waste any time. He cupped her face in his hands and kissed her soundly. She felt his strength, his love, and his hope in that kiss. It didn't hold any anger or resentment. She still resisted, not feeling worthy of any love or forgiveness, and pulled away, but he kept his hands on her face.

Averell frowned, caressing her cheek with his thumb. "I wish there was something better than I'm sorry, but I don't have any other words." Then he dropped his hands and lowered himself onto his knees. "But I am truly sorry."

She stood there, eyes focused on the top of his head. She felt a shiver run through her, as if she wanted to explode. She wanted to yell, curse, hit, cry and beg him, but she found herself speechless. She didn't know which was the correct response. Her brain started working again after Yunji had broken the spell, but this situation was more heart oriented and hers hadn't found its north yet.

Averell continued, "I can never understand what you had to go through to take on such a responsibility. What that choice did to you. I only know now that it explains so much and I understand your choices better. I hope, I pray that after this is over, that you and I can work together to find our way back to each other. I don't want to lose you, Zawnie."

"How can you still want me?" she demanded, her voice shaking.

He looked up at her, tears streaming down his face. "Because nothing can ever make me stop loving you. I have loved you ever since the moment we met and I will never stopped loving you. I am here, I am sorry, and I am yours."

"I have lost so much, Averell. I don't know how to keep anything."

"My love, no, there is so much you haven't lost. You never lost your kith. You never lost me."

"I don't deserve your love."

"Deserve? Zawnie…"

"I am still the villain."

He rose to his feet, cupping her face again while shaking his head. "No, you are my love, my light, my mate. Nothing villainous."

"Tell Rynan that."

"He will come to that realization on his own. He's smart. Like his mother."

Her lip quivered and tears started to spill. She looked up at him and her heartbreak crushed him. Averell grabbed her into his arms, his heart shattering as she sobbed against his chest. "My son is gone."

"Oh, my love," he whispered against her hair. "I am so sorry."

~   ~   ~

He had removed his armor, pulled her to the chair, and held her. She straddled his lap as he wrapped his large arms around her. His heartbeat sounded so strong against her ear and she let herself get lost in the rhythm, which helped ease her tears. He whispered words of affection here and there, apologies for his actions mixed in. When she finally caught her breath, she told him in a hoarse voice what had transpired between the time he left and when he returned.

"A spell?" he demanded, incredulous.

"Apparently Rynan... I mean Prince Bryant wasn't the only one who had magical abilities. They hid them from everyone, even the College."

He stroked her hair gently, pushing away the wayward hairs that clung to her tear streaks. "It must have been very convenient that the College blacklisted them after the insurrection. They didn't have to worry about any nosy theurgists hanging around."

"For all we know, it could have been part of Crenast's plan all along. He probably had Gwen murdered to protect his secret. He just never knew Gwen shared it with me and the College."

"Do you believe that Rynan did not leave on his own accord?"

"That I do not know. Yunji can't sense him but he isn't sure if that's Valena's doing or if it's because he is at the castle. He cannot even confirm if he is alive or not."

"What does your heart tell you?"

She scoffed. "It's too confused."

"Even with me?"

She sat up to look him in the eyes. "I know the things we said to each other were instigated by the spell. I know that. But I fear there had to be some underlying source for those feelings and words that the spell took advantage of."

"You have thought about breaking things off with me?"

"There were days where I thought you would be happier without me. Nights where I thought about the children you could have, the stability of someone who could live with you in your kith. I was haunted with the thought that I should let you go because I was unworthy of your devotion."

"So you could give me up so easily?" he asked, his eyes clouding with tears.

"Not without dying immediately."

He cupped her face and kissed her soundly.

"And you always thought me a thief?"

Averell stammered. "No, I didn't..." He took a deep breath. "I always understood that you kept secrets from me. I knew not just me, but even after we became lovers, knowing that you still didn't tell me everything hurt. I told myself to give you more time. Yet time didn't seem to be the issue. It was your lack of trust. Now knowing the truth, I see that it was a sense of protection. Not only for Rynan but for those who held the secret. How the truth would have endangered everyone's lives and your fear of it ever coming to light. I'm sorry I didn't trust you."

Then he moved his fingers to her ears and she jerked away quickly, shaking her head.

"Zawnie, I still mean it," he responded, pulling her back to him. He ran his fingers tenderly along her ears, causing more tears to pour out of her. "I love you."

With shaking hands, she returned the caresses and the words, which left him in tears as well. They clung to each other, quivering in their pain and love.

~　　　~　　　~

The next morning, with fresh eyes and their hearts in tourniquets, the two leaders worked together with other kithlin to make plans on how to protect their kiths and their allies. Maps, notes, and communications decorated Zawn's work hut, from walls to tables to even the bathroom counter. Everyone but Taylor and Zawn took a break for lunch, leaving them to discuss details alone.

Zawn squeezed her eyes shut for a moment, rubbing her temples. "Yunji said we'd have headaches. Didn't think they'd be this bad."

"Everyone's feeling them," Taylor replied. "But I'm sure you've got it worse than the rest of us."

Suddenly, there was a ruckus near the entryway to the kith. Voices and gasps filled the air as someone arrived unannounced. From her work hut, Zawn and Taylor glanced up from their maps to see Rynan, with Eriselda and Minee, stride into the kith square. She felt Taylor's gaze turn to her, concerned. Zawn's first instinct was to grab the boy's face and review the blade mark on his chin, but she quelled that instinct. She wasn't his mother, he told her as much. Her only option was to treat him like the human prince he claimed to be when he left.

She exited the hut, catching their attention and causing the trio to turn toward her. Eriselda and Minee bowed their heads, out of respect not requirement, but Rynan stood straight, his eyes steadfastly locked with the Leader's.

Zawn glared at him. "Prince Bryant."

"Leader Haley," he responded, bowing his head respectfully. "I came to warn you that Valena leads an invasion on your lands."

"I am aware."

"It was decided against my wishes. You are your own sovereignty. Mehdehra needs to mind its own damn business. When she arrives, I will handle her myself."

"Who says I want you here?"

He stared at the woman he called Momma all of his life, seeing her fury. His regret for what he said to her in the heat of anger misted his eyes but he had to offer something other than tears. "Who would you rather have fight by your side, if not your own son?"

Zawn continued to glower at him, until movement behind him caught her eye. She saw Eriselda standing a few lengths away, her attention on both of them. When their gazes met, Eriselda bowed her head again then lifted proud eyes back up to the elven Leader's.

"Since Valena leads the charge, is it safe to assume Crenast is dead?" Taylor asked.

"She killed both Crenast and Kemberly."

"Valena will not be the first to step foot on our lands," Zawn responded, "she will straggle behind to ensure her own safety."

"Then we'll follow up from behind and if she tries to save her own skin, she'll have no choice but to face me."

"Are you willing to take the life of your sister if it comes to it?" Zawn asked.

"She is my sister only by blood. My true family was created by love," Rynan replied. "She is no better than Crenast, no better than what my father was. Proof in her decisions and her actions, including killing her own mother. It's time to end the reign of those who wish to destroy instead of collaborate."

"Then I would suggest that you clean up, Your Majesty. Your hut is still yours, for now. And clean that wound. We'll reconvene once you're refreshed and we've had lunch. Our allies should arrive by then."

Rynan blinked, maybe a little too fast, then bowed to Zawn. He glanced over at Eriselda and Minee before running his eyes over the kithlin gathered around. Solemnly, he walked to his hut as the kith leader had directed him, unsure if he was kithlin or prisoner.

After watching him enter his hut, Zawn turned on the two young women. Minee and Eriselda straightened, ready for the reprimand.

"You followed him without my permission?" Zawn demanded.

"May I be honest, Auntie?" Minee inquired.

Zawn gestured consent.

"No one was in their right mind when he left. We had to make a decision, let him walk into a trap or watch his back as he would any of us?"

Taylor snorted, making Zawn glare at him. "Minee isn't wrong."

"Did we miss something?" Eriselda piped up.

"Valena bespelled us, causing the emotional breakdown of the entire kith."

Minee frowned. "Is that why we have headaches?"

"Yunji broke the spell," Zawn replied. "We've all been suffering migraines as an after effect."

Minee looked over at Eriselda, who appeared shaken. "We weren't making the right decisions, then. But Auntie," and she returned her attention to Zawn, "following him was the right decision. You can punish us however you see fit, but, it was the right thing."

Zawn groused, folding her arms across her chest. "If I was thinking straight, I would have asked someone to follow him, this is true. However, taking off like that without letting anyone know…"

"Weren't thinking straight," Minee retorted, with a half-smile.

Taylor tried not to laugh at his daughter, but his eyes sparkled with amusement. "You helped raise her."

"Go," Zawn snapped, but her tone was not malicious, "get out of my sight."

Minee smirked, bowed her head then sprinted off toward her hut.

However, Eriselda didn't move, the tears finally rolling down her cheeks. "I didn't want to lose everything," she whispered, trembling.

Zawn grabbed the young woman into her arms, hugging her tight. "I could never banish you, my child." Zawn leaned back, then wiped tears from Eriselda's left cheek. "Did you talk him into coming back?"

"I only reminded him who he was."

"And who is he?"

"He is the man we both know and love, Momma. He is Rynan, our stargazer."

The elf nodded, then pulled Eriselda in, kissing her forehead. "Go, wash your face."

"Yes, Momma."

~   ~   ~

The door to his hut opened, causing him to freeze. He listened to the rustling and realized it was the familiar sounds of Eriselda. He finished treating his wound then stepped out to find her sitting at the foot of the bed, on the farthest side, staring at the fire. He approached the bed, trying to say something, but once he was close enough, she stood and brushed past him. She disappeared into the bathing room. Listening to her clean up, he fought back tears and made himself sit in the chair next to the fireplace that faced her way. Once she exited, she noticed that he was watching her. She hovered near the kitchen, leaning against their dining table.

Rynan stared at her, heartbroken. "You had to know."

Eriselda glanced away, folding her arms across her chest.

"You helped Valena bathe and dress. You had to have seen her brand and knew it matched mine."

"I thought you were keeping a secret from me," she responded, after several breaths.

"What?"

"I saw it but you never said anything about it. Never mentioned it, never questioned it. So I thought you were keeping a secret from me. And I... if it didn't matter enough to you to talk about it then why should I question it? It didn't change who you were, not to me."

"It wasn't a secret, it was just another lie my, um, Leader Haley told me to protect my identity. But even if I had told you, would you have corrected me?"

"Why? It isn't who you are. I knew you were royalty but you never acted like it. Never treated me in that way. Until... until you ordered me to leave."

"I wish I could explain that it wasn't me. That I have never felt superior to you, but that night, I did. I thought you owed me loyalty as your mate. Fealty. No more than that. I wish I could erase the whole incident, but I can't. I can only apologize."

"I appreciate your apology, but I don't know what we are right now. I love you, you are the love of my life, but we've all been hurt with the words we've said."

"So you meant it? That you are no longer my mate?"

Eriselda paused. "I don't know."

Rynan nodded, slowly, knowing that she had every right to question their relationship. The only thing he knew to do was simple in its action even though it was the right thing to do. He approached her, carefully, making her straighten and drop her arms. She looked concerned, unsure what he planned to do. He tried to assure her that his intentions were not cruel, by holding his hands down at his sides. When he was close enough, he didn't touch her. He lowered himself to his knees. Hearing her gasp made him quiver, but he didn't look up at her face for fear of seeing her hatred for him.

"Thank you," he finally said. "Thank you for following me. Thank you for helping me escape and for talking me into coming back. And… and I'm sorry. I wish I had better words but that's all I have."

"Words mean little," she whispered. "Prove through your actions, Rynan. That's why I fell in love with you. It was what you did, not what you said."

He looked up at her, his heart filling with hope. "I will do what I can to prove to you that I am the man you fell in love with."

"I will hold you to that." She stepped away from him, making sure not to touch him, and walked toward the door. "Come. Momma said to come to lunch once we've cleaned up."

~   ~   ~

Lunch was solemn but there was a sense of relief. Even though the truth of who Rynan was had come to light, the fact that he returned and admitted he belonged to the kith brought some peace to the kithlin. Once she finished, Zawn returned to her work hut, not speaking directly to Rynan throughout the whole meal. He had kept glancing over at her while he sat between his mate and Minee, but Zawn didn't give him any attention.

She stood at the table that she and Taylor had been poring over when the trio had returned. A soft knock at the doorframe made her look up. It was Rynan, standing on the porch nervously.

"May we speak, Leader Haley?"

She frowned, her heart stinging. She still wasn't sure how she felt about his return or knew what his true intentions were at the moment. But she knew she had to hear him out. "Yes, please come in."

He entered, closing the door for privacy. He stared at her in silence, eyes wide but voice missing.

"What did you wish to speak to me about?" Zawn prompted, somewhat impatient.

"I wish to apologize but I know words are hollow. I was a monster for what I said to you."

She thought of what Minee had said. "None of us were in our right minds."

"No, we weren't. I found out later that I had been bespelled by Valena. She admitted what she had done to me. I hate myself for not realizing it and reversing it immediately."

"None of us realized it."

"But I am a theurgist, I should have been aware."

"Well, I appreciate your apology, Your Majesty."

Hearing her call him that made his lower lip quiver and his shoulders drop. "Please don't call me that."

"Then what should I call you?"

"I don't know."

Zawn sighed, long and hard, her barriers breaking down at the sight of this young man who was lost and confused. Young man. Even that seemed odd to think, when she had always called him her son. She hated seeing him doubt himself. She approached him, reaching out to grasp his arms. But he rushed into her arms instead, hugging her tight. She had a flashback to when he had reached the age of going to the College, how terrified he was about leaving.

"Yes, you do," she responded, wrapping her arms around him. "You know who you are."

"I can't be him. Not if you…"

"Rynan," she interrupted, leaning back to look him in the eyes. "You may be the heir to the throne of Mehdehra, but you are also the heir to the Haley family. My stargazer. My son."

"But that's not enough, is it?"

"Isn't it? You may see human in the glass but in here?" And she laid her hand on his heart. "You are elven. You are my son. And the man I loved, who died protecting you, instilled in you a good heart the moment you were born."

"What do I do now?"

"You fight. For both your human and your elven people. I do agree with one thing. It's time to put the rightful heir on that throne. You will face Valena and you will win." She stepped away from him, reaching for a book on her shelf, next to her keepsake journal. "Yunji wanted you to have something, if you came back to us to fight by our side." She handed over a small book.

Rynan took the book from her, then glanced through the pages. The color in his face drained, making Zawn grasp his arm, concerned.

"What is it?" she asked.

He closed the book and held it against his chest. "Uh, it's one of the books I read at least once a year while at the College. They were…" He hesitated. "They were lessons he wasn't supposed to teach me."

"So it's a message?"

He nodded.

"He had warned me that you were being taught ways to fight."

The sound of wings flapping outside drew their attention away from each other.

"Come," Zawn urged. "We've friends to speak with."

They exited her work hut to find four gargoyles standing in the middle of their kith. Greetings were shared by elf and gargoyle alike, then they turned to see Zawn approaching.

"Zawnie," Nicholaus's voice boomed. "Your letters seemed to conflict in such a short time."

Zawn nodded to Marassa, Dia, and Irai before replying, "A lot has transpired in a very short time. But you understand the most recent request?"

"We will protect our allies as well as our own borders," he confirmed.

"Good. It's time to put the Mehdehran princess in her place."

"And where is that?" Marassa inquired.

"Next to the bodies of her father, uncle, and mother."

Nicholaus looked over at Rynan, frowning. "Will that cause an issue?"

"No," Rynan responded, without hesitating. "Her wishes are to kill and subdue. That does not align with my beliefs. The reign of terror must end here and with her." After he said those words, he felt someone grasp his hand. He glanced over to find Eriselda taking her place at his side.

"Members of the Whispering Hornbeam Kith," Zawn announced, drawing everyone's attention to her. "The Kingdom of Mehdehra marches onto our lands, breaking our agreement. They arrive with the plan to battle and dominate us. Along with our allies from the Whistling Cedar Kith and of Brazen Fort, we will meet this threat with the strength and perseverance that we have honed all of these years. Archers, aim for their weakest points. Fighters, disarm and subdue."

"Are we aiming for leverage?" Ehdzia inquired.

"No," Zawn responded. "No more mercy. Because they will not show us any."

~   ~   ~

Rynan, Eriselda, Minee, and a few others moved as fast as they could along the trees and foliage. On the road between them, they watched as the marching militia headed toward their kith. However, that group would meet the fiercest warriors of kith and clan.

Rynan's group only had one target.

Rynan and his small army darted behind the large grandfather trees that lined the road. Zawn had been right, Princess Valena brought up the rear, apparently too fearful to meet her enemy face to face. She rode a magnificent stallion in full Royal Family war regalia, looking the part of a mighty queen. However, it was all a facade... at least as long as Rynan still lived. He knew that would be her goal, kill him to be the last family member standing. Then she could change the Kingdom of Mehdehra into her own image.

But she had to get through Rynan first.

His friends and mate agreed before heading out to take down her guards and leave Valena for him. He nodded the order for them to take their places, then he jumped out into the road behind the army.

"Valena!" he shouted, causing her to stop her horse and turn it around. "You have trespassed into Whispering Hornbeam Kith territory. Return to yours or suffer the consequences."

Valena started laughing. "Do you think your little warning will frighten me? I will tremble no more at the likes of you." She made a swift gesture to her chaperons.

Suddenly, the soldiers around her rushed him. Before they could get close enough, his group burst from the forest and took them down. Once they completed their task, they returned to the protection of the trees.

Left unprotected in the middle of the road, Valena held the reins a little too tightly.

"I might not scare you," Rynan retorted, "but the elf queen you disparage?"

Down the road, the sounds of arrows hitting their targets, men screeching and groaning as they died, and the clashes of blades filled the forest.

"She is reminding you why you fear her as we speak."

Another scream of someone dying of a terrible wound broke the generally peaceful atmosphere. Then "RETREAT!" followed. Men in their armor, some wounded, some covered in the blood of their fellows rushed past them back to the castle.

Valena seethed, then struck her steed, making it bolt down the road. Rynan had to jump out of the way to avoid being run down. Eriselda rushed to Rynan's side, pulling him back to the safety of the foliage, then both watched as the Mehdehran forces fled as quickly as they could.

"Now what?" Eriselda asked, helping her mate to his feet.

"She will fortify the castle," Rynan answered, glancing around as the last man ran by. "Let's regroup with the others."

~   ~   ~

Hearing their foe's retreat, it was time to regroup. Zawn gathered her kith and their allies, doling out final orders and instructions. When she heard footfalls, her eyes landed on the small group returning.

"She's running back to the castle," Rynan announced as he and his group jogged back to their kithlin. "I need to follow quickly, make sure she doesn't have time to think."

"We're going with you," Eriselda replied, while Minee nodded agreement.

"I don't know what I'm walking into."

"All the more reason for you to have someone watching your back," Minee responded. "And they will not be suspicious of two females."

"Valena will know."

"But she won't expect me," Eriselda countered, with a wry smile. "We will have surprise on our side."

Taylor chuckled. "There is no arguing, Rynan."

"We'll take the fight back to her," Zawn assured. "She thinks she has the upper hand, going back to her power source."

Rynan frowned. "I don't know if I can beat her if she is able to tap in."

"You will," Zawn replied, sounding resolute, "because she will have no power."

Taylor looked worried. "Zawnie?"

"I know what I have to do," she responded, firmly. "But I need you to have my son's back. Will you do that for me, Tay?"

"As long as I draw breath."

"Averell?"

Her mate nodded. "As long as I draw breath."

"Our kithlin will remain here, keeping the border locked down and our kith safe. Nicholaus, Marassa, will you help us make a path for Rynan?"

Both gargoyles nodded.

"Then let's end this."

CHAPTER 79

They met with little resistance. They didn't know if it was ignorance or ego. They took no comfort with the ease they had. Keeping a sharp eye out, they checked for traps or an ambush. After all, they didn't know what awaited them inside.

The elves and gargoyles surrounded the outer courtyard, weapons at the ready. Then three figures marched up the stairs that lead directly into the castle's throne room.

Valena stood on the top dais, in front of the King's throne, wearing a massive gown with full royal regalia. Her tiara, earrings, and pendant were teardrops made out of diamonds and rubies, while her dress was a deep burgundy. Her hair was braided away from her face, entwined with and held in place by red ribbons. Even her slippers were a deep red, with gold and black swirls stamped on the material.

Rynan could smell the illusion.

Above her head, on the rod hanging from the ceiling, swayed the family crest. It also had burgundy, black, and gold… the Mehdehran crest had replaced the one that had been Crenast of Garadni's. Around the room, the royal guard lined the walls, standing at attention, their uniforms with the Mehdehran crest on the right breast. Between them hung mirrors of various sizes and shapes. And the captain and two top lieutenants stood at the foot of their queen.

Flanked by Eriselda and Minee, Rynan strode down the aisle toward the dais with a confidence mustered from a deep place in his heart. The show by Valena was intimidating. However, he knew who had his back. Not just his family, but entire peoples, from kiths to clans. He wasn't alone. And he wasn't powerless.

"What do you want?" the captain demanded, glaring down at the trio in disgust. "Wasting the queen's precious time is punishable by death."

"By Mehdehran law, she is nothing but a usurper," Eriselda responded.

Valena, glowering down at her servant, finally spoke. "So I had a spy in my midst."

Eriselda smirked, almost a perfect reflection of the elf queen.

"This ends now, Valena," Rynan announced.

Valena scoffed. "Who are you to order me? You have no rights here, no power." She raised one hand, sparking lightning from fingertips to thumb. "No magician, no sorcerer could match me, could ever beat me." Then she snapped her fingers, making the sparks fly up into the ceiling. "And especially some savage-raised mediocre theurgist."

Rynan reached out toward Valena, purple and gold flecks of light swirling around his own hand. "You forget, I am King of Mehdehra. That is my throne, these are my people, and this is my birth right. I know what powers you, they run and converge under our feet, and I know it powers me too."

With concerted concentration, Rynan threw his arms out toward the guards and shouted two words. Those two words, simple in their syllables, opened up large enough portals to suck the guards out of the room. Once they were removed, he dropped his arms, causing the portals to close immediately.

Valena and the guard captain stared in shock, mouths unhinged.

"Now, that makes this a bit more fair," Rynan said, with a grin.

"Hardly," Valena snapped. "Captain Marqut, remove this trash."

"With pleasure, my Queen."

The three remaining soldiers rushed toward them. Eriselda and Minee stepped in front of Rynan, weapons drawn. The captain attacked Eriselda, while the two lieutenants ran toward Minee. Knowing they could take care of themselves, Rynan kept his focus on Valena.

~　　　~　　　~

With Valena and the castle guard focused on Rynan, her movements were undetected. She left her friends and family behind to hold the line, knowing they would support Rynan. Zawn kept her steps as stealthily as possible as she made her way around the castle grounds alone.

She arrived at the collapsed entrance quickly to find the large rocks that she and Gwen had placed there were unmoved. It confirmed that no one knew about this other entrance and that would buy her some time. She touched the edge of the large boulder that blocked the slip of an entrance and whispered an incantation that she learned from Gwen. The massive rock budged slightly, but not enough to let her through. She grimaced, then closed her eyes, focusing her intention clearly on her goal. Repeating the words softly, she felt the boulder lift a little too much too fast. Instinctively, she jumped out of the way as the rock jolted out of its position and plummeted down the ravine that ran along the back of the castle grounds.

Annoyed, she glanced around to ensure she hadn't attracted any unwanted attention. Seeing that the noise seemed blocked out by the magical fire fight inside, she climbed through the opening and entered the cave. The intersecting energy lines seemed to radiate brighter than ever. She realized they were drawn up so strongly that the lines almost shivered out of the rocks. She blinked against their shining light, then approached the large wall where multiple lines converged.

Something caught her eye. A trunk in the corner, almost hidden in shadow. She opened it up, finding notes and containers. This must have been Crenast's supplies while working the energy lines. Zawn snapped her fingers, causing a spark to fly from them. It landed on the items inside the trunk, burning them to ash instantly. Then she turned back to the energy lines shimmering brighter and brighter still.

Accepting her fate, Zawn took a deep breath. "Help me, Gwen."

~ ~ ~

The two lieutenants ran toward Minee, who held her haladie to her side and her short sword protecting her chest. All that armor made them ungainly and easy targets. She assumed they were top of their class. It really wasn't going to be a fair fight. Minee was the top of her kith. She couldn't wait to have some fun with them.

They rushed her simultaneously, one swinging his sword, another a mace. She blocked the mace with her sword while bashing the sword with her haladie. She twisted her sword just enough to lock the mace's chain around her blade before yanking it free from the guard's hand. She kicked at the other guard, freeing him of his sword, then gave it a brief glance to see how far it clattered. Then she dropped and swept out her leg, knocking the two men down. They hit so hard, groans and grunts escaped them before they stopped moving.

Minee scoffed, disappointed at how easy that was.

~ ~ ~

She laid her hands on the energy lines, feeling the heat of their power. It was like touching lightning. The incandescence exposed everything under her flesh. It illuminated every muscle, tendon, vein and bone. Touching the energy lines felt like grabbing a scalding pot, but without the obvious damage to the skin. Then, oh so gently, she swore she felt hands lay on her shoulders.

"I'm here, Zee," a wispy voice answered.

She closed her eyes, let down every single barrier she had built over the decades, and began to whisper the incantation she memorized over the years for this very moment…

~ ~ ~

The captain approached Eriselda, broad sword drawn and looming. Short sword in one hand, dagger in the other, the former servant stood her ground. She knew she couldn't take a direct hit by the sword, considering its size and the power behind it. But Zawn taught her early on one vital trick when facing an opponent: let them show their vulnerability with their first attack. Patiently, she waited, keeping her eyes on the man in front of her.

Suddenly, he swung heavily toward her and she jumped to the side, avoiding the blow easily. But there it was, his weakness.

She felt the smirk widen and she quickly pounced. Before he could raise the sword again after it bounced on the cobblestone, Eriselda leapt and landed on his arm, driving her dagger into the gap between his shoulder armor and gauntlet. Blood burst from the wound as she stabbed multiple times, making the captain scream in pain. As he threw his head back in agony, she swung around onto his back and slit his throat with her sword. He dropped to his knees and she shoved off his back to land on her feet behind him.

Taking a moment to watch the blood gush out of the man who allowed his guards to harass, terrorize, and assault many of the servants over the years, she spit on his corpse and relished in the vengeance she didn't know she needed.

~   ~   ~

Touching the energy lines took her breath, making Zawn struggle to get enough air. She felt like each layer of derma started to peel off, as if by a dull grater. The intensity turned from peeling to something similar to acid eating away. There was sizzling against bone without the sound or smell. Fat and tendons melted. Muscles spasmed and cramped. She became light-headed, feeling her grip on consciousness slipping, but she chanted the incantation louder.

Slowly the ebbing brightness faded. The energy that flowed underneath the castle flickered out. It was no longer in the ground.

It was in her.

~   ~   ~

Valena screeched in anger as she watched her captain and lover bleed out. Suddenly, the throne room seemed to flash with light of different colors. Red, gold, purple, green. Light flashed on one side before volleying over to the other side. In turn, another bolt would shoot back across in response. It almost seemed as if their power was limitless.

Eriselda and Minee stood near the door, watching the volleys as they bounced back and forth. No one was making headway, no one was winning.

"Should we help?" Minee asked.

"No. He must fight for what is his," Eriselda answered. "Even if it means killing his own sister."

"I don't think either of them are getting very far."

Eriselda sighed. She knew that with the energy lines joining underneath their feet powered the two conjurers infinitely. She didn't know what Zawn had planned to stop the flow of energy, but she hoped the elf would succeed soon. Nausea gripped both girls as they tried to breathe through the ozone caused by the magical clash.

The even fight started to falter. Rynan's exhaustion began to show. Seeing that she had gained the upper hand, Valena called out for her goddess to help her, shocking the mirrors around the throne room to life. Hands no longer laid on the glass, but reached out. As she struck at Rynan again and again, the ghastly ghouls tried to break free. Another incantation and the magic residing in the mirrors started to flow around Valena. The voluminous sapphire and onyx smoke swirled around her like a layered skirt before absorbing into her skin. A maniacal cackle escaped her before she struck again.

Valena focused all of that power and anger at the boy in front of her.

Valena hit Rynan's shield with several waves of energy until he could no longer stand. He was blown away and landed on his back, knocking the air out of his lungs.

Seeing that weak excuse for a brother laying listless on the floor, the princess crowed. But taking him out wasn't enough. Valena realized she could hurt Rynan in other ways. She charged up and took her aim at Eriselda. She deserved it after killing Marqut.

Minee watched in horror, but as the energy crossed the distance, Eriselda reacted instinctively. "Sel Gumae!" Eriselda shouted, creating a bubble of protection around herself and Minee.

As her attack dispersed against the curve of the bubble, Valena seethed. On the other side of the dais, Rynan's initial terror at seeing his love in danger changed swiftly to pride. Eriselda's protection faded away and the former servant stood straight with arrogance, goading Valena even more.

Her anger getting the best of her, the princess screamed. Then Valena raised her hands, about to lash her brother to death with another wave of electricity. But nothing came out. She gasped, tried again, only to find nothing.

And the magic feeding into her from the mirrors quivered, gasped, then dissipated. Chaotic shrieks ricocheted through the room until the reflective surfaces shattered into millions of pieces.

Rynan teetered to his feet, panting in pain, but his eyes were resolute. He stormed up the steps toward the princess, drawing his short sword. Valena pulled a dagger from her belt and lunged at Rynan. Without hesitation, he blocked her strike and grabbed her wrist. The anger on her face shifted to fear before he pushed her back. She stumbled back then straightened as if to attack again, but he gave her no chance. For kith and kingdom, he swung his short sword swiftly, lopping her head off. Just like Crenast's, it bounced down the steps of the dais and stopped in the same spot as his had. As Rynan stepped back and watched her lifeless, bleeding body collapse, he sensed a tremble directly under him.

"Get out of there!" Taylor bellowed from the courtyard.

Suddenly by his side, Eriselda grabbed his arm and all three ran for the door.

~   ~   ~

Blisters, burns, charring, swelling.

She couldn't hold it in much longer. The power ripped through her muscles, decimated veins, and cracked bones. She felt her body breaking apart. Her skin burned and seethed, as if trying to shed itself from her body. The immense pain nearly won. She almost let the energy escape back into the earth.

But she couldn't let it go, not with them inside or nearby. Her son, her daughter, her family, her kithlin. Her lover, her allies. They were all in harm's way. They could be hurt or worse, killed, if she gave in.

She had to hold on long enough until she knew they were safe.

They were the only ones that mattered.

Not her, not her pain, nothing else mattered. Only them.

"It's time, Zee. Let go," he whispered.

Hoping he was right, that it was the right time, she released the energy back into the earth.

~   ~   ~

They had made it out just in time. They stopped in the outer courtyard, where their kithlin had secured the guards Rynan had transported out of the throne room. They turned, in horror, toward the monstrous noise behind them. The castle, layer by layer, rumbled and glowed. Then each stone lifted up into the air, separating from each other in voluminous confusion, until even the foundation levitated. With one last wave of heat, the building crashed into the earth, almost swallowed by the caverns underneath.

When the dust began to settle, the onlookers found nothing left but rubble.

~   ~   ~

Her name echoed through the massive crater that used to be a castle. Marassa took to the sky while Nicholaus followed Taylor and the others on foot. They searched near where she had accessed the cave, hope dwindling with each unanswered call. Taylor stumbled, almost landing on his face, when he saw her hand, the one that still wore Gwendin's ring.

"Zawnie!" Taylor shouted, heartbroken.

He began to dig, begging her to be alive. As he pulled the rubble off of her, other hands joined and they pulled her from her prison. Rynan embraced her as Taylor handed her over, still trying to free her feet, but she didn't move. She didn't react. She didn't breathe. She just laid limp and lifeless in her son's arms. Averell collapsed on his knees next to Rynan and Taylor, wrapping his arms around his mate and her son.

Nicholaus watched the heartbreaking scene, her closest family clinging to each other and her, the others sobbing around them. "She has gone to the other side of the canopy."

"No, Momma, no," Rynan begged. "Don't leave me."

Taylor choked, grasping her hand in his. "She is with Gwendin again, finally."

Whispers of "Safe journey" filled the air as the tears flowed and the dust settled.

CHAPTER 80

Taylor carried her back. Several friends offered to help, but he refused to let her go, even to Averell. It was his place, as her heir to the leadership and as her brother by love, to ferry her home. As he entered the kith with her in his arms, he heard the gasps, sobs, and wails of his kithlin. It shook him for a moment, because he had been trying to hide his own pain and grief the entire time he walked. He made sure he didn't stumble, Zawn would have hated him for that, setting one foot in front of the other as surely as he could.

He took her straight to her personal hut, the one she had lived in most of her life. Gently laying her down on the bed, he took time to remove her weapons, boots, and gauntlets. That gave him glimpses of damage to her body, caused by whatever she had accomplished in the caves. Frowning, he set it all on her small table, then caught sight of her keepsake journal that she had kept all of her memories. He pulled it loose and cradled it lovingly in his arms like he had her body, before making way for his mate. He glanced up at the doorway and watched as Averell's bravery deteriorate again and the younger elf walked away.

Rynan took his place in the doorway, his tear-stained face almost breaking Taylor's resolve.

"If anyone were to take the lead of our kith, Momma wanted it to always be you," Rynan admitted, watching as Chae and Meagan readied Zawn's body.

"I can only hope to make her proud," Taylor admitted.

"Me too. She had a high bar."

"You are now the patriarch of the Haley family, stargazer of the Whispering Hornbeam Kith."

"No, I am King of Mehdehra. That is my title."

"My boy," and Taylor chuckled, mirthlessly, "You are both. Don't ever forget that. Or your Momma will haunt you for the rest of your days. Especially if you refuse the expectations as her son at her funeral. Come, we leave her in good hands and we must be ready for our duties as her family."

~ ~ ~

After leaving her in the care of her friends, Averell entered her work hut, wishing she was still sitting at her table. He expected to see her poring over her financial records, fussing over the details of the next growing season. Or worse, heading out to deal with the irrigation system, half-dressed and completely annoyed. He would have given anything to see her look up and smile, that loving expression that always welcomed him home.

But she wasn't there.

She laid in her personal hut, on her bed, being dressed for her funeral.

A rather large, thick book sat on her table, with pieces of leather sticking out in different places and in various directions. Numb, he opened it to one of her bookmarks. Drawings with notes and diagrams laid out before him. Scribbles about someone of different magical lineage. How they could manipulate magic and nature around them. His breath caught when he recognized the details about energy lines. Her own writing was tucked into the pages, instructions to herself on what to do. He felt his knees weakened and he collapsed into her chair. She knew. She knew exactly what she was doing… and as he turned the page, her notes informed him that she had accepted the consequences.

Tears rolled down his face. She had sacrificed everything, every day, for her kith, her people, her friends and her son. And with one last sacrifice, she saved them all.

~ ~ ~

The evening came upon them quickly, somberly. Few could manage appetites but each forced themselves to eat. They needed their energy to honor the woman who led them with patience, open-mindedness, and sometimes exasperation. Speaking of interactions with their leader made the kithlin smile, laugh, and weep. Along with food, mead and apple wine flowed, making toasts erupt throughout the group.

Taylor slowly approached Averell, who stood alone staring at the spot where he and Zawn often shared their meals together. He hesitated but knew he had to give his fellow kith leader the item in his hand. He made it to the other elf's side and handed Averell a note, folded neatly and the edges worn from being bent for so long. "I found this. It is addressed to you."

Averell took it, almost hesitantly, then sat down slowly, as if he had aged decades within the few hours of Zawn's death. He unfolded it.

My dearest Averell, my love, my mate. If you are reading this then I succeeded, which resulted in my death. I knew the consequences long before we ever met, and no, you would not have been able to talk me out of it.

You were right. I became the light that guided the kiths. But I had to let my light fade to let all of yours continue to shine. Fear not, my love, I will continue to shine. Look up, through the canopy, and that star? The one that winks at you late at night? That will be me. Watching over you, over my son, over my friends and our kithlin, from the other side of the canopy.

Thank you for spending the rest of my life with me. I hope to see you again, but please, not too soon. Live your life, my heart. Grieve, but do not forget to live. That is a hard lesson to learn, I would know, but our kithlin will help you as they had helped me. As you had helped me. And find love again. Find someone who can be what you were to me.

Lastly, watch over Rynan, as he is as much your family as he was mine. Knowing that you and the rest of our family will be there for him means I can rest well.

Goodbye, my dearest heart ~ Zawnie

The sobs bursting from the large elf were heartbreaking. But every single kithlin moved forward to comfort him. As much as he needed it, so did they, and they grieved together by the fire.

~   ~   ~

Zawn didn't write a letter only to Averell. Taylor had found other letters tucked away in her keepsake journal: one addressed to himself and Chaelene, one to Rynan, and one to Eriselda. Along with Averell, Rynan took his hard. Taylor caught the first few sentences before Rynan hunched over in tears.

Dearest Rynan, my son, my stargazer. When you were a baby, you looked at me as if I were the only person in the world that mattered. When you were a boy, you said I was "inwinsseble." When you were a teenager, you told me I was immortal. But one of our last conversations, in the home where you grew up and where we loved each other as family, you called me what amounted to a monster.

One person's honorable actions aren't always seen that way by others. I recognize that. I loved Gwendin and when he begged me to save your life, I could only honor his wishes. But ultimately, what he gave me was something I could never fathom. His wish gave me a family of my own, a family he and I would never have...

Then Rynan changed his position and Taylor lost sight of her words. However, he knew the words were the right ones at the right time based on Rynan's reaction.

Then Taylor caught sight of Eriselda, her back against the same tree she used to hide behind to read letters from Rynan while he was at the College. Tears were streaming down her face as well, but a small smile, one full of love, was there too. He knew Zawn finally let Eriselda know how proud she was of the young woman and how much she regarded her as a daughter. Something he was sure Eriselda believed, but to have Zawn express that, meant the world to the girl. And now Eriselda could cherish those words, in writing, for the rest of her days.

With a heavy heart, he approached his mate, their letter in his hand. She frowned at first, then saw their names scrawled on the envelope. Tears welled up. Chae took a deep breath, to steady herself, and nodded. "Let's read that somewhere private?"

~   ~   ~

Washed with reverence and dressed in the garb that defined her, Taylor carefully carried Zawn into the kith square. He laid her down on a mattress of the sweetest grasses, surrounded by flowers and pine cones, ribbons and her weapons. She wore her topaz-colored tunic and suede pants, leather breastplate with buckles and the skirt made of four large panels. Her overly darned socks and her worn out boots covered her feet. Her neck was adorned with the necklace of a matte blue stone and the black leather band with matching stones was tied on her left, upper arm. Her emerald, peridot and onyx hair had been braided into different plaits before twisting together in one large swirl. And on her finger, a ring of polished stone and patinaed metal glistened.

First Rynan, with Eriselda by his side, walked up to the funerary. He knelt down, saying something softly then kissed his mother's forehead. Eriselda was next, taking a moment to wish farewell and safe journeys to a woman who treated her with kindness, respect and a love of a mother she had never known until they had met.

Averell came up behind them, watching as they clasped hands and parted. After kneeling beside her and tracing one of her ears gently with his fingers, he tucked an envelope under her hands as they laid on her stomach. His letter, addressed to "his light" was his last to his beloved Zawnie. He choked back another sob and stood, leaving her to others' attention.

Taylor, Chaelene, and Minee were next. Then each family approached, from Satria and her child to Sileas hand in hand with Amna. Every kithlin shared their words and thoughts to the lifeless body, but each knew their words were carried directly to her on the other side of the canopy.

Suddenly, a chaotic crash broke the reverent silence. From the barn, an army of four legged warriors exploded out. The goats spilled out into the kith square, circling the funerary. They jumped around, catching sight of Zawn. Their mournful bleats seemed to beg her to get up, even though the reality sunk in. They knew she would never corral them again. The goats resigned themselves to their new reality, laying around her funerary, guarding their friend and leader one last time.

The sun marched overhead in its perfectly timed path, keeping light on her motionless face. It made her glow, as if the sun tried to power her back to life. But not even the sun could bring her back.

As Zawn laid in state, friends and allies from all over came to pay respects. Even Taikin, with his ill health, trekked to say farewell to his very dear friend, assisted by Talor and Chaen. Each ally sent a representative, even those on the very edges of the forest: Riders, gargoyles, theurgists, along with the other elves. As each individual walked past her body, they whispered farewells, caring words, and hopes for her life on the other side of the canopy.

The Brazen Fort clan each took their moment with Zawn, too. Marassa brought up the rear, walking several lengths behind her fellows. When she took her turn at Zawn's side, she laid a wreath woven from sweetgrass, cattails, and hornbeam twigs that was in the shape of a heart. Laying it on her former lover's chest, she also set a small bag of sunflower seeds in the middle of it – Zawnie's favorite snack. Then after a kiss to the forehead, Marassa left her friend's side for the last time.

Taylor hadn't given Averell the letter addressed to Taikin, knowing that in the younger elf's current state of grief, it would have gotten misplaced. However, as the retired kith leader entered their square slowly but proudly, Taylor slipped him the folded note. Taikin tucked it into his armor, near his heart, and thanked Taylor. Then he made his way to his heir in leadership, supporting him while he grieved too.

That night, Averell and Rynan stood nearby, her love at her foot, her son at her head, as was customary for a mate and child of the deceased. The prior night, Taylor and Chaelene held court, as was the right as her kin. The stars and moons blessed her with their light in loving sadness, glittering and glowing throughout the night.

~   ~   ~

That next morning, the sun returned, shining down on the grieving kith. Gasps filled the air as new visitors walked slowly into the kith. They were led by sentries, who looked just as surprised as everyone else. Behind them, four of the five were very different individuals but they were from the same kind. One had the appearance of a tree, another amphibious, one of fire, another of stars, and the last swirled like a wind storm.

Among the Sedoran nymphs was a young woman, who had engaging dark brown eyes and swirling blonde hair. She was taller than her companions except for the tree nymph. She solemnly approached Taylor, recognizing him as the new leader of the kith, and bowed her head in respect. Behind her, each nymph followed her lead.

"My name is Parni, I am here on behalf of Sedora in the stead of our Queen. I am also an Elemental. I am here to translate for our sisters, the nymphs."

The jahla stepped forward. "We share our condolences as well as our Queen's. All of Sedora grieves the loss of our ally and friend."

"How did you know?" Taylor asked.

"She was one of us," the eahzal answered, through their Talented translator. "Her grandmother was an Elemental. We knew the moment she came to life and when that life left her."

"She never liked talking about that," Taylor said softly.

"She embraced what she could," the jahla agreed. "We met with her when she was quite young, at the forest edge, at the request of your mother. Inari knew there were parts of her she needed to understand and without her parents to help her... She controlled her abilities by suppressing them... And eventually, she found herself having to fight for survival and for the lives of others." The woodlen nymph looked over at Rynan. "And then love took its place in her heart and she knew nothing else."

"But how can you...?" Eriselda began, then stopped herself out of fear for offending their guests.

"How can we what, child?" the aetha responded in a singsong voice.

"How can you be away from your tree? From your land?"

The nymphs all smiled, impressed by the young woman's knowledge.

Then the halha swirled around her and whispered, "Magic."

Parni gave the halha an amused look, but tried to return her face to its stoic expression. "Thanks to our Queen, we are connected at all times even outside our borders. As long as there is an Elemental with them, they can even travel outside of Sedora."

"Will you stay for the pyre?" Taylor asked.

Parni bowed her head. "We would be honored. Her bravery and sacrifice will never be forgotten by Sedora and her people."

As the others moved away, Parni reached out and laid a hand on Rynan's arm.

"Forgive my familiarity, but I was asked by our Queen to confirm that Kalo did not return to our realm."

Rynan's eyebrows furrowed together. "Who?"

"A god who fell. The dark winds whispered of her impending return, but since those winds had died down, we couldn't tell if she was still imprisoned."

The hands reaching out from the mirrors flashed in his mind. "The moment when the energy lines were disrupted, the mirrors shattered and it sounded like someone was dying."

"Then she is still caged," the Sedoran responded, with a sigh of relief. "That is good news. Thank you for confirming. I am sorry to have brought it up so soon in our meeting but I can return home with good news amongst the grief."

~   ~   ~

Taylor and Chaelene approached Zawn's body. Chae removed the flat blue stone necklace from their friend's neck, then secured it around her mate's. Next, she untied the armband and tied it around Taylor's upper arm. They hugged, their grief blinding them momentarily. Taylor took a deep breath and let his mate go, then he reached down and gathered a few items up.

Taylor stood and walked over to Rynan, handing over a small object. When Rynan opened his hand, he found his mother's ring laying there. A ring given to her by the man who loved her. Rynan sniffled, closing his hand and holding it against his heart. He grabbed Eriselda's hand and slipped it on. Both Rynan and Eriselda sobbed, hugging tightly. Lastly, Taylor turned to Averell, handing over Zawn's short sword and dagger. Taylor would keep her haladie and khukuri, she wanted him to have it, but Averell was to have her other weapons.

Once her possessions were distributed per her wishes, the final step was the final farewell.

Rynan shared the honor with Averell, touching the leaves with their torches' flames. The fire slowly crawled to her body, but once it caressed her arms, it devoured her without hesitation. Saronin stepped forward and began singing the "Song of Farewell," her lone voice soaring above the sorrow. Then other voices joined her, lifting the melody almost high enough to break through the other side of the canopy, even though they choked on tears and sobs. In addition to the voices of elves, nymphs, and humans, the trees and wildlife around them joined in. The rustling of leaves, creaking of limbs. The animals tweeting, bleating, baying, and chittering.

A fitting goodbye for the leader of the forest.

CHAPTER 81

A few days later, things started to return to normal. As normal as it could be without their cherished leader. Each kithlin went about their chores, slowly and sadly, but determined nonetheless. Even the goats, who had mourned at the funeral beside elf and man, understood life had to go on. Afterall, Zawn would have expected them to keep going, to stay proud, and to make sure the kith survived.

Rynan did not make a spectacle of his ascension to the throne. While spending time in his mother's hut, he had found a seal among her belongings. It did not match the mark on his leg, however he came to realize that it was Gwen's family crest. He used that to secure the announcements he sent to all the townships in Mehdehra of his elevation in status and what his hopes were for the kingdom now that it was under his care and supervision.

He also spoke with Taylor and Nicholaus regarding his hopes for their continued support of each other. Taylor suggested that he take a representative from kith and clan to make sure all voices were heard when he had to come to a decision. Rynan agreed, but only if he could bring Minee and Irai into his counsel. He knew both as well as they knew him, and he acknowledged the need for individuals who were not afraid to land him on his back when needed. They would keep him grounded and appreciative. Eriselda of course remained at his side, as counsel and as his mate and queen. His actions at the castle and their shared grief reconnected the young couple, bringing them even closer than before.

Rynan, in his new role as King, took the lessons he learned from Zawn and tailored them to fit his situation. He traveled throughout Mehdehra, with Eriselda, Irai, and Minee by his side, speaking with each leader and governor, to find out what they needed and how he could help. Taylor allowed him to keep the kith as his base until he figured out where to settle. Knowing what ran under the old castle, Rynan refused to rebuild there and ordered that area be considered a dead zone and off limits. The gargoyles took responsibility of patrolling the area to keep trespassers out.

The Whispering Hornbeam Kith continued to flourish under Taylor's leadership. He designated two seconds upon his taking the mantle of leader: Satria and Ehdzia. They both had worked closely with Zawn and he knew she would be delighted by his choices. Both women promised to make him, and Zawn, proud.

Averell's kith also thrived. Working together with Aric, the Whistling Cedar Kith grew into one of the largest in the forest. After a few years, Averell even found love again. Taylor had assigned Avari as his diplomat to Averell's kith. Averell and Avari grew close, falling in love after years of friendship, and they had a daughter, Haley.

Rynan worked hard every day to prove he was worthy of the throne, not just to his own people, but to those in neighboring Kingdoms. And when he had a moment of doubt or forgot who he was, he could always count on one of his friends, or a dream of Zawn, to remind him.

~ The End ~

ACKNOWLEDGEMENTS

This is the weirdest thing for me to do, because even though I am a writer, words never feel right or enough. Always appreciative to those who support me and my silly dreams, but there are a few people that need to be thrown under the bus.

Sioux, my sister from another mister, putting her own time into giving me feedback and slapping me (from many miles away!) when I have a bout of imposter syndrome. Your faith in me is epic and does not go unnoticed.

My mom, the most honest book reviewer in the world. Your patience with my insanity and home cooked meals help more than you know.

And to those not named, to those who say "Oh no" when I say "I did a thing," as I have said before, and I'll say it again, to ALL of you who have supported me, this is all your fault.

ABOUT THE AUTHOR

Living among the cacti and coyotes in Arizona, Kassandra spends her free time writing. Besides entertaining her two Dobermans (that's the breed you pick when you're a cat person, right?), the author enjoys photography, hiking, traveling, music, visiting ghost towns and staying in haunted hotels.

www.ingramcontent.com/pod-product-compliance
Lightning Source LLC
Chambersburg PA
CBHW060243030726
47493CB00025B/1581